PRAISE FOR

KRIS NELSCOTT

"Nelscott's series setting, in the turbulent late '60s, gives her books layers of issues of racism, class, and war, all of which still seem to remain sadly timely today."

—The Oregonian

"Nelscott has her own, very distinct voice, and her series creates its own deeply satisfying pleasures and cogent points."

—Seattle Times

"Nelscott is good at conveying the edgy caution that blacks once brought to their movements among white society."

—Houston Chronicle

"(A) crime writer deliberately taking chances."

—Chicago Tribune

"Like Walter Mosley and George Pelecanos, Nelscott is a chronicler of America's great racial divide, one concerned not just with solving the crime on the surface of the story but also (more so) with developing the historical backbone that gives the story its power and resonance."

—Mark Weingardner, National Book Award finalist

Protectors

Published 2017 by WMG Publishing
www.wmgpublishing.com
Cover and Layout copyright © 2017 by WMG Publishing
Cover design by Allyson Longueira/WMG Publishing
Cover art copyright © Jimfeliciano | Dreamstime, Srnicholl | Dreamstime
ISBN-13: 978-1-56146-785-3
ISBN-10: 1-56146-785-5

PROTECTORS

Also by
Kris Nelscott

PROTECTORS

KRIS NELSCOTT

WMG PUBLISHING

"Not to have confidence in one's body is to lose confidence in one's self."

—Simone de Beauvoir
The Second Sex

VAL

If you talk to people, they'll tell you their life has a dividing line. Maybe the first date with their spouse. Maybe failing to get into the top college on their list. Maybe winning the big game in high school.

Something they can point to. Something important to them. Without it, they say, their life would be completely different. They'd have no kids or they'd live somewhere else or they'd be rich.

Me, I don't have a dividing line. I have a fucking crater. My life was shredded, ripped in half, completely destroyed. Shattered into so many tiny pieces that reassembling them is completely impossible.

I am not the same woman I was in November of 1968. Back then, I'd've had a dividing line. Depending on the day you asked me, I might've said that line was the divorce from my high school sweetheart. Or the decision to drop out of law school. Or, most likely, the fact that none of the med schools on my list would take me—not because of my grades. No, I graduated number one in my college class.

The med schools wouldn't take me because I'm not only female, I'm black too.

Two strikes, one admissions idiot told me. *With your record, we'd take a risk on giving you a slot with one of those strikes. But two? No one'll take you for an internship. You won't get a residency. We'll be wasting that slot on you, honey. So sorry. Maybe the nursing school will look at you.*

If you'd asked me in November of 1968, I would have said that conversation with that administrator was the worst thing that had ever happened to me. It convinced me to marry Truman, consider having some babies. Made me apply to law school. Made me the best damn legal secretary in Chicago.

Made me give up.

I was so precious. So delicate. As if these things that happened then were adversity. As if these things were the worst that could ever happen to anyone, let alone someone like me.

Then, in early December, I humored my two sort-of cousins and best friends, Marvella and Paulette, by accompanying them to the Grand Nefertiti Ball at Sauer's Brauhaus. Marvella and Paulette, they looked gorgeous dressed in long gowns, wearing gold Egyptian bands on their upper arms. Marvella and Paulette, they're tall and stately women; I'm small, and that same outfit drowned me.

I felt ugly and silly and out of place.

Maybe that's why I danced with him. Maybe I danced with him because he was persistent. Maybe I'd had just a little too much to drink.

And no, I'm not going to tell you his name. I try not think his name. That makes him real, a person.

He wasn't a person.

And he wasn't a dividing line. That gives him too much power.

Maybe the dividing line came the next day, when I gently told him he didn't interest me. Or maybe it came at the end of January, when that son of a bitch forced his way into the hallway of my apartment building and raped me.

The rest of it—the friend from med school who said he could help me get rid of the pregnancy, the horrid, horrid fever, that ride to the hospital in the back of a car—plays in my mind in freeze-frame Chiaroscuro images:

The sharp pain in my abdomen, and my med school friend saying, *It's nothing, Val. It should feel that way.* Marvella, telling me she'll be right back. A big man carrying me down a flight of stairs. The smell of blood. A white woman in a shimmering blue pantsuit arguing with a white doctor.

And then waking up, feeling scraped and battered and empty. Finding out that I not only got rid of that pregnancy, but all possible pregnancies.

Forever and ever, amen.

Not a dividing line at all. That damn crater opened, right then and there. I don't remember hopping it. But I ended up on the other side, looking back at who I had been, and barely recognizing her.

As soon as I could after the surgeries, I sold everything, put the money my ex, Truman, had left me in his will into interest-bearing accounts that I wouldn't have to think about, and, one bright Sunday morning in early June, got on a bus heading west.

I didn't tell anyone. Not my friends. Not my family.

I just vanished.

Or rather, my body vanished.

I had disappeared a long, long time ago.

EAGLE

The scream made her sit bolt upright in bed. Captain June Eagleton looked around in the darkness, but couldn't see anyone else moving. Had she dreamed it? Then the scream came again—terrified, long, incoherent. Was there a word? Was it in English or Vietnamese?

She couldn't tell; all she could tell was the voice probably belonged to a woman. The scream came a third time, followed by some thuds.

Eagle launched herself out of the bed, reached for her clothes, which should have been on her footlocker and weren't, then realized that she wasn't at the 71st Evac Hospital, wasn't in Pleiku, wasn't even in Nam any more, hadn't been for more than two years.

She froze, her heart pounding. She'd awakened damn near every night out of a screaming nightmare since the Sikorsky flew over her apartment on May 20 and dropped CS gas all over the Berkeley campus. She had managed to make it outside to help injured students, some of whom had been shot, but all that work she'd done on calming herself, taming her inner demons, coming home—all of it had disappeared as if it had never been.

The presence of National Guard troops on the streets of Berkeley for an entire month hadn't helped. She saw the M1 Garands with their bayonets glinting in the sunlight, and her brain would leave the so-called safe streets of American to arrive in Saigon all over again, a baby nurse with big dreams, ready to save the world.

Eagle stood beside her bed, hands shaking. Coffee wouldn't be good, but coffee would be better than brandy, better than beer. Maybe someday, she'd be able to get herself a drink of water and call it sufficient. But right now, she needed to self-medicate, and she was trying to avoid the bong that sat on her wobbly coffee table—

The scream again, this time several short bursts, in English—

"Help! Help, please! Help, somebody help me! Help!"

Woman, terrified. And maybe on the street below.

Eagle shoved her bare feet in her penny loafers and grabbed the Walther P38 she had gotten in Nam. She chambered a round, then kept the pistol at her side, so she wouldn't shoot any civilians. She scurried across her apartment, opened the door, careful not to close it and lock herself out, and emerged in a dark hallway. The overhead lights had burned out weeks ago, and she had pretended she didn't care.

She cared now, as she clattered down the wooden stairs, hoping she didn't miss any, not with her hand on her pistol. Last thing she needed to do was tumble, ass over teakettle, into the lobby below.

She was probably waking her neighbors, but if the screaming hadn't awakened them, nothing would. And the screaming hadn't brought those cowards out of their snug little beds.

If the clattering woke them up, too damn bad. They were students. They certainly wouldn't complain.

The screaming continued but the words were gone, and there were grunts that didn't belong to the screamer. Eagle couldn't parse the sounds, couldn't quite figure out what was happening, only knew that something was.

No one was in the hall or the narrow opening that passed for the lobby. No lights here, except one thin ray from under an apartment door. Someone was up, but the screams weren't coming from inside.

She passed the row of metal mailboxes, and shoved the front door, trusting her neighbors' carelessness. They usually left the damn door unlocked. She figured they would do it again.

And they had.

The door opened so fast that it banged against the outside wall. Maybe that would give whoever was doing what to whom some kind of pause, and a pause was all Eagle needed.

Then the scream, a "Help me!" so strong that it made Eagle's heart pound harder.

She burst onto the street. Streetlights worked, so the street was in a perpetual twilight. But she was the only person here.

She took a deep breath, heart pounding. She hadn't dreamed this. She *hadn't*. She kept the pistol at her side, and slowly did a 180. She had to blink to see clearly. The mixed architecture—houses alongside duplexes alongside small apartment buildings like hers—made it hard to take everything in. Lights were mostly off. A few windows were open, but the only cars were parked cars. For a brief moment, a horrifying moment, she thought her night terrors had brought her to the street with a loaded pistol in her hands.

Then a scream and a thud, and the scream cut off. She ran toward the sound, to her left, closer to the goddamn park, in time to see a man standing outside a gigantic one-ton pickup, holding a woman by her hair. She was struggling, so he slammed her face against the side of the truck.

"You stop!" Eagle shouted and raised the pistol. She wasn't sure if she was a good enough shot to hit him and spare the woman—hell, Eagle had never taken a shot outside of a gun range or what passed for a gun range—and the very idea of shooting on these streets, crowded with apartments, scared the piss out of her.

The man looked over at her. He had one arm wrapped around the woman's waist, the other still pulling her hair back so that her head was tilted at such an odd angle that her neck shown whitely in the thin light of nearby streetlight.

He was big or, at least, bigger than the woman. His arm looked beefy, his face ruddy in the gloom.

"Let her go," Eagle said, moving just a little closer. She didn't want to get too close, so that the guy could rip the gun from her.

He stared at her for a moment, as if measuring her willingness to shoot him. Then, as if it were the most natural thing in the world, he swung the woman he was holding into the bed of the pickup truck.

She landed with a thud against the metal bed, and she no longer cried out. Which meant she was either unconscious or dazed and unable to help herself any more.

"Shit," Eagle said, and ran toward the truck.

The man yanked open the driver's door and jumped into the cab, starting the truck and putting it into gear in the same motion.

She was going to lose him. She was going to lose the woman. If Eagle were someone else, a crack shot or something like that, she'd shoot out his tires, but she wasn't.

She jumped into the street, hoping she could get in front of it or grab the gate and pull herself inside. But the truck peeled forward, sending dirt and broken glass and whatever else was leftover from this spring's goddamn war flying her way.

She ran after the truck, knowing she wouldn't catch it. All she had left was her brain. She had to memorize the damn vehicle.

Big. Ford F-350, according to its back end. Maybe black, maybe navy, no rust, no dents, weirdly big tires. Looked new. Might've been a 1969. The gate was closed, and there was nothing in the back that she could see to make it even more distinctive. Not even a gun rack.

And the woman wasn't sitting up, wasn't trying to get out, wasn't trying to rescue herself.

Eagle's breath was coming in huge gasps. She was out of shape, never much of a runner, her side aching. She had to get the license plate. The plate was blue with yellow lettering—California, definitely, and new. One letter—an F—and five numbers.

She couldn't get them. Then the truck swerved, the yellow of a street-light catching the back bumper. The yellow numbers flared, and she whispered them to herself before they disappeared.

The truck sped up. She ran, hoping the truck would stop at a cross street, something, but all the pot she smoked, all the burgers she ate, all the exercise she hadn't been doing caught up with her.

She bent over, wheezing, trying to catch her breath as the truck zoomed around another corner and disappeared into the night.

"Sonofabitchsonofabitchsonofabitch," she muttered with each exhalation, trying to regulate it all, hoping her damn heart wouldn't stop before she could get back to her apartment and call the cops.

Not that it would do much good. They'd come to her place, smell the lingering pot oil, see how messed up she was, decide she wasn't a credible witness.

But she had a duty. And Captain June Eagleton of the 71st Evac Hospital was excellent at duty. And mission. And following orders.

Only there were no more orders, past what she knew to be right.

Finally, she got enough air that she could stand upright.

"Son of a bitch," she said, her hands shaking, knowing that she had already failed. "Son of a goddamn bitch."

PAMMY

The black woman hovered outside A Gym of Her Own like a starving child in front of a candy store window. Pamela Griffin had seen the woman loitering outside the gym all week, but really noticed her today, because everyone else, it seemed, was staring at the television.

The television showed views from space—in theory, anyway. Right now, CBS was showing mostly drawings and its anchors, talking nervously. Apollo 11 was orbiting the moon, but that wasn't the big news.

The big news was that today, human beings were trying to *land* on the moon.

Pammy had a TV set up on her counter, facing the mats and the punching bags. All of the six women in the gym crowded around the tiny set, trying to get a glimpse of the lunar lander.

Pammy had put folding chairs on the floor facing the tall counter, but the women were standing. The tension had grabbed all of them. Pammy didn't want to stare at the TV, so she moved to the back of the group.

Pammy couldn't watch, though. The whole thing made her nervous. So she looked out the gym's gigantic plate-glass window instead.

The front part of the gym had once been a store. She had spent months clearing away the shelving, leveling the floor, and securing the ceiling so that the beams running lengthwise could handle the weight of the punching bags.

If only she had taken out the plate-glass window then. But she hadn't considered it. She had not had any idea how many times people would stand outside and stare into the gym. That huge window took away her sense of privacy, and often made the women themselves uncomfortable.

She could have removed the window. She owned the building, and she had done an extensive remodel. She had converted the two studio apartments in the back into a locker room, offices, and some private areas. She had transformed part of the space into a real kitchen, with new appliances. Initially, she had thought the kitchen would be for her, but everyone used it.

She had used the last of her money to buy proper gym equipment, modifying as much of it as she could for women's smaller frames. The gym ended up a place she was proud of before she even opened her doors in May of 1967.

The dry, flat voice of astronaut Neil Armstrong reciting the distance to the surface made her tense. He had just mentioned some dust and a shadow, and that was when she had to step away from the television, not that it made a difference. She could still hear his eerily calm voice.

In his shoes, she wouldn't have been calm. She would have been utterly terrified. She was just a little terrified right now.

If the lunar lander crashed into the moon's surface, no one could do anything to help, not even the men in Mission Control. The entire joyous event would end in a gigantic disaster.

The moon landing party hadn't even been her idea. The suburban women who (surprisingly) made up the bulk of her clientele decided it would be more fun to watch in a group.

Pammy had apparently had a moment of crazy, because she had agreed, thinking that the landing would be over and done with in less than an hour. Instead, the group had arrived two hours ago, and there was no end in sight.

She wanted them to leave, and she couldn't tell them to go. She had agreed to this, after all.

Everything about the entire day felt out of Pammy's control.

Including the woman standing outside the plate-glass window, staring in. No one else stood on the street. Just the woman, leaning forward slightly as if she were trying to get a better look inside.

The woman stood with her arms wrapped around her torso, hands gripping her ribcage. She seemed unnaturally thin. Her collarbone stood out prominently, the dark skin pulled tightly across her chest. She had cropped her hair so short that it looked like she was wearing a stocking cap made up of tight black curls.

She had an upturned nose and delicate, elfin features. Her large brown eyes weren't looking at the television; they were peering in at the exercise circle where, up until an hour ago, Pammy had been teaching her Sunday beginners' class the value of Tai Chi and being mindful.

Pammy wasn't always mindful. In fact, she wasn't very good at Tai Chi. She found it boring. But her unofficial medic, June Eagleton, had insisted on some kind of stretching routine for the women who came to the gym, so they wouldn't get hurt as easily. Eagle insisted that Pammy do more to keep the injuries under control. Eagle was terrified that the City of Berkeley would use the sprained wrists, black eyes, and occasional broken thumbs as an excuse to shut the gym down.

Pammy felt that the City of Berkeley had other things to worry about besides one business just off Telegraph Avenue. As long as no one complained (and even if they did), she figured she was okay.

But she had implemented the Tai Chi class anyway.

Something beeped on the television screen. The women—all dressed in shorts and sleeveless blouses—remained motionless. Three had their fingers pressed against their lips. Two clasped their hands together against their breasts in an unconscious imitation of prayer, and one was biting her thumbnail.

"Houston, Tranquility Base here," Neil Armstrong said from hundreds of thousands of miles away, "The Eagle has landed."

The women burst into cheers. Pammy turned back toward the television, but couldn't see the screen. Two of her students were hugging each other and jumping up and down.

Pammy didn't quite feel the elation. This was just the beginning of something incredibly dangerous. After the two men finished whatever they were supposed to do on the moon (and if they survived that), they would have to get the lunar lander back to the spaceship somehow, and then they all had to return to Earth. She wouldn't feel elated until those men walked on Earth's soil again.

But she did know that what had just happened was momentous. In spite of herself, she felt the solemnity of it, as well as the sheer magic. She let out a small breath. Whatever happened next, Americans had landed on the moon. That, by itself, was pretty incredible.

Then she glanced out the window again. The woman was now peering at everyone else, looking surprised. Hadn't she known about the moon landing? How could she not have known that?

But Pammy had a hunch. Women caught up in their own trauma didn't pay attention to the street around them, let alone the world or, in this case, the universe.

Pammy pushed past three of the women who were still staring at the television, and walked to the glass front door. She pushed it open and felt the warm summer air.

"Hey," Pammy said.

The woman stepped back in surprise. She gave Pammy a sad, startled look, then started down the sidewalk.

Pammy realized that the woman believed Pammy was chasing her away.

"Wait!" Pammy said, louder. "I wanted to invite you in. We just landed on the moon. You have to see this."

The woman stopped, her back mostly to Pammy. Two blocks ahead, some cars passed on Telegraph Avenue, but this street was empty. No one except her and the woman.

The woman turned slightly until her gaze met Pammy's.

"*We* didn't land on the moon," she corrected, with that earnestness so many of the University of California-Berkeley students had.

"America did," Pammy said. "I think that counts as *we*. C'mon. You have to see this."

The woman opened her mouth, and Pammy half expected her to say, as so many of those self-righteous students would have, *I don't need to see anything.*

Then the woman closed her mouth, nodded as if acknowledging something someone else had said, took a deep breath, put her head down, and charged forward.

Her arms were still wrapped around her torso, and she was so thin, Pammy could probably break all of her ribs with a well-placed shove.

The woman slipped inside the door, then stopped, saw the women still dancing to the news of the moon landing, and said softly, "I'm sorry. I don't belong here."

Pammy wasn't sure if the woman was saying that because she was black and everyone else in the room was white or because everyone was older than she was or because everyone was dancing.

"Sure you do," Pammy said. "This place is for anyone who wants to step inside."

The woman looked at Pammy sideways. The woman's gaze moved slightly, as if she were trying to size up the situation. Pammy could feel the fear radiating off her.

Pammy had learned in the years since she opened the gym that the actual situation here wasn't what frightened women who came through that door. The women who came into A Gym of Her Own were often already terrified.

Pammy had learned to treat them gently.

"I'm Pamela Griffin," she said. "I'm the owner of this place."

The woman looked up at her, then over at the other six women, who were now staring at the television again.

"You own a gym?" she asked, not giving her name in return. "Why would a woman own a gym?"

Pammy had encountered that question dozens of times before, but it still overwhelmed her. There were a thousand answers. *Because I want to* was perhaps the most accurate one. Pammy had combined her business and physical education double majors into something she actually believed in, something she was good at.

But there were other answers as well. *Because there was a need. Because women need to learn how to defend themselves. Because I can't imagine doing anything else.*

And, of course, those were just the superficial answers. The real answers took a lot more time to explain.

Pammy smiled at the woman, and didn't give any of those answers—superficial or deep. Instead, she shrugged.

"Come on," Pammy said. "This is history."

The woman glanced at the television again, then at the door. Pammy could feel how hard the woman was fighting with herself just to stand inside the threshold.

Then the woman gave that odd little nod again, lowered her chin, and stepped forward. She hovered near the edge of the group of women, in a place where she couldn't see anything on the screen.

Pammy let the heavy door close on its own.

"Did you see this?" Opal Curlett turned toward the new woman as if she had been here all along. "You have *got* to see this."

Opal had been one of Pammy's students almost from the start. When she had come here, she was heavyset and not athletic at all. She was still solid— she had probably never been thin—but now she looked strong instead of squishy. She wore her graying hair short, and she never wore makeup.

The new woman looked at Opal with a bit of alarm. Opal grinned. She'd been through introductions like this before.

Opal had never been one of the terrified ones. Instead, she had been one of the strong ones from the very beginning. She had fought her way through a terrible divorce and was slowly rebuilding her life. She had come to Pammy after finishing an automobile repair class. Opal had had visions of herself driving the interstates around the San Francisco Bay Area, stopping with a box of tools and rescuing women stranded at the side of the road.

She had never done it, but just the fact that she had thought of it pleased Pammy.

The new woman glanced at Pammy, then at the door as if measuring the distance to an escape.

"Here," Opal said to the new woman. "Take my spot. You can see better from here. I've got to pee anyway."

Opal had seen the new woman's terror, then. Opal was doing what she could to put the new woman at ease, including the casual mention of peeing, as if she and the new woman were old friends. Opal walked away from the television to the locker room.

The new woman watched as Opal opened the locker room door and stepped inside. Then one of the beginners—Pammy couldn't see who—said, "C'mon, move up," and for a half second, Pammy thought the new woman would bolt.

Then she stepped into the very space that Opal had just vacated.

"They just landed," the beginner was saying, "and now they have this equipment stuff to do inside the lander. It'll probably be hours before they walk on the surface of the moon."

"I'd be terrified," said Celeste Boutelle, which really didn't surprise Pammy. Celeste was also one of the beginners who had come to the gym after People's Park in May.

Surprisingly, Pammy had gotten an influx of suburban students during May and June. The entire city of Berkeley was under martial law, and people drove down to Telegraph to join Pammy's gym. She had thought the armed military presence down here would discourage people from taking classes. Instead, everyone from students to professors to employees of nearby businesses decided they needed to learn self-defense, and they had all come to Pammy.

Celeste ran a hand over her home-dyed red curls. She glanced at everyone, including the newcomer.

"Can you imagine?" Celeste asked. "Being so far away from home, in a tin can, with no help nearby? We could've heard them die today."

We still might, Pammy wanted to say, but didn't.

The new woman was watching the television, a small frown creasing her brow. She had nodded just a little as Celeste spoke. The new woman could imagine, apparently, and probably had.

She no longer hugged her own torso. She had lowered her arms, but she still held them in front of her, this time with one hand clutching the elbow of the other arm, a protective stance.

Pammy lifted her gaze from the new woman's posture to find Jill Woodbridge looking up at the same point. Jill had become one of Pammy's de facto assistants. Jill was tall and athletic, with short-cropped brown hair and a hard jawline.

She used to work in her husband's business on Telegraph but he shut it down during the Free Speech Movement four years before. He hadn't liked the chaos and disorder, the constant protests, and the coarse way the students had started speaking to adults.

He had planned to move the business to one of the outlying areas but hadn't yet completed the work when he fell dead from a heart attack, leaving Jill with life insurance, a paid-off house, grown children, and nothing to do with her days.

She had said that finding Pammy was a saving grace. Sometimes Pammy agreed, especially as the number of women who used the gym grew in June.

Pammy knew what Jill was thinking: the new woman was exceptionally guarded and deeply frightened. Jill would argue that they could help her.

Pammy wasn't sure. She never stepped into other women's lives unless invited. And so far, the new woman hadn't invited her, and maybe never would.

"You know what?" Jill asked. Pammy braced herself for an inappropriate comment. That was the downside of Jill, who occasionally stuck her foot so deep in her mouth that you couldn't even see her knee. "We need food."

Pammy let out a breath of air.

A couple of women went to get their purses, which they had placed behind the counter. The new woman glanced at the door again.

Jill saw that too. "Don't worry, I got it. I'll just take sandwich orders, and I'll pay for them. My treat."

The new woman had stepped to one side and was going to leave. Pammy could feel it, but she wasn't sure what she could do about it.

Jill looked at the new woman and said softly, "I got it," apparently thinking the new woman was going to leave because she couldn't pay.

Then everyone looked at the new woman, and she tilted her head slightly. It seemed like the assumption of poverty annoyed her.

"I think orders are a great idea," Pammy said to Jill. "You should probably start a list. I'm pretty sure Yale's Deli is open today."

"We've got a menu somewhere," Jill said. "That'll make things easier."

Her cheeks were pink. She realized she had blown it with the new woman, but probably didn't know how.

The other women crowded the counter, although a couple kept their gazes on the television. Right now, the reporters were talking about the landing, while there was chatter in the background from Mission Control.

Someone said, "You know, Kip's is closer."

Pammy let her gaze meet the new woman's, so she couldn't just sneak out. But Pammy didn't approach her either. When people were as terrified as the new woman was, talking to them head-on about anything could often make them run away.

The new woman gave Pammy a hesitant smile, then glanced at the door. As the women got involved with choosing a different restaurant, the new woman took one step toward the door, then stopped herself.

She put her head down, and Pammy was convinced she would walk out. Instead, the new woman walked toward her, watching her feet as she moved.

Trembling, her hands clenched into fists. Pammy had seen only a few other women this deeply frightened come into the gym, and none of them returned.

The new woman stopped in front of her. She was shorter than Pammy realized, maybe five-three, maybe less.

"Do you really teach women how to defend themselves?" the new woman asked softly. She had an accent that Pammy didn't quite recognize. Midwestern, long vowels, but with a cadence that was unfamiliar.

Apparently, when she had been staring at the large plate-glass window for A Gym of Her Own, she had been reading the mimeographed class schedule that Jill had pasted in the corner. That was the only place which mentioned self-defense classes.

"Yes, I can teach women how to defend themselves," Pammy said, knowing simple was best. If she tried to convince this woman of anything, the woman would back away.

"Even someone who looks like me?" the new woman asked, raising her head. Her brown eyes seemed even bigger than they had before.

She wasn't specific, but Pammy knew what she meant. Pammy had gotten the question a dozen times before.

The new woman was referring to her petite build, not her skin color.

"Especially women who look like you," Pammy said.

The woman frowned, then glanced at the cluster of women, still discussing lunch. None of them were as petite at this woman. Some of them were a little too heavy to exercise much, which was something Pammy wanted them to work on.

"It's a small class," Pammy said, making sure her tone wasn't apologetic, "on an unusual day."

The new woman didn't nod. She barely looked at Pammy. But the new woman frowned, and took a deep breath, squaring her slight shoulders.

"How," she asked quietly, "can a woman like me ever defend herself? Really defend herself? I mean, I can probably take on another woman, maybe, but men…"

Her voice had a thrum to it, a deep emotional undercurrent, an intensity that Pammy rarely heard in these early discussions with other women.

"I mean," the new woman said, "men are so much bigger."

For this woman, all men were bigger. Some women could take on men, size for size. Those women just had to realize it.

But some women were so small that even the shortest man could overpower them.

"It's not about size," Pammy said, deliberately avoiding the old cliché that her father taught her. But she was thinking it. *It's not about the size of the woman in the fight; it's about the size of the fight in the woman.* She used to quote it to her students, making it clear that the cliché used to be about small men, but she had altered it.

Too many women thought the cliché flip, though, and sometimes they even left after Pammy spouted something like that. Pammy later learned they thought they were going to get platitudes rather than actual help.

"Well, let me restate that," Pammy said. "In some ways, it is about size."

The new woman tensed.

"Men don't expect small women to be tough," Pammy said. "No one expects small women to be strong. It gives us an advantage."

She deliberately included herself in that statement, so the new woman before her realized that Pammy didn't have a lot of physical advantages either—at least, she hadn't had them when she learned how to defend herself years ago.

The new woman studied her, and Pammy could feel her uncertainty. The woman still wanted to bolt, but she seemed to be holding herself in place by sheer force of will.

"I still don't know what I could do," the woman said. "I'm scared of guns."

"So am I," Pammy said. "I know of too many people who don't know how to use them or who drop the gun at the wrong moment or who get overpowered because they are too afraid to shoot. Guns are only good in the hands of someone trained."

The woman swallowed. She was so thin that Pammy could see the muscles in her neck move. Pammy had hit on something.

"I would teach you what to do," Pammy said. "First, though, we teach how to de-escalate."

"Huh?" the woman asked.

"There are ways to confuse someone who is about to attack you or to get them to back down, ways that sometimes work before the physical attacks happen."

The woman let out a small half-laugh. "Yeah, I know all about that. Those things only work against someone who is not crazy."

Pammy now recognized the thrum of emotion. This woman had a particular person in mind. She was in trouble. But Pammy didn't want to scare her away by asking what the problem was. The woman would say something if she ended up trusting Pammy.

"That's why I teach other methods," Pammy said. "We start with de-escalation, and then we move to non-lethal self-defense moves."

"Non-lethal," the woman said softly.

Pammy braced herself for the next question: *There are lethal moves?*

"Are you worried about the legal ramifications of teaching lethal moves?" the woman asked. "Is that why you don't do it?"

For a brief moment, the woman seemed like a different person: smart, capable, and no-nonsense. Pammy had a sense that she had just gotten a glimpse of the woman's Before personality—Before whatever it was had happened. Until now, Pammy had been talking to After.

"I teach those moves too," Pammy said, deciding not to answer the entire question. "Mostly I demonstrate them on the last day of a self-defense class. Every now and then, I get enough interest in learning how to perform those techniques well, and I teach an additional class."

So far, she had only taught one such class, and if she were honest with herself, it had made her nervous. It had been in early June, just after the horrible, bloody events of May, when no one thought the next few weeks would be peaceful.

The woman made a small sound in the back of her throat, a sigh or an acknowledgement. She extended a hand.

"I'm Val," she said.

Pammy took her hand. Val's grip was surprisingly strong. "Pammy."

"Pammy," Val repeated, as if the name surprised her.

It surprised a lot of people. They expected something butch, probably, or at least something without the diminutive. But her father called her Pammy, so the name meant a lot to her.

She had learned along the way that if she approached her name with confidence, everyone else did too.

"How do I sign up?" Val asked.

And Pammy smiled.

EAGLE

Eagle had stayed up half the night, cleaning her apartment like she was going to perform surgery in it. She found a forgotten bottle of bleach beneath her sink and used it to scrub everything—furniture, floors, walls. She had to get the smell of pot out of this apartment before the police arrived, and once she started, she couldn't stop.

First, she cleaned up the mess on her coffee table. She stowed the bong in her footlocker, and hid the baggie of pot inside her Raisin Bran. She probably should've gotten rid of the pot altogether, but she didn't know where to stash it, and when she cleaned the living room of her apartment, she had still been expecting the cops at any minute.

Such an illusion.

She had returned to the apartment at quarter to one in the morning, still shaking from the encounter with the guy and the truck, terrified for the woman he had beaten into submission. Eagle hadn't even set her pistol down as she ran for the phone, taking the receiver off the wall cradle, and dialing zero for the operator, demanding the police department *now*.

She should have had the emergency numbers taped to the fridge. Even her mother had had emergency numbers taped to the fridge in every apartment they had ended up in. Captain June Eagleton would have as well, but Eagle wasn't that woman any longer.

She had let so much of herself go.

The police had brushed her off. The dispatch said they'd send someone, and Eagle offered to meet them, and when the dispatch had said not to worry, the police would come to her, Eagle felt the opportunity to rescue that woman slipping away.

Eagle had hung up, then grabbed her phonebook and thumbed through it, making sure she had the right police department. When she got the same dispatch, she tried again, and the dispatch had snapped at her.

They would take care of it. Someone would come to her.

Eagle had let out a shaky breath, and that was when she realized what she had done.

She had lit a fire under the Berkeley Police Department, who wanted to visit her in her apartment. An apartment filled with seeds and clips and the not-so-faint odor of the joint the kid next door had given her in a rare moment of kindness.

Hence, the cleaning. And the dawning realization that she was so far from Captain June Eagleton as to be someone else.

She had become a lot like the women she'd fled from when she'd left the res. Her grandmother's friends liked a good smoke, liked their drink, and liked a lazy afternoon. Life at the Pine Ridge Indian Reservation hadn't really been lazy, but it had seemed that way to ten-year-old Eagle. She hadn't understood the tribal business or the fact that the meandering discussions actually had a point.

She only realized that later, when she got older.

She had fled the res when her mom died. Her mom had hidden there, when her father had started divorce proceedings after he got back from Europe in 1946. He wanted full custody of Eagle. When her mom got wind of it, she fled with Eagle, surviving in a thousand horrible ways. She finally brought them both to Pine Ridge, getting there just in time to die.

Eagle called her dad, just like she had done a dozen times before. Only this time, her mom wasn't around to spirit her to a new place before her dad arrived. Her dad had come for her and driven her back to California. She learned then he had come the previous times too, but they had left before he arrived, and he hadn't been able to find them.

Her mother's death made Eagle's rescue possible.

Her dad had been happy to have her live with him, although his bitch of a second wife hadn't been. Eagle had to put up with nasty comments about her skin color, her dark hair, her black eyes—all outside of her dad's presence, of course.

Her dad had treated Eagle like he treated his other kids, her four pure-white half siblings. He had expected her to perform well (she had) and he had paid her way through UCLA. At UCLA, no one had known her Lakota roots and no one guessed. She didn't look that different from everyone else.

Since then, she had not discussed her heritage at all, and she had left it off the forms when she joined the service.

Ironic that they'd nicknamed her Eagle at Basic. Ironic that she'd clung to the nickname like a brand.

Her father had been proud of her service. It had been because of him that she joined up in the first place. And she hadn't seen him since she got back, even though he begged her to visit.

She didn't want to tell him about her war. It was so very different from his. He wouldn't understand.

And he wouldn't like who she had become.

She knew, because she didn't.

But that didn't stop her from having expectations—of herself and others.

Just like she expected the police to show up when someone called them in the middle of the night with an emergency.

It was now thirteen hours later, and still no one had shown up at her door. She had done the superficial clean in the wee hours. After she got rid of the drug paraphernalia, she had done her dishes, piled up her laundry, and picked up all of the newspapers, magazines, and books littering her chairs.

She picked up the box of photos she'd found in the garbage, probably tossed out by a bitter roommate, and put them under her desk. She couldn't bear to throw them out like the roommate had done.

Even with the box beneath the desk, the apartment hadn't been that clean when she moved in.

At 4:00 a.m., Eagle had called the police again, and asked if she needed to go to the precinct to give them the information she had on the man, the woman, and the truck. The dispatch or whoever she talked to had reassured her that someone would come see her.

She hadn't heard the word "shortly" but she had expected shortly. Good God, they'd already missed their window. Maybe someone had let the squad cars know to watch out for the truck. Maybe they'd already found the guy and rescued that poor woman, getting her to a hospital.

It had been the thought of a hospital (which she had at 7:00 a.m.) that reminded her that she needed to clean the smoke residue out of the apartment before the cops arrived. That was when she broke out the bleach, and scrubbed until her hands were raw.

At noon, she called a third time, encountering a new voice on the other end of the line. She repeated what she saw, wondered why no one had spoken to her, and added something she hadn't said before (to her everlasting chagrin),

How come you people don't care about a woman who was beaten to unconsciousness? She might still be in the back of that damn truck, bleeding to death. She needs medical assistance. I can tell you that much; I'm a nurse for godssake. I know when injuries can be life-threatening.

She wasn't talking to some dispatch this time. The person who had answered claimed to be a sergeant. Probably a desk sergeant.

We'll send someone, ma'am, he'd said.

I hope you have someone looking already, she'd snapped.

First I heard of it, but then, I don't always thumb through the night's calls. I'll make sure we get on this, he'd said.

Unlike the person she'd spoken to first, he, at least, didn't sound disinterested. He sounded like he might actually do something. Of course, he might've been so experienced with working with the public that he could make her feel like her call mattered to him, and still not do a damn thing about what she had told him.

That call had taken the starch out of her. That, and the long night. She had finally settled on her dumpy old couch, and closed her eyes.

The next thing she knew, someone was pounding on her door.

Even then, she didn't jump to her feet. She started to rub her eyes, then stopped because her hands still smelled of bleach. She grabbed some Kleenex off the end table, wiped her face, and stood up.

The knock sounded again.

"Coming," she said. She got to the door, peered through the spyhole, and saw two rumpled men standing in the hall. She had a hunch they were detectives, but she didn't know that for certain.

So she left the chain lock on and pulled the door open until the chain caught. "Yes?"

One of the men, a redhead with a drunk's florid face, held up a badge. He held it long enough for her to see that it was legitimate, and for her to memorize the badge number.

"You called us," he said, his tone flat. He didn't say "police." He didn't identify himself at all. Just those ice-cold words, as if she had done something wrong by even calling him.

"Yeah," she said. "Let me open the door."

She closed it, removed the chain, and pulled the door open. The redhead came in first. He was short and squat and smelled faintly of cigars.

The other detective walked behind him with military posture. He was also younger by nearly a decade, his hair too short for Eagle to determine that its color was anything other than dark.

"I'm Detective Brunsan," the redhead said. "This is my partner, Detective Stuart. Heard you had some trouble this morning."

She closed the door behind them, then swept her hand toward the living room. She wasn't going to talk to these men this close to the door. She had enough trouble with her neighbors, and their disrespect. They called the cops the Blue Meanies, a term that came from the Beatle's *Yellow Submarine* movie, and always said with contempt.

Of course, after the past few months, the cops didn't always deserve respect, but Eagle knew that the community wouldn't survive without them.

"I called the police department shortly after midnight, Detective," she said, keeping her voice emergency-room level. Then she extended her hand. "I'm Captain June Eagleton, U.S. Army, Retired."

She should have said *former* captain, because as a non-com, she didn't keep her rank when she was discharged, but she didn't. She wanted these men to take her seriously.

Not that they were.

Brunsan raised his eyebrows in disbelief, looking at her hand as if it were something that might contaminate him.

Then the other detective—Stuart—stepped in front of Brunsan, and shook Eagle's hand smartly.

"Captain," he said. "Forgive my partner. We thought you were a college student."

As if that made his rudeness more acceptable.

"Until recently, I was a college student," she said, deciding to give them personal information. "I came here on the GI Bill after my tour."

She didn't explain any further. They didn't need to know that she had dropped out or become too lazy to move. Not that there was somewhere else for her to go.

"I'm sorry," Stuart said. "If we had known that an adult had called, then someone might've gotten here sooner."

She felt a wave of anger, but she had learned long ago how to keep that to herself.

"Your neighborhood worked against you, honey," Brunsan added.

Eagle gave Brunsan her best get-yourself-together-Mister stare. To his credit, he didn't look away. Most people did when faced with that look.

She straightened, wishing she was wearing something other than jeans and t-shirt. This was one of those moments when her uniform would have given her strength—as well as some respect from the red-headed idiot.

"If you haven't investigated this," she said in that emergency room tone, "you've already lost fourteen hours, and your best chance of tracing that truck."

Brunsan looked away from her. He wasn't going to admit he was wrong, but he knew it. He knew they had screwed up.

Stuart's mouth thinned a little. She took that to be disapproval of the way the case was handled, not disapproval of her outspokenness.

"Tell us what you saw," Stuart said. He hadn't moved away from his partner. He was still half-blocking the older man.

She bit back her first retort: *Tell you* again, *you mean.* She took a deep breath, and repeated her story.

She ended with, "I brought my pistol. I did not fire it, although I did point it at him. That was when he decided to toss her in the flatbed and zoom out of there."

Brunsan shook his head, as if he couldn't believe what she told them. "You didn't shoot, did you, Miss Oakley?"

As in Little Annie Oakley, the Wild West sharpshooter, as in dismissing a woman who knew how to use a gun. Eagle raised her chin and was about to respond when Stuart said to Brunsan, "That's enough. Captain Eagleton deserves our respect."

Brunsan made a derogatory noise through his nose. "And how the hell do we know that Calamity Jane here really did serve?"

Eagle's eyes narrowed. She'd encountered this kind of bigotry before, and she hated it. She usually expected it from college students, though. They were why she kept her uniform in her footlocker and never took it out for any reason.

Stuart said to Brunsan, "Why don't you let me handle this?"

Brunsan made that snorting noise again and straightened. He was clearly not comfortable with the way Stuart was treating him.

"We don't need civilians running around the streets with weapons." Brunsan stepped around Stuart. Stuart turned again, looking frustrated, clearly about to say something, but Brunsan wasn't done. He glared at Eagle and added, "May I see your pistol, ma'am?"

The sarcasm pissed her off, but she answered him in her calmest voice. "Certainly."

She had nothing to hide. Besides, she hadn't fired the weapon in months.

Stuart was shaking his head, but Eagle ignored him. Instead, she walked into the bedroom, feeling a little lightheaded. She took the Walther from her footlocker and carried it back, along with her military identification.

Stuart was speaking softly to Brunsan. Brunsan's florid face had turned even redder. He was being reprimanded.

She couldn't quite tell their relationship. Was Brunsan, clearly the older man, also the superior officer here? Or was Stuart?

And was that really any of her concern?

"Would you like to inspect my weapon to see if it's been fired lately?" she asked, managing a tone that she had learned when dealing with the brass. It was *Hey asshole, I'm complying with your dumbass request. So back the fuck off.*

Stuart looked at her sideways, a small smile on his lips. He, at least, knew what she was doing.

"No need," Brunsan said without much of a glance at the pistol. He was actually looking at her identification as if he couldn't believe it. He managed, "Sorry, Captain."

She inclined her head toward Brunsan, acknowledging his apology without accepting it. He was an ass. She didn't need to give him too much credit for behaving like a human being.

She set the Walther and the ID down on her newly cleaned coffee table.

"So, Captain," Brunsan said, "how do you know that this man and woman weren't having a domestic, y'know. Maybe they were married or something."

She was still half bent over from setting down her weapon. Good thing, too, because she felt a surge of anger. She caught the anger, held it, hid it, and rose slowly.

Her glance at Stuart told her that he too was curious about her response. Jesus Christ, these men. Every once in a while, she understood why Pammy Griffin had opened up her goddamn gym.

"So, you think it's perfectly all right for a man to beat his wife into unconsciousness and toss her, bleeding, into the back of a pickup truck?" Eagle asked in her reasonable, let-me-look-at-your-injury voice.

Brunsan's skin got redder, but Stuart's expression didn't change.

"A man's allowed to do what he needs to in his own home," Stuart said.

"He wasn't in his home," Eagle said, a little charge to her tone. She wanted to clear her throat, to get rid of the tone, which surprised her. She hadn't expected it. But then, she had cast Stuart as the reasonable one. The fact that he wasn't pissed her off.

"True enough," Stuart said, "but you don't know if this man and woman had left their home and brought their fight to the street."

"I know that she was screaming—*screaming*—for help," Eagle said, punctuating each word. "She was screaming long enough for me to wake up, get some clothes on, find my weapon, and run a block and a half—"

"Why didn't anyone else respond?" Stuart asked. "If it were as dire as you say, then others should have—"

"Have you looked at the neighborhood?" Eagle asked, no longer trying to keep the anger from her voice. "You are in the People's Republic of Berkeley. That's what you guys call it, right?"

Brunsan opened his mouth, but Eagle didn't let him speak.

"We were under martial law until a month ago. People were screaming for help every day, and they were screaming not because their husband was beating them or they were having a—what did you call it? A *domestic*. They were screaming because they were being beaten by cops—"

"There's no proof of that," Stuart said.

She stopped, because a blatant lie tended to do that to her. "I saw it."

"The National Guard did occasionally get out of hand," Brunsan said. "I will give you that."

"Shooting unarmed civilians," she said. "Dropping CS gas on an entire neighborhood. Sending little kids to the hospital with chemical reactions that I haven't seen outside of Nam. You call that a *little* out of hand, Detective?"

"They were provoked," Brunsan said.

Eagle took a step toward him, then realized he wanted to goad her into fury. She made herself breathe. She squared her shoulders and summoned her alter ego. The unflappable Captain June Eagleton, no matter what she saw. And the good captain had seen things no human should ever see.

"We could argue all day," Eagle said. "I was here, on the street, treating the wounded. You probably were not. Not that it matters. Because politically, I don't agree with the student shitheads, Detective, pardon my French. I *served* my country, and when I came home, some of those shitheads spit on my uniform. So I'm not defending them."

Stuart looked away, but Brunsan kept staring at her.

She met his eyes. She wasn't done yet.

"I am telling you that what I saw last night was out of control," she said, "and I wouldn't be surprised if that woman was dying of her injuries. Or if she was already dead. And some of that blame will go on the Berkeley Police Department for not responding."

She whipped a piece of paper off the coffee table and held it out to the two men. "Here's the license plate number of that truck. It's a Ford F-350 one-ton. I've given this information to your dispatch twice, and to your desk sergeant or whoever took my call this morning. So the information should be at the station, although I doubt it is. Find the goddamn truck. Find the guy who drives it. See if there's blood in the back. I'll wager there is. And see if you can find this woman, because someone needs to, and unlike you people, I don't have the resources to do it."

Brunsan was staring at her as if she had grown a third head. He was probably going to comment on her language.

"Even if there is blood," Stuart said, "there's not going to be any way to know whose it is."

She waved the paper at him. "You've given up before you started, then, Detective?"

Stuart's lips had gotten even thinner. "We don't even know who that woman is."

"Yeah," Eagle snapped. "Doesn't that concern you? Because it sure as hell concerns me."

"It's a needle in a haystack," Stuart said.

She nodded at the piece of paper. "If you take this, you'll at least know which haystack to look in."

Brunsan pulled the paper from Eagle's outstretched hand, to her surprise. Then he nodded, a slight frown between his eyes.

"You're right," he said quietly. "We should at least track down the truck and its owner."

She felt a knot loosen in her back.

"But," he added, "don't you go off half-cocked with that weapon of yours. No shooting—"

"Detective," she said sharply, cutting him off. "I didn't shoot the asshole last night. You should see that as proof that I am not going to indiscriminately use my weapon. Although I must say, if I had shot that son of a bitch, then the woman would be in a hospital right now, getting the care she deserves."

Brunsan clutched the paper tightly. "You have an attitude problem, missy."

"Not as bad as yours," she said.

Stuart was shaking his head. Then he headed for the door. Brunsan was still staring at her.

She took another deep breath.

"Look," she said to Brunsan. "You don't have to like me to believe me. Just find this woman, okay? Make sure she's got medical care. That's all I ask."

Brunsan nodded. She had the odd feeling that she had gotten through to him.

Her opinions had shifted. Stuart might have military posture, but Brunsan was the one who was listening to her, even if he did have to establish dominance over her every fifth sentence.

"We'll see what we can find," he said. "Chances are it's nothing."

Nothing. Beating a woman nearly to death was nothing to them. Eagle bit her lower lip. She waited until the two men let themselves out before she opened her mouth again.

Even then, she didn't say what she was thinking.

She was thinking that it wasn't nothing.

She was also thinking that it was probably too late.

PAMMY

To Pammy's surprise, Val did not leave after she signed up for the beginner's exercise class. Val contributed a few dollars to the lunch pot that the women had set up. Instead of getting sandwiches, Jill and Opal had walked the few blocks to Kip's to get pizza. Someone had called ahead and ordered three pies, which Pammy thought was too much, but she wasn't going to argue.

As the women had been saying, it was a special day.

The women were still standing in the middle of the room, keeping their eyes on the television. The excitement had died down a little, but it still felt electric in here, as if the events thousands of miles away had occurred inside Pammy's little gym.

She wished she could shut the television off and send everyone home. Because the special day had an hours-long hole in the middle, as the astronauts did whatever they were doing on the lunar lander to prepare for a walk on the moon. The very idea made her stomach twist. The experts on television were talking about all the dangers—if the men fell over, could they get up? What happened if a rock punctured their suits? What if they couldn't climb back into the lander?

What if it couldn't take off?

Most of the women ignored that, preferring to believe that everything would work out. But Pammy didn't.

She had learned the hard way to prepare for the worst.

People could still surprise her, though. Val did. Pammy had given her the sign-up form. Val had taken a magazine and a pen, then sat in one of the chairs, and carefully filled the form out. As if it were important.

Which it wasn't.

Pammy didn't really care if her new students filled out the form or not. She had it because one of her regulars, Stella D'Arbus, convinced her that women expected it.

Pammy soon discovered that women who had ventured down to Telegraph from the suburbs expected it, as did the women who worked at the university. University students, hippies, and street people balked at filling out the form. Sometimes they drew a fist with the middle finger raised all over the front of the form. Sometimes, they looked at her in disbelief.

Several crumpled the form and started to leave; Pammy would stop them by telling them filling it out wasn't necessary. A handful offered to fill it out after they had taken a few classes and realized that Pammy didn't work for The Man.

Val was so skittish that Pammy had expected her to refuse to write down anything. But Val handed in the form, covered with neat handwriting, with every space filled out, including address and phone number.

Pammy had learned not to look at the details until later. If Pammy studied it, she made everyone nervous. She set the form in a folder that she would take to her office when she had a moment.

Then Val gave her a tentative smile. Pammy smiled back.

"How do I start?" Val asked.

Pammy wanted to say that Val needed to eat more. But lunch would come shortly, and Pammy could watch how Val actually ate without intimidating her.

Besides, Pammy wasn't the body police, much as Eagle wanted her to be.

"I'd like you to come to an exercise class first," Pammy said. "I just want to assess where you're at."

Val looked down, hands still clasped in front of her torso. "I'm not anywhere," she said softly. "I don't think I've exercised in my life."

"You'd be surprised what you've done," Pammy said, but the response was by rote. Some schools never had Physical Education for girls. Even in the schools that required Phys Ed, girls found a dozen ways to get out of it. All girls were exempted for their periods, because common wisdom said that girls couldn't exercise while they were having their menses.

Pammy didn't exempt anyone for any reason. She had looked at history and realized that historically, if women had stopped exercising for a week every month, nothing would have gotten done and nomadic tribes wouldn't have traveled.

Even in this day and age, a lot of women walked everywhere, especially if they lived down here, near campus. Walking gave them a stronger cardiovascular system than the women who sat and drank coffee all day.

Val bit her lower lip, then asked, "Will I hate it?"

Her tone seemed level, but that thrum had come back. Val was afraid of everything, it seemed.

"I hope you won't hate the class," Pammy said. "I try to make class enjoyable."

But she didn't want to make promises that she couldn't entirely keep. Some people did hate the exercise class, on principle, Pammy sometimes thought, and she had no idea if Val was one of those people.

At that moment, Opal and Jill pushed open the exterior door, carrying three boxes that smelled heavily of garlic and tomato sauce. Pammy's stomach growled. She hadn't realized she was hungry.

Val slid back, almost as if she were trying to disappear. The other women moved forward, taking the boxes and laughing. Jill also carried a greasy white bag that, if Kip's came through like it usually did, probably held red pepper flakes, napkins, and some parmesan cheese.

Pammy had to move closer. She used to frown on food in the gym, but she soon learned that didn't help some of the women, especially the students and street people. Sometimes, someone else's treat was the only meal they got all day.

"No food on the mats," Pammy said. She silently cursed herself. She should have brought a table out here.

Jill set the greasy bag on top of the counter, then headed toward the foldup tables stacked against the wall. Celeste joined her. Shirley Pettit walked over to the folding tables beside the extra foldup chairs. She was a thin woman with dyed blonde hair, who had taken up exercise to quit her chain-smoking habit. In the six months she'd been coming to the gym, she'd quit smoking seventeen times, each time vowing the latest one would stick.

"Need help here," she said to the three women still staring at the television.

They ignored her. Pammy was about to start over when Val went ahead of her.

"Where do you want it?" Val asked Shirley, taking one side of the first table on the stack.

"In front of the counter, I think," Shirley said. "I'm pretty sure Pammy doesn't want grease all over her workspace."

"You're right." Pammy moved one of the smaller mats near the punching bags, but kept an eye on Val. Pammy wanted to see how hard it was for Val to lift something.

She handled the folded table just fine, but had trouble walking with it. That didn't surprise Pammy; women who had men in their lives often didn't do a lot of lifting, hauling, and maneuvering.

Small details told Pammy a great deal.

Pammy wiped her hands on the back of her shirt, then helped with the table, putting the legs down. Celeste and Jill moved the chairs around the table, facing them toward the TV.

"Ah, hell," Opal said. "Can't we sit around a couple tables? They're saying nothing's going to happen for a while."

Shirley went back for another table, and this time, Jill helped her. Celeste moved the chairs into place as Opal opened the pizza boxes.

"You still got paper plates in the back?" Midge Thornberg had torn herself away from the TV. She adjusted her thin white t-shirt over her cutoffs. She could wear the outfit beautifully, although Pammy had tried to discourage her. Once she moved into the more strenuous classes, the cutoffs wouldn't protect her legs from bruises and the occasional rug burn. Pammy wanted her to wear loose exercise clothing, but Midge was one of those women who liked showing off her spectacular figure, even when there were no men around.

"Paper plates are useless against good pizza," Opal said. "We brought back enough napkins for everyone."

Midge made a slight face. Pammy smiled at her. "I have paper plates and paper cups, but I'll get them. I'll bring some water out as well."

She didn't have beer or soda, at least not for the group. She tried to keep the food at the gym healthy, saving most of her unhealthy splurges for home.

She headed toward her private area in the back of the building, taking Val's file with her.

Pammy unlocked the door to her office, then set Val's file on the desk. Pammy closed the door again quickly and went to the kitchen, removing a stack of paper plates and paper cups from the storage shelf on one side of the kitchen. Paper plates would quickly dissolve into a soggy mess of pizza grease, but they were better than nothing.

She brought the plates to the nearest folding table. The women had already chosen their seats, leaving one for her nearest the television. She handed out two paper plates stuck together to each woman, then set two separate plate piles on each table. Pammy grabbed a slice of pepperoni and sank into her chair.

The pizza was still warm, but a little too thin. Kip's had skimped on the cheese. Or maybe that was just her opinion. She preferred Shakey's or Pepe's whenever she got take-out pizza, but she hadn't been part of the discussion.

The men on the television were recapping what had happened earlier, plus updating other bits of news from the day. She turned her chair so she didn't have to watch them.

Val was at the other table, her chair pushed back just enough to separate herself from the group. She wasn't participating in a conversation either. She was scanning the entire gym, taking it all in as if she were memorizing it.

Her gaze seemed to focus on the row of sweatshirts and t-shirts that had the gym's name emblazoned across the front. Pammy hadn't done that for advertising. She didn't really want to promote the gym too much. The very idea of the gym seemed to drive some men completely crazy.

She kept the shirts, along with sweat pants and some baggy shorts, for women who needed looser clothing but couldn't (or didn't try) to find it elsewhere. She always felt a bit embarrassed about the shirts, though, as if they were a touch of Madison Avenue that did not belong in her by-the-bootstraps place.

Then Pammy realized Val wasn't looking at the shirts as much as she was looking at the boxing gloves. Pammy kept boxing gloves in all sizes, with an emphasis on the smaller sizes—boy's sizes, the sports equipment makers called them. There were no women's sizes. She had a lot of extra tape and chalk, and an entire row of women's tennis shoes, since most women didn't even own a pair.

She also had mimeographed handouts stacked on one shelf, telling women the various places in the Bay Area that sold sports equipment—and, most importantly, sold it to women.

Midge said something to Val and she smiled just a little, returning her attention to the table. She took two more slices of pizza, something Pammy was glad to see. Pammy had worried that Val was one of those women who starved herself just to maintain some unachievable standard of beauty.

Maybe her thinness came from a long illness. Or maybe, like Shirley, she smoked too much, although Pammy hadn't smelled it on her.

Pammy took two slices of sausage and set them on a brand new paper plate, which she placed on top of the old one. She ate and half-listened to the conversation, not really paying attention.

Usually, she enjoyed the camaraderie of the women who came to the gym. Today, though, she felt just a little out of sorts. If she were honest with herself, she had felt that way all spring, ever since late April when it became clear that the transformation of a nearby vacant lot into a park by students and hippies was becoming an issue with the city.

Ever since People's Park blew up into an international event, Pammy had felt like real-world events were taking over her life.

Even this moon landing, as joyful as the rest of the women seemed to find it, annoyed her. She just wanted a normal Sunday. She wanted to spend time with her classes, do her accounts for the week, and head home for a glass of wine and a little reading.

But she wasn't going to go home until the moon events ended, how-ever they were going to end. And, although she could excuse herself from the group, she probably wasn't going to get her accounts done either. The accounting would have to wait until morning, which meant she would have to arrive early, which meant she would have to go to bed early.

She sighed softly, her entire schedule shifting because of Jill's idea to let women watch the moon landing.

Val stood, wiping off her fingers as she did so. She asked Jill where to put the paper plates. Jill grabbed one of the boxes, now empty of pizza, and flipped the lid up. Val set her plate in it.

Then she wandered toward the sweatshirts, stopping for just a moment at the gloves, as if they worried her. Pammy watched her, but didn't walk with her.

A lot of women did this when they first came to the gym, both famil-iarizing themselves with everything here, and also silently satisfying their curiosity. Most women had never been inside a men's gym.

Pammy had practically grown up in them.

Her father had trained her to fight alongside her brothers. He had started her training at age eight, seemingly on a whim. Her brothers abandoned the fighting and sparring by the time they reached their teens, but Pammy never did, even though her mother had objected because it wasn't ladylike.

Pammy didn't care about ladylike. She was good. She could take on the men at her father's favorite gym, and she actually made a bit of money by betting someone bigger and stronger that she could take him down.

She had never been wrong. By the time she graduated from high school and left to attend college on the other side of the country, she was one of the favorites at the gym. Regulars bet on her as well, and were never disappointed by her show of strength.

So she was surprised to get to liberal Berkeley, only to find that no one wanted to help an athletic girl retain her athleticism. She finally found a gym in a bad part of town that needed her money more than they wanted to exclude her. It didn't hurt that the day she arrived, she elbowed one of the regulars so hard in the gut that he couldn't catch his breath for nearly an hour.

She had smiled sweetly at him and said, *Try grabbing my ass again, and I'll hurt you worse.* Since he was still gasping for air at the time, he believed her and never tried to touch her again.

Pammy couldn't remember exactly when she had gotten the idea for a women-only gym, but she had realized early that the city needed one. She had tried to bring a female friend to the men's gym once, and the woman had fled in terror. Pammy then realized that her willingness to take on male harassment in a male environment was unique.

Pammy chewed on her now-cold piece of sausage pizza. Val had wound her way around the rows of shoes and gloves until she got to what had initially been the practice dummy.

Pammy had made the dummy so women had something with a face to hit. But the dummy wasn't very effective, and within a few weeks, she retired it.

Shortly after that, she had arrived at the gym one morning to find the dummy sitting on a chair, with a nightshirt on over its cloth body. Someone had drawn a calligraphy treatise on the shirt in magic marker:

I am not a different species, yet people call me chick, bitch, and cow.
I am not something good to eat, yet people call me cookie, honey, and tart.
I am not a mindless sex object, yet people call me cunt, whore, slut, and tramp.
I am not something other than an adult, yet people call me baby, girl, hag, shrew, doll, and old maid.
I am a woman.
I am a person.
Treat me like one.

Pammy loved it. She had tried to thank whoever it was who made the shirt, but no one confessed. She later learned that the poem came from a poster, but she could never find out who originally wrote it. Or who copied it onto the shirt.

Women who were new to the gym always stopped in front of it and read it. Some commented on it. Others walked away as if they couldn't believe what they were seeing.

Val was staring at it now, too far away for Pammy to see her expression. But Val had grabbed her own elbow again, holding her arms in

41

front her body. Not quite hugging herself, like she had done before she arrived, but still, protecting herself.

The poem had stirred something up in Val. Pammy wondered if she would ever find out what it was.

"Hey, Pammy?" someone said.

Pammy turned.

Shirley leaned forward. "I know there's no classes scheduled this afternoon, but would you be willing to run a sparring class?"

Pammy looked around the room. Most of the women here had not graduated to sparring yet. And Pammy didn't feel like running a class.

She couldn't quite refuse, though. They had hours to kill.

"Not a sparring class," she said. "Not everyone's qualified. Um, maybe…"

"I'm the one who is new." Val had returned to the group. "I could just go, and then you can run your class."

Pammy stood. She didn't want to be sitting down to have this conversation.

"No," she said. "A sparring class is pretty specific, and only a few women here are ready for it. Maybe Jill wouldn't mind leading another Tai Chi class…?"

Jill was gathering grease-covered paper plates and stuffing them into that open box. "I don't mind."

"Wonderful," Opal said. "I'll help you clean up and then we can start."

Pammy smiled just a little. She'd be able to get her accounts done after all.

"Nonetheless," Val said from beside her, "I think I'm going to go. Class is at eleven tomorrow?"

She had spoken so softly that the others hadn't heard her.

"Eleven," Pammy confirmed. "Wear some loose comfortable clothing, and if you have Keds or sneakers, wear those as well."

Val nodded, and smiled. "Thanks for everything."

"You're welcome," Pammy said. She was going to add that Val wouldn't have trouble with Tai Chi, but Val had already turned her back and was heading toward the door.

Pammy watched her go. Val's arms were at her sides now, and she wasn't scanning the room for hazards. Pammy hoped that was a good sign.

She wanted Val to come back.

VAL

The street seemed dusty and dirty after the interior of the gym. I'd been in a dozen gyms over the years, always with Truman, and I had never seen one so clean. Everything had a place, and the places seemed organized to the point of obsessiveness.

I liked it more than I probably should have, but the thing I liked the most was the punching bags. I could reach them. I'd never been able to reach punching bags before—not and maintain what Truman called "proper form."

I'd never really punched one without someone handing me a stool or holding me up, and I'd always wanted to.

I'd always wanted to spend time in a gym.

I ran a hand through my close-cropped hair. My heart was fluttering, but for the first time in my recent memory, it wasn't fluttering with fear. It was fluttering with excitement.

I'd made a choice. I'd made a major choice.

I had joined the gym. Pamela had told me to bring money for my fees tomorrow, but I could have paid her this afternoon. I think Pamela wanted me to think about it, see if I changed my mind.

I wouldn't change my mind.

This was the most alive I'd felt in six months.

All right, that wasn't entirely true. This was the most alive I'd felt without terror being involved. It was amazing how terror focused down every sensation, from intake of each breath to twitch of an eyelid.

It was also amazing how terror snuck up on you, even in the most mundane situations.

Just walking through the door of that gym had so terrified me that I hadn't been able to do it all week.

When Pamela came outside and spoke to me, I thought my heart was going to burst out of my chest. I almost ran away.

I almost ran away several times this afternoon.

Just going inside was a major victory. *Staying* inside was even more of a victory. And eating lunch with women I didn't know—*white* women I didn't know—so far beyond a victory that I didn't have words for it.

They were kind to me; I hadn't expect that. And no one asked me awkward questions, about myself or about my skin color or about my reasons for coming to the gym.

The women simply assumed that I wanted to learn, like they did. Two of them were trying to sell me on Pamela's classes, as if the women were afraid I would leave and never come back.

I suspected a number of women had done that over the years.

Still, I had to leave before the rest of them did. They felt like a unit, and I felt like an outsider, even though they were trying to convince me I wasn't.

And I wasn't that interested in the moon stuff, not enough to wait around.

I walked over to College Avenue. The streets were amazingly quiet. They hadn't been quiet since I got here two weeks ago.

I usually craved quiet. But now that it had arrived, it bothered me. I knew it wasn't normal.

Berkeley was usually a hub of activity—and not activity that I enjoyed.

If I had known what Berkeley was like, I would never have come here. But I'd stopped watching the news after *he* raped me. I couldn't bear to think about all the pain and suffering in the world. I'd read books I'd read before, so I wouldn't have to worry about how they came out.

I had protected myself—I thought. Of course, I had been wrong.

After I had gotten on the bus in Chicago, I had decided that Berkeley would be my destination. I'd heard about Berkeley over the years, how liberal it was, how it was all about education and thinking and study. Maybe, I had thought, I would go back to school, learn something new, make something of myself.

Maybe.

The bus terminal was in Oakland, not Berkeley. I had disembarked, thinking I'd catch a cab. Then I stepped outside the bus terminal into an area that made Chicago's South Side look safe. I almost turned around and bought a ticket to somewhere else.

But I had promised myself Berkeley, so I decided to give Berkeley a chance.

Even then, I hadn't paid attention to all of the changes. I'd been thinking I was going to a university town.

I loved universities, I always had, and I knew that the University of California at Berkeley was one of the best schools in the country. I ended up with a lot of money when Truman died. I didn't want it since we had been divorced when he was murdered, but I couldn't say no to it either. And, as Marvella said to me, it wasn't like I could work. Truman had died shortly after I was injured. I needed to recover—not just from the physical injuries, but from the emotional ones too.

Marvella argued that the money would let me do that.

Still, I knew how hard Truman had worked for every dime. Even though we were no longer married, I still cared for him. I wasn't sure I had ever loved him, but I valued him, and his opinion.

He had been a good man.

At the very thought of him, I teared up. My emotions had been on the surface ever since I woke up in the hospital with the baby—and all the chances of other babies—gone forever.

I turned onto College. I preferred walking this way, because it took me away from People's Park and that gigantic mess. Even though the mess had ended by the time I moved here, it still reverberated.

Which was probably why I had been able to get a furnished apartment so close to campus and relatively cheap. The neighborhood made me nervous, not because it was bad (it wasn't. It was lovely), but because there was so much constant movement. People on the streets at all hours. Shouting, laughing, cursing. Partying.

I was afraid it would get worse once school started.

My walk from the gym to the apartment took about ten minutes. It was a lovely day—as far as I could tell, Berkeley didn't get excessively hot in the summer—and no one was on the streets.

They must have been watching the moon landing like everyone else. I would've thought that the silence on the streets made me calmer, but instead, it started my nerves again. I felt like I was missing something.

The skin on the back of my neck crawled as I walked past Dwight toward the zigzag on Parker that would lead to my street.

I'd spent enough Sundays in Berkeley to know that students should've been everywhere, sitting outside with their books, sharing their music, eating while sitting beneath the large trees that seemed to grow all over this part of town.

But there were no students. I clenched my fists, glad that I had gone to the gym. I needed the classes. I needed to feel safe.

Particularly in situations like this one. I had been attacked on an empty street right in front of my apartment building. *He* had shoved me through the doorway of the building and into the quiet hall, and the one thing I didn't do, the one thing I was proud I hadn't done, was let him into the apartment, even though he wanted me to. Even though he...

I shook my head, forced my thoughts away from that night.

It was nothing like now. That street had been dark, the streetlight broken. It had been cold. It had been in Chicago. I had been alone.

I was alone here too. But it was a beautiful sunny day. The sidewalk was wide and visible, despite the overhanging trees and the beautiful, unfamiliar blooming plants. Windows were open, and I heard voices, faint male voices. They had to belong to the announcers on various televisions.

A few tinny notes of music came from some of the apartments, so some of the people on the block were ignoring the Big National News story. The music was so loud that they wouldn't be able to hear anyone crying for help on the street either.

I let out a breath, wishing I hadn't had that thought. I was trying to control my mind, my panic. I'd learned that if I let thoughts like that escape, they became the focus.

I made myself inhale. The air smelled faintly of the ocean, but over it was the dusty green scent of the willow trees I'd been walking under. Nice day. I had spent some time with nice people. The neighborhood was nice.

But it was *loud*. That was one of the things I hated about it. People talked too loud when they were outside. They played their music too loud. There were a lot of transients—or so I guessed, since no one introduced themselves to me after I moved in.

Although the introduction-thing, that might've been for other reasons. Even though Berkeley was liberal city, with an even more liberal college, it didn't seem to have as many black students as I expected. Maybe that was just the summer. I saw a number of blacks, but not nearly as many as I had seen in Chicago.

I felt out of place in Berkeley, and people watched me go by. There were a lot more Asian students than I expected, and a lot of hippies. The entire neighborhood smelled of pot sometimes. But only a handful of people looked like me.

And usually when blacks were in short supply, anyone new seemed suspicious, not someone to say hello to.

I finally reached my building. It was a lovely old house, built at the turn of the century. Someone had painted it an ill-advised lime green, but at least it had been painted. An apartment service my hotel recommended had rented it to me without a problem, so maybe my worries about discrimination were not an issue.

Or maybe paying three months in advance, along with the security deposit and first and last month's rent, did a lot to ameliorate any issues some rental agent might have with someone who looked like me.

It didn't matter. I had fallen in love with the apartment.

The apartment was on the second floor of the old house. I looked both ways as I came up the walk, and checked to see if anyone was watching me before I ducked past the weeping willow tree in the front yard.

I hated that tree at night. If there was the smallest of breezes, the fronds moved. They made a soft rustling noise, which scared the crap out of me.

Today, though, they were motionless, and I could see through them. I walked up the concrete stairs to what had once been the above-ground entrance to the old house. (The lowest level had been built for either a carriage or an automobile, and if I had a car, I could have used my little section of it as parking.)

I used my outdoor key to unlock the steel main door. It opened to reveal stairs on the left wall, which headed up to my apartment, and a door on the right that led into the other apartment. My neighbors were a Korean couple here on some kind of study visa. I'd only met them once. The wife was so unnerved by the neighborhood that she rarely left the building.

I took the stairs up and unlocked the deadbolt on my door. I had installed a chain lock as well. Before I rented the place, the first thing I had looked at was the ease of access from the outside, and I felt reassured.

Anyone who wanted to break in would have to go through a window on the lower levels. That steel door was unbreakable.

All of the windows opened outward, and none of them opened onto a roofline or any kind of balcony. None of the neighborhood trees were near the windows, and the fence that blocked off the tiny outdoor garden from the neighbor's property wasn't tall enough to allow someone to get purchase on the side of the building.

Once I was inside my apartment, I was safe.

And as important, at least to me, I felt like I was home. The door opened right into the middle of the apartment. To the left was the large living room and a large bedroom. To the right was the bathroom and an extra-large kitchen with a space big enough for a gigantic dining room table.

The furniture was old student furniture, which the rental company would let me swap out for my own if I decided to stay past the three months I'd paid for. The bed was the first thing that would probably go. It sagged in the middle, and I tried not to think about the generations of students who had slept (and done other things) in it.

What I liked best about the apartment were two things: the built-in bookshelves that lined the long hallway between the kitchen and the living room, and the fact that the unit had one of those new modern mini washer and dryer units that cost a small fortune.

I didn't have to go into a scary basement or an even scarier Laundromat to clean my clothes.

That might've been enough to get me to rent the apartment right there, even without the space and the built-ins. Once I was in the apartment for the day, I was in for as long as I needed to be.

I shut the door, locked it, and leaned on it. Somehow, on my short journey from the gym to the apartment, I'd managed to go from triumph back to terror. It was as if my body had rewired itself in the past year to be comfortable with terror.

I hated that thought. I hated what I had become. In the past, I hadn't been the most courageous woman on the planet, but I hadn't been afraid of everything. I couldn't have been a policeman's wife if I had been.

I made myself take another deep breath. It was warm up here. I had sun pouring in the windows on three sides, and it beat in during the afternoons. I usually didn't mind; I found the sun healing.

Today, after that walk (after the renewed panic) it almost felt like too much.

I made myself step away from the door. I had already filled a lot of the shelves with new books. My old books were in storage in Chicago. I'd spent some of my days here in Berkeley haunting the plethora of used bookstores. Cody's Books on Telegraph had become a second home.

I was reading at least a book a day, but that wasn't keeping up with my buying habits. This afternoon was unusual, in that I hadn't brought anything home with me to read.

I almost went into the kitchen and turned on the television, but I didn't. There wouldn't be anything on besides the moon landing, and I'd seen enough.

I had two televisions in the apartment, both of which I had bought. One was small and portable. I had it on one of the kitchen counters so that I could watch while I cooked.

The other was in my bedroom. I couldn't sleep most nights, so I often watched until the test pattern forced me to shut the television off. Even then, I couldn't stand the quiet, although logically, I should have let the room remain quiet so I could listen for whatever was outside to threaten me.

I kept the radio on, usually tuned to KPAT for the music. The radio in the kitchen was tuned to KPFA, and I found I listened to that more than watched the television. I liked the eclectic listener-sponsored programming and the volunteer DJs. I actually felt tied into the community, listening to KPFA.

I wasn't hungry—I had eaten more this afternoon than I had eaten in days—but I felt at loose ends. I was too restless to read. I paced the apartment's long narrow hallway, my mood alternating between jubilation and panic at the decision I had made.

For the first time since I'd left Chicago—actually, for the first time since I'd left the hospital—I was choosing to interact with people. It had felt good this afternoon. Odd, but good.

I still felt fragile, but I was hoping that the exercise, the *training*, that Pammy Griffin said she could provide would make that fragility go away. Before, I never thought about how strong I was. Now, all I thought about was how weak I was, and I hated it. It needed to change.

I needed to change—again.

And this time, I had to initiate that change, and I had to follow through.

No matter how hard it was going to be, I had to do the work.

Because I wasn't going to spend the rest of my life hiding alone in my apartment, wherever that was. If I did, then I was still being terrorized. Even though I'd moved. Even though *he* was dead. I would still be keeping him in my life.

He had changed me, but he couldn't defeat me.

I wouldn't let him.

It was time for him to move out. For good.

EAGLE

After the cops left, Eagle couldn't stay in her apartment. She had too much energy. She wanted to hit someone, and she knew the perfect place to do it.

She stuffed her regular identification and a few dollars into her pocket along with her keys, and headed out of the apartment. As she stepped into the hall, she could hear televisions blaring. It sounded like they were tuned to the same channel, and the voices sounded like newscasters.

She wondered what was going on. Usually when all the TVs were tuned to the same channel, the Raiders or the Warriors were playing. But that was in the fall and winter, and it was July. Right now, the Giants were playing the Dodgers at Candlestick, but that game wouldn't have been on television. Local games were blacked out.

She shook her head slightly, not in the mood to find out what national tragedy had hit on a sunny Sunday afternoon. She was shaken up enough by the damn cops.

She hurried down the stairs and out the door. She walked to the edge of the street, then stopped, startled.

It was sunny and 75 degrees, just about the perfect summer day—and no one was on the street. That was weird. Even when the National Guard was everywhere, people were on the street.

She couldn't remember the last time that people had stayed home.

Her stomach twisted. Something really bad was happening, then. She pivoted, and walked to Pammy's gym.

Even if Pammy wasn't there, Eagle had a key. Pammy wanted someone else to be able to get in at a moment's notice. She sometimes let street people stay in the gym, something Eagle thought was a mistake. Vagrants were desperate, and at some point, one of them would either trash the place or steal all the important stuff from it.

But Pammy was the ultimate bleeding-heart liberal, and nothing Eagle could do would change that. She walked the half block in the strange quiet, and turned at the alley, to let herself in the gym's back door.

She hated going through the front door. She felt like a fraud when she did that. She usually didn't work out in the gym, and she didn't spar. She didn't want to hurt her hands.

But on a day like today, when the night's events crowded her, she needed to let out the anger. If she didn't, she'd smoke too much dope and maybe move to drinking too much. If she did that, she'd end up just like her mother.

Cleaning the apartment showed Eagle that she was too damn close to the edge as it was. The pot residue on the surfaces had been thick. She'd been smoking every night before bed to calm herself. She had to stop that. Nothing good would come from it.

At least, the detectives hadn't said anything. The smell of bleach must have overpowered the oils left by the smoke, but it was damn close.

Or maybe the cops just expected every apartment in this part of Berkeley to smell like pot and patchouli oil.

Eagle passed the garbage cans, which reeked of rotted food and dirty cat litter. Two giant piles of dog crap drew flies near the mouth of the alley, and she suspected she walked across some dog urine as well. Students around here who had dogs had stopped running them in the park since the troubles started in early May.

Since then, Eagle had walked in more dog crap than she wanted to think about.

She reached the gym's back door and unlocked it, stepping inside. The back entrance opened into the small kitchen that Pammy kept for her personal use.

Eagle wiped her feet on the mat and took a deep breath, figuring she'd smell it if she tracked anything inside. The small room smelled of Palmolive and Lemon Pledge, just like it usually did. There was no coffee on the stove, like there often was when Pammy was here.

Eagle let out a small breath. She was relieved to be alone. She wasn't sure she was up to a discussion with Pammy. All Eagle wanted to do was slide on some gloves and hit a punching bag for a while. Pammy had shown her how to hit one and protect her hands, and right now, Eagle needed to blow off that steam before she did something crazy.

She opened the door and let herself into the main part of the gym. Female laughter reached her, along with another sound, lower, just outside her normal hearing range.

She stopped, startled. All the signs had indicated that no one was here. Her entire body froze.

It was Sunday, wasn't it? Pammy rarely ran classes on Sunday. She liked to take Sundays off when she could.

Eagle debated disappearing through the back door and finding some other way to let out all of her energy. Then she heard her name.

She looked up. Pammy was gesturing at her.

"We have pizza, and a TV," Pammy said, as if those were things Eagle would want.

Eagle didn't like the "we" and she didn't know why they would need a TV. Pammy really wasn't a sports fan, and there were no fights in the afternoon—at least, not professional level fights that were being broadcast.

But Eagle's stomach growled. She could smell the garlic and tomato of the pizza. She wasn't sure when she had eaten last.

She stepped in farther, thumbs hooked in her back pockets. A group of women sat at two different card tables, picking at pizza and laughing as if they were having a fantastic time.

Eagle had trouble processing that. The television on in the middle of the day, and women at A Gym of Her Own, sitting down, not participating in a class. It was just too weird to contemplate.

Pammy walked toward her, smiling. Pammy was a good woman. A little too muscular to be considered feminine, but she didn't entirely care. She might have cared once, back when Eagle met her, when Pammy actually wore her light brown hair in a flip-do and put on makeup every morning.

But as the gym became more and more successful, Pammy dropped the rollers-at-night hairstyle and stopped putting on anything except a touch of lipstick. She also stopped wearing dresses. Either she was in loose-fitting pants and a comfortable top, along with a pair of Keds, or she wore blue jeans and a t-shirt, just like the students did.

Her hair had gotten wash-it-fast short, and she didn't wear any jewelry at all. Yet she looked a lot more comfortable with herself than she had in years.

"I didn't expect to see you today," Pammy said. Whatever was on the television, it wasn't a national crisis. Pammy had cried her way through the assassinations of 1968 while Eagle had watched stoically, unsurprised.

People shot each other. People hated each other. If growing up half-Native hadn't taught Eagle that, then Nam certainly would have. And had.

"I thought this place would be empty," Eagle said, then wished she hadn't. That sentence was more revealing than she wanted it to be.

Pammy tilted her head slightly. "You don't remember, do you? I invited you here today to watch the moon landing."

Eagle let out a small breath. She had forgotten all about that particular idiocy. Let's send a bunch of men to the moon, rather than put money into helping wounded vets reintegrate into society or the thousand other uses those millions could have been put to. Hell, if they'd used the entire NASA budget elsewhere, maybe LBJ would have won his War on Poverty and had had enough courage to run for reelection.

"Oh, yeah," Eagle said when she could trust her voice. "I forgot."

Pammy frowned. "Everything all right?"

Eagle suppressed a sigh. When Pammy's blue eyes focused on someone like that, there was no getting away without an answer.

"Everything's fine," Eagle said, knowing her tone was too dry, but unable to do anything about it. "You got pizza, huh?"

"It's cold now, but I could warm it up," Pammy said.

Which meant turning on the oven and waiting. Waiting meant conversation, not that Eagle knew how to get out of it.

"Naw," Eagle said. "Cold is just fine."

She'd said *fine* twice, which was probably some kind of red flag to Pammy that Eagle wasn't fine. So Eagle walked away from her, heading to the gaggle of women.

For some reason, Pammy's place just off of Telegraph, in the heart of radical Berkeley, attracted housewives. The gaggle had at least five of them that Eagle could see, women who wore the right clothes, had their hair just so, and went home to hubby every night. No conversations about real life or what they had done with their day. Just spending pin money on their little exercise hobby, thinking it made them stronger or safer at night or fulfilling some empty time that Eagle could never imagine.

She smiled at them, knowing the smile didn't reach her eyes. Then she looked at the open cardboard pizza boxes. They were stained with grease and had cheese attached to the lid. Someone had consolidated two pizzas into one box.

She took a paper plate and grabbed two pieces of pepperoni. The pizzas looked a little thin and grease had congealed on the top.

She'd eaten worse.

"Did you see it?" one of the women asked her, nodding toward the TV.

Eagle glanced over. Walter Cronkite was talking to some other man, gesturing with whatever passed for excitement in Cronkite's world.

If Eagle said no to the woman's question, then Eagle would be regaled with stories of the landing. If she said yes, then they'd want to know what she thought of it all.

She smiled at them again, as she grabbed a few napkins.

"Great day for America, huh?" she said, like she used to say to visiting brass in Saigon, just before she shipped home. She hoped the women didn't hear her sarcasm.

Then she moved away from them, thinking maybe she'd sit in the kitchen.

Her skin was crawling. She still felt that pent-up rage, and she wasn't sure what to do with it.

Pammy hadn't followed her to the table. Instead, Pammy still stood near the locker room door.

"What's up?" Pammy asked, placing one hand on Eagle's back, directing her to the kitchen.

Eagle stepped slightly sideways. She didn't like to be touched, and normally Pammy was good about that. But Pammy seemed to have made a calculation—touch Eagle and get her to do something that she wasn't going to do otherwise.

Pammy opened the kitchen door and waited. Eagle couldn't very well sit in the main room. Near the chairs, she'd have to converse. And if she went to the mats, then someone was bound to follow her. She didn't want to go into the locker room.

So now she was going to be interrogated by a well-meaning Pammy.

Eagle bit back her irritation and went into the kitchen.

Pammy followed her. "You want some coffee?"

"I'm fine," Eagle said, and silently cursed herself. She had to forget that she even knew that word.

"Well, I want coffee." Pammy grabbed the percolator, took off the lid, and carried the body to the sink. She turned on the faucet and filled the body to the highest water mark.

Eagle looked longingly at the door. Maybe she could just walk out. Pammy might ask her about it the next time, but Pammy might forget.

"You gonna tell me what's up?" Pammy asked, looking at her sideways.

Caught. Dammit. Eagle sank into a wooden chair near the small kitchen table. Once Pammy asked that question, there was no getting away.

"Frustrating day," Eagle said.

"I'm gathering that." Pammy set the body of the percolator on the tiny counter, grabbed the basket, and measured some Folgers into it. "You want to tell me about it?"

No, Eagle didn't want to tell her about it. Eagle wanted to punch something.

She took a bite of pizza. It was lukewarm, not cold, and better than she expected.

"You don't have to," Pammy said, clearly lying. Because Pammy would push her forever to say whatever it was. Or make Eagle feel guilty about it.

Eagle wasn't sure how the two of them became friends, because they were so damn different. Except in one thing: they both stood up for the people they cared about.

And right now, Pammy was showing care for her.

Eagle sighed. "Cops," she said.

Pammy turned, still holding the coffee scoop. "You had a run-in with the cops?"

"Not a run-in," Eagle said. "They didn't believe me."

"About what?"

"I saw a woman get beaten and tossed in the back of a pickup last night," Eagle said.

Pammy closed her eyes for a moment, absorbing that news, then nodded, and set the scoop in the sink. She finished putting the percolator back together and set it on the stove, turning on the burner.

"You called the cops," Pammy said.

"Yeah. Happened just after midnight. The cops showed up less than an hour ago."

"God," Pammy breathed.

Eagle took another bite of pizza, then she got up and grabbed a glass, filling it with water. She kept her back to Pammy as she asked, "You hear anything about a guy in a pickup truck randomly grabbing women?"

"No," Pammy said. "The women who come here right now are more afraid of the authorities than anyone else."

Eagle nodded. She could have told the government that, even if anyone had listened. The show of force, the untrained young men with guns, the sheer harassment and terror of the past few months, led to more distrust, not less.

She drank the entire glass of water, then filled it again.

"The police think that this was something they called a *domestic*, meaning—"

"I know what it means," Pammy said curtly. Of course she did. Her father had been a police officer back east somewhere. She probably would have followed in his footsteps had she been a boy. "Did it look like a husband and wife fighting?"

"No." Eagle turned around. "It looked like this guy was kidnapping her."

Big word, kidnapping. She felt her skin grow warm. Pammy didn't seem to notice, though.

"She was fighting for her life," Eagle said, then sank back into her chair. "I should've shot the son of a bitch, I swear."

Pammy gave her an empathetic look. "Have you ever shot anyone?"

"Intentionally?" Eagle asked.

Pammy didn't smile. Pammy never smiled when Eagle made a dry joke like that. A joke that wasn't really a joke.

"No," Eagle said after a moment. "I have never shot anyone."

"You don't have that kind of training," Pammy said.

"I know how to shoot," Eagle snapped.

"I meant that you don't have the training it takes to shoot another human being," Pammy said. "In fact, your training is the exact opposite. You're not supposed to harm anyone. You're supposed to save them."

Pammy was doing her magic empathy trick on Eagle, and Eagle didn't like it.

"Well, I fucked that up," Eagle said. "Because that woman is probably dead now."

She looked down at the pizza crust on her plate. She didn't remember eating all of the first piece. Stress eating, yet another sign of her mental health.

"You did what you could," Pammy said.

"No, I didn't." Eagle stood. The restless energy was back. "I should've driven to the goddamn police station and sat on those assholes until they sent someone out to investigate. Instead, I went back to my little hole and expected the Good Guys to solve it all."

Just like she always had. Part of her believed in the Good Guys— enough to join up and become one of them. Then she'd seen what the Good Guys did under duress, and she had felt her illusions crack. Apparently they hadn't entirely shattered, or she wouldn't have waited for the damn cops to show up at her door.

"You don't know," Pammy said softly. "Maybe they looked."

"They didn't look," Eagle said. "They aren't looking now."

The percolator started humming as the water boiled.

"We could do a flyer," Pammy said. "Maybe find someone to draw the guy."

"And say what?" Eagle asked. "Help us find this guy? He might've killed someone?"

Pammy shrugged. "I don't know."

She glanced at the water bubbling in the glass globe on top.

"I can't...." Eagle stopped herself. She didn't want the full sentence to come out of her mouth: the fact that she couldn't get that woman's screams out of her head.

Of course, they blended with lots of other screams, screams she had brought home from Pleiku, screams she had heard in May when she was trying to help kids on the streets outside this building.

"Do you have the license plate number?" Pammy asked.

"I gave it to the cops." Eagle didn't tell Pammy that she had also kept the number. What good would that do?

"Maybe we could just put up something in here," Pammy said. "Watch for this pickup truck."

"Why?" Eagle asked. "What would we *do*, Pammy? Call the cops? They're not going to want to hear it. Go after the guy ourselves? I couldn't shoot the bastard. I couldn't save her. What are your little housewives going to do? Henpeck him to death?"

"Eagle, that's not fair." Pammy moved the percolator, then shut off the burner.

"Fair." Eagle spit out the word. She hated the word *fair*. "This fucking town. There's nothing fair about it."

Or about any other part of the life she had known these last few years. She'd thought of moving after the People's Park riots, and ruled it out.

Maybe ruling it out had been hasty.

There was a timid knock on the outside of the door.

"Hey," someone said, not waiting for an answer. "It sounds like they're getting ready for the moon walk."

Pammy glanced at the clock on the stove, and frowned. "That's early," she said softly.

The knock sounded again.

"Thank you," she said, louder. "We'll be right out."

Eagle stood. "I'm not watching that. Thanks for the pizza."

Pammy sighed. "Wait. Tell me exactly what that truck looked like."

"So you'll make a flyer? It won't do any good," Eagle said.

"If this was a *domestic*, as the police think," Pammy said, "then you're right, Eagle. It won't do any good. But if this man is picking up women off the street and hurting them somehow—"

Hurting them, then grabbing them off the street, Eagle corrected, but didn't say.

"—then the more information we have about him, the safer everyone is." Pammy grabbed a cup and saucer for herself, then found another for Eagle, even though Eagle hadn't asked for any coffee.

Eagle ran a hand over her face. Pammy was right. If what Eagle saw was what it seemed—a kidnapping—then the man might do it again. And what could it hurt, having the information out there?

Eagle answered her own mental question. It could hurt a lot if the guy knew they were looking for him.

"You promise me you'll keep the information inside this gym, and not staple flyers to telephone poles or something stupid like that," Eagle said.

"I promise," Pammy said.

Eagle cursed, then shook her head. This was how Pammy roped her in. Always. Pammy sounded so damn reasonable, and then Eagle was doing something she had initially thought a terrible idea.

Like providing medical help to the hens out in the main room. Like helping Pammy keep this ill-advised place running.

Like putting up a flyer about some guy who nearly beat a woman to death.

"I didn't see the truck as clearly as I wanted to," Eagle started, as Pammy grabbed a sheet of paper and a pen, and took down every detail Eagle told her.

Every detail Eagle could remember, details she knew would never be enough.

PAMMY

Pammy felt oddly out of sorts the following morning. She'd been up half the night thinking about Eagle's story. Eagle was worried that if they did anything, talked about the guy, put up flyers, asked questions, he would come back and get them.

Underneath her tough exterior, Eagle was exceptionally paranoid.

Pammy had arrived at the gym earlier than she had planned. When it became clear that she couldn't sleep, she had gotten up and gone through her routine, making her arrive an hour early.

She brought a newspaper with her. The headlines, on all the papers, concerned the moon landing. Everything from *The Eagle Has Landed* to *One Small Step For Mankind* to *Two Men Explore Dead Moon* stared at her from the newspaper boxes.

All of the moon euphoria wasn't keeping Eagle's comments about taking on the guy from playing over and over in Pammy's head. Eagle's story bothered Pammy, though, because it didn't fall into any category. Like the cops, Pammy would have thought it a domestic until Eagle described the level of violence and the way the man had treated the woman.

Something was really off.

But then, something had been really off in Berkeley—hell, in the country—for years now.

The gym still smelled faintly of pizza, although the women had cleaned it up before they left. Pammy had taken the garbage out herself, hoping to get rid of any lingering odors.

But she couldn't open windows in the front part of the gym, and she hated leaving the door open. It only invited transients and people who felt like they needed to make some sort of comment on everything she was doing.

She had the radio on in the gym, but all she was getting was more news. Discussion of the moon landing, the Giants' win over the Dodgers, and some strange story about the only surviving Kennedy brother leaving the scene of an accident. She didn't care about any of it, but she was too lazy to change the channel to some music.

She wiped a few surfaces and put out more sign-up sheets. She thought again about doing some kind of warning flyer about the man that Eagle had seen and taping it to the check-in counter, but didn't act on it. Obviously, Pammy was feeling a little paranoid too.

Instead, she set out small tumbling mats for the beginners' exercise class. She also put out some jump ropes, knowing she would probably get protests.

As she moved deeper into the gym, she touched the gloves that had attracted Val's attention the day before. Val was an intriguing woman, but that hadn't caused Pammy to treat her any differently from anyone else.

Pammy hadn't taken Val's payment for the class. She never did with impulsive first-timers. She wanted them to have twenty-four hours or so to think about their decision since so many of them never returned to the gym.

Unlike some of her male colleagues, who considered walk-ins found money, Pammy hated taking cash from people who ended up changing their minds. She didn't think it was an "indecision tax" as Mountain Phillips, the man who owned the gym she used to attend, called it.

She would rather let the woman keep her money and decide when to spend it. Pammy always thought of the initial payment as a down payment in courage.

And sometimes, it took a few attempts for people to tap the courage inside of them.

She suspected it would take Val a few more weeks before she returned.

Which showed just how wrong Pammy was. Val arrived ahead of everyone else. She wore a loose Chicago Police Department t-shirt, which surprised the heck out of Pammy, and a pair of sweatpants that were tied tightly to her too-thin waist.

She carried a shoebox under one arm, and Pammy knew without looking that the box held a new pair of sneakers.

Val's eyes were bright. She looked both eager and terrified in equal measure. She had been waiting outside the front door when Pammy unlocked it an hour after she arrived. Val slipped inside as if she didn't want anyone to see her.

Now she stood in front of the counter, her gaze drifting to the moon landing headline, her new sneakers resting on one of the sign-up sheets. She rocked from foot to foot as if she couldn't keep still.

"Do you take checks?" she asked. "Because I have cash if you need it."

Pammy smiled reassuringly at her. "I take checks."

Val reached into the macramé bag she had slung diagonally across her torso. "Do you want just the class fee, because if there's a member-ship fee too, I'd rather pay it all at once."

Everyone assumed the gym had a membership fee, but it didn't. Jill said that Pammy made a mistake by not charging even a token fee. But Pammy didn't want the hassle of renewals and collecting money for no real reason.

Instead, she made a rule: If a woman took classes, then she could come to the gym any time it was open. If she didn't take classes, she wasn't welcome.

Not that Pammy enforced the second part. Eagle had never taken a class, but she came to the gym all the time. Of course, she helped with the medical emergencies. In fact, all of the women who came to the gym without going to a class seemed to help Pammy in one way or another. They had all started out taking classes (except Eagle) and they all had stuck around.

"No gym membership fee," Pammy said. "If you take a class, you're welcome to use the gym outside of class."

Val looked at her, wide-eyed, then surveyed the entire gym, as if seeing it for the first time.

Pammy braced herself for the inevitable unsolicited *You should charge fees*. Instead, Val said, "Wow. This is really special, you know?"

Pammy smiled at her. Finally, someone who understood. "Yes," Pammy said. "It is."

Val opened her mouth as if she were going to say something else, but she stopped. She opened her checkbook, which she kept in a tooled leather holder. Her hands were shaking.

Pammy wanted to tell her everything was going to be all right. But Pammy had banned that phrase from her patter when the first of her students went home after class, told her husband where she had been, and landed in the hospital with a black eye.

One class did not a fighter make, although the student had defended herself well enough to get out of the house and over to a neighbor's. Jill had said that the student probably would have died if she hadn't gotten away.

Pammy had thought the student wouldn't have been hit at all if she hadn't taken the class.

Opal had been the one who added that they wouldn't have known if they hadn't met the woman, who never did come back.

So many students never came back.

Pammy's stomach twisted as she watched Val write *A Gym of Her Own* in the check's "to" line, and then, in one of the most lovely cursives Pammy had seen, added the amount, and signed her name.

She ripped off the check, and handed it to Pammy. The act of writing the check seemed to stop the shaking.

Pammy nodded at the shirt. "Chicago PD?"

Val's cheeks grew red, and her eyes seemed just a bit brighter. "I shouldn't have worn that shirt down here. I knew it."

She sounded like she had made a major faux pas.

"No, no," Pammy said. "You're fine. No one's going to mind."

"But all the problems with the police here," Val said. "I'm being insensitive."

She had that run-away energy again.

"No, you're not being insensitive," Pammy said. "My father was a police officer. Philly PD."

The desperate look on Val's face faded. "Really?"

She sounded almost childlike.

Pammy nodded. "He's the one who taught me how to defend myself. We spent years in gyms."

Val swallowed. "This shirt was my…husband's."

Pammy wondered what the pause meant.

"He, he always wanted me to learn how to fight. He even took me to a few gyms, and I told him…" Val closed her eyes, then took a deep breath, as if she were steeling herself. Then she opened her eyes again. "I told him that I would never need to learn to fight. I had him."

She gave a mirthless chuckle, then shook her head. She said nothing else.

"I take it," Pammy said slowly, waiting for Val to give her a clue as to whether or not she should stop speaking, "you don't have him anymore?"

Val's eyes filled with tears. "That's right."

She slapped her hand lightly on the checkbook, then put it back in her purse. She sniffled, grabbed a tissue from the countertop, and lifted one strap of the purse.

"Any place I can put this?" she asked.

Pammy nodded toward the locker room. "Back there is relatively safe."

Val nodded, grabbed her shoebox, and headed to the locker room.

Pammy wasn't sure if she had screwed that conversation up, or if she had done the right thing. Sometimes some of these new students were so fragile that the wrong look could make them leave.

It didn't help that most women felt like they shouldn't be in a gym in the first place, or that exercise was something ladies didn't do.

Pammy put the check in the cashbox, and slid it in the drawer behind the counter. She'd take it into the back once class started.

The main door opened. Pammy glanced over, then felt her eyebrows go up involuntarily. A man had walked in.

Men almost never came in here. Either they stood outside and laughed as they pointed at the gym's name, or they walked in and then walked right out again.

The handful who did come inside and stay were usually business-men. Pammy's lawyer came in once to inspect the place; her insurance broker came in several times last year, looking—Eagle thought—for ways to cancel her policy; and the mailman stopped in daily, usually resting his elbow on the counter and making some derogatory comment that he seemed to think was funny.

This man wasn't anyone she recognized. He was older, balding, and bulky, although she couldn't tell if the bulk was fat or muscle. He wore a thick plaid shirt over olive green work pants and boots that had seen better days. He brought with him the scents of garlic and pipe tobacco, which she suspected would get stronger as he got closer.

He was twisting rolled up papers between his hands, and he looked around as if this place didn't make any sense to him. Finally, his gaze rested on Pammy.

"Can I help you?" she asked.

"I—I'm looking for my daughter," he said.

Pammy felt her heart sink. She'd had these kinds of conversations before: worried spouses, worried parents, who didn't want their wife or kids to interact with the "hippies" down on Telegraph. Pammy had learned to treat these people kindly, but firmly. She would clear up any misconceptions, but she wouldn't tell anyone to stop coming to the gym.

"What's your daughter's name?" she asked, making certain her expression was pleasant and her tone non-threatening.

He had a crease between his eyes. They were swollen. He kept looking around, his gaze never really landing on anything for very long.

"Darla Newsome." He sounded breathless. He walked over to the counter, still twisting the papers. "She's Darla Newsome."

Pammy had been right; his body odor was stronger up close. Beneath the pipe smoke and garlic, he also smelled of sweat and raw onions.

"I don't remember a Darla Newsome," Pammy said, "but that doesn't mean she hasn't come here. So many kids today have taken on nicknames. Is there some other name she might have used?"

He started to shake his head, then stopped, and shrugged. "I don't know."

He sounded hopeless, as if the idea of his daughter with a nickname he didn't know were one thing too many.

He set the papers on the counter, unrolling them and flattening them with his big callused hands.

"This is her," he said, pointing at a black-and-white high school graduation photo. The girl had a broad face and the same kind of flip hair-do that Pammy used to have before it became too much work. "She's missing."

The distress in his voice made Pammy's heart twist. She hadn't expect this. She thought about Eagle's story from the day before.

"When did she disappear?" Pammy was still looking at the photo, running through images in her mind. The girl didn't look familiar, but so many kids changed their appearance between high school and college, the fact that Pammy didn't recognize the girl didn't mean anything.

"I don't know," he said, then he clenched one of his hands into a fist. "She came here, and…"

His voice trailed off.

"Here," Pammy said. "You mean the university?"

He nodded. "National Merit Scholar, all expenses paid. We couldn't afford something like this."

Pammy looked up at him. His nose was red. He tilted his head, shrugged again.

"When did you last speak to her?" Pammy asked.

"Her and me, we aren't speaking." He was almost whispering now. "But her ma, she got calls every week, and then tells me about it. Until June."

"June?" Pammy asked. "Beginning or end?"

He swallowed. "End," he said. "Two weeks before the Fourth. Darla was saying nutty stuff about America, and I didn't like it. God forgive me."

They had split over politics. That was happening so much these days. Pammy tried not to talk about any of it so she could keep her students, but sometimes the day's events—whatever they were—spilled into a confrontation between her homemakers and her hippies.

He said, "Her roommate hasn't seen her for a whole month. That's how we knew. Her roommate wanted us to pay the rent."

"Did you?" Pammy asked before she could stop herself.

"Of course," he said. "Her stuff is still there. Her *purse* is still there, and nobody thought nothing of it. And the police, they won't listen. Her boyfriend, he's moved on to some other girl, so they think she ran off with a broken heart, went to Ashbury Haters or whatever—"

"Haight Ashbury," Pammy said softly. Two years before, a lot of kids went to the Haight for something the media called The Summer of Love. But those kids had moved on to other places. It wasn't the "happening" place anymore.

Besides, if Darla was in Berkeley, she would have stayed here. The center of the hippie universe had moved to Telegraph, not the Haight.

"Do you know her?" he asked, his voice cracking. He gripped the edge of the counter. His fingernails were bitten to the quick.

"Not from this photo," Pammy said. "But that doesn't mean anything. She might've changed her look—"

"Oh, she did, but we don't got no pictures," he said. "Her ma, she wouldn't take pictures of Darla looking like that. She said when Darla cleaned up, then she'd get her picture taken again."

The locker room door clicked open. He looked over, and some part of his face shut down.

He had seen Val. Pammy didn't look, didn't want to draw more attention to her.

"What was so different about your daughter?" Pammy asked, hoping this might give her a clue as to the girl's identity.

He focused back on Pammy. "Her hair was in her face all the time, long, uncombed, no makeup, and those dresses, big and sack like, and all that ropy stuff hanging off her, you know, with the knots and stuff."

It took Pammy a moment to understand "ropy." "Macramé, you mean?"

"Yeah, whatever they call it. Sometimes she had some of it tied to her hair." He shook his head. "She didn't look like our little girl any more. But this is the only picture we have."

His description could've been one of a hundred girls Pammy had seen. "Did she say she came in here?"

"No," he said. "I just been going down the street from store to store, asking people if they seen her. I don't even know what this place is."

"It's a gym," Pammy said. "For women."

He shook his head, then looked in Val's direction again. His face continued to shut down whenever he looked at her.

Pammy couldn't see Val at all, but she didn't hear her walk away.

He glanced at the entire building, clearly trying to take it in.

"I don't understand nothing," he said mostly to himself. Then he blinked and raised his gaze to Pammy. "But I gotta say, you been really nice. Some of these people, they won't even talk to me. One kid, he said she probably didn't want me to find her."

Pammy did her best not to nod. The idea that Darla had disappeared of her own free will was definitely a possibility.

"I'll tape one of your flyers to my counter," she said. "A lot of people come through here. Maybe they've seen her."

His mouth turned up in an attempt at a smile. "Thank you, honey. Bless you."

He peeled one of the flyers off the stack, his fingers lingering on the missing girl's face.

"She doesn't even got to come home," he said. "We just gotta know she's okay."

The pain in his voice made Pammy wince. She wondered what his daughter would think if she knew how much he cared.

"If anyone knows anything," Pammy said gently, "I'll make sure they call you."

"Thank you." His voice was so soft it almost sounded like a whisper. He picked up the rest of the flyers and rolled them up again. He backed away, then nodded at her, another silent thank-you, before turning, and heading out of the gym.

She watched him go, his back hunched as if he were warding off a blow.

She got out tape and stuck the flyer to the top of the counter. She'd show the flyer to Eagle, see if this girl was the one that Eagle had seen.

The timing was wrong, but it wouldn't hurt to check.

Val approached the counter, moving almost silently in her new sneakers. She glanced at the flyer, and shrugged. Clearly she hadn't seen the girl—or, at least, a girl who looked like that.

"Think she ran away?" Val asked.

"No way to know," Pammy said. "He seems pretty broken up about it."

"Sometimes people just have to leave," Val said, staring after him.

"And sometimes people get hurt," Pammy said, more to herself than Val.

But Val stiffened. "You think someone hurt her?"

"No," Pammy said. "I think we only know a tiny tiny part of that family's story."

"You'll call him if she gets found?" Val asked.

"If the daughter wants me to," Pammy said. But she had a hunch she would never get to ask the missing girl what she wanted. She probably would never see the missing girl. So many kids had disappeared, usually of their own free will.

Pammy couldn't keep track of every poster she'd seen, every concerned relative she'd talked to.

And she wasn't police. She wasn't anyone in authority. Some of her friends at the university were dealing with this all the time.

It was pretty normal for kids to drop out of school—they'd been doing it forever. They had no idea how hard the university would be or they didn't like it much or they preferred their newfound freedom.

But those kids usually went home or stayed in touch with home. This silence, that was new in the past few years.

Val looked at the door as if she could still see the man. "You're taking this pretty seriously," she said to Pammy.

Pammy shrugged. "I can't imagine anything worse than waiting for news of a missing loved one, news that might never come."

Val stiffened. Then she nodded, and turned slightly, her expression blank. "Is there something I need to do while we wait?"

She had deliberately changed the topic. Pammy frowned, just a little. She'd hit some kind of chord with Val, but she didn't know what it was, and she wasn't going to ask.

"Take a look around," Pammy said, "maybe find some gloves, get familiar with the punching bags. But don't use them. I'll train you on them when you're ready."

Val nodded and wandered away. She didn't ask about being ready. She didn't ask anything.

Pammy found that a little odd. But then, the whole morning had been odd. Hell, the whole *year* had been odd so far.

And horrific. No improvement over the previous year, with all the protests and assassinations.

Pammy suppressed a sigh. She had no idea why she expected an improvement over the previous year. Or even over May. Nothing had improved at all.

It had just gotten quieter.

And as that man had just shown her, quieter might not be better.

EAGLE

The damn shrinks said talking was good. Eagle knew that piece of advice like she'd come up with it herself. Hell, she'd even told her boys that, mostly in Pleiku, mostly when there was nothing else to say.

She'd heard the phrase from the dozens of shrinks she'd worked with, first in Hawaii, then in Saigon, always trying to deal with the mess that the war had created. And those years didn't count her stint in psych wards, although she'd tried to avoid them after her hellish two-week stretch at one during nursing school.

Talking was important, listening more important, letting the pompous shrinking assholes tell you what you already knew deep down apparently even more important.

All morning long, Eagle had been arguing in her head with every one of the damn shrinks she had ever known. She argued with them as she showered. She argued with them as she stood in her kitchen. She argued with them as she stared at the Raisin Bran box, her baggie still stashed inside of it. A doobie would make her feel better. Or a hit from her bong. A long comfortable day on her couch, thinking of nothing—

Or feeling fucking paranoid and worrying if the cops would come after her or the stupid asshole with the truck. Then she'd get the munchies and eat her way through everything in the apartment.

She didn't want to do that. She hated being this woman.

And she hated most that talking hadn't helped her at all. She'd told the cops, then she'd vented to Pammy, and still, the knot in Eagle's stomach remained.

Eagle was convinced she'd seen something criminal. Not some goddamn domestic.

And when she woke up in the middle of the night, cold sweat, hands shaking, it wasn't because she had some dream about Pleiku. It was because she felt like she failed, like that girl was still out there, calling to her, like maybe she had been the last person to see that girl alive.

Eagle had gotten out of bed then, paced the apartment, looked out the window, tried to focus her brain elsewhere. She'd been great at compartmentalizing when she'd been In Country, but since she got home (as if this was home; this America wasn't one she recognized; hell, she didn't recognize anything), her mind would latch onto one thing, cling to it, swirl around it, and then ratchet her emotions to a fever pitch.

Only two things eased the fever pitch. Booze of some kind. Or pot in whatever form she could get it.

She had headed straight for the bong at 3:00 a.m. when an image flashed across her already overheated brain.

Her mother, lying on the piss-smelling, cat-scratched couch, in what passed for their last home, slurring her words and telling Eagle that *you can't do nothing, baby, there's always some kinda shit comin' at you, nobody will love you, and nobody sure as shit will unnerstand, so you just gotta take care of yourself, you know? You gotta make yourself feel better, unnerstand, baby? It's the only way to survive.*

Eagle's hand had pulled away from the footlocker where she'd stored her bong so fast that she nearly sprained her wrist. She had taken a shower instead of a hit, then tried to go back to bed, then found herself staring at Raisin Bran, wondering why the hell talking to Pammy hadn't worked.

Maybe because Eagle hadn't punched anything, even though that had been why she had gone.

That thought—the only thing she'd been able to latch onto in nine hours that had nothing to do with drinking, toking, the girl, or oblivion—made her grab her black little-old-lady purse and flee the apartment.

The gym would be filled with eager students, probably housewives, all trying to be Jack LaLanne or Muhammad Ali or something completely unattainable. She'd do her best to avoid them, because she sure as shit wasn't going to put on loose clothing and Keds and make slow-motion floral patterns with her arms.

She almost decided right then and there to give up going to the gym that morning, but she didn't. She forced herself.

Because those shrinks might've been wrong about the way that talking could help, but they were right about one thing: when you felt the need to harm yourself, you needed to get to a new environment.

She stopped at the door out of her building. She finally heard the thoughts that had been going through her brain, really focused on them, and the thought that caught her, the *words* that caught her were "the need to harm yourself."

She closed her eyes for a moment. So that was what she'd been doing. The same goddamn slow-motion suicide that had taken her mother.

At least Eagle had a reason, unlike her mother.

And then Eagle caught herself again.

Those thoughts were excuses.

Lots of people came back to the States, bruised and battered, and led productive lives. Her life was her own goddamn fault. She was wallowing, and she wasn't a wallower.

Was she?

If she stepped back, out of herself, she would have to admit, yes, she was a wallower. And worse, she was on that road which led to eating her pistol.

She opened her eyes and put her hand against the grimy wall near the door. No one stood on the wooden staircase. For once the hallway in this busy building was empty.

No one saw her, shaking as if she needed a drink. She didn't need a drink.

She needed—God, she wasn't sure what she needed.

She tried to step out of herself again, and think. She'd talked to a lot of soldiers who'd said they had no reason to live. The worst, the one she'd gotten in trouble for, had been six months before she left Pleiku.

The boy—and he had been a boy, maybe twenty—had been in a three-bed "care" unit, really a supply closet that they'd made over when the casualties were too numerous to handle. The boys in that room were always the ones who needed special treatment, an extra look, just so they wouldn't get lost in the shuffle.

And that one boy, Reggie Something—Jesus, she couldn't even remember his last name now, and she'd thought she'd never forget him. Two weeks before, he'd stepped into a rice paddy, tripped a mine (or a buddy had tripped a mine, no one knew exactly, since Reggie was the only survivor of the incident to ever regain consciousness), and lost both his legs. Shrapnel had hit his face, his torso, his arms, narrowly missed important organs, and stayed stuck under his skin so he didn't bleed out. He'd lost his legs not because they were blown off, but because they'd become strings of flesh and bone, the main arteries remaining miraculously intact until his unit's medic managed to find him, tie tourniquets around what remained of his thighs, and save his life.

Hey, honey, Reggie had said to her that evening, his voice soft with the rhythms of his Georgia childhood. *Could you do me a favor? Could you get me my kit?*

Why do you want your kit? she'd asked instead of saying no, like she should've.

He'd looked away from her then, and she knew, even before he spoke, what he really wanted. *Just wanted to make sure my Colt was still there.*

You don't need your Colt, she'd said, maybe a bit harshly.

His lower lip trembled. He closed his eyes. He said, *Ah, honey, yes I do. I need it something awful.*

She'd stared at him. If he lived through that night, his life would never be the same. He'd clearly been a pretty boy once, strong and used to dealing with things. He wasn't pretty anymore, and he needed to learn how to live in a wheelchair.

You gonna use that gun on yourself? she asked.

Not in here, he'd said so softly that the words were almost inaudible.

You want to end it all? She'd asked, her tone harsh.

He'd shrugged one shoulder.

You know what they say depression is, don't you, soldier? It's anger turned inward.

He'd opened his eyes and looked at her then, a frown pulling on the stitches that made his face look like someone had written all over him in crayon.

Your anger doesn't deserve to be turned inward, she said. *You're not mad at yourself.*

Oh, yeah? He'd asked loud enough to make one of the men asleep near him moan. *If you're such a fucking know-it-all, what am I mad at?*

You're mad that you're here, she said, and his lips had curled sideways, creasing his ruined jawline. *And you didn't put yourself here. You should direct your anger outward, Reggie.*

Oh, I am, he said. *Your colleagues tell me that I'm treating them badly. Poor little souls that they are.*

She had smiled at that. Everyone had complained about Reggie, but he hadn't been unique. She'd seen this behavior a dozen times before, the angry man who was totally out of control and flailed out in fury at everyone, and finally at himself.

No, she had said to Reggie. *I'm not telling you to continue berating my colleagues.*

Then what are you telling me, hon? he'd asked. *To grab a rifle and go shoot me a few gooks?*

She shrugged. *Are they the ones who put you here?*

Someone did, he said. He didn't remember all the details of his injury. That was one of the things that had made him so angry.

A whole lot of someones, she said. *The someones who ordered you to that rice paddy, the someones who drafted you, the someones who—*

Enough, Eagle.

She turned. Doc Fenn stood behind her. He had been one month away from the end of his tour and looked like a scarecrow. He would re-up—he didn't want to leave the boys—and he would return, just as Eagle was leaving.

They had grown to hate each other personally, but rely on each other in the operating theater.

He had glared at her. He had never believed that straight talk would help the patients.

Looks like you need a little rest, he said to her.

For speaking truth? Reggie had asked the doctor. *Because, brother, I gotta tell you. If I could get up and walk right now, I'd take that Colt, and maybe I wouldn't eat it. Maybe I would—*

Eagle shook away the memory. It didn't help after all. Yeah, she'd gotten Reggie to focus his anger outward, and he never talked of suicide again. But then, she'd never checked on him either after he finally got transport out of the 71st.

She had no idea if he was alive, no idea if he'd eaten that weapon after all.

She glanced up the stairs at her apartment. A little oblivion would be nice. It would get rid of all the people, all the memories, marching around in her head.

And keep her anger directed inward, where it wouldn't explode, remove a few limbs, and send shrapnel flying.

She swallowed hard, made herself take a deep breath, then stopped bracing herself on the wall. She wiped her hands on her jeans.

She had to keep moving. It had worked in Nam. It had to work here.

She shoved the building's door open and stepped onto the street. Sound enveloped her. Laughter, conversation, cars swooshing by a few blocks away.

Unlike the day before, the street was crowded this morning. Students carried books, heading toward campus, strolling in twos and threes. A Hare Krishna group, colorful in their orange and white robes, paraded toward the park. Some hippie girls, just as colorful with their beads and flowing tie-dye skirts, watched the Krishna walk by.

Not too far away, someone was banging drums. Nearby, a radio blared some Hendrix, and Eagle tried not let it take her back. They'd been blaring Hendrix in the truck that took her to her first posting in Saigon. They'd been blaring Hendrix outside the 71st when she arrived.

They'd been blaring Hendrix—

77

She bent her head and plowed forward, feeling overwhelmed, over-stimulated, and in desperate need of something. She couldn't even identify what that something was. It was almost as if she were crawling around inside her own skin.

It took her a moment to identify the feeling—panic. Sheer panic. The kind she'd felt half a dozen times since she'd come home and never felt in Nam, not even when she was overwhelmed or under fire or had soldier after soldier die while she helplessly held their hands.

Tears pricked her eyes. She needed to be busy, that's what it was. If she was busy, she didn't have time to think, didn't have time to dwell, didn't have time to feel anything.

She pushed past a group of kids wearing ragged jeans and loose tops, reeking of incense and unwashed clothing. They didn't even seem to notice her, and for that she was grateful. She wasn't sure she could meet anyone's eye at the moment.

She had to skirt nearly fifty people on the short walk to A Gym of Her Own. She'd actually breathed a sigh of relief when she hit the alley, because it was empty. People were adding to that crawling sensation beneath her skin.

The back door of the gym was unlocked, even though she told Pammy to keep the damn thing locked permanently.

But did Pammy listen to her? Of course not. And someday, Pammy would regret it.

Eagle shoved the door open and stepped inside. The scents of Lemon Pledge and Palmolive washed over her, chased by the smell of stale coffee. Eagle let the door bang closed, then she locked it, flicking her wrist hard, as if proving a point to Pammy, even though Pammy wasn't present.

She was probably teaching a class out front, and if Eagle went there to say hello, she'd be dealing with people. Dumbass housewives, who saw Eagle as some kind of freak, more of a freak than the hippie girls who came to the gym, because Eagle had gone to war.

These women were trying to learn to be tough, yet they didn't respect a woman who *was* tough, or who had been tough once upon a time, before something in her broke, and her brain wouldn't stop playing the same goddamn tapes over and over and over again.

She gripped the edge of the sink and made herself breathe. Fucking panic. Fucking senseless panic. She'd banish it if she could, but she didn't know how. At least, she didn't know how without alcohol or drugs or the sweet oblivion of a medicated sleep.

She squared her shoulders and stood upright. Then she touched the handle of the percolator, still sitting on the stovetop. The burner was set on warm. The handle was too hot to touch. She picked up a crocheted potholder, vaguely wondered which of the bored housewives had brought *that* in, and then wrapped it around the handle, picking the whole thing up.

She poured the old coffee down the sink, tossed the grounds into the garbage, rinsed out the percolator, and started assembling a new pot, just as the door to the kitchen opened.

Pammy came in, smiling. How that woman always managed to find something to smile about, Eagle would never know. Sometimes she wanted to slap the smile off Pammy's face, just because Pammy looked so goddamn ridiculous.

And sometimes Eagle wished she could be as cheerful, even for a single afternoon.

"I thought I heard someone in here," Pammy said. "How're—"

"You got a class out there?" Eagle asked quickly. She had to make sure that Pammy never finished the question. Because if she did, then Eagle would be duty bound to answer it. Or to avoid answering it. Either way, Pammy would notice and pry like she had the day before, and Eagle wasn't up to prying.

Eagle was barely up to making fucking coffee.

Pammy tilted her head a little, clearly seeing through Eagle's ploy. Pammy's smile shifted, fading slightly, taking on a tolerant air.

"My beginners' class is going to start in a few," she said. "But I have a minute."

She opened a box on the countertop to reveal five plain donuts. Clearly there had been more in the box, but they had been eaten. And Eagle knew Pammy never brought donuts for the group. Pammy was all about healthy eating and proper lifestyles, and donuts, she believed, were good sometimes but never in the gym. But Pammy never said no to a gift either.

She took one and set it on a plate. (Only Pammy would put a donut on a plate.) Then she put that plate in front of the chair that Eagle usually used at the table.

"I don't need sugar," Eagle said, thinking that might make Pammy back off.

"You need something," Pammy said. "You're moving like an old woman and you're surly."

"I'm always surly," Eagle said.

"Surly-*er*," Pammy said. "Eat."

Eagle ignored her, finished making the coffee, and set the percolator on the stovetop.

"Stop taking care of me," Eagle said.

Pammy opened her mouth, probably to deny that she had been taking care of Eagle, then smiled slightly and raised one shoulder in yet another shrug.

She took out a second donut and put it on a second plate.

"Something weird happened this morning," she said.

"Someone landed on Mars?" Eagle asked, hoping she could deflect. "Isn't it a little soon to change venues in outer space? Shouldn't we explore the moon first?"

Normally, if she brought up the space program, Pammy ran with it, expressing her disapproval at the financial waste—a rare political something that she and Eagle both agreed on. It was a safe topic, one guaranteed to divert the conversation.

And Eagle needed to divert the conversation. She didn't want to hear about weird. She just wanted to sit and wait until the housewives left so she could punch something. And she didn't want to tell Pammy that, because Pammy would parade her out there and supervise as she put on the gloves and walked up to one of the girly punching bags.

"I'm serious, Eagle," Pammy said.

Eagle felt her heart sink. Apparently, Pammy couldn't be diverted today.

"Some guy came in this morning." Pammy sounded...uneasy? Alarmed? Uncertain? Eagle actually couldn't tell.

She looked over at Pammy to find the smile gone.

"He threaten you?" Eagle asked, maybe a little too fiercely. It had happened before.

"No," Pammy said. "His daughter is missing."

Eagle let out a breath she hadn't even realized she'd been holding. "I thought you get those guys all the time."

Pammy bit her lower lip. "Not all the time. Sometimes. And this one felt different."

Eagle straightened. "How come?"

Pammy shrugged "They'd had the usual political rift. The daughter is the first in the family to go to college, I think, and got radicalized, and her parents don't approve—"

"So she dropped out and isn't contacting them." Eagle grabbed her donut. It was still soft, the chocolate frosting not even set yet. These were recent donuts. "So what?"

"I don't think it's a so-what," Pammy said. "She disappeared from her apartment one day. Left her purse, her identification, all her stuff. Her roommate called the parents, and now the father's looking for her."

"This week?" Eagle asked.

Pammy frowned at her. "What?"

"Did she go missing this week?" Eagle sounded even more on edge than she felt.

"No, no," Pammy said. "Not this week. June sometime. Late June, after martial law got lifted. It sounded weird, Eagle."

Eagle bit into the donut. Not warm, but not stale either. Perfectly caked. She couldn't remember the last time she'd eaten, which was probably why the damn thing tasted so good.

"Eagle," Pammy said with a bit of urgency. "It was off."

"I heard you the first time," Eagle said. "But it's not the woman I saw. Sounds like this girl vanished a month ago."

"And that woman you saw is the only important missing person in the Bay Area?" Pammy asked with a bit of an edge. "I just thought it was weird that two women would go missing from the neighborhood—"

"According to the police, my woman isn't missing at all," Eagle said. "She was probably involved in a domestic, and her husband had the legal right to use her as a punching bag."

She spoke around the bite of donut that she'd eaten, and that managed to moderate the bitterness somewhat. She didn't want to hear about some other missing girl. She didn't want to think about the woman she'd seen.

"I'm not talking about the police," Pammy said. "I didn't even think to ask the guy if he'd contacted the police."

"Maybe you should," Eagle said, stopping herself before she added, *if you care so goddamn much.*

Pammy frowned at her, the smile a distant memory. She picked at her donut, then ripped it in half.

"He left a flyer," she said, after she'd ripped one of the halves into thirds. "Maybe you could look at it."

"They're not the same person," Eagle said. "One month—"

"And what if she got involved with some weird guy?" Pammy asked. "You know, like that weird guy that came through a couple of years ago, the guy with the eyes?"

She had mentioned the guy with the eyes a few times. Just before Pammy had opened the gym in 1967, she'd seen a creepy short man with intense eyes who had scared the crap out of her and a friend. She had said if her friend had encountered him alone, he might have harmed her, but Pammy had taken a step forward, menacing him, and the creepy guy with the eyes had backed off.

Eagle had never seen him. She hadn't even been stateside when that happened. She always suspected that Pammy and her friend had merely run into someone who was tripping, but she had never said so. It had scared Pammy and was part of the origin story of the gym, and Eagle hadn't wanted to question something so important.

"There are a lot of gurus around right now, Eagle," Pammy was saying. "Some of these kids are hooking up with seriously bad people. The drugs, the fake religions—"

Eagle waved her hand, silencing Pammy.

"I know," Eagle said. She had put all of that into the *I can't do anything about it so I'll ignore it* category.

"All I'm saying is maybe this girl dropped out for a month, had second thoughts, tried to get away—"

"And the guy beat her for that?" Eagle asked.

"People have been beaten for less," Pammy said drily.

She had a point. And she also had a determined look. Eagle recognized it. Pammy would keep pushing until Eagle examined the flyer and made sure the girl wasn't the one Eagle had seen.

"Okay," Eagle said, trying not to sound as reluctant as she felt. "Bring it back here. I'll take a look."

"Thanks," Pammy said and got up. She let herself out of the kitchen, just as the coffee started to percolate.

Eagle ate the rest of her donut, then grabbed a second one from the box. She finally remembered the last thing she'd eaten. Pizza yesterday. And she'd eaten it here, ironically.

If anyone had asked her about where she ate most of her food, she certainly wouldn't have said it was A Gym of Her Own.

Pammy came back in, clutching the flyer. Someone had spent some serious money on it. It was professionally printed, the high school photograph in the center looking like it had been designed for the flyer.

In big black letters at the top, it listed a Sacramento exchange along with these words:

If You've Seen This Girl, Please Call.

Under the photo, it said in smaller type,

Darla Newsome. 5'4" 110 lbs, brown eyes, light brown hair.

Then in even smaller type, it read:

Darla went missing on June 22, 1969. If you know her, please have her call her parents. If you have any information, please call the number above. We don't want to bother her: we just want to know she's okay.

Not a standard plea at all. And it touched something in Eagle. The Sacramento phone number, the willingness to believe that their daughter might have dropped out, the undertone of sheer terror.

The photograph was next to useless, though. High school graduation shots were staged, and Eagle would've bet money that Darla Newsome didn't look anything like that carefully made-up girl with her tentative smile, tilted head, pearls, and perfectly straight hair which ended in a perfectly rolled flip.

"Have you seen her?" Pammy asked, carefully avoiding the *is this her* question.

Eagle closed her eyes, tried to remember the image she'd captured in her memory of the screaming woman and compare it to the picture of the happy high school girl.

Eagle had gotten a good look at the woman's face, but it had taken a while for the image to register. She'd thought about it a lot that night as she waited for the cops.

Eagle wasn't sure she'd recognize the woman in any circumstance, because her face had already been bruised and swollen. She had had a fat lip, and maybe a cut along her jawline. Her hair had been tangled and her shirt ripped.

Eagle tried to mentally measure the screaming woman's height but it was nearly impossible. If she had to guess, the top of the cab was about six feet high, and the woman's head hadn't reached that.

But the scumbag had held her by her hair, arching her back, and pulling her sideways. It was impossible to measure height from that. Plus, she kept lifting her legs and kicking, as if she were trying to get away.

Maybe the woman had been five-four. Maybe she'd been five-seven. Eagle had no idea.

But the woman had been thin. Her hair color had been impossible to determine, and Eagle hadn't been close enough to notice much else.

Eagle opened her eyes. Pammy was peering at her intently.

"I have no idea," Eagle said. "This photograph, professionally done, this girl, she could be anyone. Hell, one of the hippie-dippy girls I saw heading to the park this morning might've been her."

Eagle's finger hit the flyer, tapping the photograph.

"I mean, look at her. She probably ironed her hair before she curled the ends. And if she did that, there's no way to know if her hair's naturally curly or naturally straight. No one would dress like that down here, and—"

"I know," Pammy said. She sighed and took a tiny bite of donut. "I was just hoping…"

"To solve two mysteries at once." Despite herself, Eagle smiled. Pammy liked order. It would have been nice to wrap everything up in a neat little bow. But those things didn't happen.

The coffee finished perking. Eagle got up and poured them both cups.

"I came here to punch something," she said, as casually as she could. "I don't suppose your students will leave right after class."

"This place is never empty on a Monday," Pammy said, understanding what Eagle wanted. "There's always someone around. You want me to help you?"

Eagle almost said, *Never mind*, but she stopped herself just in time. She could stay, finish her donut, have some coffee, and maybe get rid of some of this panic, or she could go home, and get back into the cycle again.

Intellectually, it didn't sound like a choice. In reality, however, it felt like a mammoth decision. Leaving would be the easier path.

But, Eagle reminded herself, she didn't want easy. She didn't need easy.

She turned around, cups in hand, pleased that she wasn't shaking. Pammy was staring at her with an expectant look. It took Eagle a moment to remember that Pammy had asked a question.

"Um, no, thank you," Eagle said. "I don't need any help. Just need to blow off steam."

"Pretend the punching bag's the truck driver," Pammy said.

"Yeah, I suppose," Eagle said. But she wasn't really thinking of him. She was thinking about the girl.

She set the cups down, then sat, feeling the weight of the last two days on her.

"We're never going to find out what happened to that woman, are we?" she asked quietly.

"Probably not," Pammy said. "Or poor Darla either. It's not really our business."

Eagle sighed. Always a good excuse. *It's none of my business. I was just following orders. I'm not in charge.*

"When does it become our business?" Eagle asked.

Pammy broke another bit of donut apart. "When you figure out the answer to that," she said quietly, "be sure to let me know."

VAL

I stood on the edge of the mat, along with six other women, waiting for the class to start, getting more and more nervous by the minute. The women were all bigger than me. I was too thin, and my skin was much darker than anyone else's. Two of the women glared at me as they walked past without even saying hello.

They went to what seemed like prescribed areas on the mat, leaving me and the other short woman in the back. At least, I'd call it the back. We were facing the far wall, through a thicket of punching bags and those little bags that looked like an upside-down balloon.

The far wall had no windows on it—the only windows in the entire place seemed to be along the front, as if the gym had been a car showroom or something. But at least Pammy had moved the big mats away from the windows.

The area back here was darker, partly because of the big punching bags hanging from thick chains from the ceiling. The big punching bags—*all* of the punching bags (even the upside-down balloons) hung lower than any I'd ever seen, so it felt a little like I was standing on a mat, staring into a forest of stubby upside-down trees.

I didn't mind the back. At least intellectually. Emotionally, I hated not being able to see the room behind me. It made me even more nervous.

I wasn't sure how I could be more nervous. I felt so terribly out of place, and now, with Pammy's words echoing in my head, I felt guilty too.

I can't imagine anything worse than waiting for news of a missing loved one, news that might never come.

I had never called Marvella or Paulette. I had let them know I was leaving town, but I didn't tell them where I was going or why.

Of course, I hadn't known. But they were bound to be worried.

I had put them out of my mind, like I had put Chicago out of my mind, like I had tried to put *him* out of my mind.

Only I hadn't been successful with *him*. He was why I did half the things I did. Like now. I looked over my shoulder to check the room behind me even though I *knew* I was safe.

The big counter dominated the other part of the room. But without Pammy there, the counter didn't seem like such a focus. Besides, the chairs that had been out yesterday were folded up and put away. The portable television with its gigantic rabbit ears was gone as well.

That part of the building seemed a lot more businesslike than it had just the day before, and more businesslike meant it was a little less friendly.

And, if I were honest with myself, that plaid-shirted white man who had come in all upset earlier hadn't helped my mood any. I empathized with him, I really did—or at least I had until he glared at me with such hatred.

But Pammy had been polite to him. I would've been too, although I wouldn't have given him nearly as much time as she had. Not with that glare. But Pammy hadn't seemed to notice. Or maybe she had. I didn't know for sure because I hadn't been able to see her face.

A few other women milled near the locker rooms, talking softly. Pammy had just come out of the back room, walking toward us with purpose.

I made myself take a deep breath, and turn back toward the front of the mat.

The other women in the class were standing still, legs slightly apart. All of the women were much heavier than I was, and seemed significantly older, although from their conversations, they probably weren't. A few might've been in their forties, but most were in their thirties, like I was.

They wore shorts that they probably shouldn't have, revealing pasty white legs that had blue veins and fat bulges. No one wore a t-shirt except me. The other women wore sleeveless blouses that matched the shorts. Their arms looked like their legs, only a little less pale, some kind of summer tan.

Pammy got to the front of the mat and grinned at everyone. She had a pretty smile that accented her blue eyes. Her hair glistened like a brownish-blonde cap. She seemed so confident.

I envied that confidence. More than that, I wanted that confidence for myself.

Pammy put her hands on her hips and nodded at us.

"Welcome, everyone. Happy Monday. You're in the basic exercise class. We will work, but I will make sure you don't overdo, either. I want you to come back every day this week, and next week as well. I am hoping that, over time, you will enjoy this class and continue to make exercise part of your daily life."

Her tone was friendly, her gaze resting on each of us in turn. Finally, it landed on me. I braced myself for a big introduction.

I hated being the center of attention. I had always hated it. I hated it more these last few months.

Then Pammy's gaze left mine. Pammy's gaze had fallen on one of the women up front. I let out a small breath, not quite a sigh of relief, but close. Maybe she wouldn't introduce me after all.

I would be happy with that.

Pammy said, "Some of what we're going to do will seem simple to you, and some of it will be unbelievably hard. Some of you will do well on one thing, and will have trouble with the next."

I hated having trouble with things. I used to be the best student in any class I walked into. My mother used to say that it was essential for a Negro girl to be better than everyone else just to be considered good.

Whether I liked it or not, she had been right—and I felt that pressure here. Just the word "class" made the old perfectionism rise up.

A slight frown creased Pammy's brow. For a half-second, I thought she had noticed how tense I had become. Then I realized she was looking at a woman to my left. That woman's pale skin seemed even paler than it had a moment ago.

She was the other short woman in the class. She had auburn hair cut into an unattractive bowl that circled her face. Her skin was mottled, that red and pale coloring that some white women got when emotions swirled inside them.

Pammy's gaze on that woman made it seem almost as if she were talking directly to the woman.

"Don't worry about how hard some of these exercises will seem." Pammy's voice remained calm. "You don't have to be perfect."

I jolted. She might've been looking at that other woman, but that sentence went straight into my core.

Pammy still wasn't looking at me, though. She was saying, "You just have to try. You'll be amazed at what you can do when you try. You'll gain strength as time goes on."

I was missing something here, something Pammy knew.

Then I glanced at the woman's feet. She wore brand-new white sneakers. They didn't have a single scuff mark, like mine.

She was new, just like I was.

I felt a small degree of tension leave my shoulders. I was happy to have company.

"We're going to start with something that seems easy, but isn't always," Pammy said. "Please. Sit down. And I want you to sit cross-legged."

A tall woman in front of me shifted slightly. She had a bouffant hairdo that was a silver-blonde that did not occur in nature. The hair didn't move either, no matter what the woman did. The style had to have cost her a pretty penny. I couldn't believe she would jeopardize it here.

She crossed her legs at the ankles and sank to the mat, ending up in a cross-legged position. Pammy watched, mouth tight as she tried to control a smile.

I clenched my hands into fists, then realized what I was doing. I couldn't sit easily if I did that.

But I had never seen anyone sit down like that woman had—not men, not little children. It looked easy, hardly any wasted movement.

The other new woman looked at me, green eyes wide with panic. Normally, if a white woman looked at me like that, I would think she wasn't used to being around people of color. But there seemed to be an element of camaraderie in her look, almost a pleading alarm: *Can you do this? I'm not sure I can.*

I smiled at her and shrugged a little. Then I tried the standing ankle-cross thing just because I always had to emulate the best in the class (on my way to *being* the best in the class). I eased down, and nearly fell over sideways. I caught myself, and my cheeks heated. Moving like that was a lot harder than it looked.

I finally gave up and sat down like the other women had. Then I shifted my legs so that I could sit cross-legged, something I hadn't even tried in years.

Turned out I could do it, but it hurt, tugging at my upper thighs.

The other new woman sat down heavily. She managed to cross her legs too. Four of the women sat down, then tried to cross their legs. Two grabbed their ankles and pulled, finally succeeding. The other two women were unable to cross their legs at all.

Pammy watched us all as if sitting cross-legged were a matter of life and death. I realized, looking at the others, that in some ways it was.

It told Pammy whether or not we were limber, and all of us except the bouffant woman were not.

Pammy did not comment on our awkwardness. Instead, she clasped her hands together, almost as if she were moved to applaud, and then decided against it.

"Good job," she said. "Movement is essential to life, but most of us don't do much of it anymore. So don't feel badly if something that seems simple turns out to be hard."

The auburn-haired woman snorted beside me. I smiled at her. She smiled back and shrugged.

Pammy said, "I'm going to take you through a series of exercises. I'm not going to allow you to do them the way that your gym teacher used to, if you even had a gym teacher."

One of the dark-haired women nodded. I couldn't tell if that meant she had had a gym teacher or she hadn't had one.

"If your gym teacher was anything like mine, she made sure you did everything the girls' way. Simpler, easier, not taxing on female bodies. Well," Pammy said with a bit of energy in her tone for the first time, "I don't believe that there are girls' exercises and boys' exercises. There are only effective exercises and ineffective exercises."

"What about our breasts?" the bouffant woman asked. I could only see her from the back, but I assumed hers were worth asking about. Mine certainly weren't.

"For some of you, on some exercises, your breasts might get in the way," Pammy said. "Do your best. If your breasts turn out to be a serious hindrance, we'll wrap them. We have found that wrapping breasts makes a big difference. Talk to me after class if you're interested."

The auburn-haired woman looked at me, eyebrows raised. Her breasts were bigger than mine but they certainly weren't in trouble territory.

I indicated mine, and shrugged. She grinned, and mimicked my gesture, then shrugged too. I grinned back.

A friend. Or at least, someone friendly.

I hadn't realized how much I had craved it.

Yesterday, today, all that socializing. I was a bit shocked at myself. I hadn't realized that I had been lonely.

"We're going to start with sit-ups," Pammy said. "You'll need a partner to do this."

I looked at the auburn-haired woman. She nodded.

"Pick a spot," Pammy said. "Then decide who will go first. The person doing the sit-ups will lie on her back with her spine touching the mat. Make sure your lower back makes contact with the mat. That's where most people make their mistakes."

The auburn-haired woman looked like she was having trouble getting out of her cross-legged stance. So I scooched over toward her. She shook her head just a little.

"This is harder than I thought," she whispered, "and all we've done is sit."

"I know," I said softly.

The others were partnering up as well, whispering as they did so. No one was really paying attention to Pammy. She was trying to say something about the other partner. She finally shook her head and waited, watching us partner up.

It only took a moment, because we all moved quickly. Except the bouffant woman. She remained in her cross-legged position like a tin-pot Buddha. The only remaining woman—the heaviest in the group—looked at the bouffant woman, and then at the rest of us, as if she longed to have any other partner instead of the bouffant woman.

Somehow it didn't surprise me that the bouffant woman remained partnerless. I hadn't wanted to partner with her either.

"I'm Val, by the way," I said to the auburn-haired woman, extending my hand.

"Joan," she said. "This is your first class too, right?"

"Oh, yeah," I said.

"My husband didn't want me to come," she said. "He said I couldn't do this. No girl could."

I raised my eyebrows. When I heard things like that, I was grateful for Truman. Even though we had our differences, even though I had married him for all the wrong reasons, he had always treated me with respect.

I touched my Chicago PD t-shirt, in silent homage to him.

"I'm going to prove to him that I can do all of it," the auburn-haired woman said. Then she rubbed her upper thighs. "Maybe just not today."

I chuckled appreciatively.

"All right," Pammy said loudly. "It looks like everyone's in place."

Joan and I both looked in her direction. The heavyset woman and the bouffant woman sat side by side. Mutt and Jeff. I hoped it would work out for them.

"One of you lie back, as I said," Pammy continued. "The other must hold her ankles in place. Your legs should be bent, your heels about a foot from your tailbone. Your arms should be flat on the ground beside you. When it comes time to do the actual sit-up, cross your arms over your chest. Do *not* put them behind your head."

"Like they taught us to do in gym class," Joan said.

Apparently, she had said it loud enough for Pammy to hear. "Exactly," Pammy said.

I didn't remember doing sit-ups in gym class. When Truman did them, he kept his legs outstretched, and leaned forward so that he could touch his toes. He had been such a big man that he had had trouble with that.

Pammy said, "The other woman will hold her partner's ankles. Your job is to make sure your partner's feet do not leave the ground for any reason. The person doing the exercise will sit up slowly, keeping her head in alignment with her spine. Once you're in a sitting position, count to two before lying back down."

"Sounds complex," Joan whispered to me. "Who knew that sit-ups were complex?"

I was beginning to think everything physical was complex.

"Do no more than ten sit-ups," Pammy said, "and wait for me before switching positions. Do *not* do these fast. You'll get hurt if you do."

"I might get hurt no matter what," Joan whispered.

I grinned. I had been thinking the same thing.

The mottling on Joan's skin had grown worse. She was actually panicked about this.

I found it oddly reassuring that someone else was more uncomfortable with a procedure than I was.

"I'll go first if you want," I said.

"Would you?" she asked. "Because it sounds so complicated."

It did sound complicated, which confused me. I remembered doing sit-ups as a child, and they seemed straightforward. Of course, I had learned to do them the way that Truman had done them.

I scooted down on the mat so that my head wouldn't hang off the edge. Then I put my hands flat at my sides. I had to concentrate to press the small of my back against the mat. That felt weird, almost like I was holding it in place.

Joan looked at my feet as if she were visually measuring the distance between my heels and my bottom.

"Ready?" she asked.

"Yeah," I said.

She wrapped her hands around my ankles. I jerked a little. I couldn't remember the last time someone had touched me at my request. It felt odd.

Her fingers held tightly. Her skin was warm through my socks.

I made myself think of something else.

"You have to cross your arms," she said.

"Oh, right." I did, crossing my arms in front of my chest. Then I tried to sit up. I leaned to the right. The scars on my abdomen ached. If I still had stitches, I might have pulled them out.

Tears filled my eyes, and I blinked them back. I bit my lower lip. I would do this. I would do it right.

Somehow I managed to sit all the way up, but I felt the movement in my stomach and my back.

"One…two!" Joan said, then looked at me.

She immediately frowned.

"Are you okay?" she asked.

"Yeah," I said, and eased back down. I wasn't going to tell her about the surgeries or the attack or the butchery both doctors had done on me.

I was still blinking as my back hit the mat.

"You going to go for a second one?" Joan asked.

"Yes," I said, and was surprised at the determination in my voice. Yes, I was going to do this. Yes, I was going to heal my stomach. Yes, I was going to conquer all of this.

I was going to do everything it took to make myself strong.

I sat up, and it was easier this time, although the aches hadn't gone away.

"One…two!" Joan looked at me and grinned. I grinned back, and hoped that it wasn't a grimace.

I laid back down. My body cried for rest, even though I had only done two sit-ups.

But I wasn't going to let it rest. I could do this.

I *would* do this.

I wobbled my way up.

"One…two!" Joan said, looking pleased. "You're good at this."

I wasn't good at it. But I made a promise to myself then and there.

I wasn't good at anything physical, but I would be.

I would be better at exercise than bouffant woman.

Better than Pammy.

I would be the best, no matter what it took.

No matter what the cost.

EAGLE

Three donuts later, Eagle folded the pastry box closed. Three donuts and two cups of coffee. Enough caffeine and sugar to keep her going for a while.

She leaned against the counter in the small kitchen, and glanced at the tiny alarm clock Pammy had placed on top of the stove. Most of Pammy's classes lasted an hour. She'd left the kitchen forty-five minutes ago.

So, fifteen minutes left in the class. Then, afterwards, the class would need time to talk, pat each other on the back, and then vanish into the street or the locker room.

Eagle sighed. And, as that class was leaving, members of another class would start trickling in.

Just like Pammy had reminded her, Mondays would be filled with students and talkers and June Cleavers. If Eagle wanted privacy, she'd have to come back at night.

And she didn't want to come back at night.

But she didn't want to talk to anyone either.

As if on cue, the kitchen door swung open. Jill Woodbridge saun-tered in, carrying two bags of groceries. Her gaze met Eagle's and they assessed each other coldly, just like they usually did.

Eagle knew that Pammy relied on Jill, and Jill knew that Eagle provided needed medical services here. But they didn't like each other. Jill had a stick wedged firmly up her ass. She thought everything should be just so, and the definition of "just so" was *her* definition, and no one else's.

Jill had been arguing for months that Eagle needed an official role. She either needed to be on a payroll or to be paid as a contractor or to sign off as some kind of volunteer. Jill thought she knew everything about anything business, and she was afraid that Pammy's insurance wouldn't cover some problem that Eagle caused.

Jill was right to be afraid that Pammy's insurance wouldn't cover something that was Eagle's fault, but not because Eagle wasn't on the payroll. It would be because the asshole insurance agent that Pammy had been assigned had given them a slap-dash policy and had told Pammy that was the best she could get.

Eagle wanted Pammy to shop around, but Pammy said she didn't have time. Eagle thought Pammy was screwing up. If something happened at the gym, then Pammy would be on the hook for it.

Of course, some other insurance company—no matter how good— might leave Pammy on the hook for it anyway. Most would think she was running an illegitimate business. Women shouldn't fight. Women shouldn't enlist either. Women shouldn't go to war, and women certainly shouldn't own businesses, unless they were cooking or sewing related.

Even in the People's Republic of Berkeley.

That attitude was why Eagle was volunteering in the first place. The black eyes and sprained thumbs around here would add up. The hospitals would report Pammy, and then she would lose everything.

Best to keep the authorities from looking too closely at A Gym of Her Own because sure as shit, they'd try to shut it down.

"Didn't expect to see you this morning." Jill's tone suggested she didn't want to see Eagle *ever*, not just this morning.

"Good morning to you too," Eagle said, and mentally added, *asshole*.

Jill walked to the counter. She shoved the donut box aside with her forearm and set the bags of groceries down.

"Someone hurt?" Jill asked, her voice even frostier than it had been a moment before.

Not yet, Eagle thought.

"No," she said.

"Hmm," Jill said, her back to Eagle. "I didn't think you liked spending time here."

As if Eagle had no reason to be here at all unless someone was hurt. As if Eagle didn't belong here.

I don't like being here when you're here, Eagle almost said, and had to actually bite her lower lip to keep from adding, *Besides, I have as much right to be here as you do.*

She set her plate beside the sink.

"You're going to wash that, I hope." Jill was pulling some bread and bologna out of the bag, putting them next to a gigantic jar of mayonnaise that she had already removed.

"I would wash it," Eagle said, hoping her tone sounded measured, "but this is a tiny kitchen and there's no room near the sink."

"You could help me put the groceries away," Jill said.

"Why did you even get groceries?" Eagle asked before she could stop herself. "Are we feeding the classes now?"

"No." Jill's response was curt, and Eagle suddenly understood. Someone was going to sleep in the gym overnight.

Eagle hated it when Pammy approved overnights. If Jill and Pammy wanted to discuss possible liabilities, this was the one that made Eagle the most crazy. Several of the women who had stayed here in the past were tripping or coming down from some kind of high.

Others were running from someone, or had an abusive spouse, or had been thrown out of their apartments. Both Jill and Pammy were a soft touch. That sweet-sister mentality would bite them both on the ass at some point.

Over the past year, Eagle had tried to explain her worries. She knew it was only a matter of time before an angry husband would break in, or a careless druggie would light a candle and set fire to the whole place. And then what would Pammy do? Her insurance guy would probably deny her coverage because the event could have been foreseen.

Besides that, women—who weren't supposed to fight or defend themselves—were really not supposed to flee their spouses either. Or do anything without some kind of male approval.

Hell, Eagle had had enough trouble just opening a checking account without a man to vouch for her. She couldn't imagine how the authorities would treat a woman who was trying to flee her man because he had threatened her.

Eagle took a deep breath. She was going to have to give her lecture all over again, and she knew it would fall on deaf ears. She would have to find a way to speak to Jill, maybe talk about insurance or fires or some other kind of *business* liability. Because talking to Jill about misplaced compassion just pissed her off.

The kitchen door banged open. One of the hippie girls swanned in, her long brown hair held back with two hairpins, dying daisies tucked in each as decoration.

"You see that flyer?" she asked Jill, and then saw Eagle. "Oh, hey. You're that doctor woman, right?"

Eagle never knew how to answer that question. She didn't want to tell someone wearing a tie-dye shirt tucked into a skirt made of dirty white gauze that she had been a combat nurse in Vietnam. But Eagle also felt like she had to correct the idea that she was a doctor, because she wasn't. Although she did have more medical knowledge—at least of traumatic wounds—than any doctor she had ever met stateside.

"She's the medic," Jill said, managing a tone that was both informative and disapproving at the same time.

"Groovy." The hippie girl shoved the bag of groceries she was carrying into the crook of her left arm and extended her grimy right hand toward Eagle. "I'm Strawberry. I've heard a lot about you."

Strawberry had introduced herself as if they were equals, as if Eagle should have heard of her. And maybe Eagle had; she usually tuned out when Pammy discussed the students.

Eagle looked at the girl's outstretched palm, thought about not shaking it for just a moment, and then decided she didn't want to be rude. Eagle took Strawberry's hand. It was dry and warm. Eagle shook, just once.

"Eagle," she said.

"Hey, cool," the girl said. "You Native or something?"

Eagle flushed, her breath catching. It had been years since anyone had asked her that. No one here ever had.

She almost felt like she'd been caught lying.

Jill half-turned, eyebrows raised.

Great. Just great. Eagle had to answer the question, and Jill was here.

If Eagle was going to lie, now was the time. But she had a code. She believed in truth. And yet, at this moment, she didn't want to divulge it. She didn't feel like her heritage was anyone's business.

"Something like that," Eagle finally said.

Strawberry half-smiled, and tilted her head, studying Eagle. Strawberry's clear brown eyes had no telltale sign of drug use, not even the redness that came from smoking too much pot. She had a golden tan, and her cheeks were flushed with good health.

Eagle probably had that pot-smoke redness, and the sallow skin of someone who drank too much and never went outside.

For the first time in a long time, she felt inferior to someone. And that someone had been named after a fruit.

"Well," Strawberry said matter-of-factly, "you got the hair. That rich black stuff. Only Oriental girls and Native girls have it. And you don't have the eyes for Oriental."

Eagle wasn't used to such rude honesty, not about herself or about anyone, really. Although she had met a few other people like Strawberry, mostly young men. They just said whatever came into their heads, without censoring any of it.

Eagle took a deep breath, reminding herself that Strawberry was just trying to make conversation. She hadn't said "gook" or "chink" or any of the other slurs, although Oriental bordered on it. And she hadn't said Indian either. Eagle hated that word, as did most anyone who had some Native American blood.

"Oh, wait, I forgot," Strawberry said. "You could be Mexican or something too. But your face is a little too flat. Maybe—"

"Lakota." Eagle couldn't take the girl's babbling any longer. "My mother was Lakota."

Jill turned the rest of the way, clearly interested.

Eagle sighed silently. Jill would tell everyone. *You hear that Eagle is Indian?* she would say. People would treat Eagle differently. They'd watch her, especially if they hadn't considered it. And then, a few of them would ask her rude questions, just like Strawberry was doing.

A few others would stop talking to her altogether.

Jill was already giving Eagle The Look. Jill was assessing, trying to see the Native American characteristics in Eagle's features. And as usual, just Jill's expression made Eagle feel defensive.

"So your dad wasn't Native?" Strawberry was smarter than Eagle had realized. She had heard the distinction in Eagle's answer, only listing her mother as a Native American. Not her father.

Jill was frowning.

"Was he white?" Strawberry asked. Then she nodded, as if she were having the conversation all by herself. "Of course he was white. That's what makes it hard to guess your heritage completely."

Eagle felt her heart sink. She had never had anyone make such astute judgments based on her looks before. She wasn't sure if she liked it.

Strawberry set her bag on the table. "That's so progressive of him, marrying a Native woman. I bet they had bigots peeing their pants."

Eagle had no idea. Her parents had never talked about that. Not once.

Maybe no one had known. When her mother was young, she wore her hair short and dressed well. She could have passed for some other more "acceptable" ethnic group.

Or maybe her parents hadn't had enough time together to deal with bigots. Her father certainly tried to ignore them. His second wife was a big fucking bigot and he never put her in her place.

"Lakota," Strawberry was saying. "That's like middle of the country. Sioux or something, right?"

Jill crossed her arms and leaned against the counter. She seemed to be enjoying Eagle's discomfort.

Strawberry didn't seem to notice. "I'm majoring in archeology and it's kinda amazing how little we know about the native peoples here in the States. I mean, how little *I* know. Y'know?"

Jill's mouth had gotten thin.

"You mentioned a flyer," Jill said to Strawberry.

Eagle looked at Jill in surprise. Jill shrugged one shoulder, and Eagle suddenly realized that Jill had been upset at Strawberry's inadvertent bigotry.

For the first time, maybe ever, Jill and Eagle were allies. If only for a moment or two.

"Oh, yeah, the flyer." Strawberry reached inside the bag and pulled out three cartons of fresh raspberries. "Pammy has it taped to the counter. Didn't you see it?"

"No," Jill said. "I usually don't stop at the counter."

"Unless you're working it." Strawberry's tone was blithe. Apparently she'd been here enough to know that Jill helped Pammy whenever she could.

Eagle sighed. She missed a lot. She didn't know most of the routines around here. She was grateful for that. She almost wished she hadn't missed a previous encounter with Strawberry, though. Someone else's encounter with Strawberry, so Eagle would have known to avoid her.

Ah, well. Eagle knew now. She hated prattlers and Strawberry didn't seem to shut up.

"What's on the flyer?" Jill asked with barely disguised impatience.

Strawberry took one of the raspberries and popped it in her mouth. "Some girl vanished. Again."

Eagle felt her heart rate increase.

"Again?" Jill asked at the same moment that Eagle said, "You know the girl?"

Eagle's heart lifted. It would be wonderful if the solution were so easy. At least one missing kid would be going home then.

"No, of course I don't know her," Strawberry said in a tone that implied Eagle was dumb for even asking. "I mean, I don't think so. Because, y'know, not everyone is using their real name these days."

She winked at Eagle, as if they had set the trend themselves.

"I noticed," Jill said with that same tone of disapproval she had used earlier.

"So maybe I met her, but not, y'know, with the hair and makeup and stuff." Strawberry opened the small refrigerator and put the raspberries inside it, taking one more raspberry before closing the door.

"But you said 'again,'" Jill said.

Eagle nodded before she could stop herself.

"Huh?" Strawberry reached into the bag and pulled out two cartons of small, squished blueberries.

"You said some girl vanished *again*," Eagle clarified.

"As if you knew her," Jill added.

Eagle glanced at her. How odd that they had both come to the same misunderstanding.

"Oh, y'know, I meant some new girl vanished. Y'know, like I mean, *again*. Somebody vanished. I mean, lots of people vanish. Y'know?"

Eagle parsed the sentences out, wishing the girl didn't use so much jargon. Strawberry didn't seem to notice Eagle's confusion.

Strawberry raised her shoulders a little, grimaced, and then shuddered. "It's getting creepy around here."

"I think it's been 'creepy' for a while," Jill said in her pedantic way. "With martial law, and everything…."

"Yeah, *that's* not creepy." Strawberry picked up the empty bag and folded it along its lines. Eagle hadn't expected that level of neatness from her. "That's just…y'know…scary dangerous. When I say creepy, I mean *creepy*. People just disappear."

Eagle glanced at Jill, who was frowning.

"Maybe they went home," Jill said. "I'm not sure I'd want to stay in Berkeley right now."

"Yeah, I get it. Old people think it sucks here," Strawberry said, her back to Jill. Good thing, too, because Jill straightened, two spots of color appearing on her cheeks, her eyes sparkling with something like fury.

Eagle shook her head, then waved Jill off. It wasn't worth either of their time to get mad at Strawberry. Eagle had learned long ago to let prattlers prattle.

"But it doesn't suck here," Strawberry shut the fridge, then turned around. "I mean, *everyone's* here, and there's always some kind of action or something, and if you want to change the world, this is the place to do it."

Not Washington D.C.? Not New York? Not Vietnam? Eagle glanced at Jill and wondered if Jill was holding back responses as well. Jill's eyes had narrowed, and she did not look pleased.

"You probably don't understand," Strawberry said with a younger version of the same pedantic tone Jill had used earlier, "but this is a happening place. If you gotta fight the Man, this is the place to do it. I'd rather be here than, say, y'know, Denver or somewhere. Totally Dullsville."

Denver. That was an interesting choice. It was amazing how much information a person revealed about herself in a casual conversation.

But Eagle didn't remark on that. Instead, she gripped the back of one of the chairs. She needed to return the conversation to the missing girl.

"You said other people have vanished?" Eagle asked.

"Yeah," Strawberry said. "People you wouldn't think would go. They would, y'know, leave their stuff and everything. Not that most stuff is worth taking, but they wouldn't tell us, 'Hey, take my stuff and use it for the general good' or whatever. They'd just split, and then we'd never hear from them again."

"I'm sure they went home." Jill turned around and pulled both mustard and catsup from the nearest bag. She was clearly done with this conversation. It probably made her uncomfortable.

Strawberry caught Eagle's gaze, then rolled her eyes. Apparently Strawberry didn't respect Jill any more than Jill respected her.

"Maybe one or two went home," Strawberry said, "but not everybody. The people I'm thinking of, they're, y'know, Movement people. Deep inside, very committed. Some had dropped out to protest all the time, y'know."

"And drop acid." The phrase sounded odd coming from Jill, as if she were trying to be cool and failing.

"Well, some of them, sure," Strawberry said. "But acid freaks, they have their own pattern, and they burn out really fast. Most people in the Movement don't want anything to do with acid freaks. I mean, those folks are seriously fucked up. And I don't get it. I mean, why would anyone *do* that? Mess up their brains and stuff. I had laced Kool-Aid at the Fillmore once. It was a Dead concert and Jesus, I *never* want to do that again. It was *horrible*. Everyone's faces were melting and the lights bled into their eyes, and I *still* have nightmares about it. Everyone was tripping and no one was helping and the music..."

Her voice trailed off as she got lost in the memory. Eagle was grateful. She didn't want to hear any more about drugs or this girl's opinions. Eagle just wanted answers to a few questions.

"You said Movement people." Eagle kept her voice neutral. Her nonjudgmental how-did-you-get-that-injury voice. "Are you referring to a particular movement?"

"You mean like AIM or something?" Strawberry asked.

She clearly thought Eagle knew what she was talking about. Once again, Eagle felt inferior. She knew it was because Strawberry had discovered Eagle's Native American roots, because she felt Strawberry saw her as a Native, and Eagle's experience was that whenever someone discovered her heritage, they would treat her badly. Strawberry wasn't treating her badly at all, but Eagle couldn't shake the feeling.

"What's AIM?" Jill asked.

Strawberry looked at Eagle. "Tell her, man."

I have no fucking idea, Eagle almost said. But she managed to hold that back, and say calmly, "You brought it up."

Jill looked at her a little too knowingly. Jill knew that Eagle had no idea what AIM was but Strawberry seemed oblivious.

"The American Indian Movement, trying to stop that red ghetto shit. Y'know? The Minneapolis stuff, Rainbow Coalition, Fred Hampton, all that?" Strawberry looked at Jill. "Y'know?"

Jill looked confused. Which relieved Eagle, because *she* was confused. Strawberry's explanation explained nothing. Eagle had no idea what the "Minneapolis stuff" was. She had never heard of a rainbow coalition, and she had never heard of this Hampton person. She hadn't heard of a red ghetto either, but she had a hunch she knew what that meant.

Jill was shaking her head, as if she were trying to clear it.

"So," Jill said after a moment, "let me see if I get this right. You think the girls who disappeared were American Indians."

Strawberry let out an exasperated sigh. "I didn't say that. I didn't say girls disappeared either. I said *somebody* vanished."

Eagle couldn't take this particular girl much longer. "Initially," Eagle said, struggling to maintain that non-judgmental tone, "you did say 'girl.'"

Strawberry sighed again. This sigh was deeper and even more dramatic. "Because, y'know, this time, it *was* a girl. But it's been guys too. Movement people. And I don't mean AIM."

And then she pinned her gaze on Jill, clearly making her point about ignorance without saying anything.

"If you haven't heard of AIM," Strawberry said, "maybe you know the Native American Student Organization? They're, y'know, real active."

"Here in Berkeley?" Jill asked.

"God, yeah," Strawberry said.

"And people from that group are disappearing?" Jill asked.

"*No. Jeez.*" Strawberry looked at Eagle, as if she thought Eagle could help explain Strawberry's point.

Eagle felt like she'd fallen down the rabbit hole. She half expected Alice to land beside her at any moment.

She shrugged. Strawberry sighed a third time, as if the burden on her in this conversation was immense.

"The people who vanish," Strawberry said. "They're, y'know, hardcore Movement people. SDS or Third World Liberation Front or Diggers or complete radicals. One or two acid freaks went missing too, but acid freaks do. They just vanish, like you said."

Eagle followed some of that, but not all of it. She had heard of the Third World Liberation Front because of their violent protests earlier in the year. She'd heard of the SDS—the Students for a Democratic Society—because of the protests that had turned violent at the 1968 Democratic National Convention. But Diggers? She hadn't heard of them.

At least she knew what acid freaks were.

"You're saying that kids are disappearing," Eagle said.

Jill shook her head and opened her mouth. Eagle could almost see the thought balloon: *They didn't disappear. They gave up and went home from college. People do that.*

"Kids," Eagle added, "who have a real life here. They're the ones who vanished."

"Not just a real life," Strawberry said. "They've renounced the conventional shit. They're *active.* They're *involved.* They're the soldiers for the good war, y'know? They'd never go back to Dullsville. They might leave Berkeley, but only for something important, like a march or something."

This time, it was Eagle who had to blink hard to keep from rolling her eyes. Since when had a march become important? They were a waste of time.

"Could you make a list of the people who've disappeared?" Eagle asked.

"For what?" Strawberry's tone had changed. "Who would want a list?"

"Me," Eagle said. "Something's going on here—"

"And what are you, a cop?" Strawberry asked. "I thought you were a doctor."

"A medic," Jill corrected. "But she is former—"

"I'm not a cop," Eagle said quickly. She knew if Jill mentioned that Eagle was former military, Strawberry would clam up completely. "I agree, though, something weird is happening here—"

"Former what?" Strawberry interrupted, in that same cold tone.

Eagle sighed. Again, one of those moments when a lie would be the best thing. But she didn't want to lie exactly. "I'm a nurse. I don't work at a hospital here in the city, which is probably why Jill is saying former."

She glanced sideways at Jill, hoping Jill was smart enough to take the hint. Jill crossed her arms and leaned against the counter, her expression flat. She clearly wasn't sure what to make of this.

"So why do you want a list?" Strawberry asked.

In for a penny, in for a pound. Eagle had never completely understood the expression until this discussion. She felt like she couldn't escape it without giving more than she was getting.

"Because of what happened a few nights ago," Eagle said.

"What happened?" Jill asked.

Strawberry looked at her, clearly surprised. But Eagle wasn't sure what surprised her. The fact that something had happened that Eagle hadn't shared with Jill or the fact that adults didn't form a solid group or the fact that Jill was even in the conversation still.

Eagle took a deep breath. What she was going to say seemed so dramatic in the cold morning light of the kitchen.

"Late Saturday night," she said, "not far from here, I saw a man abduct a woman."

"*What?*" Jill raised her voice. "And you didn't think to warn us?"

The irritation Eagle always felt around Jill returned. *It's not about you*, Eagle wanted to say.

Strangely, Strawberry was the one who asked the reasonable question. "What happened?"

"I heard a woman screaming," Eagle said, keeping it short. "I ran out of my apartment, trying to find the source of the screams, and saw this woman being held by a man near a one-ton pickup truck. He saw me, hit her against the truck a few times, and threw her into the bed of the pickup. Then he drove off. I followed, but I couldn't stop him."

"I don't know why you thought you could," Jill said. "Haven't you listened to Pammy? She said never engage. Get help if possible. You can't defeat a man like that with your fists. I hope you called the cops."

Eagle ignored the implied question. She didn't want to tell Strawberry that the cops were already involved. Given her reaction a moment ago, Strawberry would stop talking if she knew.

Strawberry's gaze remained on Eagle. Strawberry's expression was hard. Now that she was quiet, the intelligence in her eyes came out. The girl was really bright. She just hid it with all that random chatter.

"You saw a Ford F-350," she said to Eagle.

Eagle's breath caught. "Yes."

"Black," Strawberry said.

Jill stood up straight, as if she finally realized she wasn't part of the conversation.

"I think so," Eagle said. "It was night, and the streetlight wasn't real close. The truck was dark, though. California plates."

"Yes," Strawberry said.

"You've seen this truck," Eagle said.

"Everyone has," Strawberry said, with maddening lack of precision.

"When people disappear?" Eagle asked.

Strawberry glanced at Jill. Jill was frowning at her.

Strawberry stood a little taller, as if she had made a decision. She kept her gaze on Jill as she said, "I'm not calling the cops, so if this conversation bugs you, get out now. Because I want to talk to the doc here."

Eagle winced at being called "doc." But she was intrigued too. What about her last question prompted that response from Strawberry?

"I'll stay," Jill said.

Strawberry studied her for a moment. Eagle could feel Strawberry withdrawing. She didn't want to talk with Jill in the room, and Jill was too dense to see it.

Eagle knew what Strawberry sensed about Jill. Strawberry knew Jill was a woman who had no qualms listening to the conversation, and then calling the police herself.

"I think we all need to hear what you have to say," Eagle said to Strawberry in her most businesslike tone.

Strawberry opened her mouth to protest, but Eagle wouldn't let her. She turned to Jill and added, "Jill, why don't you get Pammy? The class should be done now, and she needs to hear this."

Jill's lips thinned. She glanced at Strawberry but Strawberry didn't move.

Eagle wanted to give Strawberry some kind of signal, something to show her that she shouldn't give up on the conversation yet.

Eagle hoped Strawberry was bright enough to get the subtext.

Jill wasn't. She nodded once and said, "Don't say anything until I get back."

"Okay," Strawberry said, her voice choked and strange.

Jill smiled grimly, then let herself out of the kitchen.

"We only have a minute," Eagle said.

Strawberry stared at the door, as if she half-expected Jill to be listening in. Then Strawberry took a deep breath and said, "Everyone's seen the truck. We think it might belong to a cop or something. He started showing up here in January, but nobody noticed anything until March/April. Nobody saw him after the Park. We figured he got busy with guarding the streets or whatever. I hadn't heard he was back."

All the hippie jargon had left her voice. She looked deadly serious. Eagle had a sense she was finally seeing the woman that Strawberry was underneath the tie-dye and gauze. Serious, committed, and determined.

"Has he threatened people?" Eagle asked.

"No," Strawberry said. "People just kind of put it together that they'd seen the truck and then someone would disappear."

"But no one saw anyone get abducted." Eagle said.

"Except you," Strawberry said. "You saw it."

"Why did you have suspicions about this particular truck?" Eagle asked.

"It doesn't fit," Strawberry said. "Nobody has a truck like that down here. Some of the Movement people say it shouts The Man, y'know? But I think that it's worse. I think it screams redneck. And I don't know about you, but the rednecks I know are dangerous sons of bitches."

Eagle knew a lot of rednecks. She'd saved a lot of their lives. She'd liked them, for the most part, when she'd met them in the service. They were good, committed men, who were actually disappointed by what they had seen In Country.

But she had also encountered a lot of rednecks here in the States, and they treated her the worst when she would go into Rapid City from the res. They knew she was Native, and they said things to her no one had said before or since. They also said it with an undercurrent of violence, as if they wanted her to know they meant business.

"I do understand." Eagle was speaking softer, listening for Pammy and Jill to return. "What about the driver? Has anyone seen him?"

"I haven't," Strawberry said. "I haven't even seen the truck."

Eagle let out a small breath. "But you know about it."

"*Everyone* knows about it," Strawberry said again.

"You mentioned that," Eagle said. "What I want to know is how come you know about it if you've never seen it."

Strawberry took a deep breath. Voices outside the door were getting louder.

"Because we've all been told to stay away from it," she said. "We've been told the son of a bitch driving it will kill us if he gets too close."

"And you believe that?" Eagle asked.

"After this spring?" Strawberry let out a small sound of disbelief. "E-yeah."

That last had a raised up tone, as if she were surprised that Eagle asked the question.

"Hell," Strawberry said, "everyone is trying to kill us. Cops. National Guard. Crazies. I thought you knew that."

"I did know that," Eagle said. "I just don't want to believe it."

And she still didn't. That woman inside her, the one who liked rules and regulations, who wanted to believe in the inherent goodness of people, the one who had enlisted in a fit of patriotism. That woman was doomed to perpetual disappointment.

She heard Jill's voice, strident as it got closer to the door. The conversation was over, or at least, the part that Eagle wanted to hear.

"How do I get in touch with you?" she asked Strawberry.

"For your list?" Strawberry's tone was snide.

"Please," Eagle said, surprised the word came out of her mouth.

Strawberry was about to answer, and then the door opened. Jill and Pammy joined them, and Strawberry clammed up, maybe forever.

PAMMY

Class had just ended when Jill came to get Pammy. Jill bulldozed her way into the mingling group of women, all of whom moved like their muscles hurt, and all of whom had questions.

Only Val remained at the edge of the crowd, looking up at the speed bags as if she wanted to try one. Pammy had planned to go to her, but Jill had touched Pammy's shoulder, telling her she was needed in the kitchen.

Pammy made excuses. She wanted to talk to the class, but she also knew they wanted to leave as quickly as they could. Usually after the first class, though, she made sure everyone had done all right.

"I'll be right back," she said loudly.

A few of the women looked disappointed. Pammy wasn't even sure Val had heard her.

Jill flanked Pammy's side, and practically pushed her off the mat, and onto the hard linoleum floor. It took a moment to get out of hearing range, but as they reached the counter, Pammy figured it was okay to ask questions.

"What's going on?"

Jill looked over her shoulder, lips so thin that they looked strained. Apparently someone was following, because Jill assumed a fake smile and said, "Well, what isn't going on?"

That was so unlike her, it made Pammy nervous. Jill stopped beside the counter and glanced at the flyer.

Joan, the other new student, slid past them and walked into the locker room.

"You know this girl?" Jill asked, nodding toward the flyer.

"No," Pammy said. "Her father dropped that off this morning."

"Well, Strawberry might know where she is." Jill moved away from the counter and flanked Pammy again, forcing her forward.

"You were talking to Strawberry about this?" Pammy couldn't have been more shocked. Jill had made her disdain for the students, hippies, and street kids very clear.

"Yeah, me and Strawberry and Eagle, believe it or not." Jill put an emphasis on both names, one that showed just how much she disliked them.

Pammy allowed herself a half-second of disbelief. The fact that the three women had had something close to a reasonable conversation surprised her.

"Did you know Eagle is an Indian?" Jill asked.

The non sequitur almost stopped Pammy in her tracks. She hadn't known Eagle's exact background, and she didn't care.

"She told you that?" Pammy asked.

"She told Strawberry." Jill sounded almost hurt.

They stopped just outside the door. Jill looked at Pammy as if expecting a greater response from her.

"Did you *know* that?" Jill asked.

Pammy wasn't sure how to answer or even if she should.

But Jill didn't wait for a response. "I mean, don't you think it's just strange? I didn't think Indians could serve in the military, did you?"

Pammy's breath caught. *That* was what Jill thought of first? A misguided—no, a stupid—response like that.

Pammy gave her a little smile, because she had no idea what else to do, and pushed the door open.

Strawberry was standing near the refrigerator, looking focused. Eagle stood near the door, and glanced at Jill with annoyance.

Pammy felt her cheeks warm. Eagle and Strawberry had to have sent Jill out of the room so that they could talk in private.

"Jill said you needed me," Pammy said before Jill could speak. She wanted to give Eagle and Strawberry an out.

"We got it," Eagle said, but Strawberry shook her head just a little.

"That flyer you have?" Strawberry asked Pammy. "That girl? Did you know her?"

Pammy shook her head, and stepped all the way into the room. "Her father dropped it off."

"Her father...?" Strawberry sounded surprised. Pammy had no idea why.

Jill pushed Pammy forward, so that she could close the door to the tiny kitchen. Three people made the kitchen uncomfortably close. Four made it almost impossible to breathe.

Eagle was watching Strawberry closely. Jill had shoved her way to the counter and continued unloading groceries. The rattle of the bag annoyed Pammy.

"What's her name?" Strawberry asked Pammy.

"Darla Newsome." Pammy wasn't about to forget it.

"And she just vanished?" Strawberry asked.

"Almost a month ago," Pammy said.

Strawberry looked even more surprised. Eagle's eyes narrowed as if Strawberry's reaction was important.

"Newsome." Strawberry spoke the name slowly. "It doesn't sound familiar, but, I mean, she could've had a nickname or something."

It almost sounded like Strawberry was talking to herself.

"A nickname?" Jill asked, with an edge in her voice. "Like yours?"

Eagle closed her eyes as if Jill had said the exact wrong thing. But Strawberry didn't seem to notice.

"Yeah," Strawberry said. "Like mine."

She looked directly at Pammy. Pammy wasn't sure she had ever noticed how blue Strawberry's eyes were.

"Her dad, was he, like, I mean, did he, y'know, say she was in the Movement or something?"

"Which Movement?" Jill asked. "You told us there were a lot of them."

"Jill," Eagle snapped. "Enough."

Strawberry let out a small sigh. She looked like she was nearly done talking, so Pammy decided to answer her question quickly.

"Her father said Darla had political opinions, and that she dressed like you, but he didn't say anything about activism." Pammy hoped her voice held respect. She had learned that the hippie girls in particular were sensitive about getting respect. "He might not have known, though."

"True," Strawberry said. "Did she leave everything behind?"

"Yes," Pammy said.

"Was there a truck nearby?" Strawberry asked.

Pammy refrained from glancing at Eagle. Now she knew why Eagle had wanted to talk to Strawberry alone.

"What is with this truck?" Jill said. "People own trucks."

Eagle said tightly, "Jill, I swear—" but Pammy waved her silent.

Not that it did any good because Jill whirled on Eagle. "You swear. You swear what? People own trucks, and kids drop out of school, and not everyone is political."

Jill glared at Strawberry, who looked a bit taken aback at Jill's vehemence. Pammy certainly was. She'd never heard Jill so charged.

"You're the one who said it," Jill said to Strawberry. "You said it was creepy down here, even if you denied that the martial law was the creepy part. But it was scary here in May and June, and frankly, I think most of the kids went home because they didn't want any part of the violence and the protests that you people are causing—"

"Jill!" Pammy spoke a little more loudly than she intended. But she had held this gym together with spit and glue, mostly by making her students keep politics outside the door.

"Well, they *are* causing the trouble," Jill said, a bit defensively.

"That's enough," Pammy said. "We're not talking about riots or politics. We're talking about a missing girl."

"At least two missing girls," Eagle said, her tone flat. Pammy had learned to pay attention to that tone. "One of them might be dead."

Jill shook her head, her mouth pursed. "You have no way to know that."

"For Chrissake." Eagle took a step forward. The table stopped her momentum. "I know it better than you ever could. I'm a nurse. I know what injuries do. And she was injured. That animal slammed her head against the side of the truck, and then tossed her in back. He'd been punching her. Any one of the injuries I saw could have put her in the hospital, and left unattended for too long, might have killed her. For all I know, she bled out in the back of that truck."

Strawberry let out a small, somewhat frightened sigh. Pammy felt her own skin crawl at the thought of a girl dying after a beating like that.

"I thought you meant this Darla girl." Jill almost sounded chastened. "There's no way to know if she's dead."

"I agree," Eagle said quietly. "There's no way to know. Just like there's no way to know about the girl I saw. But letting your prejudices get in the way of figuring out what's happening here—"

"We're not the cops," Jill snapped.

"Thank God," Strawberry said. "Thank *fucking* God."

Her vehemence shut down the entire room. She looked at each one of them, turning her entire head to stare at them for a full twenty seconds before looking at someone else.

She ended with Pammy, and spoke to her as if they were the only ones having the conversation.

"The cops," Strawberry said, "don't care any more than Jill does. In fact, they'd probably say good riddance."

"I care," Jill said. "I just think—"

"Shut up." Eagle's voice was soft. It was even more commanding when it was soft.

Jill squared her shoulders. She swept a hand at the grocery bag in front of Strawberry. "Make sure you take any refrigerated items out of them. They're getting warm."

Then Jill shoved Pammy out of the way for the third time, and let herself out of the room. The door slammed behind her.

None of the three women said anything after she left. Pammy almost felt like she should, but if she did, she would simply apologize for Jill, because that was how Pammy was raised. She'd learned to placate—they all had—and she didn't want to placate.

Nor did she want to be aligned with Jill right now.

"So," Eagle said into the silence. "Did anyone mention a truck when Darla disappeared?"

She spoke to Pammy, their gazes meeting. Pammy understood. Eagle wanted to calm Strawberry without patronizing her.

"The father didn't know," Pammy said. "He didn't seem to know his daughter at all. Or what he thought she had become."

"Become?" Strawberry's question was charged.

"He didn't understand anything about her," Pammy said. "He didn't even know she was gone until she failed to pay rent, and her roommate contacted him."

"Did he drive a truck?" Strawberry asked.

Pammy felt cold. She hadn't thought to ask. And she had spoken to Eagle the night before. Pammy had known about the truck.

Both Strawberry and Eagle were waiting for Pammy to answer.

"He walked in," she said. "He told me he'd been going from business to business. I never saw what he drove."

"I drive a truck," Eagle said flatly. "It's not an indictment."

"You drive a Ford F-350?" Strawberry asked.

"No," Eagle said with just a touch of condescension.

Eagle's truck was one of the smaller varieties. It was old, but she kept it up. Pammy had ridden in it a few times. She didn't really like it. It had uncomfortable bench seats, a broad dash, and it rattled a little as it made its way down the road.

Eagle's voice was tight. "I'm just saying that not everyone who drives a truck is a redneck, just like not everyone who drives a VW is a hippie."

"Freak," Strawberry said.

"What?" Eagle's tone grew frosty. She clearly thought Strawberry had called her a name.

"Hippies don't call themselves hippies." Pammy spoke up quickly before this situation could escalate further. She had learned the nomenclature the hard way. "They call themselves freaks or heads or flower children."

"Freaks?" Eagle said to Strawberry. "I thought you said you didn't take acid."

"I don't," Strawberry said.

Eagle shook her head as if it were all too complicated for her.

"Look," Eagle said, "I want to find this guy."

"The father?" Pammy asked.

Eagle glanced at her as if she had asked what happened to the Man in the Moon.

"No," Eagle said, her tone still frosty. "The guy in the truck."

She turned back to Strawberry. "You said your friends told you to avoid this specific truck."

"Hell," Strawberry said. "It got mentioned at meetings all spring. Before the Park."

"But not since," Eagle said.

Strawberry frowned. Then she slowly shook her head. "Like I said, I thought he was gone. *We* thought he was gone."

"Any theories?" Eagle asked.

"About…?" Strawberry asked.

"Where he went?"

Pammy had been right. They had initially sent Jill out of the room so that they could talk without her. They were just coming back to that early conversation now as if Pammy wasn't even here.

"I didn't even think of him, to tell the truth," Strawberry said, "until you mentioned him. That's when I remembered. I mean, really, I hadn't heard a word about him in like two months."

"Did anybody know him?" Eagle asked. "Did anyone identify him by name?"

Strawberry's hand brushed the top of the grocery bag. She was clearly growing more and more uncomfortable.

"I don't know, man," she said. "I don't know any of this."

"Can you introduce me to someone who does?" Eagle asked.

"Why do you care?" Strawberry's voice went up. She sounded almost panicked.

Pammy let out a breath. Strawberry didn't know Eagle. Eagle hid how much she cared about things.

Eagle had shown up at the gym one afternoon over a year before, absolutely furious. She had found a woman walking down the street with a cold compress on her bloody nose. Eagle had stopped the woman, made sure the nose wasn't broken, and then asked where she had gotten the bloody nose.

Eagle had charged into the gym, determined to put a stop to whoever was hurting that woman.

"Why do I care?" Eagle asked in that soft voice she had used earlier. She was looking directly at Strawberry.

Pammy was wrong. The voice wasn't just commanding. It was deadly.

"*Why* do I care?" Eagle repeated.

Apparently Strawberry didn't hear the danger. She nodded, then shrugged as if Eagle were asking a stupid question.

"Why do *I* care?" Eagle mused. Then she snorted and leaned toward Strawberry. "Why don't *you* care? You *profess* to care about so many things. The oppressed, the Park, the war…. Yet, somehow, you can't be bothered with two women who have vanished. Yeah, that's caring. That's *fake* caring."

Pammy gasped.

"That's not fair." Strawberry looked at Pammy. Apparently, Strawberry had heard Pammy's reaction. "Are you going to let her talk to me like this?"

Pammy had stopped Jill for precisely the same reason. Pammy should stop Eagle as well. But Jill had been reacting out of bigotry. Eagle actually had a point.

Or rather, she had a point that Pammy agreed with.

She opened her mouth, uncertain what to say.

But Strawberry sighed, deeply impatient. She had apparently given up on Pammy's response.

"Look," Strawberry said, using that *you're stupid* tone. "It's not just two women who vanished. It's not just about women. It's men too."

"And that makes it less of a crisis?" Eagle asked.

"I didn't say that!" Strawberry shook her head, sounding like a teenager being grounded. She looked at Pammy as if she thought Pammy would take her side.

Pammy didn't want to take sides. Or maybe she already had.

"What are you saying, then?" Eagle asked.

Strawberry's mouth thinned. "I'm saying you don't know what's going on and you don't know what we're doing to stop it."

"All right," Eagle said. "What are you doing?"

"*I don't know*," Strawberry said. "It's not my area."

"But something's being done, that's what you're telling me?" Eagle asked.

Strawberry opened her mouth, then closed it and looked at Pammy again.

Pammy decided to wait before jumping in. Eagle was right: women were missing, possibly dead. *People* were missing. Pushing Strawberry was appropriate in this situation.

"I don't know," Strawberry said again. "It's not my area."

"And I return to my original point. You care so much about Biafra and the situation in Vietnam that you can't even look at what's happening on your own doorstep." Eagle's sarcasm cut the air like a blade.

"It's not my fault that these people disappeared," Strawberry said.

"It will be," Eagle said, "if you don't work with us. If you continue to stop me from trying to figure this thing out, then whatever that asshole in the truck has done—or whoever is making kids disappear—is on you too."

"That's not fair," Strawberry said softly.

Eagle laughed once, a cold, hard sound. "Under the law, if you're protecting someone who committed a crime, you're an accessory."

"I don't care about the law!" Strawberry said.

"And clearly, you don't care about those women either," Eagle said.

Strawberry's face was red. Her eyes were filled with tears. She looked at Pammy.

"What are you afraid of?" Pammy asked Strawberry.

Strawberry opened her mouth again, then shook her head, and shrugged.

"We can't help if you won't tell us," Pammy said.

"We handle our own shit," Strawberry blurted. "We're not supposed to involve anyone with the Establishment. I get enough crap for coming here."

"So you're afraid for yourself and your relationship with your hippie friends," Eagle said.

"Shut up," Pammy said to Eagle, surprising herself. She kept her gaze on Strawberry. "We're not the authorities. We're not going to the authorities."

She looked at Eagle then, making a point of the gaze. "Right?"

Eagle nodded, as Pammy knew she would. Eagle had tried the cops and they had failed her.

"You've got to choose now, between your friends and saving some women you don't even know," Pammy said. "It seems to me, that's no choice at all."

"You don't understand," Strawberry murmured.

Eagle started to speak, but Pammy held up a hand, stopping her. "We all have a moment in life where we either stand up for what we believe in or we let someone else handle it," Pammy said. "Right now, you're letting someone else handle this."

"And you're asking me to let you handle it," Strawberry snapped.

"No," Eagle said. "We're asking you to help us *solve* this. A different thing."

Strawberry looked at Pammy, then at Eagle. Strawberry's silence seemed like assent.

So Pammy said, "Go ahead, Eagle."

Eagle straightened, took a deep breath as if she were calming herself, and then said to Strawberry, "I want a list. No, scratch that. I want *two* lists. I want a list of the people who have disappeared, and I want a list of everyone who has warned you about that truck."

Strawberry swallowed hard. Her skin had gone from beet red to pale. The very idea of lists seemed to frighten her.

"And then what?" she asked. "You'll give it all to the cops?"

Eagle was shaking her head. "The cops won't help with this. You already know that."

"So what's the point?" Strawberry asked.

Eagle slammed her fist on the kitchen table. The slam sounded like a gunshot. The table bounced and banged against the floor.

Pammy reached toward Eagle, to stop her from whatever she was going to do next. Pammy had only seen Eagle like this a few times before, and mostly during the People's Park crap in the spring. Eagle had been mad at the very authorities that Strawberry didn't like.

Eagle whirled on Strawberry, who had cringed at the noise, but held her ground.

"Goddammit," Eagle said, that soft tone back. "Just how fucking dense *are* you? I'm pretty goddamn sure a woman is dead because of this guy, and you're telling me there are other people who disappeared that he might be responsible for, and you can't be bothered to give me a goddamn list because I might be connected to the government or I might be a—what do you *freaks* call it? A narc? I'm not a goddamn narc. I'm a fucking concerned citizen. I'm beginning to believe I'm the *only* fucking concerned citizen in Berkeley—really concerned, mind you, not fake concerned with all your goddamn rallies and your pretty little signs and your stupid fucking marches. It doesn't matter how much you march and prattle and tell us how to behave. If you don't fucking care about the people *you know* who are vanishing off the streets, then why the hell should I listen to you when you tell me what to do? Why the hell should *any* of us listen to you?"

She slammed her fist on the table again, and this time, Strawberry jumped.

Pammy put her hand on Eagle's shoulder and Eagle shrugged her off.

"You're not much help," Eagle snapped at Pammy. "All your high-minded fucking stupid speeches about self-defense. What does that do? It means that one woman will fight until she's fucking tired, and can't fight any more. *Self*-defense is meaningless. Your little groups that watch the stupid moon landing instead of taking any meaningful action are worthless. And the fact you don't want anyone to talk about politics? Well, that's fucking stupid too."

Eagle shoved her way past Strawberry and went around the table. Then Eagle stopped, turned, and faced them.

"All of this? Our little discussion here? *This* is why nothing gets done in this country. Or anywhere really. Because most people are like you two. Either too frightened to do something or trusting someone else to do it. And then you won't even help when someone tries."

She shook her head.

"You," she said, pointing at Pammy. "I don't care what your goddamn politics are. You're Nixon's silent majority, waiting for someone else to do the work for you and quietly disapproving of everyone around you."

Pammy felt her face flush. Eagle knew how to get to her. Nothing made her angrier than being called a Nixon-lover.

"And you," Eagle said, looking at Strawberry. "You wait. One day, you'll need someone's help, and all your little friends will vanish on you. Because *they're not your friends*. They're self-interested assholes who want the media attention. You don't even believe half of their bullshit, but you believe enough of it to worry more about what they think than you do about *the lives of two people*."

Eagle shook her head and headed to the door.

"You both make me sick," she said, and slammed her way out.

The kitchen reverberated with the remains of her anger. Pammy hadn't seen anything like that in years, and certainly never from Eagle.

Or to be even more accurate, Eagle had never directed that kind of fury at her.

Tears lined Strawberry's eyes. She looked at Pammy. "Why do you let her come here?"

Pammy let out a small sigh, her heart pounding. She cleared her throat and said, "Eagle saves lives. That's what she does."

"She had no right to talk to me like that," Strawberry said, wiping under her eyelids with the forefingers of each hand.

Pammy looked at her. Strawberry had brought a lot of people to the gym. She had helped in a variety of ways, and yet, if Pammy were forced to choose between Strawberry and Eagle, she'd choose Eagle every single time.

"Yes, she did," Pammy said. "She needs your help."

"Funny way to ask for it." Strawberry was still cleaning her eyes, but she hadn't left the kitchen. That was a good sign.

Pammy nodded. "She's frustrated. She's used to doing things alone."

"What things?" Strawberry asked.

Pammy thought of all the times Eagle had shown up here after a single phone call, splinting sprained wrists, providing cold compresses, and, more than once, ferrying a woman badly injured by her husband to a hospital outside of the Bay Area, where the husband couldn't find her.

But none of that would impress Strawberry. So Pammy said, "On May fifteenth, Eagle ran into the streets during the riot, just like she did the other night. She patched up a number of people who had been shot, but one kid, he looked like he was going to bleed out. She stopped the bleeding, and sat on the sidewalk with him for hours, until things calmed down enough to get him help."

Strawberry raised her head, just a little.

"A few days later, when Governor Reagan sent that helicopter in filled with CS gas, Eagle realized that the gym was in danger. She ran here, and shoved all of us into the showers, so that we wouldn't inhale the stuff and it wouldn't stay on our skins. We didn't have to send anyone to the hospital, because of her."

Strawberry wiped her right eye with the back of her right hand. Then she sniffled.

"She helps people," Pammy said. "In small, very real ways. She's not good at the overall picture. She doesn't like it."

Pammy didn't add that the fact that Eagle didn't like it might have come from her service in Vietnam. Strawberry didn't need to know that.

"But one on one?" Pammy said. "She's one of the most honorable, ethical people I know."

Strawberry glanced at the door, and said in a small voice, "I didn't mean to make her mad."

Pammy smiled. The smile was a bit strained, but it was real enough. "Me either."

Strawberry took a deep breath. "What do I do now? Apologize?"

"I think we give her some space," Pammy said. "But it would help if you got those lists."

"If I do that, my friends…" Strawberry's voice trailed off. Then she looked down, shook her head, and smiled just a little. "…but maybe they're not my friends, right? If they would come down on me for helping someone, even if that someone isn't one of us. Right?"

Pammy wasn't one of them either, but she didn't say that. She was going to let Strawberry come to her own conclusions.

Strawberry straightened her shoulders, and took a deep breath. "If you're not part of the solution, you're part of the problem, right?"

She was paraphrasing one of the slogans that Pammy had seen on a dozen placards. It was one of the main critiques Strawberry's friends had of the so-called Establishment.

"Right," Pammy said, realizing as she agreed that the slogan was actually true. She wondered what Eagle would think if she knew she agreed with something the hippies constantly said.

"Then I'll bring the lists," Strawberry said. "Maybe tonight or tomorrow morning at the latest. You tell Eagle for me, okay? And tell her I'm sorry?"

"You can apologize on your own," Pammy said. She wasn't sure she'd see Eagle before that. She wondered if she should make a point of it.

Sometimes Eagle needed the space to cool down.

Pammy would give her that space, before calling and telling her what Strawberry agreed to.

Maybe by then, Pammy would be calmer too.

EAGLE

Eagle staggered into the alley, the stench of urine, dog shit, and day-old garbage nearly overpowering her. She cradled her aching fist to her chest and doubled over, her eyes dry, her body shaking.

She hated it when she got that angry. Hated, hated, hated it.

The loss of control. Jesus, she had lost control. *Again*.

She made herself take a deep breath of the fetid air, and forced herself to be brutally honest.

She had hit that fucking table because if she hadn't, she would have punched that mouthy little brat who thought she knew everything. Fucking child. Fucking child with fucking *dying* flowers in her hair.

Fucking child who knew more than she was willing to say, and didn't want to help anyone, except starving children in Biafra or some other place no one had ever heard of.

It was those places no one had ever heard of that bit back the hardest. They were the ones that people got sent to, places ringed by mountains with names no one could pronounce, and skies so blue they mocked you. Places where Hueys brought wounded, and shell casings decorated the ground. Places where grinning black-haired children played in a fucking sandbag pit, their mothers looking on as if it were normal.

As if it were all normal.

Eagle braced herself with her left hand on the warm metal top of a nearby garbage can, not caring that it was coated with some kind of sticky slime. Her right hand was still curled into a fist, one side throbbing from the force of those two blows.

The violence had surprised her. *Her* violence had surprised her, although it shouldn't have.

She'd been wanting to hit something ever since the damn cops had taken their own sweet time in showing up on Saturday night. Fucking idiots, not caring about anyone. Fucking goddamn idiots.

And then that girl, not caring either, but *pretending* to care. At least the goddamn cops didn't pretend. At least they acknowledged their disinterest. Hell, they were *proud* of it.

Assholes.

Although Eagle had been mad before the cops showed up. She'd been wanting to hit something ever since she had heard that woman, screaming for help in the middle of the night.

That woman she couldn't save.

Add that woman to the nameless people Eagle hadn't been able to save in the past five years, and maybe it was a fucking straw. All those men, women, and children with their faces gone or mutilated or covered in so much blood she couldn't see their features. People, dying people, unidentifiable except by their moans of pain.

Eagle let out her own moan. She could go back to her apartment. She *should* go back to her apartment, dig that baggy out of the Raisin Bran and just forget it all. The woman, the disappearing people, they weren't her problem. When did she become responsible for the whole world?

Why couldn't she have the same fucking attitude that that holier-than-thou flower-child had? Eagle had to keep reminding herself that it didn't matter. Nothing mattered. No matter what anyone did, people died.

People died.

Soldiers died.

Children died.

And no one cared.

She slowly sank to the ground, but before she landed on the filthy concrete, hands caught her waist.

"Come on," a soft female voice said. "It's better if you stand up."

Eagle didn't recognize the voice. She looked down, saw dark hands against her shirt, frowned, not recognizing them. An hallucination? A memory? She didn't have friends of color here in the States.

They had all died in that mess over there, or had come back in so many pieces that they were unrecognizable, even to themselves.

"Come on," the soft voice said again, with just a bit of strain. "Stand up. You can breathe if you stand."

Logic. Eagle hated fucking logic.

She shook off the hands, but lifted her butt, back into her doubled-over position, wondering if she was going to puke. Those donuts had turned into concrete in her stomach.

"I'm okay," she said to the pebbled and garbage-strewn ground. "You can go."

She didn't want to see whoever it was, didn't want to have the embarrassment of her own weakness come back to her every fucking time she saw this person's face, whoever this fucking Good Samaritan was.

The hands returned, not holding her this time, but bracing her.

"I'm not going anywhere," the owner of the voice said.

Fucking goddamn do-gooder. Eagle would've thought the do-gooder had come from Pammy's gym, only Pammy rarely had anyone but white people in her classes. Bigoted white people like that stupid fucking flower child, white people who had no idea that their stupid goddamn questions aimed at "understanding" were really just ways of establishing the difference between Us and Them. Between perfect white people and everyone else.

"I'm all right," Eagle said, her tone still measured. It would be better—more believable—if she could stand upright. But she couldn't. Not yet.

She'd been through this before. The loss of control made her see stars, made her dizzy and nauseous, and worried that she was going to die. Unrealistic panic, her medical brain told her. Panic couldn't kill anyone—at least, in a situation like this where there was no real threat.

In Nam, sure, panic killed everyone, and maybe panic had contributed to that woman getting beaten by the asshole with the truck. But here, on a sunny noon in the middle of an alley in Berkeley in July, naw. Panic didn't kill at all. Panic just made Eagle *want* to die.

"When you can stand up and tell me you're all right, I'll leave you be." The voice was so calm, so patient. So non-judgmental. Like it was trained that way.

Eagle had been trained that way.

Fury bit through her, fast and out of control. She remained doubled over, not because she needed to any longer, but because she didn't want her would-be rescuer to see how fucking angry she was.

Eagle made herself take a deep breath. *C'mon, girl*, she thought firmly and strongly, making the thought dominate her brain. *You know how to pretend to be calm. Pretending is sometimes the same as* being *calm. You know that. Get a fucking grip.*

She still didn't stand up. The woman who had come to her supposed rescue stood close enough that Eagle could see her shoes.

Brand-new Keds.

The woman *had* come from Pammy's then. Had Pammy sent her? Why would Pammy send someone Eagle didn't know?

No. If Pammy thought Eagle needed help, Pammy would have come on her own.

Pammy was probably pissed as hell at her, anyway. Fucking temper. Fucking out-of-control temper. Eagle couldn't believe she had called Pammy a Nixon Republican. Pammy, of all people. Pammy was more of an Adlai Stevenson bleeding heart than she was anything else. That Nixon comment had probably cut her to the bone.

And the very thought of that, of the stupid fucking insult, sent waves of calm through Eagle. It broke the fury, or maybe turned it inward. Eagle wasn't going to examine that, and she wasn't going to analyze it.

Not with some strange woman wearing brand-new Keds standing right beside her.

Eagle eased herself upright, and took another deep breath. Her stomach had settled as well.

"Sorry," she said. "I'm all right now."

She still hadn't turned around. She didn't want to see this woman, didn't want to interact with her. They had nothing in common with each other, and Eagle didn't need the woman's pity.

"I'll be the judge of that," the woman said, her voice still soft and calm.

Fuck, who the hell put you in charge of me? Eagle managed to bite the words back before they emerged. Preventing the words from leaving this time was better than she had done in the kitchen, anyway.

She plastered a smile on her face and turned around.

The woman standing behind her was short and skinny. Her skin was dark, like a strong cup of coffee, but her features were delicate. Her brown eyes were filled with compassion.

Eagle hated the compassion. Her smile nearly slipped. But she knew she had to keep it so that this woman would disappear.

The woman's mouth twisted upward in a wry smile.

"Nice try," she said. "But we both know you're not really doing better."

Fucking busybody, Eagle thought but did not say. She let the smile fall away.

The woman tugged nervously on her t-shirt, revealing a collarbone that was too pronounced. She was too thin, her bones visible. Who the hell was she to be lecturing Eagle?

"*We both* don't know anything about me," Eagle said, and then inwardly winced at the tangled syntax. That statement was probably truer than she wanted it to be. Neither of them knew anything about Eagle, including Eagle herself.

"True enough." The woman didn't sound at all bothered by Eagle's rudeness. "I don't know anything about you and you don't know me."

Although as she said that, Eagle realized she had seen the woman before. She had stood outside the gym off and on for days, as if she couldn't make up her mind about it.

When Eagle had first seen her, she had thought the woman was holding the gym in contempt. But judging by her clothes—that dark t-shirt, light blue shorts, and the brand-new Keds—the woman had simply been trying to get up her courage to go inside.

The woman took a step forward, hand extended. "I'm Valentina Wilson."

"That's a mouthful," Eagle said, ignoring the hand.

The woman—Valentina—nodded. "I prefer Val."

"I would too," Eagle said, knowing she was just compounding her rudeness.

The woman remained in position, hand out, but she seemed to firm up her posture, as if steeling herself to continue to stand.

"It's customary," she said in that soft, calm voice, "to shake the hand that's being offered, and to introduce yourself."

Eagle snorted. "You think I've made it this far in life without knowing that?"

The woman—Val—still hadn't moved. "I think you're being deliberately rude to make me go away. The harder you push, the longer I'll stay."

Eagle felt a chill run down her back. She would have said something like that to someone who needed her, but was using anger to keep her away. Which was exactly what she was doing to this woman, and the woman was bright enough to see it.

Eagle couldn't remember the last time anyone had seen her clearly. But this woman seemed to have her number right from the start.

"What's in it for you?" Eagle asked because she couldn't help herself.

The woman—Val—grinned. "Well, you see, I made a magical deal with a lesser angel. I have to perform one good deed per day or I will go to hell. You're my good deed today. Live through it, and then we don't have to bother each other ever again."

In spite of herself, Eagle found herself shaking her head at the sheer audacity of the woman. Not to mention the woman's sense of humor, which was appealing, despite Eagle's mood.

"What do you want?" Eagle asked, trying to keep her tone just as rude as it had been a moment ago. "A document from me, certifying the good deed?"

"A gold star will do," Val said. "A big gold star. The biggest gold star you can find, in fact. Then I'll leave."

Eagle was still shaking her head and, to her surprise, she realized she was smiling too. "Who the hell are you, woman?"

"I told you," Val said. "And I'll be honest. My arm is getting tired. So shake my hand."

Eagle reached out with her sore right hand, and took Val's, making sure the handshake wasn't too firm but wasn't too weak either.

"June Eagleton," Eagle said. "People call me Eagle."

"Yeah," Val said. "It suits you better than June. Eagles are strong, but they set their own path. June—that's the month of weddings and too much pink."

Eagle let out a short laugh. She had never thought of it that way, but it was true. She wasn't a moon-in-June kinda gal. And never had been.

"Okay," she said. "You made me laugh. Now can we go our own ways?"

Val let her hand fall to her side. "I suppose. If you feel like you need to be alone. Me, in your shoes, I'd want to talk to a friend."

"That assumes I have friends," Eagle said, and immediately felt a pang of guilt. Pammy was a friend. It wasn't Pammy's fault that they weren't close.

It was Eagle's.

"Yeah, well, I'm not seeing any of them," Val said, "and you look like you need an ear. I'm new to Berkeley, and I wouldn't mind having someone to talk to."

"The white women in the gym aren't good enough for you?" Eagle asked before she could stop herself.

Val grinned. "They're just fine, and I think one or two of them might be friend material. But you're the most interesting person I've met since I've been here."

"You haven't been here long, then," Eagle said.

"A few weeks," Val said. "So, you're right. Not too long."

"It was easy to tell," Eagle said, "when the person you want to befriend is a woman feeling sorry for herself in a piss-scented alley."

"I'm from Chicago," Val said. "It just reminds me of home."

Eagle laughed, but Val didn't laugh with her. Eagle's eyebrows came together in perplexed understanding. Val wasn't bullshitting her. Val did find her interesting.

"You're not one of those rescuers, are you?" Eagle said. "One of those people who find others they consider to be wounded birds and then try to heal them?"

Val laughed. "No. No one would ever accuse me of that. I mostly like to keep to myself."

"Then what's the interest in me?" Eagle asked.

Val's pleasant expression faded. "I don't know. I guess I recognized the emotion. I've had moments like that myself in the past year."

Eagle restrained herself from nodding. Of course. The thinness, the visible bones, the soft voice. Arriving, friendless, in a new town. This woman, this Val, clearly had issues.

Big issues.

Were they kindred spirits, then? Did Eagle really need a friend as broken as she was?

"I don't take care of people," Eagle said.

"I don't either." Val's chin was up ever so slightly. She looked strong, despite her frail little body.

"You stood outside the gym for a week," Eagle said. "Why is that?"

Val leaned back almost as if Eagle had pushed her. Finally, Eagle had gotten a real reaction from her. Only this time, Eagle hadn't been trying.

Val tilted her head, as if she were trying to speak, but rejecting the initial words. She made the movement twice before saying, "I've run all the way to the Pacific Ocean. I can either get on a bus and head back to Chicago or maybe run all the way to the Atlantic, or I can get used to my new reality, and learn how to live my life all over again."

Her tone had a ring of truth. Eagle recognized it. She didn't recognize the sentiment, though. She hadn't run anywhere. She had holed up instead, burying herself in that shitty apartment and trying hard not to come out.

"So, what happened to you?" Eagle was actually curious, which surprised her. She hadn't thought she could care about anyone else in this mood.

"That's need to know, soldier," Val said, with a businesslike tone. It sounded military and not rude at all. Just the sound of a door closing, in a way that Eagle could hear.

She started. "How did you know—?"

"That you're military?" Val asked. "I didn't for certain. You might've been a retired cop. But you're awfully young to be retired, plus your eyes are a little too red and puffy, and you're not the type for tears. That and the seeds stuck to the right seam of your shirt. They look like they were washed in."

Despite herself, Eagle looked. There was a small line of marijuana seeds running down the middle of the seam on her shirt. She tugged at one seed. It didn't come loose.

Jesus. Sometimes she wasn't fooling anyone.

"What were you?" Val asked. "WAC?"

She knew the acronym for Women's Army Corps, which also surprised Eagle.

"Army Nurse," she said, declining to give her rank, which she would have done in the past.

Val raised her eyebrows. "Well," she said, "then Berkeley's a strange place for you to hole up."

"No shit," Eagle said. "I could say the same for you."

Val looked at her arms, as if noticing her skin color for the first time. "True enough. I somehow thought there'd be more people like me. Maybe because it's summer—"

"That's part of it," Eagle said. "But you're from Chicago, right?"

Val tugged on her shirt again, and Eagle looked at it for the first time, starting again. She hadn't expected a Chicago Police Department t-shirt.

"Southside born and raised," Val said. "You don't have to see white people at all there if you don't want to."

"Do you want to?" Eagle asked.

"Do you?" Val asked.

Unlike Strawberry, Val didn't ask questions about Eagle's ethnicity. Maybe Val knew it, and maybe she didn't. But she did know—and immediately accept—the fact that Eagle had mixed parentage.

"Sometimes I don't mind whites," Eagle said. "Pammy's good people."

"Yeah," Val said. "I'm beginning to understand that about Pammy. Although my muscles are calling me a liar right now."

And Eagle finally understood. Val had been in the beginner's exercise class or, as Eagle called it, Injury Heaven. She'd treated more beginners for sprains and broken bones than everyone else in the gym combined.

"So you were a cop?" Eagle asked, looking at the shirt.

Val gave her a bitter unreadable smile.

"Too young to be retired." Eagle ran her gaze over Val, then realized that this woman's frailty could have had several causes, including a great physical trauma. "Injury force you out?"

"Injury, yeah, you could say I got injured." Val laughed, only this time the sound had no mirth at all. Bitter, again. "Cop, no. Married to one. Once."

Eagle frowned. That was a strange way to put things.

"He's dead." Val's voice had gotten even flatter. Eagle's heart went out to her, and Eagle's heart hardly ever went out to anyone.

They stared at each other for a moment. The conversation had probably reached its natural end, and for that, Eagle felt another pang.

Val looked down. Then she shrugged once as if she were having a conversation with herself.

"Um," she said, suddenly sounding unsure. The caution in her voice surprised Eagle. She hadn't expected it. "I know this is…I mean…would you like to…have lunch?"

Then Val looked up, almost as if she expected Eagle to say no.

Eagle would have, too, if it weren't for Val's tone. And the fact that Eagle was hungry, which surprised her, given the stench in the alley.

But it really wasn't hunger that made her consider Val's suggestion. It was the way Val was looking at her, worried and hopeful at the same time.

That woman was as damaged as Eagle, just in a different way. Eagle felt the pull of a kindred spirit again and wondered if she would be better off ignoring it.

"Most of the places around here are hippie enclaves," Eagle said, hoping that might give her an out.

Val shrugged one shoulder. "We are in Berkeley after all. That Caffe Mediterraneum has good coffee."

"They put shit in their coffee and call it European," Eagle said.

"It *is* European," Val said, and then laughed, a real laugh this time. "There are other places too."

"Other places would be better," Eagle said, unable to believe she was negotiating a lunch date, but unable to stop. "How about Robbie's?"

"The place that the Beats used to hang out at?" Val asked. "Yeah, that sounds good."

Eagle's eyes narrowed. "You know more about Berkeley than you initially let on."

Val shrugged. "I read the wrong things before coming here. I knew about the Beats and the quality of the campus. I had no idea that the community was in such turmoil right now. I just thought I was coming to a place where I might feel at home."

"Do you feel at home?" Eagle asked.

Val's eyes narrowed. Then she slowly shook her head.

"I don't," she said. "Although I'm not sure I would feel at home anywhere anymore."

Eagle thought about that statement. Too much truth for a Monday afternoon.

"Yeah," Eagle said. "I hear you."

She straightened up all the way, looked at her left hand covered in slime, and thought about going back into the gym to wash it off. If she went back inside, she would never leave. Pammy would want to settle what had happened, maybe update her on that stupid fucking hippie-freak girl.

"Okay," Eagle said. "Let's go see if we can hear the echoes of Ginsberg howling."

Val grinned at her. And together, they walked out of the alley and onto the street.

VAL

The sunlight seemed brighter than I expected after the dimness of that squalid little alley. I let out a small breath, still a bit surprised at myself for venturing into such a dicey place.

But I hadn't given it a second thought. I had glanced down the alley, like I always did when I passed it, looking for *him* or men like *him*, and instead, I had seen a woman in slow collapse.

I recognized that slow collapse. I'd done it a lot these past seven months. You think you're fine, and then you realize you're not, but you do your best to stay upright, even though your legs are refusing, your head feels muzzy, and you can barely breathe.

If you end up on the ground, well, then it takes a long time to get back up. But if you can remain upright, you're okay, at least for a short time.

I hurried into the alley without even checking the shadows around the garbage cans, and caught the woman by the waist before she sank onto the wet concrete. It had smelled like that wetness was dog pee. There were dogs everywhere in this city, and no one bothered to take care of them, which irritated the hell out of me. If I were a dog person—and I wasn't—I would have been pulling dogs away from their drugged-out owners. I probably would have had to have my own damn doggy halfway house or something. But I didn't, although I did seem to have a thing for strays.

People strays.

Like this woman, Eagle. Now, she was striding beside me, powerful, seemingly strong. Her back was straight, her brown eyes took in everything around her. She was nothing like the woman I had found cratering in the alley, and yet, she was the same person.

The strong woman was her cover. Like I used to have a cover.

Or maybe it was her real self, and the broken part, which had appeared in the alley, just needed to heal.

Eagle had naturally straight black hair, cut short, and flat, arresting features. Her skin wasn't as dark as mine, but it wasn't white either. Her shoulders were broad for a woman, and she kept a pace that nearly exhausted me.

Or maybe the class had exhausted me. I had done all I could to keep up, but I really wasn't good at any of it. I managed two push-ups, legs and back straight, before collapsing on the mat. I jumped rope for what seemed like forever, but it turned out to be only a minute before I had to stop and catch my breath.

It would've been completely embarrassing if it weren't for Joan and some of the other women, who were having the same troubles.

The streets were crowded, even more crowded than they had been this morning. It was a little after noon, but the time shouldn't have made as much difference near campus as it would have in a more businesslike setting.

And no one could accuse this part of Berkeley of being businesslike. Even though I was only in a t-shirt and shorts, I felt dressed up, compared to the fringe, blue jeans, and bare male chests around me. The girls all wore their hair long, held back (if at all) by woven headbands, and many of them wore bikini tops that left little to the imagination.

Bicyclists passed us, dressed in brown fringed pants with fringed vests, their bare feet extended outward. Eagle clearly had a better sense of self-perseveration than I had, because she moved aside to prevent being hit by those extended feet. She gave the cyclists a glare that should have melted them into the pavement.

Not that they noticed.

I was learning, though, that the hippie types who hung around this part of Berkeley didn't notice anyone. And they *stank*. Unwashed clothes, unwashed bodies, patchouli oil, incense, and marijuana—although (honest again) I wasn't sure whether the pot hit I was getting was coming from the hippie cyclists or from Eagle herself.

It looked like she was using pot to send herself into oblivion, the way some people used alcohol. The way *I* thought about using alcohol in those weeks after the last surgery. But, in those dark days, I had known if I did drink, I would have been lost forever.

Eagle and I reached Telegraph, and it was full of people, unlike yesterday. In fact, a large crowd gathered around the entrance to Robbie's Cafeteria at the end of the block. Someone I couldn't see was playing the bongos, and someone else I couldn't see was playing a guitar badly, and some wispy-haired strung-out white girl was singing—or maybe she thought she was singing. She was making singing-like sounds, anyway.

Dogs sat on the edge of the crowd, and for a half second, I wondered if they were going to howl. Which made me smile, since Eagle and I had just discussed Ginsburg's poem "Howl."

I was about to start quoting from it as I turned to her, changing the words to reflect the dogs, when I saw her expression. Her eyes had narrowed, her mouth thinned, and she leaned forward somewhat aggressively. She was spoiling for a fight—and oddly, that didn't bother me.

I glanced across the street, at Caffe Mediterraneum, which was closer than Robbie's Cafeteria (and had better food). Usually the hippies gathered in front of Caffe Med, but today there were only a few, and they were sitting on the sidewalk. Everyone else had moved down to Robbie's, probably to watch the performances.

I touched Eagle's arm. "I hate to tell you this, but Caffe Med looks more promising."

"Fuck, of course it does," she said. "Because that's the kind of day I'm having."

She said that last in a matter-of-fact manner, not self-pitying at all. The anger that had been in her face a moment ago was gone.

She shrugged, pivoted, and crossed Telegraph in front of two motor-cyclists and a Volkswagen bug. All three of them zoomed by her as if they hadn't seen her or simply didn't care.

A tambourine and a harmonica had joined the bongo-guitar-singer mess. I hurried kitty-corner across the street, watching for traffic, unlike Eagle, heading toward Caffe Med. It took up a good part of the entire block, its gigantic striped blue-and-white sign, painted on the building itself, dominating this part of Telegraph. A billboard for Smirnoff Vodka perched precariously on the roof of the building, sunlight glinting off the metal struts.

The billboard was how I noted Caffe Med in the first place. The word *Smirnoff* in neon had shown whitely on the stripes below, making the word *Mediterreanum* look almost alive. And then I had looked down and noticed the European espresso makers lining the window. I hadn't seen those since I took a trip to Italy in my junior year of college.

We walked around a young white man with long brown hair held back by a woven bandana. He leaned against the wall between the House of Leather shoe repair shop and the café, his dirty, naked feet resting on a blanket with some crudely made silver earrings and spoon rings displayed on it. Next to him, a woman wearing a bikini top and short shorts sat cross-legged in front of a woven blanket with her wares on it. She was clearly the source of the headbands, and I could see why. They were exquisitely woven of good materials and lovely vibrant colors, priced at less than a dollar each.

I would have lingered, except that Eagle had already marched into the Caffe Med.

As usual, I had to go through a thicket of sad-looking dogs to get inside. One rather ragged mix with curly white fur had managed to sneak past the door, and was sitting behind a middle-aged man's legs, eating the remains of a pink cupcake off the pebbled linoleum floor.

One table, completely covered with dishes, looked unusable. The only other open table was near the stairs. Eagle went to it, cleared off some dirty coffee cups, and put them on the dirtier table without a qualm.

"I'll order for you," I said.

She looked up. "No need," she said. "I got it."

I let out a small sigh. What was it with everyone here, assuming I had no money at all? I probably had more money than all of them, maybe put together.

"Just tell me what you want," I said. "You guard the table. I'll let you know how much it is, and you can pay me."

Her lips thinned, but she looked at the people still milling across the street, and I could almost see her thought. We might not get another table for a while.

"A roast beef sandwich would be great," she said.

"And coffee?" I asked, feeling a little impy.

She made a face. "A glass of water would be fine. Just wait here for a second while I wash my hands."

She left the table before I had time to protest, and wended her way to the restroom. I supposed she would order when she got back, before she came to the table.

I sighed and sat down, claiming our table. To my right, a woman with a short bob sat alone, reading a thick book about Kafka. In front of our table, four kids earnestly discussed the moon landing. One of the girls kept tucking and untucking a strand of dirty blonde hair behind her ear. The boy beside her, with his curly red hair a riot around his face, removed his granny glasses and shook them at his companions to make a point.

To my left, a couple sat in silence. They were maybe my age. The woman stirred her coffee repeatedly, while he ignored her. He was reading one of the free newspapers, the *Berkeley Barb*, as if he were memorizing every word.

Eagle came directly back from the bathroom, which surprised me. She rubbed her well-scrubbed hands, and made a face as she sat down.

"There was something slimy on that garbage can," she said. "I worked hard to make sure I didn't touch anything else."

"Except the dishes you moved," I said, looking at them in their pile.

"Well," she said in a somewhat wry tone, "let's hope their dish-washer works."

If they even had an automated dishwasher. I would wager the dish-washer here was some student who couldn't get a better job. And given the students' level of personal hygiene in this town, I wouldn't trust that the dishes Eagle touched would be clean after five washings, let alone two.

My gorge rose for a moment, and then I sighed. I had to trust, even when it came to food.

"Okay," I said with more determination than I intended, "I'm getting sandwiches."

Eagle's glance at me was perplexed. She probably heard my Churchillian "we will fight on the beaches" tone in my voice.

I stood, and hurried to the small counter, skirting several tables. It smelled like fresh ground coffee up front. A young woman wearing a white gauze peasant dress was counting pennies to pay for her coffee. The young man beside her, in cut-off jeans and a loose t-shirt, swayed to music only he could hear.

I got in line behind them—if you could count them as a line—and studied the posted menu, even though I already knew what I wanted. A young couple stood outside the door, feet bare. He wasn't wearing a shirt.

There was no sign here that said *No shirt, no shoes, no service,* but there needed to be. I had no idea how this place kept going. In Chicago, the city would've shut them down or made them pay huge fines to stay open. But then, in Chicago, almost no one went barefoot on the streets—at least in my neighborhood. Too much broken glass from smashed streetlights.

I ordered for Eagle and got myself a ham sandwich and a specialty coffee drink—espresso with some foamed milk. I asked for two waters, figuring I probably needed to drink something after that exercise session.

I brought everything back to the table in two trips. Clearly, I'd never been a waitress. I shoved an ashtray to one side, moved the big glass sugar dispenser, and grabbed some paper napkins.

Eagle looked at my small cup of coffee, with the little flower the counterman had drawn in foam on the surface.

"You're drinking that crap?" she asked.

"I fell in love with it when I was in Italy for my junior year abroad," I said.

She leaned back and gave me a sideways look. "You are a bundle of surprises."

I hated it when people said things like that. They usually meant that they had underestimated me based on my appearance or my accent or my femaleness or *something*.

"Oh?" I asked.

"Yeah," she said. "I tasted all kinds of crap when I was overseas and I ended up hating all of it."

I grinned at her, relieved. She hadn't made any of the expected remarks.

So it was my turn. "Before you said army nurse. Now you mention overseas. Vietnam?"

Her face closed down. "What's it to you?"

I shrugged one shoulder. "That thing, in the alley—"

"Forget it." She hadn't even picked up her sandwich yet. She looked like she was about to leave. "It's not important."

"I've had similar experiences," I said, ignoring her. "But not because of my service. I didn't serve. I'm not qualified. I was just a regular citizen until December."

I wasn't exactly sure why I was talking to her. Except maybe some part of me thought she was the only person I had met who could understand.

"What happened in December?" Her fingers toyed with the sandwich. She didn't look quite as stressed out. She almost looked interested now.

I had only spoken about this twice before, once with Marvella and once with the med school classmate who ended up botching the abortion.

I licked my lips, then lowered my voice. I hoped the clank of plates and the low thrum of other conversations—not to mention the distant sounds of tambourine, harmonica, bongo, and guitar—would prevent people at other tables from hearing what I had to say.

"I was raped," I said. "And after that, he wouldn't leave me alone."

Eagle didn't seem shocked at all. She had probably seen worse in her life, or maybe even experienced worse.

"Is that why you moved here?" she asked. "Because he follows you?"

I shook my head. "He's dead."

Her eyes narrowed. "Thanks to your husband?"

"Friends of my husband. Not Truman, although he tried." And that got him killed. I shivered with guilt. I had treated him badly, and he had treated me well. Well, enough, anyway. He wanted a traditional wife, and I just wasn't wife material. But I wasn't going to tell Eagle the whole sordid story. It was behind me now. Or at least, I wanted it to be.

"The attacks," she said, and I was grateful for the plural, "are they the reason you're so thin?"

Most people thought the rape was my only attack, not realizing that his very presence, the way he came after me, felt like more attacks. *He* had thought the rape was consensual, and that it meant we had a relationship, so he continued to pursue it.

I looked at Eagle. Her eyebrows were up, as if they were punctuating the question.

The question. Which I had barely heard.

"Do I look that thin?" I asked.

"Honey," she said, "you look like a strong breeze could blow you into next week."

I smiled self-consciously and grabbed the ham sandwich. The bread here was thick sourdough, something I'd never had before coming to the Bay Area.

"I had a bunch of surgeries this spring," I said quietly.

"He hurt you that badly, huh." Her voice was flat. It wasn't a question. It was an understanding.

No matter how comfortable I felt with her, I couldn't tell a stranger about the pregnancy, the abortion, the fact that I nearly died, or about the surgeon, unable to save any part of my reproductive organs because of it all.

Tears pricked and I blinked them back. Sometimes I thought if I had just had the baby, then everything would've been okay. Truman would still be alive, I'd be able to have children, and I'd be fine.

But Truman would have gone after that bastard no matter what, and *he* would have killed Truman no matter what, and I would've been a single mother, raising a child I hadn't wanted, by a man I hated.

Eagle reached across the table and put her hand on mine. I didn't jump, which shocked me. I'd touched a lot of people today, and I'd been touched in return, and I wasn't having a bad reaction to any of it.

"I nearly died," I said, figuring that was what I could safely say.

She nodded. "That's why, then."

141

At first I thought she meant that was why I was so thin, but her tone seemed off for that. So, I raised my head, my gaze meeting hers. Her dark eyes were filled with compassion.

"Why what?" I asked.

"Why you understand," she said, her voice almost a whisper.

I swallow hard.

Her fingers squeezed my hand, and then she let go. She took one of the napkins, opened it, and spread it across her lap.

She put on another persona, an official one, and her voice became stronger as she spoke.

"They call it battle fatigue," she said, "or shell shock. The Army, after World War II, instructed medics to understand that every *man* had his breaking point."

I felt my breath catch. She was talking about herself now.

She ran her hands on that napkin, her gaze no longer holding mine.

"I think," she said, "that every *person* has a breaking point, and I don't think it always has to do with actual war. But some kind of warfare. Sounds like this man forced you into a war."

He had. He had forced me into a battle, and it had lasted for months. I had met him in December, and he was dead by April, but by then, the damage was done.

By then, the damage was *more* than done.

"Nowadays," she said, studying her moving hands, "they call it Gross Stress Reaction, which is maybe more accurate."

"You're diagnosing me?" I asked, mostly because I didn't want to hear any more. I hated to think about how broken I was.

She raised her head. Her eyes were clear, unlike the way they had looked in the alley.

"You diagnosed me," she said, in a way that implied she was giving tit for tat. "And you were right. I have all the symptoms, whether I want them or not."

"I don't think anyone wants this," I said.

She snorted. "No shit."

She picked up her sandwich, so I picked up mine. We ate in silence for a moment. The ham was slightly chewy, the mustard a little watery.

She finished her half of her sandwich, then met my gaze. She had a bemused expression on her face.

"So what are we?" she asked. "A two-person consciousness raising group?"

I hated that mystical hippie-dippy stuff. "Maybe just two women with something in common."

She smiled. She had some mayonnaise in the corner of her mouth. I brushed the corner of mine, to give her a hint, and she wiped off the mayonnaise with the napkin.

"I like that," she said. "Wouldn't want to be too 'mod.'"

I grinned. "The next thing you know, we'll turn into groovy chicks wearing see-through blouses and striped pants."

Her face twisted in a mock frown. "I think striped pants are out."

I looked around the café, saw at least five pairs, and said, "Not here, they're not."

She looked too, and laughed. I had to join her. The laughing felt good. It felt right.

It felt perfect.

The decisions to go to the gym, to reach out to Eagle, to come here, had all been good ones—and I hadn't had a positive thought like that in a long, long time.

It felt like I had turned a corner.

Finally.

PAMMY

Jill and Strawberry had left the kitchen, thank heavens. Pammy wiped her hands on her shorts, folded the grocery bags, and put them on a shelf. She wasn't shaking any longer, but she still felt uneasy. Eagle's anger, Jill's quiet fury, and Strawberry's tears bothered her more than she wanted to admit.

This morning felt like a continuation of the entire year, with everything spiraling out of control.

Pammy put the groceries away, as a kind of meditation. Jill had bought staples that would last a few days—Wonder Bread, bologna, hot dogs, buns, cereal and some condiments. The fresh fruit looked good, but then it always did this time of year.

After the gym closed at 9:00, Stella D'Arbus was going to bring a woman and her daughter to the back door. Stella had called Pammy the night before to set all this up.

Stella was the wife of one of men who served on the University of California Board of Regents. Stella pretended to be a dedicated, wealthy housewife, but she had turned out to be one of the gym's main supporters.

And twice, she had brought someone here to hide from a bad domestic situation. This would be the third time.

Eagle hated these overnights, and honestly, Pammy wasn't fond of them either. The first time, she had known the woman Stella helped. The second time, Pammy hadn't known the woman at all, but Stella had stayed with her.

Pammy wasn't certain Stella was going to stay this time. Pammy hoped so, because she had no idea who this woman and her daughter were.

Pammy grabbed some raspberries from one of the containers, rinsed them in her bare hand, and popped them in her mouth. Sweet and fresh. She really didn't want to face Jill or Strawberry, but she had no choice.

Pammy let herself out of the kitchen. All but one of members of the previous class had finally left. The straggler was examining the boxing gloves as if they fascinated her.

The members of the next class were filtering in. This was a three-week self-defense class that Irene Roth, one of the professors in the athletics department at the university, had arranged. It was part of a summer school class, even though it wasn't officially sanctioned by the university. Irene paid Pammy's fees, using some grant or athletic fee money.

Irene stood at the door, a clipboard in hand. She was short and squat, solid muscle. Her brown hair looked like a fringe around her head, the bottom part of her scalp buzzed like a man would do. She said it was easier to maintain, considering she sometimes took two or three showers per day, depending on how energetic she got while teaching her classes.

She wore a blue shirt over light blue shorts, and some Peds stuck out of her sneakers. Unlike most of the women who came here, Irene's legs were shapely, without an ounce of fat on them.

Pammy was relieved to see her, despite the whistle that Irene wore around her neck. Whistles drove Pammy nuts. Irene used hers like an extension of her voice.

Irene was checking off the names of students as they entered.

Pammy and Irene had run a self-defense class last summer as well, and only ten girls had signed up. After the horrid winter and spring, though, this class had twenty-five students, and no one had dropped out.

They wore cut-offs and bikini tops to the first class, and since then, they dressed more appropriately, in t-shirts, gym shorts, socks, and some kind of sneaker. The girls had gotten too bruised that first class to ever wear so little again.

Pammy watched them file in. They were thin and earnest, most with short hair or ponytails, and none of them smelling of marijuana or incense, the way that some of Strawberry's friends had.

These were the kids who continued to go to classes despite the violence and disruption of the past seven months. Some were so earnest that they even carried books into the gym. Others disappeared into the locker room to hide their purses and belongings.

Pammy squared her shoulders. She had to adjust her mood. She needed to be calm to teach a class on self-defense.

She walked to the counter, shaking out her hands and wrists, trying to ease the tension in her body. Eagle's anger had been a powerful thing, and it had left Pammy unsettled.

Particularly Eagle's most cutting comment: *All your high-minded fucking stupid speeches about self-defense. What does that do? It means that one woman will fight until she's fucking tired, and can't fight anymore.*

Eagle hated the emphasis on *self*. Of course, she hadn't mentioned that before. But sometimes it took a push to get Eagle to express her opinion.

And she had a point. All of the tricks that Pammy taught, from remaining calm to observing surroundings to sticking fingers into an attacker's eyes were just that: Tricks.

Either the victim got away or she didn't. And if she didn't get away, at some point, she would lose. Anyone—including the strongest man—could get overpowered.

And, eventually, everyone would need help.

At least, though, these classes were part of the solution, to use Strawberry's phrase, not part of the problem. Teaching women that they were strong was helpful. Teaching young college-age women to be strong was even better.

But, considering what Strawberry had said about people disappearing, maybe it wasn't quite enough.

Pammy stopped at the counter, her fingers trailing that flyer. Then her gaze caught a cash register receipt with a note paper clipped to it. A pen held that all down.

Reimbursement for groceries. —J.

Pammy frowned. Jill had never asked for reimbursements before, no matter how often Pammy had offered to pay.

Jill really was mad.

Pammy stared at that flyer, the girl's grainy image looking bright and filled with promise. Photos like that on a missing person flyer made Pammy sad. She always wanted to dive backwards through the photo to the moment it was taken, warn the person that something bad was going to happen, and then hope it all got better.

But of course, it wouldn't.

She looked up at the girls, lining up so that Irene could take roll. Irene ran everything like military boot camp: the girls sounded off before moving to their assigned positions. Irene had them so terrified that they didn't laugh, either, like they had on the first day of class.

The self-defense class wasn't the only session the girls had with Irene. There was more to the class, including other types of exercise and fitness.

Pammy worked with the girls for forty minutes, and then the class ran back to campus—whether they liked running or not.

Pammy had stopped watching that little running trip, because it made her uncomfortable. Irene drifted up and down the rows of girls, blowing her whistle, yelling at anyone who catcalled the group, and whacking stragglers on the butt with her clipboard.

She worked them hard, and in a form of exercise that Pammy wasn't real fond of.

Pammy's fingers floated across the flyer again. The girls who came for the self-defense class looked a lot more like the girl that Darla Newsome's father had hoped his daughter would become in college.

They looked nothing like Strawberry, even though Strawberry was just as dedicated. Maybe more dedicated, in fact.

And that decided Pammy. She walked around the counter, and clapped her hands together.

"Everyone, look at me," she said.

Irene turned first. Pammy recognized the frown. Irene hadn't had the girls count off yet. Pammy was ruining the established order of things.

The girls turned as well, round eager faces, eyes bright and curious. Pammy did not know their names—she left that to Irene and her clipboard—but she did recognize the faces. None of the girls had missed a class.

Pammy made eye contact with each and every one of the girls, making sure they were paying attention before she continued.

"I have a flyer up here," Pammy said, "that a desperate father left this morning. His daughter has disappeared."

Irene's frown faded a little. She tilted her head back a little as if she were realizing what Pammy was doing.

"This happens sometimes," Pammy said as she crossed the linoleum. "Kids vanish. At least, they vanish from their parents' perspective. The kids don't call home. Or they move out of the dorms into an apartment and forgot to set up a forwarding address. Or they get a new phone number and don't tell anyone."

A couple of girls turned beet red. Apparently they recognized themselves in that description.

"But I'm beginning to think this case is different." Pammy reached the mats.

The girls were watching her—everyone was watching her. Irene clutched her whistle as if it were a lifeline. The straggler had pushed up against the boxing gloves as if she were trying to remain invisible. Pammy couldn't remember her name either. Janet? Joan? Julie?

It wasn't important at the moment.

Pammy continued, "On Saturday night, a friend of mine witnessed what she believes is an abduction. She called the police, but they wouldn't come down here."

The entire gym had become so quiet that Pammy could hear the faint traffic noise from outside.

"Even if whatever my friend saw wasn't an actual abduction," Pammy said, "it was ugly. The woman was beaten and thrown into the back of a truck."

She added the part about the truck deliberately, and it paid off. Some of the girls glanced at each other, and two, standing side by side, actually grew pale. They knew something.

"We have no idea who the girl was who was tossed in that truck," Pammy said. "We have a description, kinda, but nothing more."

"Was it the girl in the flyer?" a tiny blonde on the end asked.

Pammy shook her head. "We're pretty sure it wasn't. That girl disappeared in June. She left all of her belongings behind, including her purse. Her roommate didn't tell anyone until the rent was due, weeks later."

Irene's frown had returned. She had brought these girls here because of a recent rise in campus assaults, all anecdotal of course, since no one ever thought of prosecuting or even keeping track of them. But Irene clearly hadn't heard about the disappearances.

Pammy continued, "One of the students who comes here regularly learned about the flyer, and said she knew about several real disappearances this spring. She also said she'd been warned to stay away from a man driving a dark Ford F-350. Have any of you heard that same warning?"

Six different girls glanced at each other. One looked utterly terrified. But the girls who had exchanged glances earlier stared straight ahead, as if the words were washing right over them.

Irene glared at them. "This is not a time to be silent, girls. If something's going on down here, we need to know."

Another girl, a rail-thin wheat blonde who actually had some athletic potential, looked down at her hands.

"Gail," Irene said. "If you got something to say, you better say it."

The wheat blonde glanced at the other girls. A brunette with feathered bangs that hung in her eyes nodded, as if encouraging the wheat blonde.

"This girl vanished from our dorm in March," the wheat blonde said. "Like, she was there one day, and gone the next. It was like so weird. Because she'd seemed just fine before, and then, nothing. You know. Gone."

"Did anyone report her missing?" Pammy asked and then, because everyone looked confused, including Irene, added, "Or try to find her or tell her parents?"

"The RA knew," the girl said, referring to the resident assistant. "The RA said people drop out and we shouldn't worry about that. It's normal."

Which Jill would have taken as vindication.

"Only she didn't drop out," the girl said. "She just left everything behind one day. And she's not the only one. There was this kid in my chem lab who was really into the stuff we were doing, and he just stopped showing up to class too."

Pammy frowned. Her gaze met Irene's. Irene shrugged.

"The RA's right," another girl said. "People drop out all the time."

"But I heard about the truck," a third girl said. "Did you?"

Everyone looked at her. She was short and dark-haired, a little on the chubby side. Her cheeks pinked up.

"Well, I did. People at the…" Her voice trailed off, and her green eyes moved from side to side nervously. She wasn't supposed to talk about something. "I mean, you know, people were talking about this guy in a truck. He would follow people, going really slow, and sometimes he would ask about someone."

The hair on the back of Pammy's neck stood on end. She didn't like how this sounded.

"What do you mean, ask about someone?" Pammy said.

"Like, he had names or something. Or he'd ask if someone had seen somebody who matched some description." The girl shrugged. "I kinda thought he was a cop."

"You've seen him?" Pammy asked.

The girl shook her head. "When I heard about him, I thought, that's what cops do. Only a guy who drives a regular truck can't be a cop, right?"

Pammy had no idea. She didn't think so, but she didn't know.

"All right," Irene said, her hand still toying with the whistle. "We're going to sit. I believe we need a discussion more than we need class. Am I wrong, Pammy?"

"I think we need both." Pammy didn't want anyone to sit because she would lose momentum, but she had just lost control of the class.

The girls started to sit down. They were talking softly to each other, discussing what Pammy had said. Some just sat down quickly. Others sat cross-legged. Unlike the students in the morning class, these girls were still young enough to make sitting cross-legged look easy.

Pammy needed to get them focused again. She turned to Irene. "Do you have extra paper on that clipboard?"

Irene thumbed through the class roster. "I do."

"Then would you mind passing the clipboard around?" Pammy didn't wait for Irene's answer. "I'd like a list of names of people who have vanished."

Irene raised her eyebrows. Pammy had a sense that she might protest, but Pammy didn't give her a chance to.

Instead, Pammy raised her voice. "Please," she said, "make a list of names of those people who disappeared. And, as the clipboard goes around, if you see a name on the list that you've heard of, then put an X beside it."

"What if you don't know someone's full name?" one of the girls asked.

"Put down the name you know and where you know the person from," Pammy said, improvising.

She walked over to Irene and took the clipboard from her. Then Pammy unhooked the metal clip and removed the class roster, handing it to Irene.

"I'll start," Pammy said. "I'm putting down the name that I know, the girl in the flyer. Her name is Darla Newsome."

She printed *Darla Newsome* in her best handwriting, clean and legible. Then she handed the clipboard, along with Irene's pen, to the girl on her left.

The girl held both the pen and the clipboard like they burned her. Pammy decided not to watch the girl study the paper, figuring it would make everyone nervous.

"I want a show of hands," Pammy said. "How many of you had been warned about a man in that Ford F-350? Or maybe someone called it a one-ton pickup."

A couple of girls bit their lips. Everyone seemed confused.

"Before today," Pammy clarified. "How many of you had heard about the man in the truck before today?"

Ten girls raised their hands. The girl holding the clipboard was not one of them.

"Okay," Pammy said, deliberately making her tone warm. "Those of you who had heard of the man previously, come talk to me over here."

She walked just a few yards away from the mat. She wanted the illusion of privacy, but she really didn't want privacy.

The ten girls circled her. None of them looked like hippies, although a few of them were a little unkempt. Their hair was a shade too long or needed a trim. One girl didn't shave her legs, although she kept swiping awkwardly at them, as if the fact that they were visible bothered her.

Once they'd settled into place, Pammy said, "I want to know every-thing you know about this truck."

The girls stared at her.

She had no idea why it was so hard for them to speak out.

"When did you first learn about it?" Pammy clarified.

The girl closest to her, a large-boned girl who, in previous classes, had seemed particularly adept at assaulting an attacker, said, "I dunno. Last fall, maybe?"

"It was last fall," said the girl next to her, a frail thing with coke-bottle glasses that she couldn't remove, even for class. At least she had started wearing a strap that held her glasses in place. Still, Pammy had worried about her in every class, afraid someone would accidentally hit her in the face and break those glasses.

The frail girl sounded confident though. Her magnified grayish-blue eyes looked quite sincere as she gazed up at Pammy.

"I'm sure it was fall," the girl said.

"How do you know?" Pammy asked.

"It was just before Thanksgiving," the girl with Coke-bottle glasses said. "There were a bunch of us who were going to stay in town and not go home, and as campus emptied out, one of the guys told me to be careful. He'd heard about some big truck stalking girls, and he said he couldn't protect me anymore."

"Was that Ronnie?" one of the other girls asked her.

"Yeah," glasses girl said with a smile, and both girls giggled.

"And Ronnie is…?" Pammy asked.

"Really cute," said the second girl, and blushed.

Pammy resisted the urge to tell them all to get serious. Instead, she asked Glasses Girl, "How did your friend Ronnie know about the truck?"

She glanced at the others, but they were looking at her, as if they didn't know.

So she shrugged. "What he told me was that there was this girl from his psych class who had complained about the truck following her every-where. Then one day, Ronnie was leaving class, and the truck stopped near him. A guy got out, asked about that girl, and Ronnie said he didn't know her."

"He lied?" Pammy asked, then wished she hadn't. The worst thing she could do was sound judgmental.

"Well," Glasses Girl said, "I wouldn't tell some stranger about a friend. Isn't that one of your rules for defense? Make sure a stranger doesn't know anything about you?"

Pammy smiled. Glasses Girl got her on that one.

"Yes, it is," Pammy said. "So your friend Ronnie said he didn't know the girl."

"And the truck guy, he asked some other kids. I guess someone told him where she lived or worked or something. Anyway, she never showed up to class again. And Ronnie says that was the last time he saw her."

Pammy frowned. That seemed like a strange story.

"He asked for her by name?" Pammy said.

Glasses Girl shrugged again. "That's what Ronnie told me."

Her tone pointed out that she was telling Pammy secondhand information. Pammy understood that, but it was more information than she'd had an hour ago.

"And this incident happened last fall," Pammy said.

Glasses Girl nodded.

"Have you personally seen the truck?" Pammy asked her.

Glasses Girl shook her head, and then shrugged. "Maybe. I don't know." She tapped her glasses. "It's like the boogey man, you know? I've been seeing trucks everywhere since he said that."

"Or police cars," one of the other girls said.

"Or armored vehicles," said a third girl.

"Or men with rifles," said another.

Pammy looked at them, making sure her expression was sympathetic. That terror was why they had taken a self-defense class in the first place. She probably was adding to their unease.

At the moment, though, she didn't care.

Only Glasses Girl remained focused. "I can't imagine why he'd be interested in me anyway."

That comment intrigued Pammy. Her father used to say that it was the comments which seemed obvious on their face that turned out to be the most interesting in an investigation.

On its face, the comment seemed like one about appearance. Boys don't make passes and all of that other Dorothy Parker stuff. But there was something in Glasses Girl's tone that made the truck driver's interest seem a little more unusual.

"Why do you make that assumption?" Pammy asked Glasses Girl.

"I'm not that interesting," Glasses Girl said as her skin grew pink.

"You think this guy only takes interesting women?" Pammy asked.

"I didn't mean it like that." Glasses Girl stared down at her hands. Her nails had been bitten to the quick. "I mean, you know, no one ever notices me."

And there was an implied *please, stop noticing me now*, aspect to her tone.

"This other girl," Pammy said, "she was different from you?"

"Oh, God, yeah," Glasses Girl said. "Ronnie thought she was the end. No one compared to her."

"According to Ronnie," Pammy said, just for clarification.

"No," Glasses Girl said. "According to everybody. She was, like, the most important person in her dorm. Everyone knew her and liked her. Of course, some people were getting worried about her."

A couple of the other girls were making "keep it down" gestures with their hands, but Glasses Girl didn't seem to notice.

Pammy pretended she didn't notice either.

"Why were they worried about her?" Pammy asked.

Glasses Girl looked at the others, her skin getting even redder. By now, she had clearly started to realize she was talking too much.

"I don't know," she said quietly.

"It's all right," Irene said, "just answer. It's important."

Glasses Girl stiffened up. Pammy felt her heart sink. They had an important discussion going, and Irene might have just stopped it.

"Well," Glasses Girl said, sounding miserable, "she was getting into the—you know—heavy stuff. Starting to neglect her studies and things for politics. She said Nixon had to be stopped."

She was right, Pammy thought, but didn't say. "And this was last fall, before the election?"

"I don't know exactly." Glasses Girl shook her head as she said that. "But she was going to go to some sit-in. She didn't show. And she stopped going to class. And Ronnie thought it was all really, really weird."

Pammy frowned, thinking about that. Some of the girls whispered to each other. Irene toyed with her whistle, as if she were thinking of blowing it to shut them up.

Pammy glared at her. The whistle was the last thing she needed.

But one of the other girls was nodding as she watched Glasses Girl. The other girl was tall and thin and always backed away instead of following the instructions Pammy gave to hit the practice dummies.

"I know a guy who disappeared," the tall girl said. "He walked away from everything, I mean, that's what some people thought. But I didn't think he was the kind to walk away. He cared too much. He had just participated in the Third World Liberation Protests. He was organizing some more protests, and then we never saw him again."

The Third World Liberation Protests were in January. They had gotten violent.

"Yeah," said a third girl. She was tiny, but she had started to use her size in class to disarm the taller, stronger girls. "I know a guy who disappeared too. He had dropped out of school after the protests, and he was going to lead a group of protestors at some speech Governor Reagan was going to give, justifying the changes he wanted to make to the university system."

"That was, like, March, right?" a fourth girl asked. "Because that's when I heard about the truck. I heard he was, like, killing activists, so we should all hide if we saw the truck."

Pammy's heart was pounding.

"It wasn't March," the tiny girl said. "It was earlier than that."

"It doesn't matter," said a girl beside Pammy. "I heard the same thing, about the truck driver killing activists."

She turned to Pammy, her brown eyes earnest, "Do you think that's true? Do you think that the truck guy is killing activists?"

It certainly sounded that way, but rumors made everything seem rational.

"I don't know," Pammy said. "All we have is gossip at the moment. When the clipboard comes around, please write down the names of the people you know who disappeared around the same time as that truck, and if those people were involved in some political movement."

She didn't like how any of this sounded. But she also knew it was all supposition. Still, everyone seemed to have heard about the guy in the truck.

Could he be a one-man army against political activists? Or was that pot-induced paranoia, seeping everywhere?

She supposed the paranoia didn't have to be pot-induced. Given the last year—with the assassinations, the protests, the tear gas being dropped in the center of Berkeley—paranoia almost seemed like a rational response.

A girl who hadn't joined their group stood, and handed the clipboard to Glasses Girl. She stared at it for a moment, then shook her head.

"There's, like, a dozen names here, and even more check marks." She sounded shocked. Then she sighed, and wrote something on the paper.

Pammy looked at Irene. Irene's face was drawn. She looked tense, which Pammy realized she had never seen before.

Pammy was going to give the information to Eagle. What they would do with those names, Pammy had no idea. But it was clear something was going on.

They had stumbled into something. She was sure of that now. But she wasn't sure what.

Or what a group of women, inside a gym, could do about it.

EAGLE

She laughed.

Eagle couldn't remember the last time she had laughed, really laughed with one of those deep, silly guffaws that she felt throughout her entire body.

She was a bit stunned that she could laugh, especially after that gross stress reaction or whatever she wanted to call it. Especially after she had lost her temper so very badly.

The couple at the table next to her gave her a wary glance. She always felt like she didn't fit in here at the Caffe Med. She didn't like snotty coffee and the crowd itself was either too hippie or too student-focused. And then there was the matter of the dogs.

The owner here didn't mind dogs walking through his establishment as if they owned it. Eagle believed dogs should remain outside, peering in like Dickensian waifs looking at a Christmas goose through a shop window.

Val had picked up the second half of her ham sandwich, mustard dripping out the back end onto the white china plate. When she laughed, as she had a moment before, she was utterly beautiful.

Eagle noted the thought, then set it aside. Val had made it clear that she was straight. She probably hadn't even noticed the attraction Eagle felt. It had surprised Eagle too. She hadn't felt something this immediate in years.

"You okay?" Val asked, a thread of concern in her voice.

Apparently, Eagle's smile had faded without her even knowing it. She pasted it back on.

"Yeah," she said. "It's just been a rough few days."

She surprised herself with her answer. She hadn't planned a confessional like Val had done.

"If you feel like telling me," Val said, "I'm happy to listen."

Not *willing* to listen. *Happy* to listen. Val clearly needed companionship, and was willing to go through anything to get it.

Eagle forced that thought back. That wasn't what Val had meant, and Eagle knew it. Val was trying to make her feel comfortable, that was all.

Eagle shook her head, then glanced around. A group of jeans-clad young women were cleaning the table near the stairs, removing the dishes and carting them, one small pile at a time, to the kitchen door. The women clearly didn't work here; they just wanted a place to sit.

Everyone at the tables leaned over their coffee cups and half-eaten pastries, deep in earnest conversation, speaking in low, urgent tones. Three people stood in a makeshift line near the counter, while the students behind it made coffee and filled it with milk from some hissing steam machine.

If she stood up right now, got on the table, and demanded a show of hands from anyone who had seen the truck or anyone who knew a person who had disappeared under mysterious circumstances, what would she get? Demands that she sit down? Tossed out? An actual show of hands?

Eagle sighed, then looked pointedly at Val's Chicago Police Department t-shirt—which, surprisingly, no one had given her shit about.

"Your cop husband," Eagle said, a little too bluntly, probably too insensitively, but then, that was who she was. "Did he…was he white?"

Val glanced at her own shirt, as if trying to remember. She didn't seem offended by the question at all.

"No," she said.

"Did he work in an all-black neighborhood?" Eagle asked.

"Most of the time," Val said. "Why?"

Eagle shook her head. The couple at the next table was really staring at her now.

"Cops around here," Eagle said, "they take their own sweet time responding to emergency calls."

Val frowned. "I saw a police car on my walk to the gym this morning. He was parked near Dwight."

"Oh, there's the one squad planted here to harass everyone," Eagle said. "And at the end of the month, when the squads need their quotas, they come down here to bust some of the known drug-users or issue a few fines."

Val finished her sandwich, and grabbed a napkin, but she hadn't lost eye contact with Eagle.

"But mostly, if there's a real problem, the cops aren't interested at all." Eagle sipped the water. It was lukewarm. "I would've thought that all-black areas of Chicago were like that. Oakland is."

"It used to be worse," Val said. "My grandparents would tell stories that scared me half to death. There's minimal policing now, mostly to get rid of gangs."

Her skin turned ashen when she mentioned police and gangs, as if something about that bothered her. Eagle didn't want to push to find out what it was.

"No gangs here," Eagle said. "Hippies, though. And 'domestics.'"

She almost whispered that last, but Val heard it.

"Domestics?" she asked. "What happened? Did someone hurt you?"

Eagle shook her head. She sighed, realizing that she had backed herself into a corner on purpose.

She glared at the couple. They looked down as if they were ashamed of listening in.

"Saturday night," Eagle said, "cops dismissed something I saw as a domestic."

She told the story for the third time. Val was the first person who didn't interrupt. She propped her elbow on the table, rested her chin in her palm, and kept her gaze on Eagle the entire time.

"And then this morning," Eagle said, her voice rising some, "this hippie-dippy ding-a-ling tells me she doesn't want to help out, even though she's heard about this truck and this guy, and even though she knows some people who disappeared around the time the truck was in the area. She was much more interested in protesting the war or something stupid like that."

"It's not stupid," said the guy from the next table. "The war is wrong."

"And you're fucking out of line," Eagle snapped. "This is a private conversation."

The guy looked at his wife or girlfriend or whatever she was. She looked a little pale. She stood up and so did he, grabbing his copy of the *Berkeley Barb* as he did so.

He brushed Eagle as he went by.

"You really don't belong here," he said. "You both give off bad vibes."

Val looked shocked at his anger. But Eagle wasn't. She started to stand. Val grabbed her hand.

"That's what he wants," she said quietly.

"He didn't like that I mentioned calling the cops," Eagle said.

"Maybe." Val shrugged. "Or maybe something else bothered him."

She moved her hand in front of her face, indicating her dark skin. Eagle looked around. It was an unusually white crowd in Caffe Med today.

"Tell me more about your hippie-dippy ding-a-ling," Val said.

She seemed amazingly unconcerned by the rudeness. Eagle liked her spirit, and then tried to tamp down that feeling too.

"She made you mad," Val said, with great understatement.

The anger surged back. "She professes to claim she *cares* about things, and she doesn't care at all."

Eagle nodded toward that couple. They were now outside, talking to some of the hippies who had gathered at the window near the coffee counter.

"They don't care either," Eagle said. "It's as if nobody cares. All of these forgotten and missing people. It sounds like some asshole is preying on them, and no one is willing to do anything."

"What could we do?" Val asked.

Eagle looked at her. Something in Val's tone was different. It wasn't like Pammy or the hippie-dippy ding-a-ling when they had asked the same question. Val sounded like she was asking a more fundamental question.

"What do you mean?" Eagle asked.

"If we figured out who this man is," Val said, "and that's a big if, what could we do? If he is indeed preying on young people."

Eagle's mind stuttered. She hadn't quite thought that far. She leaned back in her chair.

"I guess I thought I'd report him to the cops once I had his name," she said slowly, "but that's not reasonable, is it? They won't do anything."

"And if we report him to the cops, and they decide to investigate, even a little, we've tipped him off," Val said. "Because if he is preying on people down here, he's smart, and he can play off the cops' prejudices."

"If we tip him off, what will he do?" Eagle asked. "He knows I saw him."

"And he knows you couldn't do anything," Val said. "But if he's afraid of getting caught, or realizes that he's been noticed, then he'll just move to a new location and prey on others. We'll never find the missing woman, and we'll never know what's really happening."

Eagle took a deep breath. She had been so focused on finding the injured woman that she hadn't thought any of this through. And then she had gotten so angry this morning when she learned there might be others that she got even more upset.

"I suppose we should find out if we're making this up first," Eagle said. "Maybe he's a harmless guy with a truck."

Val shrugged again. "I think we should have several plans. If he's harmless, we do nothing. If he's the wrong guy, we find the right one. But that's where it starts getting dicey."

"In what way?" Eagle asked.

"If he is taking people," Val said, "what's he doing with them? If he's taking women…"

She shuddered, and that bright-eyed look suddenly left her face. Eagle knew what she was thinking—she was thinking about the man who had hurt her.

"But," Eagle said, trying to distract Val, "if he's taking kids of both genders, ah, hell, that's where I get confused. What could he be doing with them?"

"Or maybe he's not involved at all, and there are simple explanations, like kids dropping out or something." Val pushed her plate away and sighed. "Truman would tell me not to get involved, there are too many ifs, and I'm making things up."

Eagle had figured out that Truman was the dead husband. Apparently, he was still quite alive and well in Val's mind.

"You didn't make up two things," Eagle said. "First, I saw a man with an F-350 hurt a woman and throw her into the bed of his truck. Second, there are rumors going through the student community to steer clear of a man with an F-350. So I say, we find the F-350 and go from there."

"Without a plan?" Val sounded a bit lost at the very idea of working without a plan.

"Yep," Eagle said. "Without a plan. We need to know what we're up against first."

Val's eyes were wide.

"That is a plan, you know," Eagle said. "It's just step one."

Val didn't move. Eagle wondered if this very idea was causing more flashbacks for her.

"You don't have to help, you know," Eagle said. "Just having a sounding board was—"

"No," Val said. "I *do* have to help. I do. It's important."

"It's not your fight," Eagle said.

"It's not yours either, and yet you're going to do it," Val said.

"I saw her. I can't get her screams out of my head." Eagle didn't add that those screams combined with other screams, screams that would probably never leave her.

"I understand," Val said softly. "I'm dealing with some screams of my own."

Eagle's gaze met hers. "You can back out at any time."

"You too," Val said.

"I don't back out," Eagle said.

Two spots of color turned Val's cheeks a dusky rose. "I'm done backing out," she said softly. "Giving in did me no good. Running away..." She shook her head as if dismissing the thought.

"Think of it as running toward," Eagle said.

Val nodded once, her chin jutted forward with determination.

"So," she said, "what do we do next?"

"I guess we go back to Pammy's and find out how to talk to that ding-a-ling," Eagle said, and then she grinned. "Maybe you can keep me from strangling her."

"Or maybe I'll help you," Val said, and laughed.

Eagle joined her. The second belly laugh of the day. The second belly laugh of the week, maybe even the month.

She shouldn't have been laughing. They were talking about serious business. But Val made her feel lighter.

And after years of darkness, the light—no matter how brief—felt really good.

VAL

Eagle and I left Caffe Med, skirting the dogs outside as well as the growing crowd of hippies, all talking about some upcoming action. The odor of cigarettes mixed with the faint stench of marijuana. It wasn't hard to see the pot smoker. He had taken his hand-rolled roach and half-hidden it behind his back. A woman grabbed it from him, and he turned, pretending to be angry. They mock-fought over it, making his attempt at hiding the roach even more ridiculous than it had originally been.

Harmless play. I knew that, and yet I was having trouble with the movements.

In the distance, the music—if that was what you wanted to call it—had almost stopped. The bongo player provided a beat for the fighters, who were twirling and laughing as the man tried to get the roach, and the woman was keeping it from him.

Eagle touched my arm and urged me forward. She had a compassionate look on her face.

She'd had that look since we stood up from our table. Sitting for an hour had made the muscles of my upper thighs seize up. I had gotten out of the chair like an elderly woman, and Eagle had reached for me, apparently afraid I was going to fall over.

"Exercise," I had mumbled.

But from that moment forward, I felt a little off. After my speech, Eagle seemed fired up. She was ready to return to the gym, ready to talk to the hippie-dippy ding-a-ling, whose name was—apparently—Strawberry which, in my opinion, wasn't much better than hippie-dippy ding-a-ling.

The *idea* of facing my fears was a good one. I'd been trying to do that since I left Chicago. The reality of it, especially taking on someone who had attacked a woman, made me feel reckless.

I could hear Truman in my head, telling me that I was too small, too fragile, too *female* to deal with things like an attacker on the loose. He would've said, *Let me handle it, honey,* and in the early days of our relationship—even in the latter days of our relationship—I would have.

Truman had tried to handle *him* and it had gone horribly wrong. I had tried to ignore *him* and it hadn't worked either. *He* had died because of someone else, not us.

Who was I to take on a man who had beaten a woman and thrown her in the back of a truck? I couldn't even do three push-ups.

And my sore muscles made me feel just exactly like I had felt after the surgeries. Worthless, destroyed, powerless.

I gave Eagle a sideways smile. She nodded to the street. Several more bicycles were going by than had earlier, slowing down some cars. Kids no older than twelve were bunched near a bookstore, one of them holding a copy of what appeared to be *Mad Magazine*, and the others looking on.

I could make my apologies to Eagle, head down Telegraph, and meander my way home.

But then I wouldn't face anything. I would go back to being the little coward I had been, the girl who ran away.

My heart was pounding. I threaded my way through the growing afternoon crowd, and made it to the other side of Telegraph.

Eagle was waiting for me. She leaned into me, and said softly, "That's the kind of police protection we get," and nodded at a car parked half a block away.

It was a Berkeley police department squad car, some basic sedan thing, and if it were anything like Chicago PD squads, the engine had been removed and replaced with something that had a lot more horse-power than any other sedan on the road.

Some of the young kids hung out near the car, and one girl was leaning on it, a comic book in her hands. She looked engrossed in it.

There was one police officer inside the car. He was young, and he had longish brown hair—too long for regulation. I understood what Eagle meant now; he was supposed to "blend in." Even if he hadn't been wearing a beige uniform, he clearly wouldn't have fit in. Maybe it was his posture: superficially relaxed, but with one hand on the steering wheel. Or maybe it was the fact that he was ignoring the young kids that stood near the car, one of whom, I could tell from half a block away, was holding a joint.

I glanced at Eagle, who was frowning at the car.

"If I went and asked him to help find that girl," Eagle said softly, "he'd tell me the same thing everyone else says. People disappear. I *hate* that sentence. I hate it. People disappear, but they shouldn't."

Unless they wanted to. I suspected a lot of people around here had disappeared from somewhere, and thought they wanted to.

I had.

But I wasn't happy here, any more than the rest of them seemed to be. Or maybe I was just imposing my own opinion on everyone else on the streets. I had mostly avoided Telegraph since I'd come here, walking streets that were quieter, except when I went to the bookstores. It was too chaotic here, and too drugged-out.

I could understand how the police felt that these kids were bringing on their own problems. All those years as a cop's wife showed.

And yet…

I knew what it was like to be part of a community that had no value. Most people in Chicago believed the South Side was all gangs and violence, and didn't know about the vibrant community of people who were the best citizens possible. My friends, my family…

The people I had left behind.

I swallowed hard and pivoted, heading down the street to Pammy's gym. Eagle had to scurry to keep up with me.

"You see something?" she asked as she reached my side.

I shook my head. "I just realized…half those people live on the street, don't they?"

"I don't know for sure, but it seems that way," Eagle said.

"Including the little kids," I said.

She shrugged. "What of it?"

The question was cold, and that offended me.

I turned, stopped, and glanced over my shoulder. She stopped too, frowning at me.

"This is where people come when they're running," I said.

"Like you," she said.

I shook my head. "Not like me, so much. More like, if they're having trouble at home or can't handle life. They come here, don't they?"

"It used to be San Francisco from what I understand," Eagle said. "I wasn't in the States at the time."

Her voice was dry, her expression guarded. I waited, a trick I'd learned from Truman. If you didn't speak, then the other person had to fill the silence.

Eagle did. She shrugged.

"They'd end up in the Haight," she said. "It's a wasteland now. Drugs everywhere, a free clinic that can't keep up, kids that are mush-brained and lost. I went there once, thinking I'd volunteer…"

She shook her head, glanced over her shoulder too. People threaded around us, like we were a rock in a river. No one really seemed to care what we did.

"I kept thinking those kids brought it all on themselves. I mean, what do you expect when you shoot up?" Her voice was so soft I almost didn't hear her. "But that wasn't it, really."

She shook her head again, then looked down. The head-shaking wasn't a *no* gesture. It was more like she couldn't get a thought out of her head.

"It was…I'd seen so many guys shoot up over there."

I assumed she meant Vietnam. I didn't ask her to clarify. It sounded like she was on some kind of roll.

"I actually understand why people seek oblivion," she said even softer. "I didn't want to be around junkies anymore. It was too close."

I didn't hear those last words as much as I read her lips.

She raised her head then, her brown eyes defiant.

"You know what I've been thinking these last few days?" she asked.

It was my turn to shake my head.

"I've been thinking that if you got off on harming people, this was the place to do it. You don't harm them on the street, because the kids on the street would stop you—mostly. They take care of each other as best they can. But if you take them out of the neighborhood, nobody knows how to find them. Nobody even knows their real names half the time. If you're one sick fuck, you can find a smorgasbord of delights down here."

I shivered. She was right. And those underage kids...they disturbed me even more than the clearly drugged-out adults.

"What Pammy's doing is great," Eagle said softly, "but it's a drop in the bucket for what's needed. And honestly, the crowd she caters to isn't the crowd on the street. It's housewives and professors and students. Not those defenseless addicts back there."

I frowned.

"Fuck." Eagle took a deep breath, then glanced at the gym. She looked at me in surprise. "Fuck."

I looked around. The crowd on Telegraph remained the same. The kid leaning against the squad car, bicyclists going back and forth. The bongo player had started up again, which was worth a curse, but not one as heartfelt as the one Eagle had just issued.

I couldn't see what had upset her.

She was looking at the gym.

"Something's not adding up," she said.

And then she walked ahead of me. I looked back at Telegraph one last time. She was right: it was a smorgasbord. And it was more than that. It was a hubbub of petty crime.

The fact that the cops just patrolled or sat and did nothing bothered me in a weird way. But it was different than Chicago. In Chicago, the cops were active. They didn't just sit and watch. They rousted drug dealers or pursued the gangs—when they were in the neighborhood. Mostly, they weren't in the neighborhood at all.

And like the cops here, they often didn't respond to real crime.

I let out a small sigh. I almost felt like a traitor for having that thought. The fact that the Chicago PD didn't respond to much of what happened on the South Side had been a bone of contention between me and Truman.

One of many bones, out of a lot of contention.

I had no idea what Eagle felt wasn't adding up. I couldn't see it. Something had bothered her, though. Something to do with the smorgasbord, the cop, and the petty crime.

I hurried after her, heading for the gym.

I had made my choice. I was going to get involved—maybe for the first time in my entire life.

PAMMY

The gym had achieved a midafternoon quiet. No classes were scheduled for the rest of the day, although Pammy kept the door open for anyone who wanted to exercise. The rest of the afternoon would probably remain quiet. The only other official item on her schedule for this day was a Tai Chi class at 7:00. Jill was supposed to teach it, but if she didn't show up, Pammy could handle it.

Pammy leaned on the counter, one elbow near the flyer, her right hand splayed on the papers from the self-defense class. Behind her, the sound of running water was oddly soothing. One of her regulars, Mattie, was using the shower in the locker room after a rather intense jump rope session.

The names on the list the class had compiled bothered her. Pammy hadn't expected twenty names. Most of them had checkmarks alongside, and all but two listed the name of some organization the person had belonged to or some protest rally attended.

And Strawberry had been right about genders. The majority of the names on the list—fourteen—were female, but the six male names had at least a dozen check marks beside them. So they weren't on the list by mistake. Everyone, at least everyone in the class, had known that those boys had disappeared.

170

None of this made any sense.

Maybe Pammy could get school records for these kids. The university would know if they had officially dropped out or had withdrawn. Other students might have had no idea.

But that wouldn't help with students like Ray Brady. He was the student who had told others that he had officially withdrawn from school after the Third World Liberation Front riots. He was the one who had been planning a protest against Governor Reagan just before disappearing.

Pammy glanced at the flyer and then back at the names.

She was almost willing—maybe she *was* willing—to believe that these kids had been targeted. Or arrested in the dead of night.

The us-versus-them mentality that she had decried when the Free Speech Movement started five years ago had crept into her consciousness.

But the paranoia didn't exactly stand up to logic. Who would arrest students in a one-ton pickup truck? The Berkeley PD didn't hide their presence in the neighborhood and had, more than once, dragged students off the streets and into a squad, sometimes clubbing them hard enough that the sound carried for blocks.

Governor Reagan clearly loved the show of force; he had proven that in May and June. He'd actually made speeches threatening a "bloodbath" against the students, and then his national guard troops had deliberately created that bloodbath.

Ten years ago, she never would have believed such behavior was possible in the United States.

And yet it had happened.

She had seen it with her own eyes.

She sighed. She felt as helpless as she had felt five years ago when her friend Linda Kaputo had died after a prolonged beating from her husband. Linda had been one of three friends whose violent ends had sparked Pammy to start teaching self-defense classes. The other two friends, Sue Ellen Gerry and Barbara Springer, had both suffered random attacks in public—Sue Ellen in a park, and Barbara as she walked to class. Both women had died of their injuries days later.

Pammy had always thought if they had just known how to fight back, they would have survived. When she trained young women, she always felt like she was training Sue Ellen and Barbara. When Pammy trained housewives, she felt like she was training Linda.

But Pammy wasn't training Sue Ellen, Barbara, or Linda. Those women were gone. They had died horribly, and Pammy hadn't been able to help them.

And she had no idea how the women she was training now would use that training. *If* they would use that training.

She made herself look at the names again. None of them were familiar to her, but she wasn't an activist. She knew some professors who were, and some of the housewives who came here had found out about it through their women's lib groups or through some consciousness-raising discussion.

She had no idea how many of the women who came to the gym were activists. It sounded like Strawberry was. It seemed like some of the students from the self-defense class were, although others seemed to be very judgmental about the activists.

Pammy really did try to stay out of all the politics, but it was hard. These days, Berkeley *was* politics, and very little else.

She adjusted the papers beneath her hand. The sound of the shower continued rattling through the pipes. She almost went back to remind Mattie to leave some hot water for the next class.

But Pammy had purchased an extra-large water heater, and the hot water probably wouldn't run out. Especially since the gym was so empty right now.

Pammy tapped the photo of Darla Newsome. The photo made it seem as if she were smiling at the ceiling, as if she had not a care in the world. Darla was a starting point. Maybe she had become active in the last few months. Her father wouldn't have known.

Darla would be easier to investigate than the woman that Eagle had seen. At least they had Darla's name.

The front door to the gym opened, and Pammy looked up. Eagle walked inside, looking determined. Valentina Wilson followed her, eyes wide, but shoulders back as if she were being pulled in Eagle's wake.

Pammy had never expected to see those two together. Maybe they weren't together. Maybe they just happened to come in at the same time.

Eagle looked around the gym as if she was taking it all in. Val walked to the counter, a slight frown on her face. She was moving slower than she had in the morning. Clearly, her muscles were sore.

She had worked just a little too hard in the exercise session. Pammy wanted to tell her to slow down, but she also didn't want to discourage her or frighten her by calling her out.

Eagle finished looking around the gym. Her dark gaze met Pammy's. Eagle's expression was hard. Pammy couldn't tell if she was still angry.

"We alone?" Eagle asked.

"Mattie's in the shower," Pammy said, and then realized she couldn't hear the sound of running water any longer.

Eagle sighed. "That's alone enough, I guess."

Pammy couldn't judge Eagle's mood. She didn't seem as angry as she had before, but she did seem determined.

Eagle walked to the counter, ending up beside Val, who seemed very comfortable with her. That was a new development. Pammy had no idea they knew each other.

"I owe you an apology," Eagle said to Pammy. "I was rude."

Eagle didn't apologize. Ever. She'd said harsh things before, and she'd come in days later as if nothing had happened.

Pammy thought for a moment. Eagle had been more than rude. She had been out of line.

She said, "I'm not going to tell you it was okay. Your words hurt."

"They were supposed to," Eagle said.

Eagle's matter-of-fact comment took Pammy's breath away. Apparently the apology was hollow.

Val looked at Eagle sideways, clearly shocked at what Eagle had just said.

But Eagle wasn't done. She raised her chin.

"I say things," she said. "Mean things. Before I think about them. That's why I don't spend much time with people. My mouth gets away from me. Especially when I'm angry. I didn't mean to hurt you. I didn't."

She sounded miserable, even though her expression remained impassive. This apology was real then. And heartfelt.

Eagle broke the eye contact. She shifted, then looked around the gym. "That hippie-di—that Strawberry girl, she's not here, is she?"

Eagle's tone had changed. It was almost as if she had put on another person entirely, the way someone would shrug on a coat.

Val's lips turned up in bemusement. So she too had caught the change in tone.

Pammy was beginning to think there wasn't much that Val missed.

"Strawberry's not here," Pammy said.

"Good," Eagle said. "She drives me nuts."

That was obvious. Pammy declined to comment on it though. Val nodded slightly, as if she already knew how Eagle felt.

Pammy wanted to ask how Val had gotten roped into all of this, but didn't know how to ask. Or if it was really any of Pammy's business.

Pammy had had the sense the day before that Val hadn't known anyone, but maybe she had misread Val. Maybe Val had known Eagle. Which begged the question: Why hadn't Val said anything about it?

"You gotta get her to give us those lists," Eagle said.

Pammy blinked in surprise. She had lost track of the conversation.

"Pammy," Eagle said, apparently realizing that Pammy hadn't been paying attention. "The lists from that Strawberry girl? We need them."

The plural also surprised Pammy. Did Eagle's use of "us" and "we" mean Eagle and Pammy? Or Eagle and Val? Or all three of them?

"Us?" Pammy asked.

Eagle whirled back around, her expression fierce. She was angry again. Or maybe she hadn't really stopped being angry.

"I thought you were on board with finding the guy with the truck," she said. "Am I wrong?"

Pammy's heart pounded. Eagle was volatile this afternoon. Eagle usually wasn't that volatile.

"No, you're not wrong," Pammy said. "I am on board with finding the guy in the truck."

"Hence, *we*," Eagle said. "And Val's helping too."

Pammy looked at her. Val's bemused smile grew into something soft, and she nodded.

Pammy had no idea how Val could help, but Val seemed to have some kind of idea.

"So," Eagle said, "I don't know what happened after I left, but—"

"I got a list." Pammy patted the sheets of paper in front of her. "I have a self-defense class filled with university students and they have all been warned about this guy with the truck. Plus, many of them knew someone who has seemingly vanished without a trace."

Her words echoed in the empty gym. Val's skin had gone ashen. Pammy had no idea what upset her. The fact that the students had helped was a good thing.

Eagle's eyebrows went up. "You got a list. Already?"

"And everyone knew about this guy?" Val asked. "What's going on here?"

The scared Val had returned, not the strong woman Pammy had seen glimpses of.

Eagle frowned at Val, then placed a hand on her back. Pammy did all she could not to look surprised. Eagle didn't voluntarily touch anyone.

"I don't think we're in any danger," Eagle said softly, almost tenderly.

Pammy felt a frown crease her forehead. She really hadn't seen Eagle like this before. It was strange.

Val took a deep breath as if she were gathering herself. Then she nodded and seemed somehow stronger.

Eagle removed her hand from Val's back.

Pammy's gaze met Eagle's and Pammy tried to ask a silent question about their relationship, but Eagle tilted her head, as if she were telling Pammy to get on with it.

Pammy straightened slightly. She slid the sheets closer to her.

"It's a bigger list than I expected." Her gaze met Val's. "I'm hoping that most of these kids were mistaken."

Val didn't respond, but Eagle did. She put her fingers on the sheets. "This it?"

"Yes," Pammy said.

Eagle pulled the sheets to her, then turned them around. Val leaned over and looked at the sheets as well.

"What's this?" Eagle asked, pointing at the words across from the names.

"What activities they were involved in," Pammy said. "If they were part of the campus anti-war movement or the Third World Liberation Front or maybe a feminist group, then I had the students mark that down."

Val was standing on her tiptoes so she could see past Eagle. "They all seem to be involved in something."

"Yeah." Eagle took the top sheet and looked under it. Then she laid the top sheet flat again.

She turned to Val, not to Pammy.

"Remember when I said something wasn't adding up?" Eagle asked Val. "This, *this* is what's not adding up."

Val nodded slowly as if she didn't quite understand. Pammy truly didn't understand what they were talking about and she was starting to get annoyed.

"I wasn't part of any discussion the two of you had," Pammy said.

Val opened her mouth, then closed it and glanced at Eagle. Eagle wasn't paying much attention. She was looking around the gym again. Then she leaned back and peered at the plate-glass window.

Eagle tapped her right thumbnail against her teeth, clearly thinking about something, shook her head slightly, and then sighed.

Finally, she looked back at Pammy.

"We just came from Telegraph," Eagle said. "We had some lunch at Caffe Med and—"

"Caffe Med?" Pammy asked. Now things had gotten even stranger. "You hate Caffe Med."

"Yeah, well, Robbie's was blocked by some bongo players, and we had pizza yesterday," Eagle said. "Caffe Med wasn't the best, but it was food."

Considering how many times Eagle had railed against the bad coffee at Caffe Med, this revelation was almost as shocking as the fact that Eagle had gone willingly to Telegraph with lunch in mind.

"Anyway," Eagle said, "it's street kid hell down there, and even the Mini Mob was out in force."

The Mini Mob were a group of underage street kids, many of them already drug addicts. Pammy hated thinking about them. She'd called the state more than once about them, but the kids seemed to have a sixth sense about the arrival of authorities. Whenever someone official showed up on Telegraph to deal with the street children—and that's what they were, children—the little kids vanished.

"And," Eagle was saying, "we were talking about what Strawberry said about a lot of students disappearing, and how it wasn't making sense."

"It doesn't make sense to me," Pammy said, agreeing. "No matter what Jill says, kids don't just vanish from class. There's always a warning—"

"Yeah," Eagle said dismissively, "that's not what I'm confused over. What doesn't make sense is that the kids Strawberry seems to know are actually *doing* something. If you were picking off young women for some sick reason or if you were set on ridding the world of hippies, why would you take kids who had friends and family and were actually attending class and doing things?"

"Oh, my," Val said. She peered at the sheets again. "*That* was your revelation?"

"It's not a revelation," Eagle said to her, as if Pammy weren't even there. "It's a question."

"And a good one," Val said. "Because anyone with a modicum of criminality and self-preservation wouldn't go after kids with friends and family. That person would pick off the dropouts and street kids and no one else."

Pammy felt her heart sink. Eagle was right. These names and that sheet of paper didn't make any sense at all.

None of this did.

"Maybe someone *is* picking off the street kids," Pammy said.

"I'm sure someone is," Eagle said matter-of-factly. She still wasn't looking at Pammy. Eagle continually examining the sheets, as if shifting them would make the information change.

Pammy hated it when Eagle took that tone. That *something's going wrong, but I don't care* tone.

"That's one of the reasons I hate Bezerkeley." Eagle almost seemed to be speaking to the papers in front of her instead of Pammy and Val. "All this so-called freedom just means that people get preyed upon."

Val's eyes widened and she looked at Pammy as if shocked at Eagle's words. If someone hadn't been around Eagle much, those words were surprising. But Pammy had heard Eagle say similar things in the past.

"But that woman I saw," Eagle was saying, "she wasn't living on the street. She wore clean clothes. She seemed put together."

"How can you know that if you only saw her for a few minutes?" Pammy asked.

"A few seconds," Val corrected softly, clearly agreeing with Pammy on this.

"Time slows down in a crisis." Eagle raised her head. "You take in details. I don't know why, but you do. I saw some things about that woman. Not enough, mind you. But I keep replaying it over and over in my mind. And when you do that, you examine what your assumptions are."

"What do you mean, your assumptions?" Pammy asked.

"I automatically assumed that she was someone who could've come to the gym," Eagle said. "Doesn't mean she did. Just means she wouldn't have looked out of place here."

Pammy frowned. How would she even know if one of her gym members were missing? So many people just stopped coming because the exercise didn't work for them or because they didn't want to come to campus any more.

Pammy never checked up on them. She didn't feel that it was her job.

"So," Val asked into the silence, "she was white?"

Pammy looked at her, startled. Pammy hadn't thought to ask that. She had just assumed it.

"Yes." Eagle looked a little startled as well. "She had very pale skin."

White skin was common here. Both Pammy and Eagle assumed it. Even Eagle who, apparently, wasn't white after all. No wonder Eagle had looked startled.

Pammy didn't like how that question made her feel. It made her worry about her own perceptions of the world. She expected everyone to be white.

And even worse, Val, who had only spent two days here, expected anyone who came to the gym to be white.

Pammy looked at Val, but Val wasn't looking at her. Thank heavens. Because Val just made Pammy see something about herself and her gym, something she wasn't sure she liked.

Eagle seemed to have shrugged off the thought. She had slid the papers over and was now examining the flyer.

"Your little friend Darla here," Eagle said, "she's part of the pattern too. She had an apartment that she was paying regular rent on. Until a few weeks before she disappeared, she'd been in regular contact with her family. She wasn't a street kid. Street kids, they have either disowned or been disowned by their families. It's a point of pride for them."

Eagle was right about that too. Shortly after she'd opened the gym, Pammy would bring an occasional box of leftovers to some of the street kids until one of them started screaming at her, telling her that they didn't need her bourgeois pity. They got along just fine without Establishment assholes like her, thank you very much.

Eagle tapped the paper again. "Now you have this. These kids, all involved in different things. But your hippie-di—ah, hell, that girl Strawberry, she said they were part of the Movement, as if it's one thing. Is it?"

Pammy shrugged. It seemed like one thing to her, kids involved in all sorts of causes. But she hadn't discussed it. She hadn't discussed it with anyone.

Val saw that shrug, and added one of her own. "I wouldn't know about Berkeley," she said. "Things are very different here. There are activist college students in Chicago, but they haven't taken over the whole city."

"They haven't taken over all of Berkeley either," Pammy said. She sounded defensive. Hell, she *felt* defensive. And protective.

Even though Eagle hated "Berzerkeley," Pammy loved it, in all its strange glory.

"But the activists and the street kids have taken over an important center of Berkeley," Val said. "In Chicago, they took over Old Towne, a part of the city no one else wanted. They really weren't in the rest of the city."

"Are you saying no one cares about them in Chicago?" Pammy asked.

"I'm saying Chicago has many more issues to care about, and so do the locals. The gangs, the violence, the drug trade—if a bunch of kids march about something in the third world, most of us wouldn't have paid attention," Val said.

"Yet the Democratic National Convention, that whole debacle was in Chicago," Pammy said.

"With imported radicals," Val said. "Most of the people arrested were from out of town."

Her words hung in the air. Pammy wasn't quite sure what Val was getting at.

Val must have seen the question on Pammy's face. "If you're going to target kids, activist kids, kids who might make some kind of difference, maybe, you don't do it in Chicago. You do it here. Everyone knows San Francisco is hippie central."

"But this isn't San Francisco," Pammy said.

"No, it's not. But it's close. And *you* said," and with the emphasis on that *you*, Val turned toward Eagle, "that the center of the hippie movement had moved from the Haight to Berkeley. So if someone was up on all of that, they would have moved too."

Val had a point. But Pammy had missed so much of their conversation that she felt left out.

So she waited for Eagle to respond. Eagle wasn't saying anything, though. She was still comparing all the papers, with an expression on her face that probably mimicked Pammy's half an hour ago.

It almost felt like the solution was there in black-and-white, but she couldn't see it.

"What I've been trying to figure out," Pammy said, "is who would target the activists? And why? The government?"

"Now you sound like them. Paranoid as shit." Eagle raised her head, her eyes narrow. She and Pammy had fought about this dozens of times before. Eagle hated it when someone criticized the government, even when the government deserved the criticism.

"We *were* attacked down here," Pammy said.

"By little boys with their toys," Eagle said. "Little military wannabes. The National Guard, who were happy they weren't in Nam but liked to pretend that they're soldiers too."

Pammy didn't say anything to that. She couldn't. Eagle hadn't yet shared most of her experiences in Vietnam, but from what Pammy could tell, Eagle felt like she'd been assigned to a medical unit in hell.

Eagle leaned in toward her, hands still on the papers. "There was nothing covert about what happened down here. Shit, Pammy, police from all over the Bay Area marched in a solidarity parade last winter. And they arrested a bunch of kids for no reason at all. That's not covert behavior. They have the power—and the support of the Silent Majority—to do whatever they want to those kids."

"It's like the Jim Crow South," Val said so softly that Pammy wasn't sure she had spoken for a moment.

Eagle glanced at her, expression bemused.

"Yeah," Eagle said slowly. "It *is* just like the Jim Crow South. Or a town outside an Indian reservation."

Pammy started. She wasn't sure she'd ever heard Eagle say something like that.

"If you're so inclined," Eagle was saying, "you can do whatever you want to certain groups. You can persecute them and even if you're caught, you won't get in trouble."

Pammy was having trouble following some of this. She felt like there was a point to Eagle's speech that both Eagle and Val understood, and Pammy didn't know at all.

"And that's relevant how?" she asked.

"If your list is accurate," Eagle said, "then these kids don't belong to those groups. These are entitled, spoiled kids whose parents have enough scratch to send them to school—"

"Newsome said he didn't have money," Pammy said. "His daughter had a scholarship."

"But that's not going to be obvious to someone who is targeting these kids," Eagle said.

"*If* someone is targeting these kids," Val said. "If the missing kids are actually tied together."

"The street kids are as obvious as it gets," Eagle said. "They're easy pickins for a variety of reasons. A regular college student, even one involved in some damn movement, isn't."

"Are you saying our man in the truck is doing this for the *challenge*?" Pammy asked.

"I'm saying there's something else at play here, something we don't entirely understand." Eagle tapped the papers again. "But we have a list. Do you have a contact in admissions, Pammy? Someone who can tell you if these kids are still enrolled?"

She did. She knew a number of women who worked there.

"I can ask them if I can figure out how I can easily claim I need that information," Pammy said.

Val leaned back on her heels, her new shoes squeaking just a bit. "You said you had a student class earlier. Can't you be double-checking your enrollment?"

"With boys too?" Pammy asked. She never allowed men to take classes here. She wanted the women to feel safe.

"Just tell the admissions office that you're branching out," Eagle said.

"Yeah," Pammy said snidely. "A Gym of *Her* Own is now accepting men."

"Is that true?" A voice came from behind her. Pammy turned. Mattie was standing there, a large purse with a wet towel sticking out of it over one shoulder. "Are you taking men now?"

"No," Pammy said. "I was just making a very lame joke."

"Good," Mattie said. "Because I like this place. It wouldn't be the same with men."

Then she waggled her fingers at Pammy as a wave goodbye and headed out the front door.

All three women watched her go. Pammy waited until she left before saying anything.

"That's why they won't believe me in admissions," Pammy said.

"Oh, they'll believe anything you tell them," Eagle said. "You just present it as something new. They won't think twice."

She was probably right. Most people didn't care about what others were doing.

"So," Pammy said, "I figure out if the kids on this list are still enrolled, and then what? We're not trained investigators."

"No, we're not." Val spoke this time. "But all the trained investigators with any kind of authority don't care. I suppose we could hire a private detective. I could—"

"Kids down here won't talk to anyone official," Pammy said. "I can barely talk to them. They'd run from a detective."

"So we have to figure this out on our own," Val said, involving herself in this. Pammy didn't mind, oddly. She liked having one more person on this team. If, indeed, she could call the three of them a team.

"And that's where I get stumped," Eagle said. "Because if we find something, then what do we do?"

"We have options," Pammy said. "We can go to the authorities, or take action if it's warranted and within our capabilities. But we're not sure if this is just a rumor, right? Like that kids' parking story about the guy with the hook? Everyone believes it, so it must be true, but it might just be a collection of weird coincidences."

"I know a man in Chicago who says there are no coincidences," Val said.

"Yeah, I've heard that," Eagle said. "But at the same time, I've seen doctors misdiagnose because they thought they saw a pattern where there was none. They didn't know the culture, so they didn't know what was normal."

She was talking about Vietnam. Pammy didn't ask any more about it. She didn't want to be sidetracked.

Instead, she said, "You're saying Jill has a point?"

"Even broken clocks are right twice a day," Eagle said drily.

Val moved around Eagle and looked at the papers. Then Val ran her fingers across the flyer.

"You know," she said, "we're missing something obvious here."

She had a deceptively quiet way of speaking. Pammy had noticed that earlier. Val stated things, and to someone who was only paying a little bit of attention, it was easy to ignore what Val said. But that quiet way of speaking masked a formidable intelligence.

Eagle seemed to know it as well. She softened her voice when she spoke to Val, as if Val's very presence shaved off some of Eagle's edges.

"What are we missing?" Eagle asked.

"Darla Newsome," Val said. "We don't know if she fits the pattern, or even if there is a pattern. All we know is that she's missing and her parents are looking for her. We don't know if she was active in anything. We don't even know if she intended to stay in school."

"Too bad we can't talk to the roommate," Pammy said.

"Why can't we?" Eagle asked.

Val let out a short bark of a laugh. And Pammy smiled too. Of all the people to ask that question, Eagle was a study in obliviousness.

"We're Establishment," Pammy said. "That roommate isn't going to tell us anything more than she'd tell the police."

"Too bad we can't enlist your friend Strawberry," Eagle said.

"We could," Pammy said.

"I sure as hell wouldn't trust her," Eagle said. "Would you?"

Pammy thought about it. She had trusted Strawberry with a lot of things.

"I would," Pammy said. "I'd believe she'd tell us what she learned from the roommate."

"But would she ask the right questions?" Eagle asked.

Pammy wasn't so certain about that. Strawberry might think some of their concerns were irrelevant and not ask, even if those concerns were important.

"I could talk to the roommate," Val said.

Both Pammy and Eagle looked at her.

Val shrugged. "I get mistaken for a college student all the time. It has to do with my size mostly. But most people don't really look at my face."

"You mean most white people," Pammy said.

Val tilted her head a little. "You said it, not me."

Eagle examined Val as if seeing her with new eyes. So did Pammy. Dressed the way she was, and as thin as she was, Val could pass for a student.

"You'd have to dump the Chicago PD shirt," Eagle said.

"Obviously," Val said.

"But otherwise, yeah, you're right." Eagle looked at Pammy. "The roommate would get us information to go with the information you'd get from admissions."

"What are you going to do?" Pammy asked, partly because she was feeling a little out of sorts.

"I'm going to check the hospitals," Eagle said, "and see if any of these kids were admitted recently."

"You can do that?" Val asked.

"Yeah," Eagle said. "If I present it right. Former patients, all that."

Pammy's stomach was tied in knots. "What are you thinking?"

"I'm not thinking anything yet," Eagle said. "I'm hoping."

"What are you hoping, exactly?" Pammy asked.

"I'm hoping that Val's Chicago friend is wrong. I'm hoping that there are coincidences." Eagle rapped a fist on the counter top.

"If there are," Val said, "then that still leaves us with your poor injured woman in the truck."

"And Darla Newsome, who is missing," Pammy said.

"And twenty kids who are just living their lives somewhere else," Eagle said, "instead of becoming victims of some sick human being who gets off on harming people."

"Is that what you think is going on?" Pammy asked, her heart pounding.

"What I think and what I know are two different things," Eagle said.

"I get that," Pammy said. "I'm asking what you think."

"I'm thinking I don't like any of this," Eagle said. "I'm thinking we figure it out, not out of the goodness of our hearts, but because we have to protect our own."

"They're not our own," Pammy said.

"We don't know that either," Eagle said. "How many people have never come back to this gym?"

Pammy felt her cheeks heat. "I always thought they didn't like class."

"And that's probably true," Eagle said. "But we don't *know*, do we?"

Val was watching them both. Then she inclined her head, as if she had decided to speak up.

"I come from a place where you just take action," she said. "We never expect the authorities to help. If you have a problem, you solve it."

"Do we have a problem?" Pammy asked, looking at Eagle.

"I have a problem," Eagle said with great force. "That damn woman will haunt me for the rest of my life if I don't do something. You of all people should understand that, Pammy."

Pammy let out a small sigh. "Oh, I do," she said in a near-whisper. "Believe me, I do."

VAL

The gym's silence didn't bother me. It didn't feel like a portent of bad things to come. Normally—or what passed for normal to me now—silence was as big an enemy to me as sound. Maybe more of one, because the last thing I wanted to do was relax my guard.

And given what we were discussing—the possible disappearance of at least two dozen college students—I should have felt more tense, not less.

But for the first time in a long time, I wasn't twitching with nervousness. And I wasn't talking to two women who treated me like something broken and fragile.

They were treating me like an equal. Maybe they were a little wary—or at least, Pammy was. I would've been too, in her shoes. She didn't know me. As far as she was concerned, I was that skittish woman she'd first talked to just yesterday outside the gym, not someone with such a large brain that my cousin Marvella called me the smartest, most educated person she had ever known.

People passed outside the too-large plate-glass window, multicolored shapes that were mostly a blur of shadow and light. I had jumped a lot yesterday as people went by—fewer people than were going by right now. But I wasn't jumping now.

Maybe my attitude had changed.

Maybe I just needed something to do.

Or maybe, just maybe, I needed people to treat me like a competent human being again. Neither Eagle nor Pammy really knew my story, so they didn't feel like they had to protect me from the world.

In fact, they were reintroducing it to me, in all its hideous glory.

Eagle was the one who was shifting her body slightly. She smelled faintly of sweat, something I hadn't noticed before. The mention of that woman who had been kidnapped agitated her in a way that telling the story of the kidnapping didn't. The story of the kidnapping had become just that for her—a story—but the thought of the woman herself upset Eagle deeper than I could have imagined.

Pammy, on the other hand, seemed both calm and unsettled. That quiet way she spoke belied the passion behind the way she had answered Eagle. They both had ghosts in their pasts, ghosts of women, maybe, or ghosts of injured people they couldn't help.

I didn't want to be one of them. I was here to get stronger. I couldn't do that if everyone around me was handing me a crutch all the time.

I had learned a lot about investigation from Truman. He always expounded on the right way to do it, and the wrong way.

The wrong way, he used to say, was to wait for the information to come to the investigator. The right way was to take the same path that the average person would take to find out the information, and then expand from there.

"Do you have a phone book somewhere?" I asked Pammy.

She looked at me, eyebrows raised ever so slightly over her striking blue eyes.

"Yeah, why?" she asked.

"Because I'm going to see if Darla Newsome is listed."

Both she and Eagle looked at me like I had grown a third head.

"You don't think someone came after Newsome because she was in the phone book, do you?" Pammy asked.

I shook my head. "I just want to talk to her roommate. It seemed like the easiest way."

Eagle smiled warmly at me, and Pammy frowned at her. I had no idea what the dynamic was between the two of them, and I wasn't going to ask.

"The phone and the phone book are in my office," Pammy said. "If you wait a minute—"

"I'll take her," Eagle said, and started to walk away.

"No," Pammy said firmly. "I'll do it. If someone comes in, let them get started without me."

"And what if they're new?" Eagle asked. "I don't want to deal with someone new."

"Have them wait," Pammy said, as if it were the easiest thing in the world.

I shrugged a little at Eagle, and let Pammy lead me to the back. The gym was bigger than I had ever thought when I stood outside. Once we went past the locker room—which was a good sized room by itself, when you considered the showers and the benches—we entered a slight hallway that was still wider that the one in my apartment.

There were two doors at the end of the hallway. One, to the right, had a rectangular sign like you'd often see on office doors. It said *Kitchen* instead of someone's name. Below the sign, someone had taped a piece of paper that read:

Please do not enter without the permission of staff.

I wondered exactly who "staff" was. I thought Pammy ran the business on her own.

She didn't even look at the door to the kitchen. She went directly to the other door and pulled a key out of her pocket, unlocking a deadbolt I hadn't even noticed.

I was a bit surprised. Apparently Eagle had a key to the office, or she wouldn't have offered to bring me here.

Pammy stepped in first, then scooped some papers off the desk, put them into a folder and set it on a dusty credenza. She took a metal cash box and placed it inside the top drawer of a nearby filing cabinet.

The drawer had a tiny lock built in, and she locked that. As if it would do any good. I could pick that with a hairpin in a half second, a skill Truman had taught me when he was trying to figure out how hard it would be for "just anyone" to learn how to break into secured areas.

Apparently, as the smartest and most educated person he knew, I was also, in his opinion, the least likely to be able to learn criminal behavior, something that offended me more than I wanted to admit.

Pammy moved the phone to the middle of the now-cleared desk, then set the thick Bay Area telephone directory beside it. She grabbed one other, thinner phonebook. That one I recognized. I had gotten it when I signed up with the phone company for my own phone service.

The thinner book was for Berkeley proper. You actually had to ask for the Bay Area phonebook. They kept it under wraps like it was worth a small fortune or something.

"Thanks." I wanted to add that she didn't have to worry about me alone in here, but I didn't. It wasn't because I was out of practice defending myself—hell, I wasn't certain if I had *ever* really defended myself—but because I was worried she might do what some of those white women did when I pointed out their behavior.

They'd blush. And with that blush, I would know they had cleaned up the room because they were going to leave a black woman alone in it, not because they did that sort of thing for everyone.

"Pull the door closed when you're done," she said, "and then come find me. I'll lock it back up."

I nodded.

She hovered for just a moment, shifting from foot to foot, and then she gave me an awkward smile.

I had no idea what that smile meant—if it was supposed to reassure her or reassure me.

She slipped out of the room, but left the door open. I debated closing it, just for my own safety, then decided against it. She had already cleaned up the desk so that I wouldn't see or touch anything private; if I closed the door, she would probably think that I was digging into her files.

I slid into the room. It was small and cozy, with space for the desk, two chairs, a few filing cabinets, some shelves that had mostly bandages, bottles of iodine, rubbing alcohol, and Mercurochrome. The office smelled of antiseptic, old coffee, and calamine lotion.

I pulled out the desk chair, and sat down. The chair groaned beneath my weight, which surprised me. I had lost pounds I couldn't afford in the spring, and now weighed 110 pounds soaking wet. The chair wasn't very sturdy if it complained about me.

I grabbed the two phonebooks and looked at the dates. Both were 1969, and neither mentioned when they were issued. So I looked inside the Berkeley book first, flipping the thick paper until I got to the *N*s.

I figured finding Darla Newsome in the phone book was a long shot, but a worthwhile one. Everyone who got a phone was listed in the book unless they paid extra to be unlisted.

But most likely the phone was in the name of the landlord or a room-mate or someone I couldn't even imagine. For all I knew, Darla had been subletting the apartment and her name wasn't even on the lease.

I had stared at the flyer during the conversation in the main part of the gym, so the spelling of Darla's name had burned into my brain.

I turned pages until I reached the N-e-w names, and stopped in surprise.

There, at the very top of the page, was D. Newsome.

I looked at the previous page. That page listed Brian Newsome. Then I flipped back and looked below D. Newsome to find Earl Newsome.

There seemed to be only one listing for a D. Newsome, and I'd found it easily. The address was near campus as well.

I glanced at the phone, wondering if I should call first. Before I did, I slid the Bay Area book toward me and looked to see if D. Newsome or a variation was listed there as well.

D. Newsome was in the book, as was Earl Newsome, but no Brian. A Boyd Newsome in San Francisco, a David Newsome in Oakland, and a Deidre Newsome in Emeryville showed up on the page. And D., with that Berkeley address.

I closed the big book, and, before I could have second thoughts, picked up the receiver on the big black desk phone. The dial tone hummed at me as I placed the receiver between my ear and shoulder.

The rotary dial moved poorly—clearly Pammy didn't make a lot of calls with this phone.

Then the phone started ringing in my ear. I jumped. The sound was louder than I had expected.

Finally, someone picked up.

"Yeah," said a young annoyed female voice. "Enough already."

I almost hung up, but I made myself continue.

"Um," I said, putting on my best Midwestern middleclass manners, "I'm so sorry to bother you, but—"

"Ah, jeez. Another country heard from," said the voice. "Who're you and what do *you* want?"

"My name is...Elizabeth Styles," I said, picking the name out of the air. "I'm with the Democratic Party and we—"

"We don't want any," the voice said.

"Um, wait!" I said. "This is Darla Newsome, right?"

"Hell, no. She hasn't been here for a month. And she didn't vote."

"Our records say she had signed on with the Clean For Gene youth campaign for Eugene McCarthy," I said, letting myself sound as desperate as I felt. "Is that incorrect?"

"Ah, crap, how'm I supposed to know?" the voice said. "Like I said, she isn't here, and she didn't strike me as the voting type. That's too Establishment, you know? But I could be wrong."

"Could you leave her a message?" I asked.

"No," the voice said. "You people have just got to stop harassing me. I—"

"According to our records," I said, speaking fast, "this is our first call. Perhaps you're—"

"I don't care if it's *your* first call," the voice said. "Everyone seems to be interested in Poor Little Darla, and like I keep telling you, *I don't know where she is.*"

And with that, the connection ended.

I pulled the receiver away from my ear and stared at the little black holes for just a moment.

My heart was pounding, partly from the anger in the voice and partly with my own audacity. I hadn't thought lying would come so easily for me, but it had.

I set the receiver in the cradle, feeling a little lightheaded. I replayed the conversation in my mind. Other people had been asking for Darla. Her father, certainly. But who else?

And then I realized it didn't matter. If enough people were looking for Darla to annoy the roommate, what was one more?

I wrote the address down on the palm of my hand, then stacked the phonebooks next to the phone like Pammy had had them.

Then I got up and left the office, pulling the door closed behind me. I needed to go home and take off the Chicago PD shirt, then head to the address. It wasn't too far from where I lived.

I emerged from the hallway to find Eagle still standing at the counter, Pammy behind it. Another woman had entered the gym with a giant purse over her shoulder, probably crammed with clothes. She wore a yellow sundress that set off her black hair.

I needed to bring extra clothes next time. That way I wouldn't have to go home to change.

Then my stomach clenched. If I went home, would I leave again?

Eagle was watching me walk, her eyebrows raised. Pammy was scratching something on a piece of paper. Neither of them looked too pleased with the other.

The woman let herself into the locker room as if she had done it a thousand times before.

"Well?" Eagle asked me.

"I got the address and the roommate is home," I said, unable to keep the excitement from my voice. "I need to head over there as soon as I change my shirt."

"They're not going to notice that you exercised," Eagle said. "Have you *smelled* this new generation?"

"It's the Chicago PD logo," I said.

"Oh, yeah," Eagle said. "You think you have time to change?"

"I hope so," I said. "The roommate sounded really annoyed at any call about Darla. But if the roommate leaves, I can always try again."

Pammy set down the pen and nodded toward the rack of t-shirts in one corner. "Just take one of those. No charge."

Why was everyone trying to give me stuff all the time? "I can...I can pay for it," I said, making sure I didn't sound as irritated as I felt.

"I'm sure," Pammy said, "but that's not the issue. If you're in a hurry and you need a different shirt, I have one."

"Is that t-shirt something students wear?" Eagle asked, clearly remembering that I had said I could pass as a student.

"I've sold a few," Pammy said. "Mostly to adult women who only wear it here, but some students have picked up a shirt. I doubt the roommate will question something that says *A Gym of Her Own*. The roommate will notice something with the words *police department*."

She had a point.

"Thanks," I said, and walked over to the rack. T-shirts, sweatshirts, shorts, and some boys' athletic socks, since they didn't make socks like that for women. There were a few shoes on a shelf as well, with a note that listed places that sold sneakers—useful sneakers—in women's sizes.

The shirts were not attractive. They were white with black lettering that had been ironed on. There were some polo shirts near the back with the gym's name sewn on them in white, but I didn't want to take something that was obviously the most expensive thing on the rack.

Besides, I figured a student would be more likely to buy an iron-on t-shirt than a somewhat upscale polo shirt. I grabbed the smallest t-shirt I could find and brought it back to the counter.

"How much do I owe?" I asked as I walked past.

"Nothing," Pammy said.

"No," I said. "I pay my way. How much?"

She sighed and said, "We'll take care of it later," which she had said before. She was clearly thinking that I would forget.

I wouldn't.

I walked past the counter and went into the locker room. I had forgotten about the tall brunette, who stood near an open locker, wearing nothing except a pointed bra and a pair of white underpants. She let out an eep when she saw me and covered herself with the sundress.

I smiled at her, knowing I made her uncomfortable, and grabbed the box that my sneakers had come in. For a moment, I debated whether or not I should put my street shoes back on. Then I decided to leave the sneakers on.

I peeled off the Chicago PD t-shirt, revealing my own bra, older and not nearly as intimidatingly space-age. I slipped on the white t-shirt, the thick lettering on the front making it feel stiff.

It wouldn't wash well, but that wasn't an issue at the moment.

I ran my fingers through my hair, and decided to leave the other shirt and shoes here.

Still, I grabbed my purse, slung it over my shoulder like I'd seen some of the students do on Telegraph, and then smiled at the woman a second time.

She was still standing with her yellow sundress pressed against her breasts. She did not look happy with my presence in the locker room.

I was sure that Pammy would get an earful about me later.

I slipped out.

Eagle and Pammy were still going over those sheets of paper. As I emerged, Eagle watched me.

Something in her gaze seemed familiar, but I didn't know what, exactly, it was.

"You want me to come with you?" she asked.

I frowned at her. Had she forgotten the discussion? Didn't she remember that both she and Pammy realized they wouldn't be able to pass for students?

"No," I said firmly. "I'll be all right."

Now that I wasn't going home. Now that I was wearing a shirt that Pammy had tried to give me as a gift. Now that I couldn't easily back out.

"You get out of there if it looks like there's going to be trouble," Eagle said.

I almost said, *What kind of trouble could there be?* And then I remembered that I was being naïve. A girl had disappeared. So had several other students. And Eagle had seen yet another woman kidnapped.

"I will," I said. "I'll be cautious."

Or at least, I would try.

EAGLE

Eagle felt a little shaky as she watched Val leave the gym. Val's casual rejection—which wasn't a rejection, Eagle had to remember that—Val's casual *I'll be cautious*, augmented by a half smile that acknowledged Eagle's push, made Eagle feel stupid and awkward and sixteen again, with an inappropriate crush on one of her classmates.

Eagle let out a silent sigh. She did have a crush on Val. It had been sudden and immediate and powerful.

And Eagle knew, without asking, that Val did not reciprocate.

The gym's midafternoon stillness accented Eagle's awkwardness. Sunlight filtered in through the plate-glass window, like it did every afternoon. But usually, the gym was filled with people.

The emptiness felt unusual, although Eagle had no way of knowing whether or not it actually *was* unusual. She always did her best to spend as little time in here as she possibly could.

"What's going on with you two?" Pammy asked. She sounded annoyed.

Eagle turned away from the plate-glass window. Val had left her sight the moment she stepped through the door. Eagle was just looking wistfully at the street, like a lovesick teenager.

"Nothing," Eagle said flatly. She moved those papers around again. They were truly disturbing.

"It doesn't look like nothing," Pammy said. "Were you the one who recommended that she come here?"

"What?" It took a second for the question to register. Pammy thought Eagle had known Val before she had come to the gym? "No. I just met her."

Pammy's eyebrows went up, as if she didn't believe that. Why wouldn't she believe it? Was Eagle's crush that obvious?

Pammy didn't say anything in response, though, which was also odd.

"Really," Eagle said, feeling defensive. "I met her in the alley. After that hippie-dippy ding-a-ling insulted me."

The color left Pammy's face. Eagle wasn't sure why.

"Don't call her that," Pammy said. Her voice was tight with disapproval.

She was defending the ding-a-ling. After all Eagle had done for the gym.

Eagle sighed audibly this time. "She upset me."

"Well, you didn't exactly respond in an adult manner," Pammy said.

Eagle's eyes narrowed. "She wasn't willing to help us."

"Actually," Pammy said, "I convinced her to. She'll bring the lists back."

"Not that we need them," Eagle said.

She slid the papers to one side. She had taken out a plain piece of paper while Val was in the locker room and had started to scrawl the names of the missing on them. Now, Eagle grabbed the pen and poised it over the last name she had written down.

"We do need Strawberry's lists," Pammy said. "What if her names aren't on this list?"

Eagle's shoulders tightened. Part of her had hoped that this list in front of her had all the names on it.

"Oh, God," she said. "I don't want to think about that."

She'd been doing enough thinking already. As she had copied the names onto her sheet of paper, she had been thinking of that woman who had been abducted, wondering if her name was here.

Eagle doubted it; she had thought the woman older than the average college student. But that had been a fleeting impression, one she couldn't quite quantify.

"If we're going to do this," Pammy said, clearly still thinking they were arguing over Strawberry, "then we need as many names as possible."

"Yeah," Eagle said softly. "I know."

What Pammy probably didn't realize was that the names made people real. Before, they were hypothesis, facts, figures, occasional thoughts. They weren't actual human beings.

Their names made them someone. They still weren't as real as that woman had been, screaming on the street, but they were people now, with histories, loved ones who wanted to know where they were, and lives that could be lost.

Eagle shuddered. She might never know what happened to the people on this list. Some of them were probably in other cities, maybe at other colleges, living their lives, oblivious to the fact that their fellow students thought they were missing.

Others were probably in trouble or on the streets somewhere.

Or dead.

She closed her eyes for a moment. Dead. So many missing and dead friends. Soldiers, patients, colleagues. She once kept a list of her acquaintances who were MIA, secretly hoping they had gone AWOL and weren't in the hands of the North Vietnamese.

"You okay?" Pammy asked. "I didn't mean to pry."

Eagle looked up. She had stopped writing. She hadn't realized that. She had just stopped doing anything.

"I mean, you just seemed different with Val," Pammy said.

Eagle blinked. Her mind had gone so far from that discussion that it felt like it had happened days ago already.

"I...like her," Eagle said, hoping that wasn't a confession. Pammy didn't need to know what Eagle really meant.

"Yeah, me too," Pammy said, smiling. "She seems sensible. Damaged, though."

Eagle nodded, remembering the conversation at Caffe Med, wondering if that had been in confidence. She needed to treat it that way. The fact that they both suffered from some kind of reaction to the wars they had gone to—whatever war had claimed Val.

"We're all damaged," Eagle said. "That's why we're here."

Pammy's expression flattened. That was how she sometimes showed surprise. Or didn't show it. Or tried not to show it.

"Here," she said. "The gym."

"Yeah," Eagle said. It was true. Much as she fought the gym and the stupid, naïve things that Pammy had done, the reason most of the adult women came here was because something had happened to them, something bad. They wanted a way to combat the badness, wanted a way to make things better.

Pammy offered that. It was a service, whether Eagle approved of every part of it or not.

"That's why we've got to find these people," Eagle said.

"Because they're in trouble," Pammy said, as if she were trying to understand.

"We don't know that," Eagle said. "But we have to assume some of them are. And we know that Val is right: we need to take care of our own."

"We do," Pammy said. "We're branching out here. I don't think these women are ours."

She had said *women* even though Eagle was writing down men's names too. Pammy hadn't really thought of the men. She thought that men could take care of themselves.

Eagle had learned otherwise. She had learned it the hard way, taking care of men—boys—who should never have been marching through insect-infested jungles carrying very large guns.

Shot. Dying.

Like students had been shot here.

It was naïve to think the police would ever help. Not here, not now.

"These people are ours," Eagle said softly. "They just don't know it yet."

She didn't watch Pammy's response. Instead, Eagle wrote down the last few names, then folded the piece of paper and put it in her back pocket.

Then she met Pammy's gaze. Pammy was watching her as if she could see inside Eagle.

"This many names," Eagle said, "it'll take some time to check the hospitals. You're going to admissions, right?"

"Yeah," Pammy said. She sounded almost unwilling. "But not today. In the morning."

Eagle nodded. No one else felt this same sense of urgency that she felt. No one else had seen the truck or the woman.

No one else understood that time was running out.

Just Eagle. And she didn't have the skills to make the investigation move faster. She was groping in the dark, trying to figure out how to solve a problem she only dimly understood.

She'd been in the dark below. In Pleiku, when the power had gone out, and the back-up generators had failed. Surgery by candlelight.

Even then, she'd only been doing triage, saving men—boys—so they could head out again, or head home, lives ruined.

She had never solved the overall problem.

She wouldn't be able to solve this one either.

There were too many missing kids. They couldn't all be missing for the same reason. So even if she found one or two or that poor woman, Eagle wouldn't be able to find everyone on the list.

She would have new names to add to her old one.

Her lot in life, apparently.

"I need to get on this," Eagle said, feeling awkward. She didn't know how to take her leave of Pammy. Eagle wanted to ask if they were good, if they were still getting along.

But she wasn't going to.

Either they got along or they didn't. A conversation wouldn't help that.

"I'll call you if there's news," Pammy said.

Normally, Pammy would have told her to come back or invited her to wait. But that fight with Strawberry changed something. What, exactly, Eagle didn't know.

"Thanks," Eagle said, then pivoted, and headed out the front.

She had to go home and change clothes. She had to start thinking like an investigator. She had to figure out how to ask the right questions.

If only she knew what those questions were.

VAL

I had been wrong about the address. Darla's apartment wasn't that close to my place. In fact, it was a shorter walk from Pammy's gym than it was from where I lived. Fortunately, I had gone toward campus, thinking I would avoid my street, so I wouldn't be tempted to give up and go home.

I walked the side streets, away from Telegraph, following instructions that Pammy had given me. The streets here were an odd mixture of old houses, new apartment complexes, and square business buildings. There seemed to be no rhyme or reason for anything.

When I reached Darla's street, I was surprised to see relatively new apartment buildings on the one side of the street and an entrance into campus on the other.

The apartment buildings were that boxy, modern construction that sort of mimicked some Frank Lloyd Wright buildings I had seen in Chicago. Only these buildings weren't single-family dwellings. They were apartments, with exteriors made of gray concrete.

Even the balconies were made of concrete. Each apartment had glass sliding doors, which I supposed was a selling feature. But to me, it looked like Soviet construction that so many magazine showed these days, the kind of rebuild that you'd find in East Germany instead of in the United States.

Darla's apartment building was in the very center of the block. A parking garage slanted downward under one side of the building, and the entrance took up the other side.

I had to go up a flight of concrete stairs to get to the double glass doors. The doors wouldn't have looked safe to me if they had been closed, which they weren't. Open, they looked like the worst kind of unprotected entrance into a building.

From my position outside, I could see a wide hallway, with metal mailboxes on one side of an artsy staircase that had wood steps, which looked like they floated between two metal frames. Toward the back of the entry, through those open stairs, was an elevator. On either side of the hall were doors, probably leading into the downstairs apartments.

I would have hated living here, particularly on the lower floor. Anyone could get into your apartment. Hell, anyone could climb up the balconies on the outside, stand on the concrete railing and, if they were tall enough or smart enough to bring a climber's rope, reach up to the railing one story up. They could use the railings like a ladder, going from balcony to balcony to get to the right apartment.

I shuddered, and shook off the thought. I didn't live here. I wasn't going to live here either.

I squared my shoulders and walked to the little hand-scrawled directory beside the door. There were buttons beside each name, probably so that a guest could be buzzed inside.

Not that it was necessary today with the doors wide open.

The address in the phone book hadn't had the apartment number and of course, I hadn't asked the roommate on the phone. I only hoped that Darla's name was on the directory.

I didn't see any Newsome. But I did see a D.N. next to #11, along with three other sets of initials. From the layout of the directory, #11 was on the top floor of this four-story monstrosity.

I slipped inside, feeling like I was breaking a rule.

I didn't see anyone as I walked to the staircase. The wood steps were slick beneath my brand-new sneakers, so I grabbed the steel railing to keep my balance. The entire staircase shuddered when I did so.

If I hadn't already decided that I hated this place, the staircase would have sealed the deal. As it were, the staircase was just one more thing to dislike in a building that had nothing to recommend it.

The staircase ended on the same side of each floor, with a narrow hallway heading to the left, and two doors facing each other off that hallway. The hallways differed only by carpet color. I hadn't noticed the carpet on the first floor, if, indeed, there had been any. But the second floor had an industrial blue, the third a dirty red, and the fourth a bright kelly green.

Apartment 11 was on the left side of the hallway, which probably gave the apartment a view of the back of nearby buildings. Apartment 12 was on the right, and clearly had a view of the campus. I wondered if the placement had any impact on the rent, and decided that it probably did.

The door was made of the same polished blond wood as the stairs. I knocked, and the number 11 above my hand swung a little. The building couldn't have been more than five years old, and yet it already looked tired and worn.

To my surprise, the door yanked open. I had expected the sound of a deadbolt unlatching, the rattle of a security chain protecting the person inside from the person outside.

Instead, I wasn't even sure the door had been locked. And clearly, the young woman in front of me hadn't looked through the peephole that was a little above my eye level.

She was a slight redhead with explosive curls that haloed her face. The girl didn't wear any makeup to hide the matching riot of freckles that dotted her skin. Her eyes, a green that put the carpet to shame, assessed me.

"Am I supposed to know who you are?" She owned the voice that I had heard earlier.

I had to make sure she didn't recognize my voice. I took a little of the education out, removed the Midwestern politeness, and spoke in a soft, nervous, breathy tone.

"Hi," I said. "I'm looking for Darla?"

"Christ, you and everyone else on the planet. What the hell?" the girl said. "Is this 'find Darla' day?"

I swallowed. "You mean she's not here?"

The girl tugged on her sleeveless green top. She wore matching green shorts and her feet were bare. She looked like a student in an advertisement for the university, but she certainly didn't talk like someone the university would want to represent them.

"Ah, yeah, I'm saying she's not here," the girl said with annoyance. "I'm saying she hasn't been here for a month. So toddle off and go bother someone else."

She started to close the door, but I blocked it with my right hand. She looked at my dark skin against the door's blond wood, as if either my skin color, the presence of my hand, or my action offended her. Or maybe all three.

"Look, sister," she said, "I don't know you, and I don't want to know you, but believe me when I tell you I have not seen Darla in, like, for*ever*."

"I believe you," I said in that soft little passive voice. I wished I had chosen a different way to speak to her, something tougher. Unfortunately, I couldn't go back now. "But I've been trying to reach her for almost a month. She stopped coming to class."

"I know," the girl said. "She stopped everything, including paying rent."

"Um, maybe I can help with that?" I said as timidly as I could.

I had been thinking of my cover story for the entire walk over here. What would a student want with Darla, especially since Darla had been gone for weeks? I could only think of one thing.

The girl was frowning at me.

"I, um, I'd been talking to Darla about subletting?" I said, letting my inflection go up as if I was nervous. "She, um, she was interested? I've been trying to call her. Because I have to move on August first?"

"Bitch isn't supposed to sublet," the girl said. "Not without everyone's approval."

"Everyone?" I asked.

"There are three more of us who get a say. Jeez." The girl pulled the door back. "Darla was sure a waste of air. C'mon in."

I was surprised. I hadn't expected the lie to gain me entrance.

"I'm Lucy," she said, extending her hand. "If you can believe that."

She indicated her hair, and it took me a moment to realize her sarcasm had more to do with her resemblance to the red-headed actress Lucille Ball than with anything to do with me.

I decided not to comment on that, in case I was wrong. I almost said, *My name is Elizabeth*, and then remembered I had used that name not an hour before. I had no idea why I was stuck on the name, but I clearly was.

"Paulette," I said, giving the name of my cousin because I had to come up with something quickly.

"That's a mouthful," Lucy said.

"Yeah," I said and shook her extended hand. Her palm was warm and moist. I broke contact quickly and resisted the urge to wipe my hand on my shorts.

I stepped inside the apartment. It smelled like unwashed sheets and dirty dishes, but the main room was clean enough for a student apartment. It had regular walls—not concrete—which I knew only because Lucy—or *someone*—had decorated with political posters. Regular thumbtacks held the posters in place, although the older ones, announcing last fall's book sales, movie nights, and political rallies, were curling at the edges.

A saggy sofa sat beneath them, along with a scarred coffee table. Two mismatched stuffed chairs framed the sofa, and a console television—clearly the most expensive thing in the living room—covered the other wall. The television was off, but I could hear music coming from somewhere. The Who, maybe, or Jefferson Airplane. I wasn't that up on current groups. Not anymore.

I had been right about each apartment having a balcony. The one for this apartment stretched the length of the back wall. The sliding glass doors were in the middle of a series of floor-to-ceiling windows, letting a lot of light into the room.

I had to revise my sense of the building. The interior of this apartment was surprisingly spacious and surprisingly pleasant. The main room branched off into an L, which probably formed the dining area.

"You serious about subletting?" Lucy said. "Because I doubt I can get Darla's dad to pay for another month if she's gone for good."

I looked at her as if I didn't understand her. "What do you mean, she's gone for good?"

"Oh, hell, I don't know. She didn't come home one day. It was between sessions. Her dad thinks she's missing, but I've had roommates book on me before—not," she added quickly, "that I'm hard to live with. I'm pretty straightforward, really."

I cringed inwardly. If Lucy had to deny bad behavior, she probably exhibited a lot of it. She probably *was* hard to live with.

"But it's hard to keep roommates these days. No one goes to classes anymore." She shrugged. "I've lived here for two years. To afford it, I need three other girls. The other two are home for the summer, but they're still paying rent. It was supposed to be me and Darla for the summer session, but she split, and so it's just me."

"This is a four-bedroom?" I asked.

"Three," Lucy said, "but one room is big enough that we divided it into two spaces. You'd get that. The new girl always does."

"Darla made it sound like I'd get her room?" I said, with as much uncertainty as I could muster.

"If you want to take over this week, maybe yeah, you could," Lucy said. "Since no one else is going to be here until the end of September, and I don't want to move everyone's stuff around. They'll come back, and if they complain, I'll just say it's already a done deal. So you won't have to worry about it."

She sounded like she wanted me—or fake me—to have the apartment, without doing any vetting at all. All my legal training made me shudder. That, and my experiences this past year.

She would have no idea what she was getting into. There was no way she could. And she was comfortable and trusting.

For all she knew, I wanted to steal from her or case the apartment for someone else.

Because I clearly wasn't a physical threat.

"Do you mind if I see the whole apartment?" I asked. "I mean, Darla was supposed to show me, and then she vanished?"

"Yeah, *that* was annoying," Lucy said. "I'll show you the apartment."

We stepped farther inside, and she pushed the door closed. She swept a hand toward the living room.

"The apartment's pretty cool," she said. "We lucked into it. My dad knew the guy who built the place, and he gave my dad a deal on the whole place. We have to rent, though. Initially, my dad rented the apartment for my brother. But he transferred to UCLA after two years, and I convinced Daddy to let me have the apartment. It took a bit to get the other guys out, but we managed, and I brought in some girls. So, my family has been here since this place was built. First, though, it was my brother, and now me."

"And your other roommates," I said just loud enough so that she could hear me.

"Oh, hell no," she said. "Some people have no idea when they get a good deal. I had different roomies last year. Then I met Darla last summer, and she and I decided to rent. She found the other two girls, which was good, because I was buried. I'm an econ-poli sci double-major and I was working on election crap for my honors Presidential Politics seminar, and I had no time to, like, find anyone to live here. So Darla did."

"She's nice," I said wistfully, as if I wasn't sure I could live here without her.

"I thought so," Lucy said. "Until she freakin' booked on me."

She led me through the living room to the balcony.

"This is the best part, really," she said, sliding the doors open.

There was a grill on one side of the balcony, and some aluminum lawn chairs with the kind of nylon weave seats that clung to the skin in humid weather. I couldn't tell what color the weave had been, only that the nylon had faded with time and exposure to the elements. The nylon looked as saggy as the couch.

"I sit out here and study all the time," she said. "It's, like, perfect. A little brewski, a book, and you're good to go."

I walked to the railing. It was more of a barrier, which provided privacy. It went all the way up to my ribcage.

Unfortunately, the view from here was of the other buildings. I could see directly into an apartment about ten yards away.

Still, I could feel the sunlight on my shoulders. Lucy was right. A beverage, a book, and a comfortable chair (not those lawn chairs), and this would be a perfect place to study.

It had to cost a fortune. It was certainly nicer than anything I had ever lived in when I was in school—at least, until I married Truman and moved into his small house.

"So how much is this place?" I asked, still looking at the apartment across the way. I could see into the kitchen. The table had a giant candle in the center, made of melted wax. The tenants must have put a new candle in the old wax and kept it there, letting it melt into that amorphous ball.

"The apartment is two hundred dollars a month," Lucy said.

I inhaled sharply. My furnished one-bedroom cost me ninety-five dollars per month.

"But," Lucy said, "it includes laundry in the basement and three parking spaces. Plus, you'd only be paying fifty dollars per month."

I turned, remembering my pose. "I'm paying less than that right now. Darla made it sound like I'd be paying thirty-five dollars per month."

"Darla was high, then," Lucy said dismissively. "Because she paid fifty dollars."

Which was an amazing rate for a scholarship student. At least, I thought she was a scholarship student. Pammy had said that Darla's father had no money.

Where had Darla gotten hers?

"Can I see the room I'd have?" I asked.

"Sure," Lucy went back through the balcony doors, then waved her hand toward the left. "Let's go through the dining room and kitchen, so you can see what a great deal this really is."

The dining area was good size, with a big table in the center, covered in books and papers. It too had excellent light, since the floor-to-ceiling windows extended to the edge of the dining room wall.

A galley kitchen ran from the dining room to the hallway. The stench of rotting food was stronger here. Clearly, Lucy wasn't the most hygienic of roommates. Judging from the pile of dishes near the sink, she hadn't washed anything in at least a week, maybe more.

I had no idea what the bug situation was here, but I knew in Chicago that any apartment with a kitchen this filthy was cockroach heaven.

Lucy walked through the kitchen as if the smell didn't bother her. The smell made the ham sandwich I had eaten earlier think of returning. I cupped one hand over my nose and mouth and followed her into the hallway.

She turned left, away from the living area. Then she nodded at a door right beside the kitchen.

"Bathroom," she said.

It didn't look clean either. A mound of towels lay on the floor beside the tub. I didn't want to turn on the light to see the condition of the sink or toilet.

She pointed at the end of the hall. "That's the big room. My dad put in a floor-to-ceiling divider if you want to see."

A floor-to-ceiling divider. I wanted to say, *Wouldn't that be a wall?* but such a snide comment wouldn't go with the role I was playing right now.

"That's the room the other two share?" I asked, mostly as clarification. I wanted to see Darla's room, and then get out of here.

"Yep," Lucy said, "and if you'd come in here in October, it would be yours. But I think you can have Darla's. Serves her right, if she comes back. Then she'd have to start all over in the roommate pecking order."

Oh, yeah, I bit back. *You're not a handful. You're easy to room with.*

I smiled just a little to myself, glad I was following her so she couldn't see that reaction.

"This room would be yours," she said, stopping outside the next door. "Right beside the bathroom."

Where you had to listen to everyone go by, the squeal of the shower as it turned on, and the continual flush of the toilet.

"Mind if I go in?" I asked.

She shrugged. "Be my guest," she said, then reached around the door frame and flicked on the overhead light.

The room was a lot neater than the rest of the house. A full-size bed covered in thin pillows dominated. Surprisingly, it was made with almost military precision. A ragged stuffed dog leaned against one of the pillows and a hand-crocheted afghan rested across the foot of the bed.

A closet filled with clothes stood open across from the bed. A desk was pushed up against the exterior wall, the chair slightly askew as if someone had just been using it. A pile of books held in place by book-ends leaned against the wall, and one book, along with a legal pad and a pen, sat on top of the desk.

A purse hung off the chair. A thin coat rested on a peg beside the door.

"Wow," I said. "It looks like she just left."

"That's what her dad said." Lucy sounded unconcerned.

"But you don't think so?"

"She had a macramé purse, and it's not here," Lucy said. "And she wore these sandals that were usually kicked into the middle of the floor. I was always tripping on them when I came to talk to her."

I frowned. "She left with her purse and her shoes, but nothing else?"

"I didn't say that," Lucy snapped. "I don't inventory my roommates' possessions. I have no idea what she took and didn't take. But I thought she was coming back. She didn't *say* she wasn't going to pay July's rent. She just didn't."

I looked at her, letting her see that I was bothered by all of this. "Had she done this before?"

"Who're you? Her mother?" Lucy crossed her arms and leaned against the door jamb. Even though she sounded irritated, she didn't act irritated.

I was slowly beginning to realize that her anger was a cover for her own concern. She felt left out by the fact that her roommate had seemingly abandoned her without telling her why.

"If I'm going to rent her room," I said, "I should know if she's coming back."

"If she was going to sublet to you, then she probably wasn't coming back," Lucy said. "But she didn't say anything to us about subletting."

Because she hadn't planned on it, I wanted to say. I wanted to dump the entire lie now. But I couldn't.

"She didn't meet me, though," I said. "She never followed through."

Lucy leaned her head against the jamb.

"It's really weird," she said. For the first time, she sounded vulnerable. "She should've said something. I don't even know when she was last here. I think I remember her going out at breakfast back in June, but I don't know. It might've been some other day. Or she might not have come home for a couple of days. We all agreed that we wouldn't keep track of each other. That's what our parents did, and we're grown-ups now. So we didn't."

Then she hunched her shoulders forward and added, "*I* didn't."

My mouth opened slightly. She felt guilty about Darla's disappearance.

"You think something happened to her?" I asked.

"I don't know," Lucy snapped. Then she sighed and added quietly, "I really don't."

EAGLE

With trembling fingers, Eagle pulled out her keys and unlocked the door to her apartment. Then she stepped inside, closed the door, and locked all of the locks.

The interior smelled like someone had dumped an entire bottle of bleach down the kitchen sink and hadn't bothered to run water over it to clear out the stench. So much for fooling the cops yesterday. They probably wondered what she had to hide.

Of course, seeing the saggy couch, her red-lined eyes, and the scratch marks all over the battered coffee table, had probably told the cops exactly what she was hiding. Looking at this room from their perspective meant they had probably given her more respect than she deserved.

Her face flushed. She sat down heavily. She didn't want to leave again. If only hiding here were an option. And she supposed it was, if she wanted to stay drunk all the time. Drunk, not stoned. Because if she stayed stoned, her brain would examine everything closer and closer, with a pothead's paranoia, and she'd end up even more upset.

She didn't dare stay drunk. Not and keep what little self-respect she had left.

She got up and opened the windows. She had to get the bleach smell out of here. A warm breeze came in, along with the faint sound of bongos. That player had tireless energy. Either that, or he had traded off with someone else.

She pulled out the paper and unfolded it, the names crystal clear in her neat handwriting. Too many names to go into a hospital without an appointment, files, or some hand-written authorization. If she went to a hospital in person, they might want to see some form that gave them permission to release a record.

Not that most hospitals cared about the paperwork, in her experience. They'd tell anyone anything, provided the person had the right credentials. She had good credentials, good enough to fool most record departments if she were requesting one record.

But she'd be asking for twenty, and no one would look the other way for that.

Then an idea struck her. If she stayed here and worked the phone, she had a way to talk to records—at least for the male names on the list. Female names would be harder. But she could come up with something.

She went to the ratty desk that sat at the far end of the living room. She opened a drawer, removed a yellow legal pad, found a working ball-point pen, and then went into the kitchen. Unfortunately, the telephone was attached to the wall, so she would have to stand. Standing would probably make her sound more formal, anyway.

She grabbed the Bay Area phonebook. She preferred it to the Berkeley phonebook because it gave her more resources. She flipped through the yellow pages to hospitals and clinics, saw all the free clinics listed, and winced. Some of these places she might have to visit in person after all.

But not with her uniform on.

She decided to start with the least likely hospital. San Francisco General, a teaching hospital that was far from the UC Berkeley campus. She'd done some work at SFGH and knew it to be both cutting edge and rigid at the same time. Dealing with their records department would help her practice her spiel.

She dialed the general number and asked for records. As her call was transferred, she leaned against the wall, envisioning the dark corridors of the ancient building where the records were.

The phone rang a few times before someone picked up.

"Records, Waldon," a male voice said.

"Hello." She made herself sound tired. It wasn't much of a stretch. "I'm Rita Hall with the U.S. Army Recruiting Office. I'm trying to track down some records to see if they're legitimate. Are you the person I can talk to for this?"

"Depends," this Waldon said. "What exactly do you need?"

"I have paperwork in front of me for six young males who are trying to be classified 4-F. We've had a lot of phony paperwork come our way lately, and so I've been assigned to see if these young men have visited your hospital and if so, what exactly they were treated for."

"You don't got a doctor's slip?" Waldon asked. He finally sounded a little interested.

Eagle cursed silently. He knew how the military system worked. The military system needed a doctor's release for a 4-F classification. Often that was just a first step. But it was an important one.

"Oh, we have that," she said. "But these days too many doctors here have made a side business of selling their signatures to help wealthy young men avoid the draft."

She paused, hoping for some kind of reaction. There was none. She then suspected that this Waldon knew that.

"So, we've started requiring additional paperwork where possible. We've had the boys fill out a list of surgeries, emergency room visits, X-rays, along with dates—"

"I am not looking up a pile of paper just for you, lady," Waldon said.

She smiled. His reaction was exactly the one she had wanted. Because she could have had him go through each file, procedure by procedure, or she could get him to comment generally.

"I don't blame you," she said warmly. "I got assigned this duty just this week, and I have to say, it's not the most exciting job I've ever had."

He didn't chuckle or even make a sound. She wished he had.

"But," she said, "the woman who trained me said that we can short-circuit the procedure by having you look up a patient's records by name, and then confirming the last visit the patient made to the hospital. In theory, our records should match, or at least come close."

He sighed. "Technically, I'm supposed to have you come down here and fill out some forms before I give you that information."

"I know," Eagle said. "But considering the day I've had, I have a hunch that would waste even more time for us. Because I suspect you probably don't have a lot of these names in your records."

He grunted. Either that sound was a half-laugh or a sound of disgust. She couldn't tell without seeing his face.

"Why don't I just give you the names that I have? I don't even have to give you date of birth, because all of these young men are between the ages of eighteen and twenty-five, draft age. That would be birth years 1944 to 1951."

"Sounds so easy. You should see the files down here," he said.

"Oh, I have," she said. "That's why I don't want to come down if I can help it. You're not alone down there, are you?"

"If I say yes, will you hang up?" he asked, letting her know just by his response that someone else was there as well.

"If you're alone down there, I'll hang up after I give you the names," Eagle said. "And then I'll call you back."

He muttered something under his breath, then he said, "Hey, Sophie, need you to handle the phones and desk for a while."

Eagle couldn't hear Sophie's response, but it must have been affirmative because the phone made shuffling noises, and then he said, "Okay, how many names we talking?"

"Six." Eagle decided not to give him the girls' names because that would just confuse the matter. She needed a different scheme for those.

"Fire," he said.

She read off the names, spelling them and claiming, if he asked, that she couldn't always read the handwriting she was working off of. He seemed to understand.

When she finished, he said, "Here's what I'll do. I'm just going to pull the files that I find and bring them back. Then we can compare dates."

She bit back a half-second of annoyance since that was how she had explained the plan to him. But then she realized that it would be better if he thought it all was his idea anyway.

He didn't put her on hold. She wasn't sure the phones down in records had that capability. Instead, the phone clunked on the other side and then she heard some faint music. It sounded like Frank Sinatra, but she couldn't be entirely sure.

She didn't hear much else for several minutes. While she waited, she wrote down his name and Sophie's name, then circled them, and drew little sparklers coming off the circles.

By the time the phone clunked again, Eagle had nearly worn a hole through the top page on the pad.

Without preamble, he said, "I don't got any of those names, unless you were mistaken about age. I got a seventy-five-year-old under one of the names, and he's got some heart condition. He came in a year ago for a heart attack. Dunno if he's still alive or not."

She almost thanked Waldon cheerfully, and then caught herself just in time. "You'd better give me that name," she said. "In case we have someone using fake records."

He did, and she dutifully wrote it down, not that she thought it mattered. The name was common enough.

"You're sure you have no others?" she asked.

"Positive," he said. "I double-checked the files. Unless something is upstairs right now, none of your guys have been here according to our records. You sure they were at SFGH?"

"No," she said, "I'm not sure. That's why I'm double-checking. Half the records just say San Francisco. I was taking the easy route, and hoping that they meant SFGH, not some other San Francisco hospital."

"You in the San Francisco office?" he asked, as if he knew it.

"No. I'm at headquarters," she lied. "I get all the paperwork that they don't know how to handle."

"So your documents are coming from all over the Bay Area?" he asked.

"Looks like," she said. "Although this bunch seems to be mostly from Berkeley."

He snorted. "Figures. No wonder they had you check everything."

Finally, she knew where he stood politically. Although it was too late in the conversation to help her much.

"These college kids," he said, "they don't know nothing about the Bay Area. They think it's all San Francisco. There actually might be records, but they could be in Oakland or something."

"Yeah," she said. "That's what I'm afraid of."

"I'd just blow it off if I were you," he said, "and deny them all, send them over to Vietnam so they know what a real war is like."

It's not a real war, she almost said, a reflexive, sarcastic response, based on the fact that no one had ever declared Vietnam a war, just a police action. Except it was a real war.

People died.

She took a shaky breath. "Thanks for your help."

"No problemo," he said. "Glad I don't have your job."

Glad I don't have yours, she thought, but didn't say. Instead she hung up and stared at the names.

Her scheme would work, at least for the male names. She'd need something else for the female names.

And she would have to do it at different times. After that conversation, she couldn't call Waldon back immediately and ask for the girls' records. She'd have to wait until early morning, when a different employee manned the desk.

She tapped her ballpoint pen on the legal pad. When she had volunteered to check hospitals, she had had no idea how much legwork that would entail.

For a brief moment, she wondered if the effort was worthwhile. Then she remembered those desperate screams for help.

She bent her head over the phone book and looked for the next number to call.

VAL

Lucy stared at me, her green eyes wide and open for the first time since I'd arrived. Her admission that she had no idea what happened to Darla had calmed the anger that seemed to come up every time I spoke Darla's name.

That, and the fear my question had provoked in Lucy. Underneath all that bravado, she was terrified.

She still had her arms crossed, and the side of her head touched the door jamb to Darla's room. I was deep inside it, near the perfectly made bed. The room smelled faintly of vanilla candles, even though no one had been here in a month.

"So much could've happened, you know?" she said, "It's been really scary down here since, like, January. And then all the riots and tear gas and stuff. Darla was pretty freaked out. We got gassed in our own apartment. I mean, I was sitting on the balcony when that helicopter flew over and dropped the gas. I had to go to the emergency room. Darla took me. She wasn't feeling much better, but she helped, you know? She kept saying it would be all right."

I didn't say anything, just waited. I was glad I hadn't been here in May when all of this stuff went down.

"She was wrong, you know? It wasn't all right. There were, like, cops and *military* everywhere. I wanted to go home, but Daddy says Sanders aren't quitters." Sanders must have been Lucy's last name.

I wondered if her father had said that before or after the tear gas attacks on campus.

"And now," Lucy said, looking at the floor instead of me. "I'm the only one left."

My breath caught. Suddenly, her attitude and the mess in the apartment started to make sense. She had been frightened this spring. She had leaned on Darla and her friends. Her friends had left her to face summer school alone. But Lucy had probably felt comfortable with Darla, and then Darla disappeared.

"You think something happened to her?" I asked softly.

"I don't know," Lucy said. "I mean, people are coming and going all the time this year, and they don't tell their parents. I mean, would you?"

If my parents were still alive, maybe. Although I doubted it. I wouldn't have been able to say anything to my father about *him* or the pregnancy.

Or the botched abortion.

Lucy was watching my face through her fringe of curls. She must've seen something in my expression, because she lifted her head just enough to nod.

"You wouldn't've said anything either," she said with more than a little triumph. "See? That's what I mean. And last fall, when everyone moved in, we all promised we wouldn't get involved in each other's lives and be all nosy like our parents. Live and let live, you know? Everyone has their own shit, and we all have to own it."

That sounded well and good, but these girls were still young. They needed someone to watch out for them, and apparently no one had. They had made their little pact, not realizing what was coming for them. Hell, I had been a full adult, married, divorced, and I hadn't known what was coming for me.

"Wouldn't Darla have said something if she was just skipping out on the rent?" I asked.

"Well, if she talked to you about subletting, maybe she talked to somebody else too. And maybe she'd made an agreement and that somebody never showed. How would she know if someone didn't show?" Lucy uncrossed her arms, then ran a hand through her curls. "I mean, she never told me about the subletting, so maybe she never told me that she had actually contracted with someone. Which isn't fair, you know? Because *I* have to live with that person."

My lie was snowballing. I hated that.

"It's not fair," I agreed. "I can't imagine how it would feel to have a stranger say she had the right to move in."

"I know, right?" Lucy shook her head. "Darla used to tell me stuff. I thought we were friends. I don't know why she wouldn't've told me about this."

"Well," I said, trying to change the direction of the conversation away from my lie. "*I* thought she was going to sublet to me. She mentioned bringing me up to see you. That's the last we discussed. We were going to come up here about a month ago, and I never saw her again."

More lies. I kept spinning them, hoping they would get rid of the thought that Darla would have sublet to someone else.

"Huh." Lucy sighed, then looked over her shoulder. "I don't get anything anymore. She shouldn't've left. I mean, she knew we were all counting on her."

I didn't ask how they were counting on her. I assumed it was for rent, but I didn't know.

I touched the stuffed dog. The fur had worn off its back and sides. One button eye had been sewn back on with red thread.

"This looks well loved," I said.

"You're not supposed to touch it," Lucy said.

Then we looked at each other. We clearly had the same thought at the same time. Who left a childhood treasure like this behind?

"Did her father say anything about this dog?" I asked quietly.

"I didn't let him in here. I didn't let him past the living room." Lucy straightened, almost as if she were going to battle him again. "He was so angry, and stuff. I lied and told him that the other girls were in the back, and no man was supposed to go back there. I figured a father would want to hear that."

That was probably true. "And he listened?"

"Yeah." The word was curt.

I pressed my lips together, then looked around the room. No loose papers, nothing out of place. I bet if I looked in the dresser, I would find underwear. I bet if I looked in the closet, I would find a suitcase.

I didn't care how Darla was paying for this room, no scholarship student I had ever met had enough disposable income to leave all of her possessions behind and buy new.

Unless...

"Was she involved in that back-to-nature stuff?" I asked.

"Why?" Lucy asked. "Do you see something?"

"No," I said. "I just thought, well, I mean, if *I* were going to deliberately leave everything behind, I would do it because I was giving up material things."

"God, communes," Lucy said, her dry tone letting me know exactly what her opinion of the back-to-nature movement was. "I don't think she could have lived in one. She was all about Lysol and clean dishes and *pick up your towel* and stuff like that. Have you ever *been* to one of those communes? Some of them don't even have running water."

I hadn't been to any of them, but that sounded true, at least from what the media reported.

"I was just thinking—"

"You're thinking it's weird that she's gone," Lucy said. "I think it's weird that she's gone. But I don't know what to do about it."

"Were you the one called her dad?" I asked, deliberately misunderstanding what Lucy had told me.

"God, no," Lucy said. "Darla was happy to be outta there. She would've thought I betrayed her or something."

"Were her parents tough on her?"

"Naw." Lucy half-smiled. "They were just...Republicans. You know?"

Not exactly. I didn't know how to say that. The way she said it, it sounded like I should understand. Maybe other students would have.

I tried to figure out how to ask the question without sounding like a full-grown adult.

"So, you mean, she didn't agree with them about stuff, right?" I asked, hoping that was good enough.

"Oh, God, yeah," Lucy said. "Her folks were so Establishment. She couldn't take it, you know?"

I didn't, exactly. I was probably what Lucy called Establishment. I hadn't realized how much I was until the women at the gym—housewives, some of them—had looked at my Chicago PD t-shirt in disbelief.

"Is that why Darla left?" I asked. "Politics?"

"Oh, I don't know," Lucy said. "All of us disagree with our parents about that shit. Don't you?"

"I don't talk to them about it," I said, which was technically true. I didn't need to tell her that I couldn't.

"God, I wish I could stop talking to mine about politics," Lucy said. "My dad won't shut up about it. He thinks I'm too stupid to understand his point."

She wasn't stupid. That was clear. But she was young. I suspected that was what her father thought.

She shrugged. "But, you know, I have no idea if that's why she left home, though. I think she'd had enough of them, plus, she was like completely brilliant, you know?"

Lucy was using past tense. I wondered if she realized that. She wasn't just thinking that Darla was gone; part of her believed Darla was dead.

A shudder ran through me.

"I thought she was going to summer session because she needed to make up classwork," I said, guessing on summer session.

"Apparently, she didn't go to summer session," Lucy said, "even though that's like completely weird because she was looking forward to some econ class. I mean, like who looks forward to *econ?*"

I shrugged. Certainly not me.

"She really liked it here," Lucy said. "Her folks hated it. That much I know for a fact. They fought all the time her senior year. They hated that she was coming here. They wanted her to go to Fresno State. Can you imagine? With her grades?"

I frowned. I hadn't heard of Fresno State. I had heard of UC-Berkeley. I supposed that told me something about Darla, but it told me more about Lucy.

She cared about grades. She cared about this apartment. She wasn't into the "Movement," whatever that was. She cared about her education, and she thought that Darla had too.

"I'm really confused now," I said. "I don't know if I should take the room. It sounds like she'll come back."

"She hasn't. It's been a month." Lucy was looking down.

"I hate to…" I paused thinking about my next sentence. "I hate to say this."

Lucy raised her head, and looked at me through her curls again.

"But…" I said as timidly as I could, as if I didn't know, "shouldn't we call the police?"

Lucy barked out a laugh. "And tell them what, exactly? That my roomie skipped on the rent—oh, wait! I got her daddy to pay. So never mind on that. Should I tell them that she 'disappeared' somewhere? C'mon. Jeez, sister, for a black chick, you sound totally square."

My cheeks heated. I did sound square. Because I was, deep down. And I had finally revealed it to Lucy.

I let my fingers run across that stuffed dog.

"Yeah, I know I sound square," I said, "but I've never heard of anything like this before. What if she's in trouble? I mean, what are we supposed to do?"

"I don't know." Lucy sounded miserable. She clearly had thought about this. Those arguments she made were all arguments she had probably had inside her own head. "If she's in trouble, she's been in trouble for a month."

The words hung between us.

She swallowed hard, once, twice, and then a third time, almost like she was swallowing back words.

"I, um, I was hoping she was at home." Her voice was almost inaudible. "I was kinda hoping she went home, but when her dad came, it was clear she hadn't."

I felt a little dizzy, and I realized I hadn't inhaled. I made myself breathe.

Lucy's anger, on the phone and when I arrived, hadn't been at other people. It had been at herself.

When Darla's father had shown up, Lucy could no longer deny what she feared—that something bad had happened to Darla.

221

I patted the stuffed dog one last time. Someone should do something. And no one would.

I started to ask if Darla's dad was going to file a missing person's report, and then I stopped. That was a question Valentina Wilson, ex-wife of Chicago PD Detective Truman Johnson, would ask. Not a question that the girl I was pretending to be would ask.

"Maybe we should talk to her friends?" I said, reverting to that timid voice again. "I mean, was she in some kind of group or something? Maybe, like, protesting something? You mentioned politics."

"She studied," Lucy said defensively. "She didn't have time for most of that stuff."

And neither, apparently, had Lucy. So that single connection Eagle, Pammy, and I had thought we had found back at the gym didn't seem to be a connection at all.

"But you said she was political…?" I let the question hang, hoping it would get her to say even more.

"Like all of us. I mean, it's life and death out there," Lucy said. "Especially for the guys. You know? They could get drafted and then get shot, and not do anything. So we, like, hand out flyers sometimes or something. But I thought Darla agreed with me. It was better to get an education and infiltrate the Establishment and change it from the inside."

Her passion surprised me as much as her naiveté. I had never known any major organization to change from the inside—not like that, anyway.

"She handed out flyers?" I asked. "I never saw that."

"Like, at Homecoming, and stuff. If you did that, you got into the game for free. Not that we're supposed to care about football." Lucy shrugged her shoulders. She clearly did care about football. "I don't think she did anything since the election. We were all getting disheartened, especially after Bobby got murdered, but for a while, we thought that we could keep fighting. Or just vote. I mean, we thought our votes would count. And then, the summer, and the Democratic National Convention, and Humphrey, and the campaign and Nixon, and who has the heart for this stuff?"

I frowned at her, a little startled. Lucy had been active, and I hadn't expected it. She had clearly worked for Kennedy. She called him Bobby, and said he was "murdered," not assassinated.

I had felt that death, but not as keenly as Doctor King's death a few months before. And I never would have thought of calling him Martin, even though I believed in his cause.

"I thought…" I stopped myself before I could make a mistake. Because I almost said, *I thought you had told me that she wasn't political at all when I called from the Clean For Gene Campaign.*

Lucy looked at me.

I had to finish the sentence.

"She just never struck me as political?" I said, putting on that timid voice, partly to keep my own comments in check. "I mean, she never talked to me about anything political."

"She gave up when Bobby died." Lucy swallowed hard again. "She really liked him. She wrote letters trying to get him to run, and then he did, and she was really happy. I think she thought she might've gotten him killed."

That explained the Clean For Gene reaction. The majority of Kennedy supporters didn't move to Eugene McCarthy after Kennedy died. They had seen Bobby as their only hope, and no one could substitute for that. That was one reason why Humphrey had lost so big in November.

But Lucy's comment was a little weird. How could Darla have thought she had gotten Kennedy killed? By asking him to run?

That was a lot of misplaced guilt.

I frowned. "Was she Catholic?"

"I don't know," Lucy said. "She didn't go to Mass or anything. Why?"

And then Lucy made a face at me as a thought hit her.

"Not everyone who likes a Kennedy is Catholic," she said, as if she had explained that before.

"I know," I said. "Just something you said."

I shook my head. I wasn't very good at this.

Then I decided to be somewhat honest.

"I'm confused," I said. "You told me she was giving out flyers at Homecoming. That was, like, October, right?"

I was guessing. I had no real idea. Usually Homecoming was late September, early October at most colleges.

"Yeah, for all the good it did us," Lucy said. "They were having a 'sit-out.' No one was supposed to go to football, like football is the

Antichrist. And y'know, people listened. I don't get it. Who doesn't go to football? Jeez."

The politics of all of these movements had started to confuse me. How was I supposed to react? Was I supposed to support Lucy's opinion? Or the opinion of the students who staged the—what had she called it?—the sit-out.

"And we got called all kinds of names, you know, like about us personally, how we looked, and ah, hell you know. It was filthy." She shook her head. "I decided not to go back."

"And Darla too?" I asked in my normal voice. Lucy glanced at me, as if she hadn't expected that.

"No," she said, frowning. "She didn't say anything about it. And when I tried to talk to her, she changed the subject. I think she met some guy."

My heart started to pound and I wasn't sure why.

"You think?"

"Yeah," she said, "but I never saw him again. He was older, kinda straight-looking, but then, most guys at the football game were straight-looking. Freaks don't go to games, you know?"

I nodded, even though I didn't know. I supposed I would if I were in college.

She waved her hand, almost dismissively, but she wasn't looking at me. She was lost in a memory.

"That guy," she said, "that guy was weird. She talked to him for a long time."

"Did he drive a truck?" I asked.

She looked at me like I had lost my mind. "How the hell do I know?"

"I just thought, have you heard about that guy with the truck? Because I've been warned to stay away from him." I made myself sound scared. It wasn't hard.

She shook her head. "I haven't heard anything about any truck. But Darla, she wouldn't talk to me about the guy. And she didn't go back with the flyers, but I figured that was because it was such a bummer."

"She didn't date him?" I asked.

"She didn't date anybody that I know of," Lucy said. "If she did, she never brought the guy here. But then, who would? I mean, three other girls? Thin walls? If he had a better place, then she could've gone there."

I almost asked if she spent a lot of nights away from here, but that felt like I was crossing a line.

I didn't know what to do with the information Lucy was giving me. And I didn't know how to keep pushing without seeming completely weird.

I had to end this conversation, partly for me. I was getting really uncomfortable.

I walked out of the bedroom, musing aloud as I went. "So, fifty bucks a month. That's a lot of money."

"Not really," Lucy said, almost defensively. "Not for a place like this."

"Well, it is for me," I said as defensively. "I mean, I thought it would be cheap. Because I thought Darla was on scholarship, which I thought meant no money. But I guess I didn't understand something or something. I don't know."

"Darla *was* on scholarship," Lucy said. "She worked three jobs her first year, and bitched a lot, because doing that and the homework was tough on her. But she got some good job last fall, and she never mentioned money again."

"What job?" I asked, trying to make it sound like *I* wanted that job, not like I wanted to know more about Darla.

"I don't know," Lucy said, apparently unconcerned with this part of my nosiness. "She never said. But she didn't seem to have a lot of hours, and she had more money than all of us. It was weird."

Then she looked at me fiercely, as if I had asked another question, even though I hadn't.

"And before you say anything, she wasn't dealing. I would have known. She would've been kicked out of here."

Something in her tone made me think she had snooped through Darla's stuff when she wasn't here, to see if there had been any dope.

"No dope at all, huh?" I asked.

"Yee-ah," Lucy said as if that were the dumbest question I could ask. "If she was dealing, we could've all been arrested, and my dad wouldn't've believed me if I said I wasn't involved. That was, like, something we all had to agree to. And no smoking weed in the apartment. Because Dad said when he bought the place, he said he could just as easily rent to some other students as us, and we didn't dare forget it."

Obviously she hadn't.

"You think she disappeared because of drugs?" I asked quietly.

"No." Lucy's answer was firm. "She was getting straight As. You don't do that and toke up, you know?"

Straight As. Came into money. Stopped talking to her friends. None of this added up.

"Have you talked to anyone else about her disappearing?" I asked.

"Just the other two girls," Lucy said. "I thought maybe she was visiting them or something. She wasn't."

We reached the living room. It no longer looked like a slobby mess to me. It looked like one girl's cry for help. Lucy, who felt all alone.

I could empathize.

"I don't know if I should move in here," I said. "I don't want to take her room away."

"We'd just move her to the other room," Lucy said.

"And then what when the others come back? I mean, it seems too up in the air to me."

Lucy bit her lower lip. "I don't think she's—oh, I don't know. I get it, but I'd like company, you know?"

I nodded. "I can't move in, though, thinking I might have to move again. Sorry."

I extended my hand. Lucy looked at it like it was covered in mud. My "decision" not to take the apartment had made her angry. Which was ironic, considering she hadn't even thought about the possibility of a sublet before I came here.

"She's just screwing us," Lucy said. "Jeez."

"I think something's wrong," I said. "I think you should do something."

"You figure out what I should do, you tell me," Lucy said. "Because I sure have no *fucking* idea."

She yanked the door open and stood beside it, waiting for me to leave.

"Thanks," I said as I walked out.

"For nothing," she said, and slammed the door so hard that the wall shook.

I stood there for a moment. I would have thought that Darla moved because Lucy was so volatile if it weren't for that stuffed dog.

If Darla had hated it in this apartment, she would have taken the stuffed dog, just like she had brought it to college with her.

A straight-A student, who had come into money, who was not political, and who was missing.

I liked this less than I had when I arrived.

And I had no idea what to do with the information I'd gotten.

I had no idea at all.

VAL

I hovered in the entry of the apartment building longer than I should have. I was deeply disturbed by my conversation with Lucy. Finally, I had taken a piece of paper from my purse, and I had written my phone number on it, along with a note.

If you hear from Darla, call me.

I hadn't signed it, because I couldn't bring myself to do that, not with the false name. I slid the note under Lucy's door, and then I left.

I meandered my way home. I thought of going back to the gym, but I had no idea if the others would be there. Pammy probably would, but she would be teaching. Eagle was supposed to be visiting hospitals.

And honestly, I was exhausted. My muscles ached, and I had dealt with more emotions than I had in a long time. Not just other people's but my own as well.

Lucy had presented me with a conundrum.

Darla had come into money. Darla wasn't involved in any movement. Darla wasn't selling drugs.

Darla had disappeared, and no one knew how to find her.

I had disappeared as well, and no one knew how to find me. I had disappeared just like Darla had: Everyone thought I was doing one thing—traveling—when I was really doing something else.

I had left home for good.

The streets were filled with college kids and professors, all moving with some kind of purpose. The occasional businessman would weave his way through them, probably heading to his parking space.

I walked, and didn't weave as much as kept to the curb.

Even if the cops were interested in Darla's disappearance, they probably wouldn't investigate. They knew that most missing persons—if those persons weren't children—had either disappeared on purpose or they had no idea that others thought they were missing. It wasn't worth the manpower or the resources to search for someone who either wanted to get away or would return on their own.

I knew exactly how Truman would have handled this investigation, because once he learned how interested I was in procedure, he would tell me the unusual ways he would get information from someone unwilling to give it.

With missing persons, he would say, the questions most cops asked weren't the right ones. Questions like *Where did you last see the missing person?* only told you where the person and the reporting party had last been at the same time. Questions like that told you as much about the person reporting as the person missing.

The same with *Did she say she was leaving town?* and other questions of that ilk. Because all they did was reveal more about the *relationship* between the missing person and the reporting party.

If cops actually had the time to do lots of legwork, and managed to talk with everyone, then maybe they would get the information they wanted with those questions. Otherwise, the questions were useless.

Because, if someone were investigating my "disappearance" from Chicago, they would get different stories depending on who they asked. They would get a hundred answers from people who had "no idea" that Val was gone, let alone missing. Those same people wouldn't tell the police about my reasons for leaving, either, with all the losses that I suffered, because I had only told two people.

If the cops failed to talk to Marvella or Paulette, then they would never be able to figure out that I had left deliberately. And they certainly wouldn't be able to check with me, because neither Marvella or Paulette knew where I had ended up.

If Marvella or Paulette had guessed, they would still have been wrong, because I hadn't had any idea where I was going when I left Chicago. I only knew I was going west.

Based on past conversations, Marvella and Paulette might have told the police that I probably ended up in Madison, since I had some friends there, or that I was thinking about Boston, which I had a few years ago. I had vowed I would never go south. It frightened me down there, so they might mention that.

But I had never mentioned California—at least not as a place to disappear to—and they wouldn't consider it, any more than I initially had.

They were probably so worried about me. And they had no way to find me.

I veered into a deli I hadn't seen before to pick up dinner. It looked like they were getting ready to close. Most of the meat was out of the glass cabinets, and only one person stood behind the cash register.

I ordered a roast beef and cheddar with horseradish on rye. As the man behind the counter took the last of the roast beef out of the glass cabinet, I glanced around the deli.

Small, spotless tables. A refrigeration unit with bottles of soda. Some scattered newspapers. And a rack of postcards.

The postcards made me let out a small breath. I didn't want to call Marvella or Paulette. I couldn't talk to them—not yet.

But a postcard would solve it all. I could tell them I ended up here, send them my address, and let them know I would be in touch.

I wandered over to the rack and found a cheery *Greetings From Berkeley!* postcard. It had a jaunty hand-drawn map with the bay, the parks, and the campus. I grabbed two, and paid for them along with my sandwich.

Then I walked the rest of the way home, still uncertain about what to do about Darla. But at least I had rejoined the land of the living—as far as what was left of my family was concerned.

PAMMY

The last class ended at 8:30. The women filed into the locker room like it could fit all of them. Some emerged quickly, holding purses, car keys, an extra pair of shoes. Others lined up for the shower.

Pammy hoped Stella wouldn't show up early. In theory, Stella was going to bring a woman and her daughter to the door off the alley, but theories didn't always work as planned.

Pammy stood near the counter and glanced at the plate-glass window. The street was in shadow, but it still had some late-summer evening light. A group of her students stood just outside, talking and laughing. The laughter in particular filtered through the glass. The sound of the shower continued behind Pammy.

She should have ended the class earlier. She wanted to, and then she got involved explaining how to properly make a fist, and there were questions, and the next thing she knew, it was 8:25. Wrapping everything up took an extra five minutes, no matter how hard she tried to speed it up.

She looked at the wristwatch she almost never wore. It was a girl's Timex with a brown leather band. Her father had given it to her when she graduated from high school, telling her that being on time was as important as being honest and trustworthy.

She had stopped wearing the watch when she opened the gym, but she kept the watch here. She still used it to keep track of the time—the last thing she wanted was a clock overhead so that the students would watch it—but she was afraid the watch would get damaged because she forgot she had it on.

Tonight, she had put it on to remember to pay attention to the time. It had worked. The band felt tight against her skin. Tight and uncomfortable. The leather had hardened since she stopped wearing it regularly.

It was 8:40. The showers were still running, but no women had threaded their way out of the locker room in the last five minutes.

At quarter to, she'd go in and remind them that she had to close up shop at 9:00.

The front door opened, letting in the laughter from the group of women still congregated out front. Pammy glanced over, expecting one of them to have returned.

Instead, Strawberry walked in, wearing a gauzy white dress without a bra underneath it. Pammy winced. She hated the braless trend among some young women, particularly when they made no effort to hide their nipples.

She liked to think her response was a protective one, but she suspected her age was showing, just a bit. The few times she'd mentioned the braless thing to some of her students, they had laughed at her and called her old-fashioned.

Men can go without shirts, they would often say. *Why can't we?*

She never answered them. But she wanted to argue: *In a perfect world, women can do anything. But this world isn't perfect and women have to live in it, dealing with the men around them and the realities on the ground.*

That was one reason why she taught women how to defend themselves—the realities of the world they all lived in.

She realized suddenly that she was staring at Strawberry's torso, and flushed.

Strawberry didn't seem to notice. She walked up to the counter, and plunked her backpack on top. The backpack clanked.

"I got two lists, like you asked, and baby food," she said, sounding cheerful, as if the tensions from the afternoon had never happened.

"Baby food?" Pammy asked, heart sinking.

"Oh, yeah, didn't I tell you? Stella asked for baby food too, but the store I went to on Telegraph this afternoon didn't have any, so I had to go to Safeway tonight. There wasn't a lot of choice."

Pammy let out a small sigh. "I didn't realize that Stella was bringing a baby."

"She didn't say exactly what she was doing," Strawberry said, "so I have no idea what's going on except that it sounds bad. I feel like we've become a way station in the Underground Railroad or something. The woman's only going to spend one night before she moves on somewhere else."

Pammy sighed. She felt out of control. She should have known about the baby. And she didn't like the way that Strawberry talked. The gym was for the women who came here, yes, but it wasn't a "we." It was Pammy's gym.

Maybe she would have to remind everyone about that. A lot of rules had gotten lost since the riots in the spring.

"Take the food to the kitchen," she said, "and leave me the lists."

"Yes, sir!" Strawberry saluted. Apparently Pammy's tone was crisper than she had intended it to be.

Strawberry pushed the papers she had brought with her toward Pammy, and picked up the backpack. It clanked again. Pammy hoped that the baby food was well packed, because from the sound of that clanking, the glass jars might have cracked inside the pack.

She pulled the papers Strawberry had left toward her. Strawberry had brought two piles, both yellow legal paper with the sheets stapled together.

Strawberry walked around the counter, and said hi to someone behind her, then headed toward the kitchen, sandals squeaking.

Two women, hair wet from the shower, passed Pammy and said their goodnights. The showers still hummed behind her, though, which meant that someone was still in the locker room.

Pammy turned the papers around. One list was titled *Truck List*, and the other was titled *Vanished!* Both were covered in big loopy handwriting.

Pammy didn't care about the truck list, at least not at this moment. Where Strawberry and her friends had heard about the truck really didn't matter right now, not as much as the list of people who had disappeared.

Pammy moved the handwritten list next to the list that the students from the earlier class had given her.

Strawberry's list did not have organizations marked beside the names. Pammy couldn't exactly remember what Strawberry's instructions were. Had they known at that moment to add the organizations to the list or had Pammy just done that on her own, after the prolonged discussion with Strawberry?

"Hey, Pammy! See you next week!"

She looked up. Two more women were walking out, leaving the scent of soap and perfume behind them. Neither of them looked back at her as they left.

She glanced at the wristwatch again. It was quarter to. She sighed, wanting to go through the names, not police her gym, hustling everyone out so that Stella's friend could show up.

Pammy turned the papers over and placed two mostly empty cups on top of them. The cups had just a few drops of water in them, not enough to damage the papers if the cups fell over. But the cups' presence should be just enough deterrent for anyone who wanted to see exactly what Pammy was up to.

She went to the locker room and opened the door. A wall of fragrant steam hit her. Four women, all in different stages of undress, looked up at her. Only one grabbed a towel and placed it over her mostly-clad body, as if Pammy had offended her modesty.

One shower remained on, the dark shower curtain pulled. The other shower dripped onto the tile that she had laid herself. Water pooled slightly on the drain, something she was going to have to fix.

The room felt crowded. It was barely big enough for all four women and for Pammy. She had no idea how more women had managed to squeeze inside.

"I'm getting ready to close up," she said. "I have an appointment at nine. Would you let her know?"

She nodded toward the shower, since she had no idea who was in there.

"Sure," said the woman wearing the towel. She was new-ish. This was her second week of class. She had been doing pretty well, too, as if she already had some athletic experience.

"Thanks," Pammy said, and pulled the door closed. She rubbed her hand over her face, removing the beads of water that the steam had left behind.

She wiped her wet hand on the side of her shorts, and glanced at the kitchen door. She had forgotten to eat dinner. She did that sometimes, and she always paid for it later.

But she wasn't going in there right now, not with Strawberry setting everything up for Stella. If Stella and her friend arrived early, Pammy was counting on Strawberry to keep them out of the main room until the remaining women left.

Pammy went back to the counter and took the cups off the lists. She looked at the first name on the large list again—Britt Stevens. She assumed that was a girl's name, but she couldn't be sure. The writing was unclear in both cases. It might have been Brett Stevens.

She sighed, then ran her hand down Strawberry's list. Pammy didn't see a Britt or a Brett. There was a Steven Klepple, but that name was significantly different from Brett or Britt Stevens so that Pammy didn't think they were the same person.

Why couldn't this project be easy? With her thumb and forefinger, she rubbed the bridge of her nose, willing the tension away.

"Almost everyone's dressed."

She jumped and turned, not realizing that someone stood behind her. The new woman had a towel rolled up under one arm and a purse in the other. She was wearing a yellow sundress and sandals. She looked like someone who was heading to dinner, not someone who had just exercised.

"I think they'll be out in a minute or two," she added.

"Thanks," Pammy said, and resisted the urge to look at her watch.

The woman waved and went out the front door. Pammy frowned. The shower wasn't running any longer, which was a good sign.

She resisted the urge to go back to the locker room and demand that everyone leave.

Instead, she went over the lists again. No Britt/Brett Stevens on Strawberry's list. Steven Klepple on Strawberry's list, but not on the large list.

Although how could Pammy know that for certain? For all she knew, Steven Klepple was *Janus (Nickname)* as one person was listed, or maybe he was *Soapy (m)* as someone had listed someone else. (Who let himself be called "Soapy?" and why?)

"Thanks, Pammy!"

She looked up. The remaining four women were almost to the front door. She hadn't even noticed them passing her.

She waved at the women, then grabbed her keys and followed, noting that it was getting darker outside. No one stood on the sidewalk any longer, and the streets weren't as full of life as they had been in the afternoon.

She exchanged pleasantries with the last of the women to go through the door, then pulled it closed and locked it, turning over the closed sign.

She walked to the counter, dropped the keys on it, and then kept going to the locker room. She pushed open the door. It smelled damp inside, but the waves of steam were gone. The lights were still on, and some wet towels lay on the floor beneath the only bench that fit into the place.

Both showers dripped, and water was still puddled around the drain. The water puddle looked smaller than it had before, so the drain still worked, but it was something she would have to take care of.

Just like she would have to clean this room before she went home.

Maybe before she rebuilt the front, she could hire someone to clean on a regular basis.

She shut off the light and pulled that door closed, then glanced at her watch.

9:05.

She looked at the kitchen door like it was the enemy. No one had come for her, which, she supposed, was a good thing. At least the other women hadn't known what Stella was going to do.

Pammy took a deep breath, then headed to the kitchen. As she reached the door, she heard voices, and her shoulders sagged.

They had arrived.

She opened the door. Strawberry was on her feet, near the kitchen entrance, holding a baby in her arms. The baby had one pudgy hand wrapped around Strawberry's right finger. Strawberry was bouncing the baby and cooing at it—at her, judging by the pink footie pajamas—and the baby was staring at her as if it had never seen anyone like her before.

Stella stood near the kitchen table, her silver-blonde hair filled with so much hairspray it looked like a wig. She wore a denim day dress with a gigantic turquoise necklace around her neck. She probably had matching earrings, but her earlobes were bare—and red, which meant that the clip-ons she usually wore were in the matching denim purse that sat in the center of the kitchen table. Her rings, also silver and turquoise, glinted in the kitchen's overhead light.

Although her jewelry alone probably cost more than everything in the kitchen, the outfit was dressed down for Stella. Her husband, one of the regents of the University of California system, always insisted that she look the part of an influential man's wife. If Stella wore blue jeans and a loose top, with no jewelry at all, her husband would notice and comment.

He probably didn't like this outfit much either, but it was fashionable. And practical, at least for the things Stella was doing this evening.

There was a small woman behind Stella, but Pammy couldn't quite see her. She had moved out of Pammy's line of sight the moment Pammy came into the room.

"Pamela Griffin," Stella said, her voice as formal as it would be in a faculty party, "this is Norma, and her daughter Raquel."

Norma raised her hand, but didn't move. Pammy frowned, and Stella seemed to realize that Norma was hiding behind her, so Stella moved aside.

Norma's face was black, green, and purple. Someone had used her as a punching bag. Her left eye was swollen shut, and the left side of her mouth had a black scab over the lips.

Despite her annoyance, Pammy felt her heart go out to this woman.

"Hi," Pammy said. "Welcome."

Norma nodded, then looked down with her good eye.

"We don't have a really comfortable place to sleep, but Stella said this is just for one night, right?"

Norma shrugged.

"She can't go home," Stella said. "I'm trying to figure out a place to put her, but her husband—"

"My husband is Luciano Paolinie," Norma said, lisping the words.

Stella winced. Strawberry stopped bouncing the baby and looked at Norma. Pammy caught herself before she could gasp.

Luciano Paolinie was one of the stars of San Francisco's growing classical music scene. His performances mixed classical music and modern rock songs, and had received some international attention.

He was, in Bay Area circles, a Big Deal.

Pammy's gaze met Stella's. Stella sighed quietly, then shrugged almost imperceptivity. Usually they agreed that they wouldn't give Pammy or anyone here much information about the women who came through.

"I'm sorry," Norma said, looking at Stella. Something in Norma's tone said she wasn't sorry at all. She had deliberately not followed instructions. "It's just...I keep telling Stella...it's hopeless. He'll find me. He's friends with the mayor."

"Of San Francisco," Stella clarified.

"And the chief of police, and everyone else. I can't...they don't...no one will help, and after last night...." A tear leaked out of Norma's good eye. "I mean, look."

She extended her arms for the baby, and Pammy looked at her skin. Her arms had old yellowing bruises, and so, it seemed, did her torso, partially visible through the openings under the arms of her sleeveless shirt.

Strawberry gave the baby to Norma, who unzipped the pajama top.

"See?" she said, pointing at the baby's right shoulder.

Pammy leaned forward. The beautiful soft skin had the unmistakable image of a hand that had gripped too tightly, revealed in five separate bruises—long finger marks, and a palm print on the shoulder's top.

"I had to get her out, but I don't know, my parents, they—he'll go there first. And she cried. Oh, my God, she cried." Norma swallowed hard. "I have to get her out."

Stella wasn't looking at the bruise. She was looking at Pammy.

"Has anyone looked at this?" Pammy asked.

"The police? No, I said—"

"I meant a doctor," Pammy said.

Norma shook her head. "He'll yell at me if I take her to a doctor. He thinks that makes us look weak."

"Makes *him* look weak," Strawberry muttered. "The freakin' asshole."

"I can't go back," Norma said, mistaking Pammy's silence for disapproval. Norma waved a hand at her face. "I can't. He did this when I got in the way. She didn't cry when he did this, only after I managed to get her away from him. She's only five months and she already knows to be quiet when he's around, and I'm afraid she's not going to…"

Norma clearly couldn't finish the sentence. She didn't need to. Pammy understood.

"You can stay here," Pammy said.

"But just tonight, right?" Norma swung her head around quickly to look at Stella, probably for confirmation, lost her balance and nearly fell.

Strawberry grabbed the baby while Stella held Norma in place.

"I'm calling someone," Pammy said. "Just hang on."

"No police, please," Norma said. "Please."

"Not police," Pammy said. "We need someone to look at you."

"I'm fine," Norma said. "Really. It just looks worse than it is."

Pammy had heard that before. Her friend Linda used to say that all the time.

Pammy knew better than to contradict a woman who had been lying about beatings for years.

"I know you're all right," Pammy said.

"You gotta be kidding me," Strawberry said.

"But," Pammy talked over her on purpose. "I'm not so sure about little Raquel, given what you've been saying. Let's make sure she's okay."

"You can't take her," Norma said. "I don't want to lose her. She needs me—"

"I'll have someone come here," Pammy said. "Don't worry. She's trustworthy."

"She is," Stella said. "She's helped others in similar circumstances."

Strawberry took the baby and gently pulled the pajama top over the bruise. "She's gruff."

Pammy opened her mouth to contradict Strawberry.

"But," Strawberry continued, just the way Pammy had a moment before, "she knows her stuff really good. You can trust her."

Norma looked from woman to woman as if she couldn't believe she was here. Then her knees collapsed underneath her. Stella caught her and eased her into a chair.

"You're safe here," Stella said softly.

"What if he comes here?" Norma asked.

"He doesn't even know this place exists," Stella said. "No one does."

"Your husband—"

"Thinks I play too much bridge," Stella said with a smile. "You've even heard him complain about it."

Norma smiled as best she could with an injured mouth.

"Can I ask a weird question?" Strawberry said, juggling the baby from one hip to the other. Little Raquel didn't protest at all. Her large blue eyes remained on her mother.

Pammy shook her head slightly. She didn't want any more complications.

But Stella shrugged, and Strawberry took that as an invitation.

"I thought your husband was a musician. Don't they protect their hands?"

Pammy cursed silently. Stella stiffened. They tried not to talk about what had just happened, thinking it was probably best.

But Norma didn't seem upset by the question at all.

"He sings," she said. "He's very protective of his voice. He never yells, never raises his voice. I think that's why no one believes me. Because he's so soft spoken, and so…."

She couldn't seem to finish the thought.

"I believe you," Stella said. "I believed before you did."

That almost sounded blaming. Pammy didn't want that either. It might make Norma leave. And as much as Pammy hadn't wanted her here before, now she didn't want Norma to go back to a man who would hit his wife so badly that it was impossible to tell what she looked like.

And Pammy certainly didn't want baby Raquel to ever get near the man again.

"I know you believed me," Norma whispered. "I just never thought… I thought he loved Raquel. I did."

Strawberry looked over the baby's head at Pammy. Strawberry had gone pale.

"You got a call to make," Strawberry said, sounding like the oldest, most responsible person in the room.

Pammy nodded. She headed out of the kitchen to call Eagle.

EAGLE

The phone rang, jarring Eagle out of a sound sleep. She'd been hunched on her couch, head back, mouth with a lingering after-taste of the tuna salad sandwich she had made herself for dinner. She rubbed her eyes and glanced at the clock on her stove.

Who the hell would call at ten at night? She hadn't left any messages. Four hospitals, six names per contact, and nothing. She had given up around 7:00 p.m. when it became clear that people who worked in Records kept pretty normal business hours.

The phone rang again. Only one person was that persistent.

Pammy, with another emergency at the gym. Bring the full medical bag, she said.

Eagle didn't tell her to be more cautious, even though she wanted to. Beginners got hurt. *Women* got hurt. Pammy seemed oblivious to that.

Still, Eagle answered the summons like she always did, grabbing her large black medical bag and some extra bandages, and let herself out of the apartment.

Halfway down the stairs she realized she hadn't combed her hair, washed her face, or straightened her clothes. She probably looked as ruffled as she felt.

But it didn't matter. If someone was hurt, they wouldn't care how she looked as long as she made them feel better.

It didn't take her long to get to the gym. Force of habit took her to the back door. She stepped inside, smelled something spicy—mustard?—overlaid with old coffee and the faint hint of poop, which she didn't ever recall smelling here before.

She closed the door behind her and locked it, wondering if maybe the smells had come in from the alley with her. But they got stronger as she walked into the kitchen proper, and then realized where the poop smell came from.

The hippie-dippy ding-a-ling, Strawberry, leaned against the counter, a baby in her arms. The baby made Eagle stop entirely. She hadn't thought Strawberry had a kid, but nothing should surprise her. Even the fact that Strawberry wasn't changing the kid's diaper.

Pammy stood by the door, holding a plate in her hands with a half-eaten sandwich on it. She looked tired.

Stella D'Arbus was dumping the contents of the percolator into the sink. She wore a denim dress that probably cost more than Eagle's entire wardrobe. The belt, made of turquoise and silver, definitely cost more than Eagle had earned in her entire life.

The woman would have irritated Eagle—*had* irritated Eagle, in fact—if she hadn't managed to save at least two lives that Eagle knew about. Stella's presence told Eagle that Pammy's phone call hadn't been about the gym.

It had probably been about the woman who sat with her back to Eagle, who seemed unaware that anyone else had come into the room. She was crouched over the table, holding a glass of milk in a shaking hand.

Eagle braced herself, glad that she hadn't indulged in any weed for days now. She felt clear-headed, and she had a hunch she needed to be.

"What've we got?" she asked Pammy.

The mystery woman jumped and turned, and Eagle's words faded. The mystery woman's face was covered in bruises and contusions. Judging by the color of the bruises, they were at least twenty-four hours old. Her left eye had swollen shut. The entire left side of her face was misshapen, and not just from swelling.

"Are you the doctor?" the woman asked, sounding desperate. She spoke out of only one side of her mouth.

"Not quite," Eagle said.

"We call her the combat medic," Stella said. "She was a nurse in Vietnam."

Strawberry froze ever so slightly, her gaze meeting Eagle's. Eagle couldn't tell if that hippie-dippy girl resented Eagle's service, was impressed by it, or simply hadn't realized that Eagle was here.

"Can you look at my baby?" the woman asked.

Eagle's breath left her body. She hadn't expected that at all. But she had learned a long time ago to keep her face impassive, even when the people she was trying to help surprised her.

Eagle walked deeper into the kitchen, setting her bag on the table. She stopped beside Strawberry. The baby wasn't crying. Her eyes were clear and very blue. They took in Eagle as if they'd never seen anything like her before.

"What happened to her?" Eagle asked, keeping her voice mild.

"My husband..." the woman said softly as Strawberry gently moved the collar of the baby's footie pajamas away from the baby's shoulder.

Eagle stepped closer and didn't touch. The handprint was shockingly red and purple, the kind of bruise no child should ever have. It was also swollen just a bit.

She touched it carefully, feeling for broken bones. She didn't find any, and the baby didn't cry, which meant Eagle was either being very, very gentle or there were no fractures.

Eagle almost asked if this was the only injury the baby had suffered, and then remembered seeing injuries like this on children before. Sometimes, the parent mentioned the minor injury but not the major one.

"Let's get her comfortable," Eagle said. "I want to examine her—and she needs a diaper change anyway."

Strawberry nodded. "Where do we do this?"

"Let's take her to the bench in the locker room," Pammy said. "I'll clean it off, set down some towels, get a bag for the diaper. Do you have another?"

She asked Stella that.

Stella nodded. She set the percolator down and went to the back of the kitchen, removing a pink Pampers box from a paper bag. Beside the paper bag was a some kind of baby carrier. It was pink and made of thick material, and looked a little like a combination of a basket and a baby buggy without the wheels or the handle.

At least the kid would have somewhere to sleep tonight.

Pammy hadn't waited for Stella's answer, instead leaving the room and heading to the locker room. Strawberry followed with the baby, as did Stella with the Pampers.

Eagle waited until they had left before she turned to the woman. She pulled the other kitchen chair back and sat down beside her.

"My baby first," the woman said.

"In a minute," Eagle said. "Let them set everything up. I want to look at your face."

"I'm okay," the woman said.

"I know." Eagle set her hands on her knees. "I want to touch the injury. Is that all right?"

The woman shook her head. "Raquel first."

Raquel. What a mouthful for such a little thing.

Eagle wasn't going to argue with the woman. She needed the woman's trust.

"I'll take care of her if you tell me what happened to her." Eagle spoke softly. "The others don't need to hear."

The woman kept her head bowed. There was dried blood in her blonde hair as well.

"He...she was in her high chair. Just eating. Banging her spoon. You know. Baby things." Her voice trembled. "He put his hand on her shoulders. He was looking at me. He said I had to keep her quiet, but she was so good. She stayed quiet when he touched her. She didn't make a sound."

Eagle imagined her own hands gripping her knees to remain calm. But she didn't dare move, didn't dare show a reaction, or this woman would shut up.

"I...I tried to make him move, and he..." She raised her hand to her face. "And that's when she started to cry. He'd let go of her, so I grabbed her and I said if he touched me while I was holding her, then he could kill her, and he..."

Eagle braced herself for something worse.

244

"He...he left." The woman nodded, as if confirming her own story in her mind. "He left."

There was a lot more to the story. The bruises said that. But Eagle wasn't going to push.

She hoped that the part about the baby was true.

"I waited until I heard his car pull out and then I called Stella. She'd said she knew how to help. That was last night, but I knew if I wasn't there when he got back, he'd look for us, so I told Stella, I said we'd wait until he left for rehearsal, and she said that ..."

The woman shook her head, as if she didn't want to remember what Stella had exactly said.

"...anyway, he left. And she got us, and we came here."

Rehearsal. Eagle's brain tripped over that word. It was an odd one. Not *left for work*. Left for *rehearsal*.

"I...I could stay, but Raquel...he's never...she cried all night, and he was so mad, and finally I got her quiet, and he slept, and I thought..." The woman shrugged. "It doesn't matter. We're here, and Stella says we can be safe. If he doesn't find us."

"I won't say anything." Eagle knew that was what the woman wanted to hear, as if her husband Knew All and Saw All. Some women were like that. They'd been under their husband's thumb for so long, they figured he could read their minds.

"Will we be safe?" The woman asked.

Eagle nodded. "We'll make sure of it." *If I have to shoot the son-of-a-bitch myself.*

God, what a last few days. She hated this.

"Will you make sure Raquel's okay? I hated waiting, but it seemed wise."

If it got you out of the house, Eagle almost said, but didn't. She couldn't comment on any of it. She had to make sure that baby had no other injuries.

"Come with me," Eagle said. "She'll trust me more if you're in there too."

The woman raised her gaze to Eagle's. "I don't—"

"She'll need you," Eagle said. "I've done this before. It's better for the baby."

And it made certain that the woman wouldn't have a change of heart, search out the phone, and call the rat-bastard to apologize.

The woman put her hand on the table, started to get up, and stopped. "I'll just wait."

She had a lot more injuries than the ones on her face. Eagle pretended not to notice, not yet anyway.

"Let me help you up," she said.

"No, I can do it," the woman said, then pulled herself up, going so pale that for a moment, Eagle thought the woman was going to faint.

Eagle put a hand near her back, so that she could catch the woman if she did fall.

The woman gave her half a smile, or maybe a full smile. It was impossible to tell with those bruises.

"I'm okay," she said in such a cheerful voice that had Eagle not been watching her, Eagle would have thought she was just fine.

The lie had gotten the woman this far. God knew how many times she had used it to move herself forward.

Eagle grabbed her bag but made sure it was in the hand on the other side of the woman.

Together, they walked out of the kitchen and to the little baby in that locker room.

And the whole way, Eagle hoped that little Raquel had suffered none of the injuries her mother had.

Because if the baby was badly injured, Eagle would have to get her to a nearby emergency room. And she didn't want to do that.

She didn't want the husband to have any chance of finding them ever again.

VAL

Eleven p.m., and I couldn't sleep. I lay on the bed, the willow tree rustling outside my window, my heart jumping with each rustle. I toyed with closing the window, but it was still warm inside my apartment, even though it had cooled to the lower sixties outside.

I had fans in two windows—one in the living room and one in the kitchen—but I couldn't face having a fan in the bedroom window. The white noise hid all other sounds, and I had learned that I needed to hear each rustle, each cough outdoors, each creak of the old building.

Another legacy from *him*, one I'd be happy to get rid of.

Although, if I were honest with myself, it wasn't just the rustling that was keeping me awake. It was the conversation with Lucy. I kept replaying it in my head.

I got up and grabbed my robe off the chair beside the bed. I slipped on my robe as I walked into the living room, where the hum of the fan was reassuring rather than irritating. The living room was ten degrees cooler than the bedroom.

I propped open the double doors so that the bedroom would cool off, and went into the kitchen, flipping on the light once I was inside.

247

The kitchen sparkled. I had cleaned it after I ate dinner, scrubbing the scratched countertops to within an inch of their lives. The kitchen still smelled faintly of bleach.

My own demons were some of the reason for the excessive cleanliness, but some of the reason was the condition of Lucy's apartment. The filth bothered me and reminded me how easy it was for a single, somewhat depressed person who lived alone to spiral into such a mess that she couldn't recover from it.

I didn't want my new home to reflect my inner turmoil, so perhaps I went overboard. Perhaps I had cleaned too deeply. My hands were red and raw, and no amount of lotion I had put on them seemed to fix that.

I pulled out the loaf of bread that I'd bought the day before and cut a slice. Then I put it in the toaster and located the peanut butter while I waited. I poured myself a glass of water and leaned against the counter.

I couldn't seem to shake the thought that no one could do anything about Darla. Her roommate hadn't contacted the police. Her father couldn't confirm that she was missing—at least, not in a way that the police would believe.

Besides, so many kids ran off these days. It was all over the news. And the kids were so disrespectful to the police that the police didn't seem to care.

Or maybe they didn't care.

Truman had taught me that. He had shown me, sometimes dramatically, just how human police officers were. Even though he had darker skin than I did, he was often as dismissive of blacks as the white police officers were. When I finally challenged him on it, he had whirled on me:

People on the South Side don't see my skin color, Val. They see my uniform, and react to that. And they react poorly.

Even after he was promoted to detective, he never forgot that treatment. He would do the job as best he could—he was an honorable man—but he wouldn't go the extra mile for someone who didn't respect him or the police.

He would hate Berkeley. He would have choice words for it.

The toast popped up, and I spread peanut butter on it. I took a bite, then sipped some water, and frowned.

Truman used to say the one thing most cops never did on a missing person's case unless that case became important was to contact other precincts. Not just to check for a John Doe, but to see if there were some new hookers or junkies or homeless people around. And to see if there were any unsolved homicides that fell inside the range of the disappearance—and that range had to include the two weeks before the person ostensibly disappeared.

I couldn't get a warrant for Darla's home even if I wanted one, not that I needed one. I had gotten a good look at Darla's apartment. I certainly couldn't talk to the bank in any official capacity to find out what she was spending her money on.

But I could get information from the police. Especially right now.

Thanks to Truman, I had learned that the people who worked late at night in a police precinct cared a lot less for standard protocol than the day staff. Sure, they had a desk sergeant and someone handling dispatch. But the detective squad was thin at night, and the beat patrol officers were on the prowl.

Arrests and processing still happened, but civilians with requests were told to wait until the next day. People generally knew that and respected it.

So calls into a precinct at this time of night were either from people in trouble or from other law enforcement officials.

My heart rate increased. Impersonating a police officer was against the law in any state, but I didn't have to impersonate a police *officer*. There were lots of other employees in a precinct who handled grunt work.

I took a sip of water, got out the phone book, and looked up the general number for the Berkeley police. The phone listings showed me that Berkeley didn't have precincts. From what I could tell, it had only one police station.

I paused, wondering if what I was going to do would work. I had planned to call from one precinct to another. But with only one station, the ruse would be harder. Although there were several other police departments nearby. Oakland had one. Emeryville had another, and San Francisco probably did have precincts.

I wished I had the Bay Area phonebook, like Pammy had. Instead, I had to let my fingers do the walking, like they said in the stupid Yellow Pages ad. I dialed O on the telephone and got the operator.

"I need to reach the general number for a San Francisco police precinct," I said. "I'm just not sure which one. Can you list them for me?"

"According to the listings," she said, "San Francisco does not have precincts. It has bureaus, divisions, and stations. Which would you like?"

My breath caught in surprise. I knew that different regions had different police practices, but I didn't expect a completely different structure.

"Would you mind reading me the names of the bureaus?" I asked.

She did. Bureaus seemed to be some sort of central clearing for information, for such a large police force. Field Operations were separate from Investigations.

And none of that did me any good. I asked her for divisions, and she asked for more clarification. I was getting confused. She was getting confused, and she wanted me off the line.

So finally, I asked for the numbers of the various stations. That was probably closer to what I wanted anyway.

She gave them to me, and I dutifully wrote them down. She offered to give me the phone numbers of substations as well, but I felt bad enough taking so much of her time.

If I felt I needed the substations, I would call back.

I scanned through the numbers she had given me, trying to figure out which one to call.

Finally I decided I'd pretend I was from SFPD when I called the Berkeley police. My finger rested on the name of one of the stations in an area I had heard of.

Then I dialed the Berkeley PD general number. The man who answered sounded crisp and alert, which I had not expected at this time of night.

I ignored the pleasantries and went straight for business. I decided not to identify a rank, which could get me in trouble later.

"Carol Ann Houk calling from the Tenderloin Station," I said, slurring Carol Ann just enough that the careless listener might think I said Carolyn or Caroline. "We just collared a man who says he has information about one of your unsolveds, and he wants to trade. Before we do anything, I need to verify that you have the unsolved or if he's just blowing smoke."

"Call back in the morning," the man said. "Our information office can help you."

"I don't have until morning," I said, making sure I sounded slightly annoyed. "I either have to process this bastard tonight or let him go."

"Hold him overnight, honey, and call us in the morning," the man repeated, as if I hadn't heard him the first time.

"Maybe you didn't hear me," I said before he could hang up. I was mad now, as if I were a legitimate police officer who had just been on the receiving end of disrespectful comments from a colleague. "I'm not some secretary trying to get information for my boss. I'm working a case, and I might have information that will help you with one of yours, if this twerp is as knowledgeable as he thinks he is."

"Honey, everything can wait. You'll learn that eventually," the man said.

"Clearly, you small town police do things differently than we do," I said, "because no one here would presume to tell me how to do my job. If you don't want to talk to me, let's make both of our lives easier. Why don't you just transfer me to someone else."

"Hang on," the man said as calmly as if I hadn't spoken at all. The phone clunked. He had put me on hold.

I bit back irritation. I had forgotten that nasty part of calling for information from anyone. Even though I could dress my voice up so that I could sound more educated than anyone in the room, I couldn't lower my tone enough to pass for male—no matter how many times I'd wished for that ability in the past.

The phone clunked again. "Carter," a tired-sounding male voice said.

I repeated my name and my story.

"Jerk," this Carter said softly.

I did not sigh, but I felt like it. I snapped, "Excuse me. Maybe I didn't—"

"I didn't mean you," Carter said. "The guy who passed you off on me. He's a junior officer and should have handled it, not that you care. But he's going to get an earful from me later."

"I hope so," I said. "I certainly appreciate you taking the time."

"Yeah, well, sharing is how cases get solved. And solving cases is how we get promoted. At least here." There was a bit of a smile in his voice.

"Here too," I said.

"Well, then," he said. "You got a name on this unsolved?"

"No," I said, "and that's part of the problem. I got a description and a time period."

Here I went again, making up lies. I hoped it would get me somewhere.

"Your perp can't even give you a time?"

"He can't remember," I said. "He's coming down off of something, which is one reason I'm not entirely sure I believe him. However, his daddy has money, and judging from the file, Daddy will be here with a lawyer as soon as I let this kid near a phone."

"Gotcha," Carter said drily. "What do you need?"

"He claims he has information on a dead college girl," I said. "Light brown hair, brown eyes, thin, about five-four, give or take."

"That's a lot of info for someone who can't remember anything," Carter said.

"He also guessed her bra size and told me she had a great ass. He clearly paid attention to how she looked."

Carter chuckled. I knew I had him then. He believed me because of what I was saying, and because I knew the lingo. His tone sobered. "How'd she die?"

"That's what this twerp doesn't know," I said. "He didn't see it. Just heard about it. Can point us to the doer, which is what he's trading. Information for rehabilitation in an actual medical facility, if you can believe that."

"You're kidding me, right?" Carter said.

"Nope," I said. "That's what he thinks will fly. I know that this particular night court judge won't allow the clinic. He doesn't believe in drug rehabilitation. But he might let the kid go with a reprimand. Money talks on tonight's bench."

"Jesus, the problems you Big City folk have." The amusement had returned to Carter's voice. "Time period?"

"End of June, maybe," I said. "Maybe around the Fourth. If I were looking, I'd look at homicides for the last month. This kid smells like he's been slumming for a while, and I'm not sure he knows what day it is right now."

"Gotcha," Carter said. "You want me to call you back?"

This was the dicey part. Technically, that was what I should be asking for. It was common courtesy.

But there was no way to fake a phone number. So I had to make sure my voice didn't betray my nerves.

"You can't have that many open unsolveds, can you?" I asked, making it sound like my request was no big deal.

"Doing you a favor, Houk," Carter said. He used my fake name, which startled me, and told me he was a good cop. He had taken down my name. "Let's not go all My City Is Bigger Than Yours on me now."

"Didn't mean to imply that," I said in a tone that meant I hadn't meant to get caught.

"Sure you didn't," he said. "But you didn't answer the question. You wanna give me a call-back number?"

"I'd like it better if you could just thumb through the files real quick now." I tried to get that urgent-but-I-don't-really-care sound to my voice I'd heard when I hung out at the precinct with Truman. "Like I said, I don't have a lot of time."

"You owe me," Carter said and set the phone down. I could hear a chair slide back, and then some low-key conversation. A man laughed, and another said something I couldn't understand.

I grabbed the toast, took another bite, then wished I hadn't. Peanut butter stuck to the roof of my mouth. I grabbed the water and swigged it, relieved that Carter hadn't come back while I was eating.

I put the toast down. I would finish it when this call was done.

Then there was the squeak of a chair, the rustle of some paper, and the sound of a phone being picked up.

"You there?" he asked.

"Yeah," I said.

"We got seven female open-unsolved. I've got three with names already, all of which are a lot older. I got two hit-and-runs, one of which is an old lady, but the other might be your vic, if it's a hit and run that your guy mentioned."

My heart pounded. "When was this?"

"Fourth of July, near the fireworks. Some drugged-out girl was mowed down. Long-time junkie from the look of her. Didn't even see the car, although witnesses say the driver honked. Some thought she just jumped in front of it. Judging from the level of LSD in her system, that's probably the case."

"I don't think that's her, but let's hold it in reserve, shall we?" I said. I couldn't imagine that the Darla Lucy described would have become a junkie in the space of a week or two. But I wasn't going to rule anything out entirely. "What else do you have?"

"Girl found near the bay, possible prostitute, judging by what was left of her clothes. Looks like she went overboard from a boat. Ugh. The fish made this one hard to identify." Sounded like there were photos with that file, and not pretty ones either.

"That's six," I said. "You got one more, you said."

"You're going to love this one, San Francisco. Because it's a jurisdictional nightmare, and if your collar is in the middle of it, it just got worse." Carter was giving me an out.

I didn't take it. I made myself sound weary instead of interested. "Let's hear it."

Paper rustled as he looked through the file. "Woman dumped off a truck between 62nd and Dover, but it might've been 61st and Dover. You understand?"

Off a truck? I didn't want to focus in on that detail, not yet. I had him talking.

"I'm taking it from your description that I should know something about the block between 61st and 62nd where it intersects with Dover," I said.

"You don't got a map, San Francisco?"

"Not in front of me, Berkeley," I said, using his tone.

He chuckled. "Normally, I'd tell you to learn geography on your own time, but I'm feeling generous tonight. We don't know exactly where that body landed. If it bounced or was pushed in the wrong spot…well, let me put it to you this way. If the body was found south of 61st, it's Oakland's problem. If the body was found north of 62nd, it belongs to us. And since no one has done the hard work of figuring out exactly where this girl landed, then this thing remains in jurisdictional limbo. And…judging by the names on the file, they prefer limbo."

He had just told me that the detectives assigned to the case didn't want it. They wanted Oakland to take it.

"Maybe you'll inherit this one," he said. "Because no one wants to figure it out."

"Is there a reason for that?" I asked.

"You've never handled jurisdictional issues, San Fran?"

My turn to make that little chuckle. "You do realize that we have more stations than you have murders every year, right?"

"Except this year," he said quietly, suddenly serious. "It's been hell here."

"Yeah, sorry." I felt like I was channeling Truman. "Welcome to my world."

"No sympathy from the big city girl, huh?" he asked. I decided I liked him right then and there, at least from his attitude. For a minute, I thought about meeting him.

Then I realized that he wouldn't expect me, a little black woman from Chicago. Right on the heels of that realization came another. I had assumed he was as white as those young cops I had seen on Telegraph earlier in the day.

"I have lots of sympathy for you," I said. "I know exactly how it feels."

And oddly, I did, not because of San Francisco, which I still knew little about, but because of what Truman went through in Chicago, particularly with the South Side gangs.

"Yeah." Carter was quiet.

I let the silence hang for a minute. When it became clear he wasn't going to say any more, I asked, "So, this girl was thrown off a truck and died when she hit?"

"Hell, no," he said. "Body was dumped. Someone claims they saw it get pushed out of a flatbed, but someone else claims it rolled out. Doesn't matter either way. She was dead long before she hit the pavement. She was wrapped in a loose-weave blanket, tied at the hands and feet, and gagged."

"Okay. That puts a different spin on this information," I said. "She's not some random victim who happened to fall out of a flatbed."

"Nope," he said. "You don't tie up a corpse."

"Or, maybe you do," I said, "if you want her to fit in a rolled-up blanket. But you certainly don't gag one."

"Yeah," he said quietly. "This might not be first-degree, you know. If you gag someone wrong, then wrap them in a blanket, they could easily suffocate."

"Is that what happened?" I asked.

"Looks that way," he said. "Happened on July 10. Does this jibe with what your guy said?"

July 10. Probably not Darla, then. But the tie to the incident Eagle witnessed was fascinating.

"I have no idea on my guy's dates," I said. "But what he said didn't sound like a kidnapping gone wrong."

"All right then," Carter said, sounding like he was about to wrap this up.

"However," I said quickly, "the truck *is* interesting for a different reason. We're dealing with something else that the truck might fit into. We got some homeless claiming they've been hiding from a one-ton, likes to clear them off the street."

Another lie, especially since our Ford F-350 hadn't gone near homeless.

"Huh," Carter said. "You're actually investigating that?"

Cop attitude. Every cop I'd ever met believed that people who lived on the street got what they deserved. That warm feeling I'd had toward him a moment ago faded.

The papers continued to rustle.

"Don't know what kind of truck this was," he said. "It's not listed here. Can't even tell how big it is. You want me to have the detectives on the file call you? Maybe they got off their asses and actually talked to some of the witnesses themselves."

"I thought you had interviews from witnesses," I said.

"Yeah, from the patrol that showed up after the body got found." Carter let that hang as well, but I understood it. The detectives had caught the case, but they hadn't cared about it.

The justice system had done its thing—a patrol unit had shown up, done the requisite interviews with witnesses, reported everything, the coroner had picked up the body, figured that the body was dumped, figured they had a murder of a young unidentified woman, someone assigned that murder to two detectives who were probably already overworked. They took one look at the jurisdictional issue, the fact they had a Jane Doe, and decided to solve this one only if they got pressure from the outside, which they probably never would.

"So," Carter said, "you want them to call?"

"No," I said. "Not my case. But I know someone who might want to see the file. You want to give me their names? I'll hand them over to him."

"Sure," Carter said. "Detectives Fleenan and Ruffner. They work days, so they should be here for morning roll."

"Great," I said. "I'll let him know what you got. Thanks, Detective."

"Don't mention it," he said, and hung up.

I pulled the receiver from my ear and stared at it. I hadn't expected such a fast hang-up.

He had probably heard my tone cool. Or maybe he didn't like the fact that I bailed on the call back. Most cops probably would not have.

It didn't matter what his reaction was. He couldn't track me down. He had no idea who he really had been talking to, and he had given me a mountain of information.

I felt like I had just had eighteen cups of coffee. My heart was pounding, and my mouth was dry.

I hadn't found Darla, most likely, but I found something else. Eagle had seen a woman abducted a few days ago and put into a truck. Another woman's body was tossed off a truck not too long before that.

I wondered what I would find if I called the other police stations in the nearby towns. More open-unsolved? More trucks?

More dead college students?

I took a sip from my water, my hand shaking.

There was only one way to find out.

PAMMY

They had made a nest for the baby on the locker room bench. It was twice as wide as the baby, but Pammy still piled towels and coats on the floor around the bench in case the baby rolled off.

The baby was quiet, but watching everything. Pammy had no idea if that kind of quiet was normal in a baby. She had no experience of babies. She was the youngest of four, and had left before her brothers had married and had children. They were all the way across the country. They sent pictures of their boys every Christmas, and Pammy felt slightly guilty whenever she saw them, thinking she should probably go home and visit before her nephews became adults.

So far, that thought had not inspired her to leave Berkeley.

Strawberry had taken over the baby duties. She had put the baby on a towel while Stella made the nest. Strawberry had expertly peeled the footie pajamas off the baby and inspected them to make sure the diaper hadn't leaked, something Pammy wouldn't have thought to do.

Then Strawberry changed the diaper, placing the dirty one in the paper bag she had brought for that purpose. Somehow Strawberry had pinned the diaper together without stabbing the baby, something that completely surprised Pammy. She had no idea how Strawberry had finessed that.

At Strawberry's suggestion, they left the baby nude but for her diaper so that Eagle could examine her. The baby didn't cry as Strawberry changed her, which Strawberry said was a good sign.

Stella remained quiet. Pammy had no idea if she had children or any experience with them. Pammy was beginning to realize she knew very little about Stella, almost as little as she knew about Strawberry.

While they waited for Eagle and Norma to arrive, Pammy cleaned up the locker room. The water had drained from the shower, but Pammy wiped it all down and put everything in the hamper she kept in a nearby closet so that she could take it all to the laundry with the industrial-sized washers just a few blocks away.

The door opened, and Norma entered, moving slowly, as if everything hurt. Pammy realized that she hadn't seen Norma walk before. Pammy didn't like what she was seeing now. The woman moved like she was eighty, not in her thirties.

Stella's gaze met Pammy's. Stella's lips were thin, her expression clear. *See? We needed to come here.*

Pammy understood that, but at the same time, she wasn't equipped for this. She didn't want to be equipped for this.

Eagle entered right behind Norma, and Pammy realized that Eagle was flanking her in case she fell. Eagle set her bag down. Pammy got one of the two chairs in the locker room and slid it beside the bench. The baby waved her pudgy arms at Norma, as if greeting her.

Eagle didn't look at the baby. Instead, she guided Norma into the chair. Then Eagle knelt beside the baby and smiled at her.

"Aren't you pretty?" Eagle said in a voice Pammy had never heard her use before. It was warm and high-pitched, the kind of voice most people who were familiar with babies used whenever they spoke. "Her name's Raquel?"

Strawberry started to answer, but Stella glared at her.

"Yes," Norma said.

"Such a pretty name for a pretty girl." Eagle kept talking to the baby as if she were a wary puppy about to bite. So far, Eagle hadn't touched her, but seemed to be leaning closer.

Strawberry stayed beside her.

Eagle looked up, and Pammy braced herself. She didn't want another fight with Strawberry.

"Let me examine the baby," Eagle said in that same sing-song voice. The baby was watching her as if she were intriguing.

Strawberry stiffened. "I'm not—"

Stella touched her arm, stopping her, as Pammy said, "I think Eagle would like some privacy. Let's go into the main room. I have a few things to discuss with you anyway."

Eagle gave her a grateful look, then bent over the baby, gingerly rubbing the baby's stomach.

Strawberry picked up the bag with the dirty diaper in it. Stella opened the door. Pammy led the way out.

The main room was at least twenty degrees cooler. Pammy hadn't realized she was sweating until the cooler air hit the dampness on her skin.

"I'll toss this outside," Strawberry said, and headed into the kitchen.

Stella watched until the kitchen door opened and closed. "What's her story?"

"I was just wondering the same thing," Pammy said.

Stella went to the light switches, but Pammy stopped her.

"If we leave only a few lights on, it's a spotlight on what we're doing. If we leave all the lights on, no one notices."

She'd learned that the hard way.

Stella nodded. She tugged on her belt as if it were uncomfortable.

"I'm sorry I had to bring her here," Stella said quietly. "I know it puts you in an awkward position."

Pammy didn't deny it. Truth be told, she wanted Stella to be uncomfortable with bringing women in trouble here. Pammy wanted her to stop doing it, without actually having to say so.

Stella inclined her head just a little. "She came to my house this morning, after Roy left. He's going to some meeting in Sacramento, something to do with the governor. He'll be back on Wednesday."

Then why hadn't she kept Norma at her house? Pammy almost asked, but didn't. She wasn't sure she could ask that question without all of her irritation bleeding through.

"At first," Stella said, "I thought we could just stay at my place while I figured things out, but then Norma told me a few things, and I realized that I'm one of her only acquaintances in the Bay Area. Her husband will be at my house in a New York minute once he realizes she's gone."

Great, Pammy almost said, but caught the word in time. Instead she asked, "He hasn't realized it yet, huh?"

"Not as of this evening," Stella said.

Pammy made herself take a deep breath before asking the question she'd wanted to ask all along. "So what exactly happened to her?"

"Who, you mean," Stella said.

"I thought you knew who," Pammy said.

"I do." Stella shrugged. "I don't know the details. I just know it's not the first time. She's canceled dinner plans before, and not shown up to some galas where the wives were expected, and her husband sang. So he's got a history, and I think it's a long one."

"Great." This time the word slipped out. "Has he hurt the baby before?"

"I don't know," Stella said. "Judging by her reaction, no, he hasn't. But I don't know for sure."

"What did she tell you?" Pammy asked.

"Only that she can't take it anymore. It's gotten too bad," Stella said.

Pammy had heard that a dozen times in the past year, often from women who came to learn self-defense. Most of them managed three classes before disappearing again.

And sometimes women came into the gym seeking more information, claiming to be at the end of their ropes as well. They took the mimeographed sheet of classes but usually never returned.

Stella said, "I'm pretty convinced this might be our only opportunity to help her. She'll go back to him if she thinks she has no resources. She'll protect that baby as best she can, but my God…what gives someone the right to do that to anyone?"

"The law," Pammy said. "He's her husband. It's private. It's not something the police really can help with, unless he does kill one of them."

Her voice broke when she said that last. Because of Linda. Pammy had tried to get her out more than once, and she had always gone back. The bastard could sweet-talk her.

"I have money," Stella said, "but I don't know where Norma can go. She can't be by herself. And she can't go to see her family. She did that before. Her own mother told her that she made her bed, now she gets to lie in it."

"Jesus," Pammy said.

"Maybe I can help." Strawberry stood in the hallway.

"What could you do?" Stella asked. Somehow she made that question soft, so it didn't sound quite as rude as it was. But the undertone was there. What could *you* do, girl?

"I can't tell you," Strawberry said to Stella. Strawberry didn't put the emphasis on the word *you*, but it was implied, nonetheless.

Then Strawberry met Pammy's gaze, as if expecting Pammy to understand.

Pammy didn't understand. She swallowed hard. What a tangle.

The locker room door opened. Eagle came out, with the baby cradled in her arms. The baby softened her, made her seem almost pretty. Pammy had never thought of Eagle as pretty before.

"Can I get someone to hold the baby for a few minutes?" Eagle asked.

To Pammy's surprise, Eagle was looking at Strawberry, not Pammy or Stella.

"Sure," Strawberry said, and hurried over.

The baby had her footie pajamas on again. Her face was shiny and red, as if Eagle had washed it off. Maybe she had.

Eagle handed the baby over to Strawberry, who took her gently.

"She's okay," Eagle said to Strawberry, as if the baby were Strawberry's daughter, not Norma's. "Just the one bruise. It's a bad one, and if she were older, I'd want to x-ray the shoulder, just to make sure there's no fracture. But baby bones are soft and flexible, and something that would damage an adult probably won't hurt an infant. I told Norma that she'll have to watch to see if the baby favors the shoulder or still winces when the bruise disappears. Then she'll need to take the baby to a doctor."

Pammy let out a small breath of relief. Had the baby been injured badly enough to go to an emergency room, it would have caused all kinds of problems, especially with the famous father.

"Are you sure he didn't hurt any other part of her?" Strawberry asked, juggling her arms slightly to move the baby into the proper position.

"Yes." Eagle's tone was serious. "And I looked at everything."

The words hung between all of them. Stella bowed her head. Pammy tried to shake the image of a man deliberately twisting tiny limbs just to make someone else angry.

Eagle didn't seem to notice. She asked, "Where'd you get the diaper experience?"

Strawberry's smile was perfunctory. "Oldest of seven. And I started babysitting for neighbors when I was twelve."

"You're good," Eagle said, then pivoted and went back into the locker room.

All three women looked at each other. Then they looked at the door, together. None of them had seen that side of Eagle before.

"I thought she hated me," Strawberry said.

"You impressed her," Pammy said. "That's hard to do."

"No kidding," Stella said softly. "One problem down, though."

She meant the baby. The baby wasn't really a problem, but her injury could have been.

Strawberry cupped a hand around the baby's tiny face. "You're okay now," she whispered.

If only that were true. Pammy glanced at the locker room door. Another problem was continuing. Who knew what Eagle's examination of Norma would turn up.

"I'm going to take her into the kitchen," Strawberry said, cradling the baby in one arm and brushing the wisp of hair off her forehead with the other hand. "Looks like she's having trouble staying awake."

Pammy expected the baby to be crying by now. Especially after Eagle had examined her.

"Are babies supposed to be this quiet?" Pammy asked Strawberry.

"Babies are all different from each other," Strawberry said. "Maybe she's just a good one, quiet."

"They learn," Stella said. "They're human inside that tiny body. They know when things are bad."

"She's awfully young to know that," Strawberry said. "But the doc says she's okay, so I'm thinking she's okay."

Pammy almost corrected Strawberry again. Eagle was not a doctor. Eagle hated being called a doctor.

But Pammy didn't say anything, not with Strawberry treating the baby so well.

"I think she just needs some sleep," Strawberry said. "Her carrier's in the kitchen. I'll put her down in there until we decide what to do with her."

Her, not *them*. Pammy noticed. She wasn't sure Stella had.

Strawberry didn't look at either of them as she opened the kitchen door and disappeared inside.

Pammy stood for a moment, feeling at loose ends. She knew that Eagle needed the time alone in the locker room. Eagle had a knack for talking to injured women, getting them to admit what really happened, a knack Pammy hadn't yet learned.

"You going to go with her?" Stella asked.

Pammy frowned, looking over at Stella. She was standing, arms crossed, staring at the kitchen door.

"I don't know anything about children," Pammy said.

"I wasn't thinking of the baby," Stella said. "It sounded like Strawberry might tell you how she can help. She certainly doesn't want to tell me."

Strawberry had volunteered that information, but Pammy wasn't sure she wanted Strawberry's help. Pammy wasn't sure what kind of help Strawberry could give.

"I guess I could find out," Pammy said, but she sounded as dubious as she felt.

She glanced at the locker room door, wondering what they would do if Norma was too injured to take care of the child.

"I'll get you when they come out," Stella said. Then she crossed her arms and walked over to the plate-glass window, clearly taking herself out of the conversation.

Pammy sighed, rotated her stiff shoulders, and wished the stress would ease. This was as bad as she had imagined. No, it was worse because of that baby.

All three women had to take action, even if Norma didn't. If Norma were childless and decided to go back to her husband, Pammy would have done nothing. She'd been through that before; she'd learned not to get involved with a domestic, just like her father used to say.

But Pammy couldn't just sit by with an innocent life at stake. Clearly Luciano Paolinie was the kind of man who enjoyed hurting small vulnerable things, maybe even destroying them.

That baby had to be taken away from him, somehow. And given Norma's condition, there wasn't enough time to find a good lawyer to see if they could do some behind-the-scenes work in getting Norma out.

If, and that was a big if, the city fathers didn't get involved.

Stella looked over her shoulder. Her reflection, in the darkened window, seemed to move more impatiently than Stella actually had.

"*Go*," she said.

She wanted to know what was coming next. She knew that this part was out of her hands.

If Strawberry didn't have any realistic ideas, then Pammy wasn't sure what would happen. Because the choices she could foresee were bad ones.

Clearly that's all Stella could foresee, as well. Without a family to help, Norma had hardly any options. And the woman that Pammy had observed didn't seem strong enough to step out on her own.

Pammy didn't like the idea that the only person who might be able to help Norma was Strawberry.

But somehow, they had ended up in that position.

Pammy rotated her head, trying to loosen even more muscles. A tension headache lurked. She made herself shake her arms as she walked toward the kitchen.

The room still smelled of old coffee. Strawberry was pacing with the baby, humming a tune that Pammy recognized but couldn't identify.

"You're good with her," Pammy said.

"So I'm told," Strawberry said drily. She had moved the baby carrier to the table, and was adjusting the blanket with one hand, while holding the baby with the other.

Pammy moved to the table, and grabbed the edge of the blanket. It was soft and warm. She laid it out flat, then folded it back.

Strawberry eased the baby into it, then pulled the blanket over her, brushing the wisps of hair again.

Pammy stepped back. She didn't want to get attached to this child in any way.

"You said you might be able to help," Pammy said quietly.

"Yeah," Strawberry said. "I can't tell them, though. They'll hate me."

"Them?" Pammy said.

"The doc and Mrs. D'Arbus. They're, like, so square, and the doc, she's, y'know, military."

Pammy frowned. "I'm not sure why Eagle's military experience is relevant. She's not going to turn you in to the government."

Strawberry continued to brush the baby's forehead. "You don't know that."

"I can't imagine any situation in which she would do that," Pammy said.

"I can," Strawberry said. Then she took a deep breath and stood up.

The baby blinked at her, then the tiny eyes closed. She was tired.

Pammy watched as the child slid into sleep. Strawberry didn't, though. She was watching Pammy.

"If I tell you," Strawberry said quietly, "you can't narc."

"Narc?" Pammy asked. She'd heard the term, but never in relation to herself.

"Tell the police," Strawberry said. "Or anybody."

"I can't promise that," Pammy said.

"Then I'm not sure I can help," Strawberry said.

Pammy let out a small breath. She needed to hear Strawberry out. It wasn't as if Pammy were averse to doing something illegal. She did things on the shady side of the law all the time, it seemed. These days, that seemed like the only way to help people.

"I can't...you gotta promise," Strawberry said. "I can't tell you if you don't promise. I mean, it's like helping this baby or keeping quiet. And that *sucks,* man."

And that was true, for all of them. Norma, Stella, and that bastard who had fathered this child had put Pammy and Strawberry in a terrible position.

Pammy looked at the baby's little face, eyes closed, long lashes against the pink cheeks. Underneath that thin little shirt was a bruise the size of a grown man's hand.

"All right," Pammy said. "I promise. I won't narc."

Strawberry lifted her head, her chin jutting out just a little. She looked fierce.

"You better hold to that promise," she said, with no trace of young woman in her voice. It was as fierce as her expression. "Because if something happens in the next few days, I'll blame you."

Pammy's heart pounded. "What do you mean, something happens?"

"If the cops show up or something," Strawberry said. "It'll all be on you. And I won't be quiet about it."

Pammy straightened. "I don't like being threatened in my own place of business."

Strawberry's cheeks grew red, but her gaze remained intense. "I'm being clear. Because I'm trusting you with a very big secret."

Pammy could back out right now. She could tell Strawberry to remain silent. But Pammy didn't. She needed to know now, not just because of this baby, but also because she needed to know who she was letting into her gym.

"All right," Pammy said, although she wasn't sure quite what she was saying "all right" to. "Tell me."

Strawberry nodded. She bit her lower lip, then took a deep breath.

"I work with a group that gets kids to Canada," she said.

Pammy frowned. "Kids?"

"Guys. Who got drafted." Strawberry's voice was nearly a whisper.

"Oh." Pammy let out a small breath of air. Since they'd been talking about the baby, she had been thinking *children* when Strawberry said *kids*, not college-age boys.

"We got a system," Strawberry said in that same soft voice. "We get new identification, we get them across the border, we give them to a Canadian group, and they start new lives. It's pretty small, and we're pretty exclusive. But I know that they would help Norma. And the thing is, for her it wouldn't be illegal."

"Except for the new identification," Pammy said. "Don't you work with someone on that?"

"In Canada," Strawberry said. "We'd get her the right kind of papers."

"Then how will she cross the border?" Pammy asked. "They don't just wave you through anymore."

She noticed that a year ago, when she took an impromptu vacation in Victoria. The easy drive into Canada now required declarations and automobile inspections, probably at the request of the U.S. government.

"I know they don't," Strawberry said. "But it's an open border. And there are a lot of places that you can drive across without any border guards at all."

Pammy felt her cheeks heat. "You know where they are?"

"They're on maps. They're not hard to find," Strawberry said. "The trick is staying in Canada. I think it'll be a lot easier for Norma than it is for some twenty-one-year-old single guy."

Strawberry was probably right about that.

"Besides," Strawberry said, "she might not have to get any Canadian identification. Lots of guys survive without it. If she's worried about that."

Pammy looked down at the sleeping baby because she didn't want to stare at Strawberry. Pammy had no idea if Norma would do any of that. She would have to give up everything.

To save the child. Hadn't she already put herself in jeopardy to do that?

Pammy took a deep breath. "How do you propose that we get Norma out of here without telling the others the plan?"

"Just say I'll handle it," Strawberry said.

Pammy had no idea how Eagle would feel about that. But maybe it didn't matter.

Still, saying that Strawberry was going to handle all of this would seem arbitrary from Eagle's point of view. And Pammy had no idea how invested Stella was going to be either.

"At the very least," Pammy said, "we'll have to tell Norma."

"No, we don't," Strawberry said.

That surprised Pammy. She had always told the women she was helping what she planned to do. "You're saying that we just drive her to Canada, and leave her there?"

"Not quite," Strawberry said. "I'm proposing that we tell her we'll get her someplace safe, that it'll take a couple days to get there since we'll probably have to stop once or twice. She won't have any idea where we are, except north. Once she's in Canada, she can decide if she wants to stay or not."

It sounded sensible. It sounded like the kind of thing Pammy would plan. Make sure the woman is safe, and then leave it up to her.

That wouldn't guarantee that the baby would be safe, but it would at least take Pammy and Strawberry out of the equation. They would be able to content themselves with the idea that they had done everything they could.

There were a lot of places this plan could go wrong. Including the drivers. This underground railroad—to use Strawberry's term from earlier—was designed for young men of draft age, not for women.

Which probably meant that the drivers and the contacts were male.

"Do you have someone that you trust to take her up there?" Pammy asked.

"No," Strawberry said.

Pammy stiffened. She looked over at Strawberry. Strawberry's hand was cradling the baby's cheek softly, but her gaze was hard.

"I'll drive her," Strawberry said. "I'll make sure she and Raquel are all right."

Strawberry had bonded with this baby. That was probably good. At least, Pammy hoped it was good.

"What about school?" Pammy asked.

Strawberry smiled, just a little, still stroking the baby's forehead. "It's summer session. Everyone misses some classes. It's expected."

She wasn't wrong about that.

"You've given this some thought," Pammy said.

Strawberry took a deep breath. "Eagle said I don't make a difference. She wasn't entirely wrong."

That tension headache started working its way up Pammy's neck again. "You can't do this just because Eagle challenged you."

"Sure I can." Strawberry nodded her head, her jaw set. "I thought about it. She's right. I talk a great game. But talk's easy. Now it's time to step up."

"You're going from talking to protecting an injured woman with a baby," Pammy said. "You'd be driving them across hundreds of miles."

"I know," Strawberry said.

"I'm not sure you do," Pammy said. "I've dealt with women like Norma just a little bit, and the one thing that surprises me about them is how often they change their minds."

"What do you mean?" Strawberry asked.

"One day, they want their husbands out of their lives. The next day, they're back in the relationship, pretending everything is fine." Pammy *hated* that. Maybe that was one reason she tried to keep her distance. She had dealt with it with Linda, who bounced Pammy up and down like a yo-yo, asking for help and then refusing it when it arrived.

Strawberry played with the baby's wispy hair. "If I got her to Canada—"

"That's not as easy as it sounds," Pammy said. "It's a couple days' drive, and you'll have to watch her every second. She can't get near a pay phone. She needs to believe there's real help coming, and even then, if she calls him anyway and goes back, you can't interfere."

Strawberry's eyes filled with tears. She was looking at the baby.

"She wouldn't do that," Strawberry said, but her voice was wobbly. Part of her knew that Pammy was right.

"You don't know what she'll do," Pammy said. "I don't either. But I've seen it happen that way before. And you've got to remember, she stayed with him for a long time. She had a baby with him, and I can guarantee that he was hurting her before the child was born. He has a hold over her, and distance might not set her free from that."

"It has to," Strawberry whispered.

"I wish," Pammy said.

Strawberry swallowed heavily.

Pammy looked at the baby too. Little Raquel was sleeping peacefully. Maybe the first peaceful sleep she'd had in a while.

"Look," Pammy said. "I don't want to talk you out of this. It sounds like a good solution. But it'll probably be the hardest thing you've ever done."

"I want to try," Strawberry said, more to the baby than to Pammy.

That was all any of them could do. They could try.

Ultimately, it would be up to Norma. Because they couldn't take the baby from her. They just had to give her a chance.

"You have to make up your mind fast," Pammy said. "And you can't change it."

"I've already made up my mind," Strawberry said. "And don't worry. I won't back out."

Pammy nodded. "Well then, we're going to have to move on this now. Because Norma will back out if she stays in the Bay Area. So we have to get her out of here as soon as possible."

"All right," Strawberry said. Her voice was shaking.

"If she doesn't have to go to the hospital," Pammy said, "you'll have to get her out of here tonight."

"And if she does have to go to the hospital?" Strawberry asked.

Pammy met her gaze. She wasn't going to say what she thought. If Norma went to the hospital, then she would lose this opportunity. She would lay there and think and worry and lose confidence, and after a day or two, she would head home, deluding herself into thinking that everything would be okay.

"Just pray she's all right," Pammy said. "That's about all we can do."

EAGLE

E agle wished she had a Polaroid. She wanted to take photographs of every inch of Norma's body. The woman was covered in bruises—old bruises, new bruises, fading bruises, bruises just emerging.

Her husband was a sadist, an effective one. He liked administering pain, but he knew when to stop. He took Norma to the verge of needing emergency medical attention, but never did enough damage to make it inevitable. He gave his wife injuries that she could live with.

Eagle did not shudder. She had seen this too many times, in a variety of different ways. She'd seen it more than she wanted to here, at the gym, although not this effectively.

She'd seen this kind of damage in Pleiku on some of the Vietnamese, particularly the guides that the men no longer trusted. There was one officer who had taken torture to an art form, knowing how to inflict the maximum amount of pain for a minimal amount of damage.

It looked like Luciano Paolinie had learned that skill somewhere too.

She didn't mention this to Norma. Norma had been reluctant to show her injuries to Eagle, even though Eagle had insisted. Norma never entirely undressed. She took off some articles of clothing as Eagle needed to examine different parts of her body, but left other articles of clothing on. Eagle had had to cajole to see every inch of Norma, but somehow, she had managed.

The worst damage she had found was on Norma's face. Her husband had broken her nose, and judging by the feel of it, he had done so before. Eagle taped it up, despite Norma's protests, being exceedingly careful with Norma's left cheek as she did so.

X-rays would tell Eagle if the cheekbone was damaged, because her fingers couldn't probe cautiously enough. After the work on the nose, Norma kept moving away. The pain was too much.

But a damaged cheekbone wasn't life threatening, and it had become clear that Eagle wouldn't get Norma to a doctor unless her injuries threatened her life.

The locker room smelled of damp tile, wet towels, and industrial-strength cleaners. Pammy had managed to clean it up enough to make it presentable for the morning's classes, but it still had a dinginess that seemed unique to heavily used locker rooms everywhere.

The baby's nest of towels remained on the bench. Norma kept looking at that nest as if it had given her inspiration. Or maybe, strength.

Because God knew, this woman needed strength. She had stayed with her sadist much too long.

Her torso was an abstract painting of bruises, bruises upon bruises upon bruises. She had winced as Eagle pushed on them, feeling for swelling underneath the skin, especially around the stomach and the vital organs.

Eagle hadn't found anything on the torso, except the badly healed unevenness of a broken rib. Norma's buttocks and thighs had taken the most serious beatings. It looked like the rat bastard had kicked her repeatedly in the lower back. Two bruises shaped like footprints crisscrossed over the back of her right thigh, and that was where her limp originated.

Eagle worried about that injury. If the bone was fractured, Norma would probably be all right. But if it was broken, its sharp edges could jab an artery.

Eagle had already told Norma that she needed to get an x-ray on the leg, and Norma had said no.

He'll find me at the hospital, she said, and that was true enough.

Now, she hovered over her clothing as if putting it on again would hurt. She glanced at the showers.

"Do you mind if I take a shower?" she asked. "I haven't all day...."

"I don't think that would be a problem." Eagle stood. "Just avoid the tape on your nose, like I told you. Don't get it wet yet."

"Okay." Norma didn't sound daunted by that. Maybe she'd had her nose taped before.

"I'll get a towel for you," Eagle said. "And be right back."

Pammy kept a few towels in the janitor's closet for women who had forgotten theirs. Eagle would fetch one from there.

As she left the locker room, she grabbed her bag and carried it with her. She knew better than to leave a bag with any kind of knife or the small drugs that she occasionally used alone with anyone.

Stella was leaning on the counter, reading something—probably the lists. She raised her head as Eagle emerged.

"Well?" Stella asked.

"In a minute." Eagle opened the janitor's closet near the kitchen, grabbed the thickest, softest towel she could find, and carried it back inside the locker room.

Norma was behind the shower curtain, the rest of her clothes neatly folded on that chair.

"I'm setting the towel on the edge of the bench," Eagle said.

"Thank you." Norma's voice sounded normal, as if she hadn't been through severe trauma at all. The woman had clearly been abused for a long time. She knew all the tricks to hide the damage her husband had done.

Eagle had tried to get her to talk about the marriage, but Norma wouldn't say a word about it. She only told the story of the baby's injury and how hard she had fought to get the child away from him.

The look in his eye... she had said, her voice trailing off. *The look in his eye....*

She had come back to that statement more than once. Apparently, the look in her husband's eye had finally awakened her to what she had subjected herself to. Or maybe he had trained that eye on the child, and that had frightened her.

Although Eagle had asked for clarifications, Norma had given her none. And, really, it wasn't Eagle's business.

Eagle's business was to figure out the extent of the injuries, and she had done that as best she could, without access to an X-ray machine and more sophisticated equipment.

She let herself out of the locker room to find Pammy standing beside Stella, waiting. Eagle had expected Strawberry, too, but apparently, Strawberry remained in the kitchen with the baby.

The hippie-dippy ding-a-ling had proven herself to be pretty solid. Despite her own misgivings, Eagle was impressed.

"Well?" Pammy asked.

"Norma needs to see a doctor," Eagle said. "There's an injury on her left leg that I'm pretty worried about. Her nose is broken, and I'm not sure about her left cheekbone."

"Should I take her to the emergency room?" Stella asked.

"Even if you wanted to, she won't go," Eagle said. "And it can wait. She needs to see someone though, and I recommend that the someone isn't in the Bay Area. That husband of hers enjoys hurting her. It looks like he's been doing it for years."

Pammy glanced at the locker room door. Eagle recognized the expression. She was worried that Norma would come out to find them discussing her.

"She's taking a shower," Eagle said. "I think this is the first shower she's had in a while where she didn't need to keep the baby close or keep an eye out for her husband."

Pammy nodded.

Stella was frowning. "I don't know where to take her. Her family doesn't want to be involved, but they might—"

"You got a smart husband here," Eagle said. "He's gotten away with this for a long time. He'll want her back. Even if the family wanted to be involved, they're out of the question."

Stella sighed. "You're right."

Pammy did not volunteer anything. She was quiet, which wasn't like her. Eagle looked at her, afraid that Pammy would ask her to take Norma out of the Bay Area. Eagle had taken an injured woman out of the Bay

Area for Pammy once before. That woman had fought back hard when her husband attacked her. He had badly injured her, and Eagle had taken her to a hospital in Bakersfield, which was almost too far away.

Eagle had stayed until the woman pulled through, and then helped her get out of town.

But that woman had had her own stash of money saved up, and had been planning her escape for years.

Eagle had a hunch Norma's departure was a spur-of-the-moment thing—a run-away-now impulse that she couldn't have imagined doing one week earlier.

It made Norma's escape less likely to succeed. It also meant she probably had few friends, no resources, and no idea how to survive on her own.

"Thank you, Eagle," Pammy said softly.

It sounded like a dismissal. Eagle tilted her head. She hadn't expected that.

"You have a plan?" Eagle asked.

"Yeah," Pammy said. "We have some options."

Stella looked at Pammy in surprise. Clearly, Stella hadn't been apprised of the options either. Did that mean Pammy and Norma had come up with something? Or Pammy and Strawberry?

That last thought made Eagle deeply uncomfortable. She wasn't exactly sure why.

At that moment, the locker room door opened, and Norma emerged. Her wet hair hung over her shirt, and her bruises looked bright. The swelling on her face seemed more pronounced.

The tape did not look wet, however. Norma had listened to that instruction, at least.

"Where's Raquel?" she asked.

"In the kitchen, with Strawberry," Pammy said.

Norma bit her lower lip, then glanced at the plate-glass window. The reflections of all four women looked blurry in the glass. Someone could see them; maybe not identify them, but see them.

"Where do we sleep?" she asked.

"We need to discuss that," Pammy said.

"What about the usual spot?" Stella asked. Generally, they placed the women in the locker room, with a foam pad and sleeping bags. The room was safe, enclosed, and windowless. No one on the outside could see any light filtering under the door.

"Could you set it up?" Pammy asked Stella.

Stella glanced at Eagle, surprised. Eagle understood, though. Pammy wanted to talk to Strawberry and Norma alone.

"You need me for anything else?" Eagle asked. She didn't want to get roped into driving Norma somewhere. Unlike the woman a few months ago, Norma could change her mind at any second, putting her driver at risk.

Pammy opened her mouth, then closed it as if rethinking her initial response. She glanced at Norma.

"Do you have any questions for Eagle?" she asked.

Norma didn't meet Eagle's gaze. That behavior was pretty common after something this traumatic.

"No," Norma said, then added in a near-whisper. "Thank you."

"You're welcome." Eagle grabbed her bag and headed toward the kitchen. She was going out the back, no matter what Pammy said. "I'll talk to you tomorrow, Pamela."

"Thank you for coming on such short notice." Pammy sounded as formal as Eagle had. She didn't follow, probably waiting for Eagle to leave before talking plans.

Eagle straightened her shoulders as she walked. All those years, and she still had trouble shaking off some patients. Norma was one, mostly because Eagle had a hunch nothing she said would make any difference at all. This woman would go back to her husband, get punched until something vital gave way, and then she would die, leaving her child alone with a monster.

Eagle pushed open the kitchen door. Strawberry was sitting on a chair at the table, her finger clutched in the baby's tiny hand. The baby had fallen asleep that way.

"You've volunteered?" Eagle asked, almost before thinking about it.

"Yeah," Strawberry said. "I can get her out of the city."

"You know she's just going to come back, right? You know this will end badly," Eagle said.

"I don't know that," Strawberry said. "Neither do you."

Her voice shook just a little, though. She suspected things would go awry.

"The kid's got your heart already," Eagle said. "They always grab on, tight as she's holding your finger right now. But that kid's not yours."

"I know," Strawberry said.

"You don't know," Eagle said. "Not deep down."

Strawberry started to speak, but Eagle held up her free hand.

"You listen for a minute," Eagle said. "Because I'm thinking of you. If you're taking them somewhere, then take them there. Get them set up. And *leave*. Don't ask for updates. Don't ask to be informed if they come back. Don't volunteer your address or your phone number. You let that woman do whatever she's going to do, and you don't interfere."

Strawberry moved the baby's hand slightly. "You don't have a lot of faith in her."

"I'm not worried about her," Eagle said. "I'm worried about you."

Strawberry looked up, clearly surprised.

"Other people's shit is heartbreaking. It's just heartbreaking. And you're volunteering in the worse kind of situation. You're not careful, it'll take you down." A lump rose in Eagle's throat. She swallowed. The lump moved down just a little.

"Is that what happened to you?" Strawberry asked.

Eagle wasn't sure what the question meant. Maybe Strawberry was asking about her cynicism, maybe her rudeness, maybe her personality. Eagle wasn't going to ask for a clarification.

"They teach you when you become a nurse to let the patients go. You can't make them eat right. You can't make them follow the medical protocols. You can't even make them come back if they break a wound open and start bleeding again. Your job ends at the door, because it has to. Do you understand?"

Strawberry's eyes were big. "Yes."

She didn't understand. No one could understand. Hell, Eagle had had two years of domestic experience before heading to Saigon, and *she* hadn't understood. She'd looked up too many of them, asked too many of them to report. They had stolen her heart, some of them, and now she would never get it back.

"You won't listen," Eagle said as she walked around the table. She didn't look at that baby again. She had deliberately not called the baby by her name. Eagle didn't even want to think about the footie pajamas, the bruise on the shoulder, those big blue eyes.

She didn't want to think about them, and she wouldn't. Not once she went out the door.

"I hear you," Strawberry said.

"Yeah, you hear me," Eagle said. "But you don't *listen*. No one does on their first one. But you'll remember this conversation. Believe me."

Strawberry watched her. "Answer me one question."

Eagle hadn't expected that. She'd expected some more denials, not that strong voice.

"What?" Eagle asked.

Strawberry moved the baby's hand again. "If you think this is going to fail, why do it?"

Good question. There was no easy answer.

"Because," Eagle said, that lump threatening again. "Every once in a great while, someone proves me wrong."

VAL

There were a lot of little towns in the San Francisco Bay Area, many of them incorporated with their own police forces. Since I didn't have a Bay Area phonebook in front of me, I couldn't look up the various numbers. And I was at a disadvantage with San Francisco Police Department too.

Even though I had gotten phone numbers and a list of stations from the operator hours earlier, I couldn't figure out exactly how the San Francisco PD was organized. I supposed I could call the San Francisco PD in the morning and ask. I would have to use some general number, and lie about a reason for getting background on the stations.

Or I could go to the library when it opened and look all of that up. But it seemed like a waste of time to me.

Besides, I had a hunch the morning staff at *all* of the stations would be a lot savvier than the night crew. The night crew in the smaller towns believed that I was dealing with a demanding night court judge and a squirrely dope fiend with information on an unsolved.

Night crews understood urgency. Morning staff didn't. Everything could move at a leisurely pace, because day cops believed that there were plenty of courts and plenty of judges and plenty of time—at least, so long as that time fell between nine and five.

About an hour into my phone routine, I had brewed some coffee, which I would probably regret later. Or not. I hadn't been able to sleep anyway, and I certainly wouldn't be able to sleep now.

After I had spoken to Detective Carter with the Berkeley PD, I had gone into my living room and grabbed the legal pad I used for keeping track of bills. I brought it to the kitchen table, along with a bowl of Cheerios and a cup of coffee, and wrote down everything Carter had told me.

I figured I'd lose track of information quickly, otherwise.

Then I searched my stuff for the map I had bought of California, back when I was thinking of leaving Berkeley. The map was pretty big, so it didn't give me as much information as I wanted. But it did tell me just how many small communities there were in the Bay Area.

More than I could handle in one night's series of phone calls.

I made a list of the places I'd contact, starting with some of the smaller towns. The San Francisco cops wouldn't buy my story. They'd want to know who the judge was or why I wouldn't be able to come down to their station. I'd have to figure out a different way to deal with them.

But some of the smaller municipalities wouldn't know what the inner workings of the SFPD were any more than I did. And those were the places I wanted to target first.

Besides, I had a benefit most people didn't. I knew that cops were territorial, and they didn't like to share with other cops, even within major city police departments. Just because a woman's body had been discovered wrapped in a blanket in one municipality, no one would think to check if another woman's body had been found in the same way in another municipality.

However, I wasn't quite certain how to handle the two separate cases that I was investigating. I wasn't sure Darla Newsome had any ties to the man in the truck. If I asked about the man in the truck, I would taint the Darla Newsome investigation. If I asked about Darla first, then I would raise suspicions about the guy in the truck.

I eventually decided to do exactly what I had done with the Berkeley PD. I asked about Darla first, and then I asked about the truck—saying that it was of interest in a homicide that might be tied to Darla's case.

I made six phone calls in the first hour, none of which were as fruitful as the call I'd made to Berkeley. No one had an open-unsolved of a brown-haired woman in the right age group, and the farther I got out of San Francisco proper, the more likely it was that a truck was involved in all measure of crimes, not just a suspicious death.

More than once, the police officer I spoke to mentioned a sheriff's department, pointing out that I needed to talk to someone at the such-and-so county office. It varied by police department as to which county sheriff they referred me to, but they always did with the same kind of sentence.

The rural departments see more body dumps than we do. Usually we get the junkies, and the rural guys get the random killings.

The words were spoken with such coolness, such acceptance, that I ended up chilled. After a while, I found myself gripping my coffee cup, not because I wanted more to drink, but because I needed the warmth.

By 12:30, I shut off the fan in the kitchen window. I liked to think the chill I was feeling came from the crisp night air. I looked out over the fenced-off backyard.

The light in the neighboring house was off. It felt like I was the only person awake at this hour—me, and the police officers I'd been talking to.

Weirdly enough, the conversations kept me calm. If I had thought this through before I started making the phone calls, I would have thought that investigating would have made me more paranoid, not less.

But I felt like I was doing something. Moreover, I felt like I was doing something *useful*. I hadn't had that feeling for a long time.

And that feeling more than overwhelmed the sadness I felt at all of the unsolved cases the officers mentioned as they thumbed through their files. Some officers had no open homicides involving young women, and some had no open homicides at all.

But others had all manner of suspicious deaths. A couple had complained about lack of resources, and one wished out loud that the case I'd been discussing was related to something in his files.

Sure would be nice to have your resources, he had said. *Even for one single day.*

One officer in one of the little towns on the eastern edge of the Bay Area had told me he had nothing to offer since most of the killings that occurred in his jurisdiction were domestics, something that made me sigh quietly to myself. I still made him look up the brown-haired young woman.

Could be a boyfriend or something, I had said.

These women never got to the big city, he had replied, and I wondered how he knew. But he'd given me information anyway, and part of me wished that he hadn't.

I grabbed an apple from my stash and took a bite, then went back to the phone. My stomach was churning a bit from all the coffee. I took my legal pad and set it on the counter, then dialed the Walnut Creek police department.

After a tired-sounding man answered, I went through my usual stories, asking first for information on any unsolveds of any unidentified young women they might have, and when he told me they had none, asking about cases involving a one-ton.

"A truck?" The officer—who had identified himself as Albert Jessup—sounded wider awake now. "What kind?"

"A Ford F-350," I said.

"Well, now I can help you," he said.

My heart started to pound. I grabbed my pen and opened the legal pad to a fresh sheet of paper.

He said, "We had a weird call in June about an F-350. I remember it because I took it. Caller said some girl was screaming at the top of her lungs from the bed of an F-350. The truck had pulled into the Enco gas station and was filling up, and the girl in the back started screaming blue murder. Attendant went inside, called us, and I got dispatched."

My hand was frozen over the legal pad, pen between my thumb and forefinger. I needed to know how this turned out before I wrote anything down.

"I got there, truck was gone. The attendant couldn't figure out how to keep the bastard at the station. He had paid cash, so there was no way to track him, not that I'd expect some doer to write a check. But you never know. Perps can be squirrelly."

"They can," I agreed, mostly to keep him talking.

"The attendant did what he could. He gave me the license plate, and off I went, but we never did find the doer or the girl."

Jessup sounded a little shaken even though this had happened more than a month before.

"Why didn't the attendant help her?" I asked before I could stop myself.

"He tried," Jessup said. "Girl was under a pile of blankets. He managed to pull one back, saw a rope, attaching something—her, the blanket, something—to one of the hooks inside the truck. Then the driver grabbed the attendant by his collar and tossed him away from the truck. Bruised him pretty bad. The doer unhooked the nozzle from his gas tank and spilled some gasoline on the attendant's leg—attendant thinks deliberately."

My breath caught. My hand was still over the legal pad.

"Threw a five on the attendant, and jumped in the cab, and drove off. Attendant stood up, got the plate, had it when I got there. The whole place smelled of spilled gas. They had to put up signs everywhere, telling smokers to stay away until it got cleaned up. Called in two extra guys just to get through that night."

"What time was that?" I asked, not exactly sure why that was relevant, yet needing to know.

"About eleven," Jessup said. "I'd just come on. Spent a week searching for the bastard. Figured he'd be somewhere. Never did see hide nor hair of him or the girl."

"What do you think happened?"

"He got away, what do you think?" He sounded snide.

"No, no," I said. "I didn't ask the question correctly. The girl was tied up, right?"

"I assume so. Dunno for sure. She might've been injured or tangled in that blanket. All I know is that she was screaming for help, and the doer drove off like he'd done something wrong. Attendant said he was freakishly strong. Attendant is about two hundred pounds, and that driver lifted him like he weighed no more than a feather."

I let out a small whistle before I remembered I was on the phone. I didn't apologize, though.

"You still have that license plate?" I asked.

"Do I ever," he said. "Hang on."

He set the phone down, and I heard him say something to a person nearby. "…maybe finally catch the son of a bitch…"

And then the phone rustled as he picked it back up. He gave me the license plate number.

"You couldn't match it?" I asked.

"Asked the DMV for a match, but they said the plate doesn't exist. Most frustrating dead end of my career so far. I kept thinking about that attendant, you know? All that driver would've had to do was light a match..."

He didn't finish the sentence. He didn't have to.

I was scrawling everything down now, trying not to breathe too loudly. I was glad he couldn't see me.

My excitement would've been palpable.

"And you know what else?" he asked. "I find myself wondering sometimes about that nut in Vallejo, you know, from July? And I wonder if it was the same guy. Because that was weird too."

I frowned. I had no idea what he was talking about.

"Nut in Vallejo?" I asked.

"Yeah," Jessup said. "Fourth of July? Made the news everywhere, I thought, but maybe not San Fran. The nut who drove up to a couple necking in their car in Blue Rock Springs Park? Shot them like a million times. Killed her. The guy lived."

"He was in a truck?" I asked.

"The guy?" Jessup asked.

"The shooter?" I asked.

"Naw. A Corsair, maybe. I just kept thinking our truck guy might've dumped his truck for something more practical."

"Wouldn't he have changed his MO too?" I asked. "I mean, shooting's a long way from tying someone up in the back of a truck."

"Not as long as you'd think," Jessup said. "You'd be surprised. If you'd asked about older cases, I might've had something for you."

The hair on the back of my neck stood up. "What do you mean?"

"Lots of woods around here," he said. "Lots of ditches and mountain roads. It doesn't hurt that one of 'em's named Mount Diablo."

I got the sense he'd told this part of the story a few times.

"We find more bodies than I like to think about," he said. "But they're usually skeletal by the time someone finds them."

"Any of them wrapped in blankets?" I asked.

"Hard to tell," he said. "Cloth decomposes just like skin. And we get a lot of rain, lots of animals. We got a lot of unsolveds, but they're old. Not the girl you're looking for."

"You get calls from other jurisdictions about this?" I asked.

"Not as many as I'd like," he said. "That's why I watch the news, try to remember odd cases. Figure I can call one of the big boys with a possible when we find something. So far it hasn't panned out. But you put my name down, okay? I got information, and I'd love to leave Walnut Creek one day."

I smiled. Poor man must have been desperate to say that to someone he thought was a San Francisco cop on crummy night duty.

"I got your name," I said as warmly as I could. "I'll contact you if I need anything else."

And I hung up. Then I wrote down the rest of what he had told me, and underlined that license plate number.

I glanced at the clock on the stove. 1:30. Too late to go to the gym, obviously, and too late to call Eagle or Pammy even if I had their phone numbers, which I did not.

I wiped my hands on my robe, then walked around the apartment, trying to work off some of the nervous energy. I'd had a breakthrough.

A truck with a woman in the back. A license plate. A strong man who could toss a 200-pound gas station attendant like he weighed nothing.

The college kids were onto something.

I still hadn't found Darla. But I'd found something that might've been just as good.

PAMMY

They left via the alleyway, in an ancient Oldsmobile with great tires. Strawberry sat at the wheel as if she were born to drive. Norma huddled in the back seat, the white tape across her nose reflecting in the light over the door.

The baby slept in her carrier, unaware that she was changing locations—maybe for good.

Pammy and Stella had helped pack. They filled the car with food and blankets, keeping the disposable diapers within easy reach, and adding a stack of ripped and discarded towels in case the diapers ran out.

Strawberry took three grocery bags out of the pile that Pammy kept under the sink to use as garbage bags. She had a hunch one of the first things that Strawberry would buy on a pit stop were expensive plastic bags so that the diapers wouldn't stink up the car too badly—if they needed to change one on the road somewhere.

When the group finished, they had awakened Norma, got her ready, and taken the trio to the car. Before they drove off, Pammy had walked around the car, making sure that it was solid. The car looked all right to her, and Strawberry had said that her father made sure the car was tuned every single time she came home.

But Pammy didn't know the last time Strawberry had gone home. A two-plus-day drive to Canada would put a lot of stress on a car. Pammy wanted everything to go as well as possible. She wished she could pay for a tune-up before they left, but there was no time.

She also wished she could call Opal to join them in this tight little alley, because Opal, with her automobile repair class experience, could have looked under the hood to make sure everything was okay. But it was after midnight, and Pammy couldn't in good conscience call. Even if she wanted to wake Opal up, she didn't trust Opal to keep Norma's presence quiet.

So, Pammy would have to trust on another level. She would have to trust this father that she did not know, and hope the car was up for the drive.

Stella had done her part as well. She had five hundred dollars in cash. Apparently, she kept a stash in the house for emergencies. Those emergencies, Pammy was beginning to learn, were rarely Stella's.

Stella had pressed three hundred and fifty dollars of that five hundred in Strawberry's hands while the three of them were alone in the kitchen, as Norma still caught the last of her hour of rest.

Normally, I'd give you all of it and tell you to give half of what you have left to Norma when you reached your destination, Stella said, *but she might take off with the baby before you get there, and I don't want that child to have to spend a cold night out in the woods somewhere.*

Strawberry had looked startled at that but, to her credit, she hadn't denied that Norma's return was a possibility. Maybe Strawberry had heard Pammy after all.

The other thing that Stella didn't mention was that Strawberry was untested. Norma wasn't the only one who could run off. If Norma and the baby became too demanding, Strawberry just might leave. And if she did, Norma had enough money to make it until new help arrived.

If Pammy had to bet on it, though, she would have wagered that Norma was much more likely to bolt than Strawberry.

Before they left, Strawberry had offered to let Pammy look at the map so she would know where they were going to go. Strawberry made it clear that this was a huge offer, based on trust.

Pammy declined.

Not because she was afraid to know the route that Strawberry's draft-dodger underground railroad used, but because Pammy didn't want to obsessively think about where the trio would be as each hour passed.

For all Pammy knew, they weren't going to Canada at all. They were going to go south to Mexico or they would take a flight out of Los Angeles to somewhere else.

Lord knew that Stella had given them enough money to do any of those things.

It had taken nearly an hour to get Norma into the car, in the backseat, with the baby in her little carrier. Strawberry insisted on using some kind of origami magic with the seat belt to thread it through the carrier, to protect the baby, she said. She wanted to face the baby toward the seatback, but Norma had balked. They had the baby facing Norma, sideways in the seat, so that Norma could fuss over her.

At 2:00 a.m., the loaded Oldsmobile had finally backed out of the alley and headed off into what remained of the night.

As they drove off, Stella slipped an arm around Pammy. Pammy leaned her head on Stella's shoulder, feeling a great exhaustion wash over her.

She had a fifteen-minute drive home and then a wind-down. She had promised Eagle and Val that she would check with the admissions office in the morning, which meant that she had to be up at seven at the latest. For a moment, Pammy toyed with getting her four hours of sleep here and then she realized she hadn't brought any extra clothes.

She did have extra underwear and socks for just that sort of thing, but if she were being honest with herself, she needed to get out of here. She needed a few hours to herself, just to shake a little.

Stella squeezed Pammy's waist.

"Thank you," Stella said quietly.

When someone thanked her in these instances, Pammy used to say, *There's no need* or *That's fine*, but she didn't anymore. There was a need for a thank-you. She needed to hear it.

And what had happened here tonight was not fine. It might never be fine, and if she had protected herself well enough, she would never know if the entire venture went bad.

"You're welcome," Pammy said, and slipped out of Stella's hug. Pammy went through the back door into the kitchen. Lights were still on. The remains of a sandwich sat on a plate on the counter. Someone else had left their crusts behind. Glasses sat in the sink.

"I'll do the dishes," Stella said from behind her.

"Let's leave them for the morning," Pammy said. "We need sleep."

She ran a hand through her hair. She still had some cleanup to do out front and in the locker room. She didn't want the women who arrived for the first class to get any hint that someone was here late into the night, and she certainly didn't want them to know that someone had bedded down in the locker room.

Stella followed her through the kitchen door, and Pammy, exhausted, nearly told her to stay put. Then she remembered that Stella's purse was in the locker room.

They walked down the hallway into the gym proper. It looked both empty and weirdly bright with the overhead lights on. Pammy shut off the lights over the punching bags and t-shirts, leaving only the lights over the counter and locker room on.

"May I ask a question?" Stella was standing next to the counter, facing the locker room door. She was probably going to ask why Pammy wanted to clean up alone.

"These lists," Stella said, one hand tapping the papers on the countertop. "What are they?"

Pammy let out a small sigh. Stella had trusted her, repeatedly, with the lives of other women, to help with problems in her community. Stella, despite Pammy's initial impression of her, had done more for women connected to the gym than almost anyone, except Eagle and Pammy herself.

"Help me clean up," Pammy said tiredly, "and I'll explain as we work."

They went into the locker room first, folding blankets, putting away the nest of towels. The level of laundry that Pammy would have to do this week had gone up exponentially.

And as the two of them worked, Pammy told Stella about Eagle's encounter with the man in the truck, the possible kidnapping, and the warnings students had heard about the same man.

By the time they finished with the locker room and shut off the lights in there, Pammy had gotten to the visit that Darla Newsome's father had made to the gym and about her disappearance.

"About forty percent of students never complete their degree," Stella said as they headed into the kitchen. "That's one of the statistics that bugs Roy the most, and a reason he became a regent, not that they're working on it as much as he would like."

"I'm aware of dropout rates." Pammy suspected the number was higher for women, since so many of them had been encouraged to come to college just to marry—or get their M-R-S. degree, as Irene Roth derisively put it.

"This could be one of those," Stella said.

"I'd agree," Pammy said, "if it weren't for that idiot in the truck, and the fact that Strawberry and some of the other students had identified the kids who disappeared as participating in what they called 'The Movement.'"

She went on to explain as they straightened the kitchen how many of the students had already dropped out, but were—in Strawberry's words—committed to the cause.

Stella had paused in the middle of gathering the garbage, and looked at the back door.

"My goodness," she said quietly, "I just realized that if Strawberry decides to stay with Norma and help her and the baby get settled wherever they're going, then she'll be a dropout."

"Most likely." Pammy rinsed off her hands and put out a new towel beside the sink. She ran her fingers over the open weave.

Stella rolled the top of a big grocery bag, stained with something wet despite the fact that she had put other bags inside of it.

"Puts a whole new perspective on it, doesn't it?" she asked. "How easy it is for these kids to just…vanish. Maybe those Movement kids, as you call them, are doing something Important with a capital I, and haven't bothered to tell anyone."

Pammy nodded. She hadn't thought of that. The kids involved in all the different causes around campus would be more likely to leave on some kind of mission than other kids.

"Maybe, that list isn't important at all," Stella said. "Maybe those kids are just do-gooders."

Pammy let out a small sigh. Maybe they were. Maybe she was over-reacting because of her history, and because of Darla's father's panic.

Pammy could guarantee that Strawberry's father knew nothing about what his daughter was doing at the moment. And she wouldn't be calling him with that information.

Strawberry hadn't had time to tell friends that she was leaving. She might not have even told her roommates—if, indeed, she had room-mates. Pammy knew nothing about Strawberry's living arrangements and, Pammy just realized, she didn't know Strawberry's real name either.

Pammy couldn't contact Strawberry's parents even if she wanted to.

"It might be a crisis," Stella was saying, "but not a sinister one. The crisis might be how many kids think dealing with their causes is more important than getting an education that will help them through life."

"I have a hunch these next few days will give Strawberry a hell of an education," Pammy said softly.

"But not one she's going to want," Stella said. She grabbed another bag of garbage and carried both out the back door.

Pammy checked the fridge to see if anyone had left open containers. No one had, but one half-full baby bottle sat inside.

She stared at it for a moment, feeling sad. These rules she set for herself, not knowing what was going to happen to the women she had helped, they took a toll. She sometimes felt like she had a chip of ice in her heart, a chip that would never entirely melt.

The door banged and she whirled, heart pounding. Stella came back inside, hands extended, a small grimace on her face. She went directly to the sink and started to wash up.

"You know what?" Stella said, her back to Pammy. "I made light of those disappearances and I shouldn't have."

Pammy closed the fridge. "I don't think you made light."

Stella shrugged, still scrubbing her hands. "Yeah, maybe. But I didn't respond with anything approaching compassion."

Pammy opened her mouth, then closed it. This was an insight into Stella that Pammy hadn't expected.

Stella grabbed a paper towel and used it to dry her hands instead of the clean towel that Pammy had put out. Then Stella turned around and faced her.

"I heard you when you said that the police won't help down here," Stella said, "and I know that Eagle had trouble with them."

Pammy bit her lower lip. She wasn't sure where Stella was going with this.

"However," Stella said, "I can help with that in the right instance."

Pammy nodded. Stella had helped in January, when an arsonist had targeted the gym. Stella was the one who had gotten the police to take the call seriously.

"I'm not sure what the right instance would be," Pammy said.

"Me, either," Stella said. "But I do know, if we come up with the right cover story, I'd be able to…um…get the police to actually look at some suspects we come up with. We might be able to figure out a way to report the disappearances."

"It sounds like too much, Stella," Pammy said. "If we use you too often, then the police aren't going to listen any longer."

"Maybe not to me," Stella said, "but they have to pay attention to Roy's wife. So, the next time you need police help on something, let me run interference."

Pammy let out a small sigh. She had no idea how that would work.

"You do a lot for me, Pammy," Stella said. "I know you saved the life of at least one of my friends, and you may have just saved two more lives tonight."

"I didn't do anything," Pammy said.

"I would never have told Strawberry about this," Stella said. "And then what? I get Norma a hotel room, or something, and she goes back to that asshole, and he beats her to death? Or she goes back and he kills her by inches, harms that baby, and Norma can't come to me anymore because he knows she came before? You've done a lot, Pammy. Just the fact that you're here means a lot."

The exhaustion that had been dogging Pammy for the last few hours came back. "This place isn't some kind of rescue, Stella."

"I know," Stella said. "And I appreciate everything you've done. So, let me pay back where I can."

Her words hung between them. Pammy didn't want to say yes. That meant there would be more incidents in the future.

And that ignored the two things she, Eagle, and Val were already investigating.

Cases. Pammy's father would have called them cases.

But if Pammy did, that meant she was not only running a gym, she was running some kind of amateur detective agency, as well as some kind of rescue operation for women in trouble.

She felt pulled apart enough as it was.

"Please, Pammy," Stella said.

Pammy sighed. "All right. But I hope we never have to use that clout of yours."

"Me too," Stella said. "Believe me. Me too."

VAL

By three in the morning, I was flagging. Besides, my night court story was wearing thin. Most collars that came in this late waited for shift change and the official start of a day court.

I had given up on coffee long ago. I was too jittery. I had placed the percolator on a cool burner, and had put my coffee cup in my pristine sink. The air coming in the window was darn near cold, something I still wasn't used to, not given the oppressiveness of Illinois summer nights. My hands were chilled, but the rest of me was bathed in a light sheen of sweat.

Not because of the temperature, but because I was onto something.

What exactly, I didn't know.

Three more jurisdictions had reports of screamers in an F-350. They were all in June, and they were all near Walnut Creek, so it might have been the same screamer.

Two rural police departments had sent me to the same county sheriff's office because they both had found skeletons wrapped in blankets on side roads. The surprise was that both skeletons were male. They were bound and gagged—or had been before most of their skin sloughed off—and they were clearly dumped.

Whoever this doer was, he was smart enough to leave the bodies in places that didn't have a large detective force. And the doer seemed to know that local jurisdictions often didn't talk to each other.

I had finished the last call with someone in Vallejo, who had nothing on a truck driver with a fetish for blankets, rope, and gags. But the officer there told me about their Fourth of July shooter all over again, and reminded me to watch out for him.

Maybe that was how some information got passed between police organizations in the Bay Area. A little tit for tat—I'll watch out for your strange killer if you watch out for mine.

I didn't ask though. I didn't want it to seem like I had no idea how to play the game, even though I was beginning to think I really didn't.

I was shaking with exhaustion and overstimulation. I sank into a kitchen chair and realized at that moment that I would end up with the phone bill from hell. At least I was calling after 11:00. That would cut down on some of the expense.

But I had paid no attention to how long some of these calls ran, and some of them ran for at least fifteen and twenty minutes.

I also had no idea what to do with this information I had discovered in my late-night calls except present it to Pammy and Eagle. I didn't even know what I would have done if Truman were still alive and all of this was going on around Chicago. So many jurisdictions, so many questions—

I supposed that Chicago detectives would notify the other precincts. Here was where my knowledge of procedure broke down. I wasn't certain if I had enough information to issue something formal to other community police departments. I had no idea if an All-Points Bulletin could cover this or if the departments just sent each other flyers or if there was some more formal way of handling all of this.

Or if it really was that tit-for-tat thing.

I rubbed a hand over my face and decided to make one final call. This time, I would change my story a little and try Oakland, threatening to drive over if they had the right information.

I grabbed my trusty legal pad and went back to the counter, taking the receiver off the wall. One last call—or maybe two. I wanted to see if they would give me the body in the blanket on the border with Berkeley. I wasn't going to offer it up.

It took me three calls to get someone who was willing to cooperate. The officers answering the phones sounded surly in Oakland, and one of them made it sound like he wasn't going to help anyone from the SFPD for any reason ever.

Finally I got transferred to someone handling North Oakland, although I wasn't sure what that meant. Did it mean that North Oakland had its own precinct or did it mean that they only had one officer handling an entire region of a good-sized city? No one said, and of course, I couldn't ask without sounding like a new raw recruit—or someone who hadn't lived long in the Bay Area.

To my surprise, the person who took my call in North Oakland was female. She didn't identify herself, so I had no idea if she was a cop or some late-night dispatch.

I suspected cop just from the way she answered the phone.

"Yeah?" Her tone distinctly said *This better be worth my time, jerk.* I smiled at it.

I introduced myself as Carol Ann Houk again, and outlined my story. I tried not to make it sound practiced.

I ended with, "I'm the lucky person who gets to drive over and look at your file, if you have something open and unsolved that fits his description."

She made a pe-shaw sound with her lips. "Ain't it always the way."

She sounded as tired as I felt. But she didn't use that opening to tell me anything about her.

"Give me the details," she said. "I'll have them ready for you when you get here."

"I'll be honest," I lied. "I got shift change in three hours. If I can avoid a drive, I will. Would you mind looking in my date range first, so I know whether or not I'm wasting my time?"

"Rather waste mine, huh?" Her tone held no amusement at all.

"It's a favor to both of us if he actually has the information," I said.

"Yeah, I suppose," she said, and put me on hold without telling me. The only way I knew was that the phone sounded dead.

I couldn't resist, though. I asked if she was still there. She wasn't. I hoped she hadn't cut me off.

I paced the kitchen, going as far as the cord on my phone would let me. I couldn't reach the sink or I would have poured out the coffee. A light went on in the apartment across the backyard. Someone else was finally awake on this block. I tugged on my bathrobe. I really should have gotten dressed before doing all of this.

She returned with another click. Their phone system was clearly better than any other I'd encountered all night.

"Lots of dead girls in the last month," she said. "You didn't say. Was this one Negro?"

She was right: I hadn't said. I hadn't had to say before. Everyone else had assumed a white victim. But I remembered my one glimpse of Oakland, at the bus terminal, and realized that its complexion was a lot darker than much of the Bay Area.

I had also heard that the Black Panthers had their national headquarters in Oakland, whatever that meant. In Chicago, I had stayed as far away from the group as possible, thinking they had little to do with me.

"No," I said. "She's white."

"Well," said the woman on the other end of the phone. "That makes this a lot easier. I should've asked before I pulled open-unsolved."

"Sorry," I said. "I just assumed…"

"Yeah, you can't assume nothing around here. Ninety percent of the calls we get deal with trouble in the ghet-to." She had made it two words, and she had said it derisively. Obviously my assumptions about *her* skin color had been correct.

I could hear paper rustling through the phone.

"Sometimes I think we should just torch the entire place," she said conversationally. "Save us a lot of time and money."

My breath caught. Had she just said that?

I moved my jaw. I wanted to reply somehow, but I had no idea how.

"Okay, here's what we got," she said, as if she hadn't said anything out of line. "Two known prostitutes, no real names, just nicknames. Beat to death by the same john, we think. Interest you?"

I took a deep breath, not really wanting to continue this conversation at all. But if I wanted information, I needed to.

"How long were they known prostitutes?" I asked.

"Arrest records going back to 1967," the woman said.

"My mutt made it sound like she was a Berkeley college student," I said, using some of the same slang I'd heard from Truman.

"Then why the hell aren't you on the phone with them?" the woman asked.

"I was," I said. "They got nothing."

"Well, they should have something," she said, "because the only other thing that fits is a body dump between 62nd and Dover. We handed it over to the Berkeley PD."

They didn't think so. Or they were using the jurisdictional issues as an excuse not to solve it.

"Body dump?" I asked.

"Female, bound, gagged, wrapped in a blanket. July 10. Pushed off a truck. Witness called us. We heard the address, called Berkeley. You want the names of the officers they assigned?"

"I do," I said, only because that was what someone from another police department would ask for.

She gave me the same names I'd received before.

"Other than that," she said, "our open-unsolveds with women in your age range are known victims, not Jane Does. That all I can do for you?"

"One last thing," I said. "You mentioned a body dump off a truck."

"Yeah, I said it's Berkeley's problem—"

"I know," I said. "But I've been given another job. A shit job. Homeless claim that some man in a truck has been picking them off one by one."

"Shooting them?" she asked in that same flat voice she had used when she mentioned burning down an entire section of her city. Boy, was she charming.

"No," I said, trying not to let my voice reflect my contempt for her. So much for some kind of sisterhood. She wasn't anyone I ever wanted to spend time with—if she could even see past my skin, which I was certain she couldn't. "This guy seems to take them away, never bringing them back."

"How come the SFPD has you chasing hallucinations?" she asked. Apparently she had an even lower opinion of the homeless than Carter from Berkeley.

"Because there've been enough credible witnesses to corroborate," I said. "We're not too thrilled that some guy in a truck is using our area as some kind of hunting ground."

"That's a big assumption," she said. "For all you know, he's picking them up as free labor for his farm."

She made that sound logical. She made it sound like something she would have approved of.

"And then what does he do with them?" I asked.

"If you're lucky, he feeds them and sends them to a church or something, pulls them out of your district. Ignore that one, Houk. It's not going to get you promoted."

My fault that I had presented all of this as possible promotion fodder.

"I was just wondering—"

"I don't talk to the homeless," she said. "Bad enough I gotta deal with the Negros. You got what you want, right?"

And then, without waiting for my answer, she hung up.

Which was probably a good thing. Because my answer wouldn't have been reasonable (and possibly white) Carol Ann Houk of the San Francisco PD's answer. My answer would've been pure Valentina Wilson when she had nothing to lose.

I hung up the phone slowly, shook out my hands, and paced the kitchen.

No wonder Eagle had been pissed off at the Berkeley police. They had felt that the abduction she saw wasn't worth their time. And from her description, they had seemed a lot more caring than this woman from North Oakland.

If I had had any doubts about our investigation of Darla's disappearance and Eagle's truck driver, those doubts would have evaporated after this conversation.

I knew that cops saw a lot of crap. I knew that they got a lot of crap too. But that North Oakland cop and I had been discussing human beings, human lives, and she hadn't cared.

For a half second, I thought of reporting her for her comment about the black population of Oakland.

But who would I report her to? Oakland police investigated their own. And if she felt comfortable enough to say that to me, a stranger, then I couldn't imagine what the Oakland police officers were saying to each other.

I shivered, glad I hadn't moved there or even stayed there for one night.

My exhaustion had vanished in the face of my anger. But I knew it would return as soon as the adrenaline left my system.

So I decided to use that adrenaline while I had it.

I needed to make sense of my notes for Eagle and Pammy.

I grabbed the legal pad and sat down at the kitchen table. And then I started to write.

EAGLE

Eagle managed to get five hours of sleep, which had to be some kind of record after the night that she had had. Her dreams weren't quite nightmares, but they were filled with images of children playing in bomb craters, tossing infants back and forth as if they were sandbags, and battered Vietnamese women wearing hats, not quite a Nón Lá, but similar—woven and made of dead ferns that had decayed to black.

Everything smelled of rotted vegetation and standing water. Eagle stood in a rice paddy and watched the children playing catch with the infants, feeling a growing sense of dread.

But the dread wasn't bad enough to wake her up. It was the kind of dread she had felt every day that last year of her service, the kind that had become an inevitable part of life.

She had awakened at six. She had forgotten to pull down her blinds, and the sky was turning pink over the apartments to the east. The street was quiet, and for a moment, she basked in the silence.

The silence and the fact that she was here. In the States. Away from the madness she had experienced in Nam.

The madness here, in Berzerkeley, was a different kind of madness. An everyday madness, sadly. She wagered there wasn't a place in the world where some women did not end up looking like Norma had. Human beings battered each other. Mostly men battered women, but Eagle had even seen women batter their men.

And the children…

She sat up, knowing that the children tossing infants around in her dream had come from walking into the gym's kitchen to find Strawberry holding that injured baby.

Eagle let out a small breath. She had to shake off the image of that baby—all of those babies. The babies she had seen in much worse condition.

The problem with all she knew, with all she had experienced, memories cascaded into other memories, becoming some kind of pit that could swallow her whole.

She didn't dare let it.

Eagle eased out of bed. She had to shake off the events of the night before. As strange as everything was, it was better than it had been a year or two years before. She had to remember that.

It took one scalding shower, some clean clothes, and some coffee with extra sugar to wake her up. She had to toss out the Raisin Bran because the baggy she'd hidden in it had sprung a leak, and she didn't want to get high at breakfast.

She treated herself to two eggs perfectly fried alongside bacon, made toast slathered in butter, and found some ancient jelly that actually looked edible.

She couldn't quite believe the appetite she had. If she hadn't been keeping track of her pot use, she would've thought she'd gotten accidently high anyway. But she hadn't. She actually felt okay this morning, not like she'd been beaten and robbed, the way she felt most mornings.

Then she hauled out her notes from the day before. All of her calls, all of her notes, were about the missing young men. Why was it always easier to deal with boys?

She bit into the last crisp piece of bacon, worried ever so slightly that the ancient jelly might make her ill—and then smiled to herself. That worry gave her an idea. A good idea.

She finally figured out how to call various hospitals and give them the girls' names. Then she looked up at the clock.

Only 7:00. All that activity, and still too early to call.

Unless she dealt with the boys first. If she used the military recruiter line, she might get some early birds in the records offices, and those folks would think it perfectly normal for a military secretary to be on the job before eight.

She put her dishes in the sink, covered them with dish soap, and promised herself she'd get to them after she finished with the phone calls. Then she rinsed her hands, poured herself another cup of coffee, and sat down.

She started with the hospitals whose records offices had closed before she knocked off last evening. She started those calls with, "Oh, good, you're there. Wonderful."

She managed to sound chipper. She had no idea *how* she managed to sound chipper, since "chipper" was never a term anyone used to describe her—even when she was in a good mood, which she decidedly was not. She couldn't remember the last time she had been in a mood she would have described as "good."

Just like the day before, she got no traction on the names. None of the young men had been to the hospitals she called. She wasn't surprised. With only six male names on her list and dozens of hospitals, not to mention free clinics and local doctors' offices, she was doing the equivalent of looking for a needle in a haystack—except she wasn't even certain someone had put that particular needle in that particular haystack—or in *any* haystack for that matter.

At 8:30, she switched to female names. With those names, she called the hospitals she had called the night before. She needed to call those hospitals early because she didn't want to catch someone she had spoken to the day before, and with most records departments keeping business hours, the someone she had spoken to the afternoon before might actually be in the office this morning.

She started with San Francisco General Hospital once again. Best to follow the same pattern, so she wouldn't lose track.

Fortunately, she reached a different person in records, a woman who answered the phone with, "Records. Monica DeSouza speaking."

Eagle put on her most official voice. "Hello, Miss DeSouza," she said. "I'm Gertrude Anderson with the Berkeley Department of Public Health. May I have a moment of your time?"

"Yes, of course," DeSouza said. "What happened to Ethel? She's usually the one I deal with over there."

Eagle hadn't expected that someone from Berkeley would be in touch with someone at SFGH so often that they knew each other's names. However, it made sense, given the fact that the hippies and drugs had moved from Haight-Ashbury in the past few years to Berkeley.

"Ethel has finally been able to take that vacation," Eagle said, hoping that was somewhat true. "I'm handling some of the details right now."

"Good for her," DeSouza said. "It sounded like she needed some time off when we last spoke."

Eagle was suddenly curious when that was and what the two of them had spoken about. Her heart was pounding. That little bit of news—about the contact between the two departments—could have one of two results.

It could mean that DeSouza and this Ethel woman were used to sharing information. But they might have been doing it without following the rules, rules Eagle was woefully ignorant of.

And DeSouza might not be willing to play nice with someone else.

"Ethel had told me that I wouldn't need to contact you while she was gone," Eagle said, hoping that sentence could cover all contingencies. "But something's come up, and they want me to talk to San Francisco hospitals. I hope I'm not violating some procedure…."

She deliberately let her voice trail off.

"Procedure went out the window when LSD moved in," DeSouza said. "What do you need, hon?"

Eagle let out a small sigh. Her planned lie actually fit into the reality of what SFGH and the Public Health department in Berkeley actually dealt with.

"Our hospitals here have contacted us with something they believe is some kind of food poisoning," Eagle said, "but we can't find any common food sources among the listed victims. No restaurants in common, no grocery stores, nothing really. So we're thinking—"

"Another bad drug reaction." DeSouza did sigh. "This is where I would ask Ethel if she was as tired of this as I am. But you're new, so I'm not going to burden you. How long has this been going on?"

"Well, we have records for some cases going back to the beginning of the year," Eagle said. "Back then, the hospitals here didn't test for drug usage with food poisoning cases—"

"Yes, yes, I know," DeSouza said, "much to Ethel's dismay."

Eagle was beginning to like this Ethel woman. She sounded conscientious.

"So you understand the problem, then," Eagle said, trying to tie this around. She felt uneasy. She had a series of questions planned, and she was being short-circuited on some of them.

"I assume you've been cross-checking with police reports," DeSouza said, inadvertently helping her.

"The level of detail required is astonishing," Eagle said, not answering that question exactly. "We've ended up with a list of names, people we think might have been treated elsewhere. Maybe SFGH has the right kind of records for us."

"Here's where I get all official," DeSouza said, and Eagle tensed. "You know I'm supposed to ask you to send someone to check the records yourself."

"I do," Eagle said, and was about to make excuses for not being able to get to SFGH.

"So consider yourself asked," DeSouza said before Eagle could continue. "Now, I assume you have names you want checked?"

"Yes." Eagle felt a little light-headed. "We're not entirely sure how these people are involved, but here are the names. And I hate to say this, but I have quite a few."

"Give them to me," DeSouza said. "I'll call you back."

"Um, here's the thing," Eagle said. "I—"

"Your boss wants this yesterday," DeSouza said.

"I'm afraid so." Eagle made herself sound apologetic.

"I'm amazed that Ethel didn't quit. Are you sure she's coming back from vacation?" DeSouza asked. "Because this is happening a lot."

Eagle wasn't sure how to respond to that. "I—um—I—"

"Don't say anything, hon. It'll just get you in trouble. Fire the names to me. I'm ready."

Eagle swallowed hard, blinked a little at how easy this was compared to how much she had worried about it, and then read the list of women's names that she had.

"All girls," DeSouza said. "That's odd."

"Sorority," Eagle said, because it was the first thing that came to mind.

"Oh, that makes sense," DeSouza said. "Let me see what I have. I'll be right back."

Eagle cradled the phone between her ear and her shoulder, then ran water in the sink. She figured she had a few minutes, and she was right. She managed to fill the sink with steaming hot water and finish her coffee while she waited.

Then she went back to her chair, accompanied by the uneasy thought that this inquiry might take most of the day.

Ten minutes after Monica DeSouza had left the phone, she returned.

"You still there?" she asked.

"Yes," Eagle said, sitting up and grabbing her pen.

"We have something," DeSouza said, "but it's not what you want, I'm pretty sure. Clearly not food poisoning. But it might be something the police can use."

"O…kay…" Eagle said uncertainly, as if she were a new employee who didn't have a clue what any of this stuff meant.

"We have records for Kelly MacGivers. She came in on March 18. Does that jibe with anything of yours?" DeSouza asked.

"Yes," Eagle said, hoping she wouldn't have to elaborate.

"Well, she wasn't throwing up or having those kind of problems. She was beaten to within an inch of her life, and here's the odd thing. The attending noted rope burns on her wrists and ankles. Not to mention that some skin around her mouth had been damaged."

"Damaged?" Eagle asked, because she truly didn't know what that meant.

"Like someone had put tape over her mouth," DeSouza said. "At least, that's what the attending speculated in his notes."

"My God," Eagle said. Her shock wasn't entirely an act. "Do they know what happened?"

"Girl wouldn't say. She came in with her parents. When the attending wanted to call the police, they refused, saying it had already been handled."

"No flag on the file, then." Eagle knew how this usually went. It was considered private, something that the family would deal with, and if challenged, the family would simply deny that anything had happened.

"No, none," DeSouza said. "Although the attending did note that the family had a regular physician. When the attending wanted to give the files to the regular physician for follow-up, the family said they would make sure he contacted us. To date, no one has."

"Well, that's strange," Eagle said. "Did they check for drugs in her system?"

Pages rustled. "Yes, and they found nothing. Only used a blood test, though, not a urine test because they didn't think this was drug-related."

"Okay," Eagle said. "Wow."

"So, I guess this means you don't need the file," DeSouza said.

I wish, Eagle thought. She wanted it more than ever. But she couldn't have it.

"No, we don't need the file," Eagle said reluctantly.

"Here," DeSouza said, "let me give you the family's phone number, just in case. Maybe they're ready to talk to someone now."

Eagle doubted that, but she took the names and phone number anyway.

"You know," DeSouza said, "as I read this to you, I realize there's one other strange thing here."

"What's that?" Eagle asked.

"You didn't notice? The address? It's in Daly City."

Eagle glanced at it, and then frowned. "That's quite a ways from you," she said. "Maybe yours was the closest hospital to the incident."

"Which begs the question," DeSouza asked. "What really happened to this poor girl?"

"I guess we weren't meant to know," Eagle said.

"Huh," DeSouza said. "The things I see in this job. And I work in an *office*, away from the patients." She paused, then added, "Is that all you need from me?"

"It would seem that way," Eagle said, although she wished she could ask about the young men again. DeSouza sounded a lot more competent—and sympathetic—than that Waldon character whom Eagle had spoken to the night before. "Thank you."

"Any time," DeSouza said. "You give my best to Edith."

"Will do," Eagle said, but DeSouza had already hung up.

Eagle tapped her pen against the legal pad, looking at her hastily scrawled notes. She wasn't sure what she had expected to get from the hospitals, but this surprised her.

Rope burns on wrists and ankles. Tape across the mouth. Parents who did not want to talk to the police. Parents with an address far from the hospital.

Eagle looked at the address again. It wasn't one of the wealthiest neighborhoods in the Bay Area, but it was affluent. Daly City was proud of its vast suburban neighborhoods. The address she was looking at was in one of the nicest areas of Daly City. She certainly couldn't afford to live there.

Wouldn't someone with that kind of money go to a closer hospital, near their local doctor, with services that they expected? Or, if their daughter had been injured nearby, wouldn't they tell the hospital staff to call the police, so that the perpetrator of whatever happened could be caught?

She circled the information on the page, then made a little star next to it.

This was too strange to be some kind of odd coincidence. She didn't know what to make of it yet.

But it had her fired up. She was ready to make more calls.

She felt like she was onto something. What, exactly, she didn't know.

But she had the feeling she would know—if she just kept looking.

PAMMY

When the UC Berkeley admissions office opened promptly at 9:00 a.m., Pammy had been the only person waiting in the hallway. She had memories of long lines near the admission office, but apparently they had all dated from her time here as a student, not from any reality—at least what passed for reality on a Tuesday morning in July.

The admissions office was in Sproul Hall, a thirty-year-old, four-story, white neoclassical building designed to look old. It smelled like chalk and cigarettes, even though very few classes were held here. Mostly, students sat in the wide hallways and waited for appointments while administrators, secretaries, and the occasional student assistant scurried up and down the marble stairs on some kind of important university business.

This building had been occupied a few years ago during the Free Speech Movement, and it seemed like the administrators had been jittery ever since. Pammy had only been inside the building a few times in the last few years, but every time she was, someone had looked at her sideways as if they had known she no longer belonged.

The admissions office itself had its own set of barriers to entry. She had made it inside the office with no real problems, and once she identified herself, saying she wanted to check enrollment figures, she had to wait. There were only a handful of chairs against a wall decorated with university flyers and pamphlets, all telling her how to improve her university experience or giving helpful suggestions on everything from applying for financial aid to getting the best student housing.

The blond wood counter between her and the beehive that led to the offices beyond was clear of everything except a clipboard with a sign-in sheet. The sheet, with July 22, 1969, scrawled on the top in black Magic Marker, was empty.

Pammy hadn't signed in. Alice Sullivan, whom Pammy had known since her own freshman orientation years before, was the person who unlocked the door. Alice used to be tiny, but now she was growing square and solid. She had two children, and a husband who couldn't seem to hold a job, so Alice held hers with the university like a drowning woman clung to a lifeline.

Pammy had lied to her, and the lie felt uncomfortable. Opening A Gym of Her Own to men seemed wrong, even in theory. But Pammy tried to sell it so that Alice would investigate every name on those lists.

And, to Pammy's surprise, Alice hadn't even questioned it. She had taken the lists that Pammy had carefully copied, and disappeared in the back. Pammy paced the main room, waiting. She could just hear voices, and occasionally, her name mentioned.

She could also see over the desks that stood between her and the area toward the back where the records were kept. One woman was visible through the glass in the door, leaning over a table, thumbing through a huge ledger book with, Pammy supposed, the names of that year's registered undergraduates.

It wasn't until she got here that she realized she might have to repeat this process at graduate admissions as well, or at some of the specialized schools within the university, like the law school.

She had less pull in those offices. She might have to ask Alice or someone here to request the information for her.

The back door opened, and another woman came out. Olive Beiderman had looked old when Pammy had registered in 1956. Olive looked the same now. Her hair was a gunmetal gray, and it made her skin seem gray as well. She had never worn makeup, and her black, horn-rimmed glasses made her seem even older.

Pammy had gotten to know Olive when they had both served on some committees before Pammy had opened her gym. Olive had always been a little skeptical of the gym. But she had been supportive, in her own way. She had been the one who had introduced Pammy to Irene Roth so that Irene's students could study self-defense in Pammy's gym.

Olive strode past the desks, frowning. Her glasses rested on the edge of her nose, her faded blue eyes meeting Pammy's over those black rims.

"I don't know if we should help you at all," Olive said. No hello, no nothing.

Pammy had seen Olive in this kind of mood before. Olive had a take-no-prisoners side, which was why she had become the de facto office manager for Undergraduate Admissions, running everything, no matter what the Dean of Undergraduate Admissions and his secretary seemed to believe.

Pammy knew better than to mess with Olive in this mood. All she could do was talk to Olive directly.

"Is something wrong?" Pammy asked.

"Yes, something's wrong," Olive said. "I've listened to you too long, that's what's wrong."

Pammy straightened ever so slightly. She took a step toward that blond wood counter, resting her hands on it, but not leaning.

"What, exactly, is the problem?" she asked.

"Your list," Olive said. "Now you're admitting men into your program?"

"Possibly," Pammy said, not really wanting to lie to Olive.

"Well, unpossible it. Young men have more than enough opportunity to learn how to beat people up. They do it on their own with no encouragement from you."

"Um." Pammy felt blindsided. "I don't teach anyone to beat someone up. I teach them how to avoid such situations."

"You teach them how to use their fists, correct?" Olive asked.

Some of the office staff had slipped through the doors. They lined up like this was a televised fight, and they had ringside seats.

"Yes," Pammy said. "Sometimes a woman needs to know how to hit back."

"*A woman,*" Olive said. "I supported you when I thought it was just women, especially these young people today who get into horrid situations with their drug-addled friends. But I can't support you teaching young men."

"Well," Pammy said, "right now it's just a vague idea. Which was why I brought the list—"

"Your list," Olive said with contempt. "Your list is not valid."

Pammy's cheeks heated. Had Olive figured out that none of those kids were applying for any classes?

"What do you mean?"

"As far as we can tell, most of these students have dropped out. I won't have you teaching children to beat each other up on the university's dime."

Alice had come up behind her. She was waving the list just outside of Olive's sight, almost like a little white flag. Or maybe it simply meant *let her talk.*

"That's why I'm here, Olive," Pammy said. "I thought there was something suspicious in this group of names. I brought them to you to make sure they were enrolled here."

"Well, most of them aren't," Olive said, but she had less charge to her voice. Sometimes reason actually worked with Olive.

"Thank you for clarifying," Pammy said. "I'll deal with this from here."

"I'll talk with Irene Roth. She shouldn't be bringing these people to you—"

"She didn't," Pammy said quickly. She didn't want to get Irene in trouble. "A graduate student was proposing this class. I'll kibosh it as soon as I get back."

"What graduate student?" Olive snapped. "I'll talk with her—"

"It's all right," Pammy said. "I'll take care of it. If I come to believe that she was trying to pull something over on the university, I'll let you know."

Olive pursed her lips. "I don't like this, Pamela."

"Neither do I," Pammy said. And then, because she couldn't help herself, she added, "I am confused, though. I thought you supported the self-defense classes."

"I did," Olive said. "I made a mistake."

Pammy's hands gripped the edge of the counter. Its corners were rigid. They bit into her skin.

"What made you change your mind?" she asked.

Olive pushed her glasses up to the bridge of her nose. Their lenses distorted her eyes, made them seem larger than they actually were.

"You didn't hear about that poor girl?" Olive said.

"Which girl?" Pammy asked.

"The one they found in Tilden Park yesterday," Olive said.

"I hadn't heard anything about it," Pammy said. She hadn't heard much news in the last two days, except for some headlines this morning—something about the Apollo Crew heading back toward Earth.

"*Olive!*" a woman yelled from the back. "You're not supposed to—"

"It's Pamela," Olive said as if everyone in this office knew who Pammy was. Maybe they did.

Alice suddenly looked worried. She rolled the papers that comprised Pammy's list into a tight baton. Alice glanced from Pammy to Olive and back again.

Pammy couldn't quite read Alice's expression, but the women who had been watching slipped back into the offices as if they didn't want to be a part of this conversation any longer.

Olive came closer to the counter. "The police arrived here last night, wanted some information, so I had to stay late. I'm not supposed to tell you anything, because they're not going to tell the press anything until the family's notified, but Pamela, what I heard gave me pause."

Pammy's stomach knotted up. "The girl they found in the park, is she all right?"

"Of course she's not all right!" Olive snapped. "That's why they have to notify family. She's dead, Pamela. She died horribly, and the police believe that she fought with someone. They believe that she sealed her own death warrant by fighting back."

Pammy frowned. "How would they know that?"

"Her wounds," Olive said. "She had skin underneath her fingernails. What fingernails were left, of course. They ripped off in the struggle."

Pammy closed her eyes for a brief moment, trying to calm herself. She had heard this kind of thing from the police before. Men often got defensive wounds on their hands as well, but the police always said they were heroically trying to stave off savage blows.

When women got them, they were stupidly trying to fight back.

"It was awful," Olive said, as if she had been waiting for Pammy to look directly at her. "They showed me photographs."

Pammy started. "Why would they show you photographs, Olive?"

"They don't know who she is," Olive said. "Her identification is missing, and they don't have her fingerprints on file. They doubt she's been fingerprinted, since her hair is nicely trimmed and she has good teeth, whatever that means."

"It means," Pammy said softly, "that she hasn't been starving and she wasn't using a lot of drugs."

"Well, there is that, then," Olive said somewhat sarcastically.

"I'm still not sure why they came to you," Pammy said.

Olive raised her chin slightly, then blinked hard. The photographs had truly disturbed her.

"We have photographs of all of our students," she said. "We take them as part of their freshman class, and then again, if they want, of course, in later years. They were hoping I would go through the files for them."

Pammy couldn't imagine how much work that would take. There were thousands of students at UC-Berkeley. "Do the police do this often?"

"Sometimes," Olive said. "Usually, we have more to go on than this. You know, a name, an address, an age, something."

Pammy nodded.

"Sometimes, we have student assistants who can go through the files and pull the relevant year's worth of photographs. Or we start with students who didn't re-enroll. But this time..." Olive's voice grew hoarse, and she cleared her throat. "This time, it's summer, and who knows which students will return and which ones won't and who stayed in their apartment for the summer and who left, and what exactly is..."

She swallowed, then stopped.

Pammy didn't know what to say, so she didn't say anything at all.

"I told them that I'd look, which was my mistake. That's when they showed me their photographs—the ones clean enough for me to view."

Olive's voice broke. "I think...I think maybe...I think they thought it would galvanize me, make me look quicker."

"It might get the image out of your mind," Pammy said, hoping she was being helpful.

"*Nothing* will scrub that away," Olive said fiercely. "*Nothing*. And you, Miss Girls-Are-Strong-Too, you should see what happens to girls who fight like that. You should see...."

Olive stopped herself, her lips pressed together. Then she whirled and started back to her office.

"Olive," Pammy said, "when did she die?"

"What does it matter?" Olive asked.

"A friend of mine saw something a few nights ago," Pammy said. "Maybe this girl—"

"This girl was already dead," Olive said. "That was part of the problem, Pamela. She was already dead, and animals have gotten to her. The soft squishy bits are gone, do you understand? And the police thought I could recognize her from some photograph, compare it to *that*."

She shuddered, then walked away.

This time, Pammy didn't try to stop her. Pammy just watched as Olive slipped into the back.

Alice walked up to the counter, her expression apologetic. She unrolled the list, flattening it on the countertop with her hands.

"How often do the police do that?" Pammy asked. "How often do they come here for information like that?"

"More and more these days," Alice said quietly. "Kids just seem to vanish sometimes. Usually it's missing persons. Parents contact them, wanting to know if their child has moved or is still attending classes. Sometimes the students keep us informed, but don't inform their parents."

Pammy tried not to look at the lists, curling slightly under Alice's palms. "I can understand that."

"We can too. Students have always done these things. We're allowed to give information on the undergraduates if they're not yet twenty-one, but the graduate students—well, sometimes it's hard. I'm glad I work here and not, say, at the law school."

Pammy nodded. "I was actually wondering about the poor dead girl—"

"It's not your fault, Pammy," Alice said. "Olive's been yelling at everyone since she saw those photographs."

"Is that normal?" Pammy asked. "That—"

"Olive? No, she doesn't yell as much as you'd think—"

"No," Pammy said. "The police, showing crime scene photographs to a civilian."

Alice shook her head. "I think they're desperate. I overheard some of the conversation. I think they're worried that they might be blamed for the death."

"How could they...?" Pammy stopped herself mid-thought. "They think this happened during martial law? Has the body been in the park that long?"

Alice shrugged.

"Would there be any of it intact?" Pammy said, more to herself than to Alice. "I mean, martial law was lifted—"

"I don't know," Alice said, "and I don't want to know. The girl's dead. It's horrible. She was fighting with someone. Also horrible. Or maybe—I mean, she was off the side of a trail. Maybe she had fallen and grabbed someone for help, and scraped skin as she did so. Maybe that person was too scared to go to the police after this spring. I know I might have been."

Pammy looked at her. She hadn't expected that revelation from Alice.

Alice shrugged again. "Think about it. If you were a college kid, and right now, the police are demonizing them, and you go to the police with something simple—a friend fell. That could lead to a murder conviction as easily as an accidental death."

Pammy's mouth went dry. She hadn't thought of that at all. It seemed odd that Alice would have. But maybe the admissions office was seeing things Pammy couldn't even dream of.

"I'm glad my kids are still young," Alice said in a low voice. "Because right now, even though we get all kinds of breaks because we're employees, I wouldn't let my children go to school here. Heck, the way the country's going, I'm not sure I want my kids to go to college at all."

Pammy found herself nodding. This world certainly wasn't the one she'd attended college in. She had thought things had gotten bad here in Berkeley during all the protests of the Free Speech Movement. Those protests seemed like child's play now.

"Anyway," Alice said when Pammy didn't respond to her confession. "I have your list of names. You really taking men in your classes now?"

Pammy shook her head. "I'm rethinking it."

"If it's because of Olive, don't. Do what you need to do," Alice said. She slid the papers forward. "Now, onto this."

Pammy put her hand on the papers, spreading them out.

Alice tapped her finger on the top page. "I don't know where you got these names, but most of them aren't students."

Pammy was not surprised. Since these kids were missing only from the perspective of friends, it stood to reason that many of the kids had just dropped out of school.

"Something just seemed off about the proposal," she said, "but I couldn't think of a reason to say no."

"Well, take a look." Alice held the edges of the papers down. "I marked the current enrollees in red. Three of them are at the same address that they've been at all along. One's back in the dorms after living off campus for a while. I'm rather surprised the four of them are on the list. Good kids, it seems. The others…well, the university is better off without them, I think."

"You recognize some of the names?" Pammy asked, surprised.

"Not so much," Alice said, "but there are notations in the files. I recognize the pattern. They come, they get involved in some of the politics around here or they drug up or whatever that's called, then they flunk out. The next stage is coming back with a parent, begging to be reinstated and having the Fs thrown off their transcript. We've been getting a lot of that lately, and some high-powered attorneys trying to force us to do it as well."

"Really?" Pammy hadn't heard of any of that kind of behavior before. Maybe that would be an explanation for the disappearances. "Are any of the students on this list involving their parents?"

"No one here, yet," Alice said. "But believe me, they will. That's how the pattern works."

Pammy bit the inside of her lower lip. "Could they just be…missing?"

Apparently, Alice didn't hear the trepidation behind Pammy's question.

"Your guess is as good as mine," Alice said. "They could have gone missing. They could have gone to some hippie commune. They could have gone to some protest in Washington, D.C. They could be in some drug house off Telegraph. We have no way to know, unless someone reports something to us. All we get are transcripts and inquiries."

"And you have no transcripts or inquiries for these kids?" Pammy asked.

"Transcripts on all of them, with lots of Fs or DNFs. None of the kids formally dropped out, as far as I can tell. But the information might not have gotten to us yet."

"Okay." Pammy was trying to understand this. "Yet you mentioned these kids were all trouble."

"Oh, we have at least one note in each of the files. Some from professors citing disruptions. Some from the dorms, requesting a room be opened or closed or one of the students to be permanently barred from the dorm—"

"You can do that?" Pammy asked.

"*We* can't. The Housing Administration makes those decisions, but we do document things. Because complaints accumulate. Every once in a while, we have to tell a student they may not enroll for the next semester."

"I didn't know the university did that," Pammy said.

"We like to keep it quiet," Alice said. "Usually, these students, they go away—they don't take classes for a semester or two, and we can tell them that they're no longer enrolled. Then we make them reapply, and we turn them down. They have to go through a lot of hoops to get back into the university."

"Even though you accepted them once," Pammy said.

Alice shrugged. "It's a political process, at its core. We do have limited slots. We can use our discretion. You'd be surprised some of the former students we've turned away."

"Like Mario Savio?" Pammy asked, citing one of the leaders of the Free Speech Movement. His attempts at getting readmitted to the university made national news two years before.

"That was a particular case," Alice said primly. "Savio's request played out in the news because he was well known. Most of these requests do not make the news at all. Only the family knows. Or the student."

"Are these students as active as Savio was?" Pammy asked, thinking about those political listings that she had left off of her recopied list.

"Good heavens no," Alice said. "He was the national leader of a movement against the university—"

Pammy started to correct her, then didn't. The Free Speech Movement ultimately was about students' rights, not about trying to hurt the university. But, Pammy knew, lots of university employees, particularly with offices here, in front of the action that happened inside the building and at Sather Gate, felt otherwise.

"—no one is on par with Savio," Alice was saying. Pammy had missed most of what she had said. "But some of these kids do have marks in their files for their protest activities. And some of them, particularly the young men, were involved in some of the more violent protests."

"Did Olive know that?" Pammy asked.

Alice nodded.

"So that's why she's so against them taking my classes," Pammy said.

"She's against them, period." Alice patted the papers as if they had tried to escape. "She's not necessarily alone in that."

Alice said that last very softly. Pammy frowned at her.

"You have no idea what it's like here, Pammy," Alice said. "We got gassed in May."

"So did we," Pammy said.

They stared at each other for a moment. Something sizzled in the air between them. It wasn't quite hostility, but it wasn't friendly either. It was as if their shared experience had made them enemies rather than solidifying their friendship.

Alice slid the papers toward her.

"I don't think you should conduct this class," she said.

Pammy made a show of thumbing through the pages. Someone had written the dates of last known attendance beside each name. The red marks that Alice made showed up like flares in the middle of a sea of yellow paper and blue ink.

Pammy folded the pages and sighed, still making this a show.

"Trust me," she said to Alice, "I'm not going to teach any of these young people in any of my classes. And I'll take your advice and Olive's under advisement. I'll rethink the policy change on men."

"Thank you," Alice said.

Pammy put the folded pages in her purse.

"No," she said quietly. "Thank you. You and Olive have helped me more than you know."

She turned toward the door. Then Alice said, louder than before, "You be careful, Pammy. You have no idea what these kids can do."

Pammy stopped, wondering if it was only the kids. After all, the shootings, the gas attacks, the tanks—none of that had been the kids. No wonder the police were keeping that poor girl's death quiet. No wonder they worried that they would be blamed for it.

Given the place Berkeley had become, the police themselves were probably the most obvious suspects.

"I will be careful," Pammy said, knowing she was taking the statement a little differently than Alice had meant it. "I promise."

VAL

I didn't get a lot of sleep, but for the first time in almost a year, I didn't need it. I actually had energy when I woke up. I was looking forward to the day.

That was new, at least for this me. The old me, the pre-crater me, she used to wake up happy and ready to face the world. But that attitude had vanished after the Grand Nefertiti Ball.

I was feeling good because I was useful again.

I folded the recopied notes and put them in my purse. Then I grabbed some extra clothes, put on my sneakers, and headed to the gym.

I bounced as I walked, heading through knots of students on their way to summer school classes, and past restaurants filled with young people who thought a cup of coffee gave them the right to sit all day.

The sky was overcast, and the air had a bit of a bite to it. I hadn't brought a sweater, and I wished I had. This was July, and it wasn't even seventy degrees.

I really wasn't in Chicago any longer.

Then I turned onto Pammy's street.

A bright orange Chevelle stopped in front of the gym, and a woman got out. As I walked closer, I realized it was the bouffant woman from my class. She carried a macramé purse, and she wore shorts, despite the cool weather.

She had the kind of legs I always envied, long and just muscular enough, the kind that looked good in heels and showed off well in miniskirts.

I sighed. Clearly I had been running later than I expected. I had wanted time to talk to Pammy before class. Maybe we would take it anyway, particularly if Eagle was there.

But as I stepped inside, blinking against the harsh light of the overhead fluorescents, I didn't seen Pammy at all. Jill stood in front of the counter, a clipboard in hand, her short brown hair slightly mussed. She was in deep conversation with a woman I didn't recognize.

I glanced around the gym, searching for Pammy. A couple of young women were looking through the t-shirts. One woman with actual muscles was on the mat that looked a bit like a boxing ring to me, although when Pammy had given me the tour, she hadn't called it that. The woman was wearing boxing gloves, though, holding them up near her face and then bringing them down. She kept looking to one side, as if she were expecting someone else.

Another muscular woman was trying on football helmets. I hadn't realized the gym had any helmets at all, not that it seemed worthwhile. The helmets kept sliding on the woman's head, as if she were a child wearing her father's hat.

No one stood near the kitchen. Another woman from my class held the locker room door open for Joan, the woman I had befriended the day before. I suddenly realized that felt like days and days ago.

Jill handed the clipboard to the woman she was talking to and waved her hand toward a folding chair someone had set up near the far wall. As the woman walked to it, I headed to Jill.

"Hi," I said, suddenly feeling awkward. This was the woman who had automatically assumed I couldn't afford my lunch on Sunday. I had automatically assumed she held that opinion because of my skin color.

"Oh, hi!" she said in a fake-cheerful voice that most people reserved for young children or crazy people. "You came back."

My lips moved in a smile—or an approximation of a smile. I was used to this kind of reaction from certain types of white people. They liked to think they were being supportive, when really, they were being patronizing.

"Is Pammy in the kitchen?" I asked.

"She had an errand," Jill said in that same fake-cheerful voice. "She asked me to handle things until she gets back."

Pammy had said she was going to talk to the admissions office that morning. But I couldn't quite believe it would take hours. After all, half the class was here already, and it looked like another class had just ended.

Jill swung her arm upward and ostentatiously looked at her watch. "I hope she gets back before your class starts. I can teach it," she sighed as she spoke those words, "but I prefer not to."

Then she let her arm fall. Her gaze met mine. A slight frown had formed between her thin eyebrows.

I braced myself, although for what, I did not know.

"You *are* continuing with the class, right?" Jill's tone was the same, but she had moved from fake cheerfulness to fake concern. "I mean it is difficult at first, but—"

"I have no intention of dropping the class," I said before I could stop myself. Usually I remained silent when white people treated me like Jill had—like someone who needed to be treated gently or I would break or, I don't know, lose my temper and attack her or something.

I hadn't heard that voice out of myself, ever. Not even when the Dean at the University of Chicago Medical School told me that he didn't want me to enroll, even though I had tested better than anyone else who had applied.

Jill heard the sharpness in my voice and leaned back just a little. She *was* afraid of me, then.

"Oh, well, yes, of course. I didn't think so, but one, well, you know." She smiled at me awkwardly, then sidled away from me, and looked for someone else to talk with. She glanced at me, then nodded, and hurried toward the young women still looking at t-shirts.

"Ignore her," someone said beside me. "She's a piece of work."

I turned, half expecting Joan. Instead it was bouffant woman. I had to look up to see her eyes. I was surprised to realize that they were brown. I had expected blue or green.

She extended a well-manicured hand. "Marilyn Bakewell."

I took her hand. It was dry, and surprisingly, had calluses on the palm. "Valentina Wilson."

"And before you ask," Marilyn said, "I'm as new to class as you are. Unfortunately, I've known Jill since college."

Marilyn didn't lower her voice like I would have. But Jill didn't seem to notice. She was deep in conversation, holding up one of the t-shirts in front of the young women as if they were trying on fancy dresses for prom instead of picking out shirts with iron-on stickers.

"Unfortunately?" I asked.

Marilyn grinned at me. It was a conspiratorial look, like we were in something together.

"That's not entirely fair," she said. "Jill tries. Which is more than can be said for me."

I don't know, I wanted to say. *You don't treat me like an imbecile.*

"To be fair," Marilyn continued, "Jill is the one who told me about the gym. And believe me, I needed it. Jack LaLanne can only take you so far. And I cheat when I do it."

"Cheat?" I felt like I was in some kind of surreal conversation from one of those movies that depicted drug trips. Half of what she said didn't entirely make sense.

"Oh, you know. Do a push-up and touch your nose to the ground. I bend my elbows a half inch and call it good."

"I wish I could do it that well," I said.

"I have an advantage," she said. "I used to be a cheerleader for the Cal Bears, one hundred years ago. Some muscles never go away."

She clapped me on the back hard enough to make me take a step forward and grinned. "I'll bet you were one of the brainy ones I cheated off of in class."

My cheeks heated. At least she wasn't treating me like Jill had.

"I'm afraid not," I said. "I went to school in the Midwest. It must have been some other brainy black girl."

"And here I was thinking of the tiny smart ones," she said, her eyes twinkling. "It's so easy to see over your heads."

I laughed in spite of myself.

"I'm going to go get ready, particularly if Jill has to teach this thing," Marilyn said. "I have to keep reminding myself to take this baby weight off somehow or I'll end up as round as my mom. You want me to grab you a jump rope?"

"Please," I said, smiling. I hadn't expected to like her. Now, I felt a little embarrassed that I had called her "bouffant woman" in my head. "I have to put my purse in the locker room."

My smile faded just a little as I said that. I really wanted to talk to Pammy and Eagle right away. I didn't like to think about those lists, waiting to be seen.

I turned and headed toward the locker room. Two more women from my class came out, one tugging on the hem of a too-tight shirt.

I went inside. The locker room was steamy as if someone had taken a recent shower. Underneath that smell was the smell of bleach. A pile of blankets was neatly folded in a far corner. I hadn't seen those yesterday. Odd that Pammy would keep blankets here.

I set my purse near the shoe box with my regular shoes, the box I had deliberately left behind the day before. I checked the clasp on the purse. It was closed, but I leaned the top of the purse into the box anyway, so I could tell if someone messed with it.

I left the locker room, and almost ran into Pammy. She smelled faintly of sweat. Her shirt was slightly crooked as if she had just put it on.

"Pammy," I said. "Can we talk?"

She looked at me, and for a moment, I thought she didn't recognize me. Then her eyes focused.

"Is Eagle here yet?" she asked.

"I haven't seen her," I said.

"She's not in back, and I don't want to have this conversation twice."

My stomach clenched. "What conversation, exactly?"

Pammy half-shook her head. "Sorry. I—um…it's been a hard morning. Strange morning."

She glanced at the mats. Most of the class was already standing on the center mat, their jump ropes beside them. Joan was watching me over her shoulder. Jill had moved away from the t-shirts. One of the young women had a shirt draped over her arms.

"Let's talk after class," Pammy said. "I'll call Eagle if she's not here by then."

Pammy headed away from me before I could reply. I thought of those lists folded neatly in my purse, and I felt a stab of worry, like a surge of adrenaline.

Had I done all that work for nothing? Had I misunderstood our joint purpose? Pammy was almost rude, and I hadn't expected that.

I trudged toward the mat. Jill gave me another fake smile. But up front, Marilyn stood, smiling a real smile, an extra jump rope extended in one hand. She indicated a spot beside her.

I took the rope, thanked her, and said gently, "I promised Joan," and headed toward my spot in the back.

I wasn't exactly sure what I had promised Joan. I just knew I didn't want to be at the front of the class, next to a very nice former cheerleader who could do almost everything Pammy assigned.

Besides, I didn't want to keep staring at Pammy, wondering what she had been thinking when she put me off, wondering why she hadn't quite recognized me, wondering what exactly had happened this morning.

Of course, as I took my place beside Joan, I wondered anyway. Standing in a different position on the mat would make no difference.

I was dithering, feeling insecure and frightened, whipping myself up into some kind of lather—over what? What three other women thought?

I was back to the woman who had left Chicago, the woman who was afraid of her own shadow.

I didn't like that woman, and I didn't like how easy it was to tip the confident woman back into her.

I made myself take a deep breath and focus on the class itself.

I was here to learn how to be strong. So I would be strong.

No matter what it took.

EAGLE

Three more fruitless hospital calls. Two more people asking what had changed at Berkeley's Department of Public Health because Ethel hadn't called them instead.

Eagle certainly hoped Ethel was enjoying her fictitious vacation— and she hoped that Ethel would get a real vacation before she needed to call these hospitals again.

Everyone that Eagle had talked with was friendly and willing to help. The person at the other hospital sounded annoyed that she had to do any work at all on a Tuesday morning. Eagle could hear the snick of a cigarette lighter as the woman talked, the pauses in her sentences followed by the drag and smack of someone smoking as she spoke. Chain-smoking, judging by the snick of that lighter.

The names meant nothing, the records held no information on any of them, and Eagle was beginning to worry that she would have to call the morgues next.

The thought unnerved her. She stood up, splashing her latest cup of coffee on her notes. She grabbed a towel off the sideboard and blotted the legal paper so the ink wouldn't run and lose some of her precious notes.

Particularly the name and phone number of the girl who had gotten beat up.

Eagle tossed the towel in the sink, then sat back down and copied the name and phone number onto a different sheet of paper, just to be safe. The number belonged to the girl's parents, not the girl, but if she had been as badly injured as Monica DeSouza had said, then she might still be at home.

Eagle picked up the coffee cup and put it by the sink. She had had enough for one morning.

Then she picked up the phone, and almost without thinking, dialed the girl's phone number.

A woman answered, and Eagle's heart leapt. Maybe she would get to talk to one of the names on her list after all.

"Kelly MacGivers?" she asked.

There was a slight pause and then the woman said cautiously, "This is Carla MacGivers. May I help you?"

Eagle checked her notes. They distinctly said Kelly MacGivers. "I need to speak with Kelly, please."

"I am her mother," Carla MacGivers said. "I can answer any questions you might have."

"Thank you," Eagle said, "but I have business with Kelly."

"I'm afraid she's not here," Carla MacGivers said. "May I give her a message?"

"How may I reach her?" Eagle asked.

"Who is this?" Carla MacGivers asked.

"My name is Gertrude Anderson." Eagle couldn't think of a new name on such short notice. "I'm calling from San Francisco General Hospital."

"Yes?" There was a hint of panic in Carla MacGivers' voice now.

"Can you put me in touch with Kelly, please," Eagle said.

"Whatever you can say to her you can say to me," Carla MacGivers said.

Eagle half-smiled. If her mother had ever said that, Eagle would have gone down her mother's throat.

"I'm sorry, ma'am," Eagle said. "I'm calling from Billing and Records. I'm afraid I must deal with Miss MacGivers directly. There are confidentiality issues at play."

"I'm not sure if you have her birth records in front of you," Carla MacGivers said, "but Kelly's only nineteen. If this is something official, then you must deal with me."

"She stayed with us over a month ago," Eagle said, "and we have some follow-up questions. I don't have her birth records in front of me, so I'm afraid I must insist that I speak to her directly."

"Give me your number, and I'll make sure she reaches you," Carla MacGivers said.

Eagle nearly sighed aloud with frustration. She wasn't going to get past this woman. "At least give me her mailing address, so that I can reach her there."

"Certainly." Carla MacGivers sounded less panicked now. "Do you have a pen ready?"

What kind of question was that? Of course Eagle had a pen ready. She was the one who had asked for the information.

"Yes, of course," she said with the infinite patience of someone who dealt with stupid people all day long.

"Good," Carla MacGivers said. "Here is her mailing address."

And then she rattled off the same address that DeSouza had given Eagle earlier.

"That's the address we have on file," Eagle said. "However, several bills we have sent have come back stamped *no such address*. I need the real address, ma'am, or at least, I need a phone number where I can reach Miss MacGivers."

"That *is* our real address," Carla MacGivers snapped. "I don't know why you're getting the bills back. You've already charged us an arm and a leg for her treatment. Are you using one of those fancy code things?"

"A zip code, ma'am?"

"Yes," Carla MacGivers snapped. "In my experience, those things never work. Leave it off, mail us the bill again, and I'll make certain we pay it."

And then she hung up.

Eagle pulled the phone away from her ear, looking at the receiver as if it had betrayed her. That was odd. And it really didn't answer any questions for her. Except that the family was being very protective of Kelly, which was understandable, given the nature of her injuries.

330

Eagle hung up the receiver, then put her hands on the small of her back. She had been sitting too long. She glanced at the clock on the stove.

Pammy's beginner's class would end soon. Eagle was supposed to meet Val and Pammy after that class. Eagle had been thinking of blowing off the meeting, at least until she had more information, but now she was feeling restless.

Besides, that interaction with Kelly MacGivers' mother was just plain odd. Who was rude to a hospital billing department that had an incorrect address?

Eagle replayed the conversation in her mind. Her mother had said she would give the phone number to Kelly. Not take the number down and leave a message.

That implied that Kelly wasn't in the house.

Eagle would talk to Val and Pammy, get a little perspective, and then come back, make a few more phone calls, see what she could turn up.

Because right now, except for the strange case of Kelly MacGivers, Eagle was coming up with a whole lot of nothing.

Of course, she wasn't even halfway done with her list of hospitals. And then she still had the clinics and morgues.

Whoever thought investigative work was glamorous, thought wrong. It was a lot of digging. Rather like science classes in college. Repetition, leading to the same conclusions others might draw.

She grabbed a cloth bag, stuffed the papers inside, and found her wallet. She grabbed that as well, then went into the bathroom to check her appearance.

She didn't look like a woman who had gotten only few hours of sleep. She looked like a woman who never slept.

She hoped Val and Pammy had come up with something. Because at the moment, Eagle was regretting volunteering for hospital duty.

There had to be a better way to find the woman who got thrown into the truck.

Eagle just didn't know what, exactly, that better way was.

PAMMY

Pammy watched the door more than she watched her students. Which, she knew, was not the way to run a class. Particularly an exercise class filled with beginners. Beginners injured themselves when they sneezed wrong. Pammy really needed to pay attention to make certain they were moving correctly.

Instead, she was waiting for Eagle to arrive—even though she knew that Eagle never came in the front door.

The class remained full, which surprised her. Pammy usually lost a few after the first day, when the students realized they would have to work hard.

Pammy recited her patter, moving the students from stretches to sit-ups (holding each other's feet, keeping their backs straight) to push-ups to jumping rope. Some of the students from Jill's earlier class watched for a few minutes, no doubt remembering when they had had this class, and then, one by one, they filtered out of the gym.

Jill watched too. She hadn't said anything about the anger she had displayed the day before. She had just shown up early, as if she and Pammy had decided on it, and reminded Pammy that there was a class to teach. Her presence allowed Pammy to go to the admissions office and have that deeply disturbing conversation.

Pammy had thought about the conversation the entire way back, feeling unsettled. Not because of the missing students. That should have bothered her more than it did. But because of Olive, blaming her for that poor girl's death. As if training women to defend themselves put them in harm's way.

As if training women to be strong was a bad thing.

Pammy had heard those kinds of disparaging remarks from the day she proposed the gym. She had heard that from men, sometimes, and other women, often. She usually wrote it off, thinking it was fear of change. But sometimes—such as with this death and the skin under the nails—those remarks echoed for her.

There was no way to know whether or not that girl who died had ever been to the gym, no way to know—at least at the moment—whether or not she had died defending herself. No way to know who she was either.

And those thoughts were what had preoccupied Pammy so thoroughly that she hadn't heard Val ask a question before class started. Pammy had looked right through Val and then realized the look had startled Val.

Instead of reassuring Val, like she normally would have, Pammy had blown her off. But Pammy really didn't want to talk about that meeting in the admissions office more than once. She was half embarrassed by it, and she wasn't entirely sure why.

Finally, she looked over the rest of the gym and saw Eagle standing near the locker room door, arms crossed. From this distance, Eagle looked frail. Pammy always thought of her as strong and solid, but she wasn't a large woman. She was as tall as Pammy, but thinner than Pammy had realized.

Had Eagle lost weight? Or had she always been that thin and Pammy just hadn't noticed?

She made herself look away from Eagle. The women in the class were red-faced and sweat-covered. Some of them were breathing hard, doubling over almost every time Pammy gave them a moment to rest.

Pammy's gaze met Jill's. Pammy touched her left wrist. Jill looked at her ever-present watch, then held up her right hand, fingers splayed.

Five minutes left.

"Let's cool down," Pammy said to the class. Usually she had them do the cool down on their own, but she wanted this class over with.

She led them in a few simple stretches. Eagle leaned her head against the wall beside the locker room, eyes closed as if she could sleep standing up. Jill walked behind the counter, which was a good plan, just in case people had questions when class was over.

The final stretch was simple: hands over heads, palms pressed together. Then on a five-count, slowly separate the hands and bring the arms down until they were parallel with the shoulders. Hold that position for a ten-count, then on another five-count, bring the arms to the sides.

The women were shaking as they did this. Pammy used to wonder how women got so out of shape until Opal reminded her that most girls never got into shape in the first place. All of this was brand new.

"Great work, everyone!" Pammy made herself sound enthusiastic and pleased, although if she had to tell someone what the class had done, she wouldn't have been able to do it. "Thank you! I hope to see you all tomorrow!"

And then she walked away from the front of the class, even though it was clear some of the students wanted to buttonhole her with questions. The questions after this class were usually of a type she didn't want to answer: *How am I doing? Should I be exercising this heavily at my age? Am I going to do permanent damage to my arm/hip/leg/back? Are you sure average women can do this? Because it seems hard...*

Pammy smiled dismissively as she moved around the students. She tried not to make eye contact with anyone except Val. Val was talking to Joan, smiling easily. Marilyn Bakewell had joined them, and Val was making introductions.

Pammy didn't stick around. She walked to Eagle's side.

Pammy touched Eagle's shoulder. Eagle started, then blinked. She really had fallen asleep standing up.

Her eyes were sunken into her face, her cheekbones hollow. She looked exhausted.

"We gonna talk?" Eagle said.

"Yes," Pammy said. "Will my office do?"

Eagle frowned, staring at Jill's back. "If we don't get interrupted too much."

"I think we'll be all right," Pammy said.

At that moment, Val ended her conversation with Joan and Marilyn, and glanced over at Pammy. Pammy raised her hand, beckoned Val to come with them, and Val nodded.

Then she turned back to the women she had been talking to, maybe saying her good-byes. Pammy hoped Val wasn't saying more.

"Hear anything?" Eagle asked.

Pammy frowned. Hadn't they just said they were going to talk in the office?

Eagle raised her eyebrows, and Pammy suddenly realized Eagle was asking about the events of the night before.

"I didn't tell them to contact me," Pammy said. "I hope they don't, honestly."

Eagle nodded. "I'll put it out of my mind then."

Pammy was a bit surprised it was still in Eagle's mind. Eagle had always struck her as someone who could compartmentalize easily.

Eagle pushed off the wall. "Let's go."

Pammy was about to say they needed to wait for Val. But Val had nearly reached them. She was red-faced too, her skin covered with a layer of sweat.

"Did you want to clean up first?" Pammy asked. "We'll wait."

Val smiled. The smile softened her face. "Do I smell that bad?"

Pammy felt a flush rise in her own face.

"Kidding," Val said. "I'm okay. Are we going to the kitchen? I can rinse my face there."

"My office," Pammy said.

"Then I will rinse off and change my shirt," Val said. "I'll meet you there."

She slipped behind them into the locker room, moving much more easily than she had the day before.

She had either had some athletic training before or she had some natural ability. Pammy had seen that before with other students. The ones who either had experience or who had some ability recovered faster than the others.

"Let's wait in your office," Eagle said. "I really don't want to answer any questions about normal aches and pains."

Pammy doubted that this class would ask Eagle anything. They didn't know she was the gym's unofficial medic. Then she noted where Eagle was looking.

Some of the women were talking to Jill, and Jill would send anyone Eagle's way if they had questions about their health.

Pammy followed Eagle to the office, grabbing an extra folding chair as they walked past the pile. Normally, Pammy kept one extra chair in her office, not two.

She unlocked the door and they slipped inside. She turned on the light, handed the chair to Eagle, then went behind the desk, tidying some of the paperwork she had left lying around. Yesterday's paper, with its exclamation-point filled headline about the moon walk, seemed like it had come from the distant past.

She almost offered it to Eagle as a keepsake of the major historical event, then saw Eagle's expression. Pammy folded the paper and tossed it into the trash.

She took a deep breath, still feeling a little off-kilter.

"Do you know anything about Val?" she asked quietly.

"Why?" Eagle asked. "Did she do something wrong?"

Pammy shook her head. "It's just—"

The door opened, and Val entered, accompanied by the scent of fresh soap. Her face had a fresh-scrubbed look. She seemed even younger than she had when Pammy met her.

"Sorry that took so long," she said.

"It didn't take long at all," Eagle said, taking the folding chair near the wall. She left the comfortable chair for Val.

Pammy frowned ever so slightly. She couldn't remember Eagle being that considerate with someone who wasn't a patient.

Pammy decided to ignore it. She opened one of the drawers on her desk and removed a cardboard do-not-disturb sign she had taken from a Holiday Inn years ago.

"Put this on the door, would you?" she asked Val. "And then lock it."

Val opened the door slightly, hung the sign on the knob, and pulled the door closed. Then she sat down in the chair, set her purse on her lap, and opened it, removing some folded papers.

Eagle took some out of a cloth bag she was carrying.

Pammy took the papers she had brought back from the admissions office and set them on her desk.

"Looks like we've been busy," Val said. Her mood was oddly upbeat. She seemed more relaxed than she had before. "Who wants to go first?"

Pammy didn't. She still hadn't processed the conversation with Olive yet.

"I don't got much," Eagle said. "I've been on the phone with hospital after hospital, seeing if any of these kids have shown up in the last six months. I haven't called any morgues yet."

Somehow Pammy had expected Eagle to go directly to the hospitals. Hadn't Eagle said that was what she was going to do?

"Only one person showed up in my search so far," Eagle said. "It's a girl, named Kelly MacGivers. She was beaten within an inch of her life. She had rope burns on her wrists and ankles, and damage to the skin around her mouth, from tape, the admitting physician thought. That was in March."

Pammy slid the paperwork closer. Pammy knew Kelly MacGivers was on it because she and Eagle and Val had been working off the same list, but for some reason, that name was ringing a bell.

"Here's the strange thing, though," Eagle said. "She went to San Francisco General with the injuries. Her parents signed all the paperwork. She was going to school here, and her parents live in Daly City. There are a half dozen hospitals that are closer to her parents' home. And there are a lot of hospitals closer to here than SFGH."

"She had rope burns?" Val turned slightly in her chair to face Eagle. "Was she wrapped in a blanket?"

Pammy looked at Val in surprise. Eagle frowned.

"Why?" Eagle asked.

"Because," Val said. "I happened on some strange things—"

"Talking with Darla Newsome's roommate?" Pammy asked.

"That was something else," Val said. "Last night, I couldn't sleep, so I called police departments...."

Eagle raised her eyebrows and looked at Pammy, not trying to hide her shock. Pammy was frowning. She actually felt some disapproval rise, but she wasn't exactly sure why.

"…husband, Truman," Val was saying. She had noticed the looks, but she didn't sound defensive. "I didn't say who I was, but I knew that the late night staff wasn't as picky about protocol as the daytime staff. Anyway, I found some information about a one-ton, some women, and a murder."

Somehow she managed to say that flatly, even though the words were dramatic.

"Recent murder?" Eagle asked.

Val shook her head. "That was my first question. It wasn't the woman you saw. This body was found on July 10. It was pushed off a truck on…"

She pulled out some paper and looked at it. Pammy almost stood so that she could see something besides Val's neat printing, which showed up like ghostly backwards letters through the thin legal paper.

"…not on, exactly," she corrected herself. "Between 61st and 62nd where they intersect with Dover."

"The boundary between North Oakland and Berkeley," Pammy said, immediately understanding the problem.

"I spoke to someone in North Oakland who said the body, which was pushed from this truck bed, landed on the Berkeley side. I have the names of the BPD detectives who, so far, haven't investigated at all. They're claiming that no one knows where she landed, so they don't know whose jurisdiction it's in."

Now, Val's voice had some charge to it. Pammy's back had stiffened. She understood that charge as well.

"That's stupid," Eagle said.

"Yeah," Val said in a tone that lead Pammy to believe she'd seen that sort of thing before, and accepted it as a routine part of police work. "But here's the thing. This poor girl, who is, at the moment, a Jane Doe, was pushed off the truck, wrapped in a blanket, her wrists and ankles bound, and a gag over her mouth. The cop I spoke to didn't say exactly how she died, but he led me to believe she had suffocated."

"Ankles and wrists," Eagle said. "And a truck. Was it an F-350?"

"Don't know," Val said. "And we don't have the police report, even if they did know. There's some witness, but of course I couldn't get that."

"I'm surprised you got that much," Pammy said. And she was. She wouldn't have known how to do that.

Val shrugged. "I was in the squad room a lot. I observed. Cops are willing to help cops."

"But you're not a cop," Pammy said.

"I'm not," Val said. "And before you say anything, I do know that it's illegal to pose as a police officer. I was very careful as to how I identified myself. If they ended up thinking I was a detective, that's not my problem."

Eagle barked out a laugh. Pammy looked at her in surprise. When had she last heard Eagle laugh? Had she *ever* heard Eagle laugh?

Eagle saw Pammy's look and misinterpreted it. "I did my share of pretending last night too. The phone is nice and anonymous."

"And people are more trusting than they should be," Val said. "Even the police."

Pammy's shoulders relaxed slightly. Val was *helping*. She wasn't getting in the way. Pammy let out a small breath. She trusted people all the time. She had to go with her instincts here. Val was proving herself.

"I tried to reach this Kelly MacGivers this morning," Eagle said. "I got her mother, who put up a very effective roadblock, not that I blame her. But if we can reach her, maybe we can find out if she was in the same truck."

"Well, I think someone was," Val said. "Because I also spoke to a very nice detective in Walnut Creek. He has been looking for a Ford F-350 for over a month. The driver had a screaming girl in the flatbed, wrapped in a blanket. He stopped at a gas station, and the attendant called the police. It turned into some kind of altercation, and I'm not exactly sure of the events, but it ended with the truck driver picking up this 200-pound gas station attendant, tossing him across the parking lot, covering his legs with gasoline, and threatening to light a match."

"Holy shit," Eagle said.

Pammy had put a hand on her chest without a recollection of doing so. "Is he all right?"

"Yes," Val said, "but there was a lot of clean-up. Ever since, this Walnut Creek detective has been searching for the F-350. He has a license plate, but when he ran it, he didn't get anything."

Eagle started to reach for the paper, then clenched her fist and set it down. "Did you get that plate?"

"I did," Val said. "You want to compare it to yours?"

"Yes," Eagle said.

Pammy slid some papers on her desk, her heart pounding. "I have it here somewhere."

"No need to look," Eagle said. "I know it by heart."

Val slid a different piece of paper over to Eagle, and pointed at something near the top. Eagle shook her head slowly.

"It's off by one number," she said. "Either mine's off or his is off."

"He's the police, and he called the DMV. They said it was a made-up license," Val said. "He's really dogged about this. He's afraid for the girl."

"I get that," Eagle said drily. "So his number is off, not mine."

"He got it from the attendant," Val said. "I think the attendant was thinking about other things at the time."

Pammy shuddered. Gasoline poured all over her legs at a gas station. Yes, she'd be thinking of other things.

"How do we get that detective our number?" Pammy asked. She felt over her head here.

"I don't know," Val said. "If I call back, why would I have him run the plate when I can do it myself—in theory, you know?"

Eagle was nodding. "But we have confirmation. This is our guy. The same truck, the same everything."

Pammy frowned. "It's not really confirmation. I mean, you didn't see this man wrap a woman in a blanket—"

"No," Eagle said fiercely. "I saw him kidnap her."

The words reverberated in the small room. Then Val gathered herself and made eye contact with both Pammy and Eagle.

"There's one more thing," Val said. "There are reports of bodies, male bodies—skeletons, really—found near Mount Diablo, wrapped in blankets and tied up."

Eagle's gaze met Pammy's. Pammy had gone cold. She had never really heard of anything like this. There were spree killers, like that man in Chicago—what was his name? The one who killed all the nurses—and that shooter in the University of Texas Bell Tower a few years back. But someone who kidnapped people, young people, and then tossed them away—

"Have you ever heard of anything like this?" Pammy couldn't help herself. She had to ask.

She wasn't looking at Eagle, though. She was looking at Val.

Val half shrugged.

"I come from Chicago," she said, and Pammy tensed. She would probably find out the name of that nurse killer now. "And there are a lot of bodies that get discovered all over the South and West Sides. But those are usually gang related. The bodies get dumped as a warning. Truman—"

Her voice broke, and her eyes filled with tears. She held up her hand, then shook her head.

Eagle was watching her, as if uncertain what to do.

Val cleared her throat.

"Truman," she said, her voice a bit wobbly. "He said the gangs were an insolvable problem, and it was closer to a war than it was to anything else. So, I guess, no, I've never heard of anything like this."

"Yeah," Eagle said quietly. "A war."

Pammy wondered what was behind those three words. Eagle did not elaborate, but Pammy stared at her for a long moment.

"My experiences don't count," Eagle said.

"If you have something—"

"Honestly, Pammy," Eagle said. "My experiences don't count."

She spoke very forcefully, and Pammy had no choice but to stop pushing.

"What kind of man are we dealing with?" Pammy asked.

"As I see it," Val said, "he's doing one of two things. He's killing these people and dumping their bodies, or he's dumping the bodies of people who died accidentally. I'm thinking it's not accidental, though, given the treatment of that gasoline attendant."

Pammy shuddered. "How do we get this to the police?"

"We have only supposition at the moment," Val said.

"Well, not entirely," Eagle said. "You've forgotten Kelly MacGivers."

"You think she was abducted by this truck monster?" Pammy asked.

"Yes, I think she was abducted," Eagle said, with the same kind of force she had used before. "And here's why. I think it's really strange that her parents took her to an outside hospital, told the attending *not* to

341

send information for a follow-up to the family doctor, and she has the same kinds of injuries."

Pammy let out a small sigh. Poor girl. Pammy wondered how she had gotten away.

"These people are clearly scared." Eagle looked at Pammy. "Maybe we figure out how to talk to her?"

Pammy held up her index finger. She grabbed her own list and shuffled through it, looking at the four names marked in red, hoping as she did so that she had a reason for remembering Kelly MacGivers.

"There it is," she said, feeling an elation that she immediately tamped down as inappropriate.

"What?" Val asked, leaning forward.

"Kelly MacGivers," Pammy said. "She's back on campus."

"What?" Eagle asked.

"She re-enrolled." Pammy shook the paper at Val and Eagle. "I have her address right here."

EAGLE

Eagle hadn't expected Pammy to have Kelly MacGivers' campus address. She had thought that Kelly MacGivers was up in her bedroom in her parents' house, hiding and shivering and pretending that she was Just Fine. Eagle hadn't expected the girl to be back at the university.

Pammy's office was hot and close. Val looked a little shell-shocked. Pammy was more animated than she had been throughout the entire conversation. She held a piece of legal paper in her hands.

Eagle leaned forward, reaching for the paper. "Are you sure you have Kelly MacGivers' *current* address? Because she had enrolled before. That's how the students knew her."

Pammy gave Eagle a withering look. "I spoke to the admissions office this morning, and this is what they gave me."

She handed Eagle the sheet. The same names that Eagle had been dealing with for the past twenty-four hours were on that list, only in Pammy's neat printing. Most had notations in another hand nearby, but four were circled in red. One of those names was Kelly MacGivers.

"The address is at the bottom of the page," Pammy said.

Eagle's gaze snapped downward. There it was—Kelly MacGivers.

"This can't be right," Eagle said. "She lives in Stern Hall?"

"What's wrong with Stern Hall?" Val asked.

"It's a dorm," Eagle said.

Val shrugged. "Don't college students live in dorms?"

"She's not a first-year student," Eagle said. "And from what I can tell, her parents have money."

"Generally students with money end up in their own apartments," Pammy said. "Sometimes the parents even buy housing for them."

"Oh," Val said, her voice lilting upward in obvious understanding. "I encountered that yesterday, with Darla's roommate."

"Darla didn't have the money to buy housing," Pammy said, frowning. "Her father said she was a scholarship student."

Eagle was frowning too. She had forgotten about Darla Newsome.

"I know she didn't have the money," Val said. "But her roommate, Lucy, owned the entire building or rather, her father did. And Lucy still has to pay rent, along with three other girls. Darla's one of those girls. I let Lucy believe I was going to sublet from Darla."

"Still," Eagle said, "that sounds expensive."

Val nodded. "Darla was working several jobs to pay for school and housing until sometime last year. Then she came into money."

All three women looked at each other. Eagle wasn't understanding any of this. How did a student come into money that her parents didn't know about?

"Was she selling drugs?" Pammy asked.

"No," Val said. "Lucy has a no-drugs policy. Her father's really strict. They can't even smoke marijuana in the apartment."

Val said "marijuana" primly, and Eagle stiffened just a little. She suddenly realized that Val would disapprove of her lifestyle, if she knew about it.

"Let's get back to the point," Eagle said, not wanting to discuss drugs at all. "We need to talk to Kelly MacGivers, but how?"

"We're not sure that she knew this guy," Val said. "Something else entirely could have happened to her."

"Really?" Eagle asked. "Like what?"

"A hazing gone wrong," Val said. "Sororities and fraternities have strange rituals. It wouldn't be the first time someone got injured in one of those."

Eagle was shaking her head. "If that happened, Mommy and Daddy would be suing someone. These people have money. They would be talking to the university and they probably would not have sent their daughter back here."

"Hmm," Val said. "Then maybe what happened to her didn't happen at the university. Maybe we're looking in the wrong place."

Eagle hated all of this guessing. They needed facts, not supposition. "I think we need to talk with her before we rule her out. She's on the list, and she's a good lead."

"She's exactly what we thought," Pammy said. "We thought the students would misidentify a few students as missing when the students were actually still enrolled."

"She's not at all what we thought." A throbbing had started in Eagle's left temple, a clear sign that her blood pressure was going up. Why couldn't these two understand? "Kelly MacGivers was injured, she deliberately went to a hospital outside of her neighborhood—both of her neighborhoods—"

"Maybe whatever happened to her happened close by," Pammy said.

"If she was raped," Val said, her voice quiet and yet somehow more powerful than everyone else's, "her parents wouldn't want anyone to know that. *She* wouldn't want anyone to know that either. Maybe that's why she avoided the family doctor."

Eagle looked at her. There was a hint of dusky red in Val's cheeks. She wasn't making eye contact.

Pammy's gaze had sharpened. Her frown deepened. She looked at Eagle and tilted her head slightly as if to say, *Hmmm.*

"It's possible," Pammy said softly. "That would explain all of the secrecy, and the fact that the parents were being overprotective."

"Yeah, but it doesn't explain the medical report," Eagle said. "The file that the woman at the hospital read to me said nothing about assault, sexual or otherwise."

"Would that woman have told you?" Val's voice was still quiet.

She would have told Ethel, Eagle almost said, then caught the remark before it escaped. Val and Pammy didn't know about Ethel or the Berkeley Department of Public Health. They didn't know about all the lies she had told.

Eagle sighed. She had to be honest here, in this room.

"I don't know," she said. "The woman I was speaking to might have kept it quiet."

"Or, it might not be in the records at all," Val said. "You mentioned the parents had money. If they had enough influence, they might have convinced the ER doctor to look, but not to mention it."

Eagle's cheeks warmed. She thought of the ERs she had worked in as she trained. They had left a lot out of the reports, particularly compromising information, particularly information that had to do with some important person's reputation.

"That just confirms it," Eagle said. "We need to talk to her."

Val sat up, ran a hand over her face. Her mood had changed from earlier. She seemed smaller somehow.

"I suppose I can talk to her," Val said. "Play the student again. But I don't know how I'm going to get from 'Hi, I want to move into this dorm' to 'Hey, when you were in the hospital last March, had you just been attacked? Or were you tied up at some frat party gone wrong?'"

Eagle's face grew even warmer. Put like that, none of them could talk to Kelly MacGivers. The lead was not as good as Eagle thought.

"I can go," Pammy said.

Both Val and Eagle looked at her.

Pammy shrugged. "I can play the Good Samaritan. I can bring her a flyer for the self-defense class, say a friend asked me to talk to her because she was in the hospital last March, and just see what happens."

Eagle knew what this kind of probing did with hospital patients. They often responded angrily, as if their privacy was being invaded. She couldn't imagine what would happen with a student like Kelly.

"It could get ugly," Eagle said, not really wanting to elaborate.

"I can handle myself," Pammy said with a small smile. It sounded like bravado.

Eagle shook her head. "I found her. I should talk with her. I can speak to her as a nurse—"

"Eagle," Pammy said in that condescending tone she had somehow mastered. "We both know I'm the best choice for this."

"She's white?" Val asked.

Eagle started. For a moment, she had forgotten that Val was even in the room.

"Yeah, I…" Eagle shrugged. "I didn't ask. I have no idea."

Pammy said, "With a name like Kelly MacGivers—"

"She could be anyone," Val said, a little sharply. "But the neighborhood where her parents live, you said that was a wealthy neighborhood?"

"Yes," Eagle said.

"A wealthy white neighborhood?" Val asked.

Eagle wasn't sure how to answer that. "The neighborhoods are changing here. You know, covenants—"

"That's a yes, right?" Val asked.

Eagle hated thinking about race, almost as much as she hated ignoring it.

"It's a yes," she said quietly.

"Then odds are that Kelly's white," Val said. "And if I went in, asking impertinent questions, she won't talk to me."

"She might," Pammy said.

Val shook her head slightly. "Let's not sugarcoat."

Pammy's cheeks turned red. Val had clearly embarrassed her.

But Val seemed to be ignoring that. She shifted in her chair, and looked at Eagle. Val seemed to be growing stronger again.

"And Eagle, you would be coming at it from the medical side, right?" Val asked.

"Yes," Eagle said. "I think I could approach her as a nurse, and…"

She let her voice trail off as Val shook her head, more strongly this time.

"She was injured in March. Her parents—or maybe it was her—anyway, *someone* kept it quiet. That's over *four* months ago. If she has lingering injuries, either her personal doctor or someone is taking care of them. Or she's ignoring them. A person can do a lot of healing in four months, and being reminded of an old injury isn't what someone usually wants."

That sounded like the voice of experience. Eagle had the sense that more had happened to Val than she had confided at Caffe Med.

"I think," Val was saying, "Pammy's right. She's our best choice. If you approach her in some kind of nonthreatening way."

She said that last to Pammy.

Pammy leaned back slightly. She clearly wasn't used to having someone else be in charge. She didn't know anything about medicine, so she let Eagle handle that, but it was always Pammy's idea to bring Eagle in on some case. Eagle wouldn't take the lead until Pammy assigned it.

Val wasn't waiting for permission from Pammy to take the lead. Val was acting with initiative, the kind that someone who was used to being in charge took naturally.

Pammy's lips thinned. She looked slightly distressed, even though she had been the one who had initially suggested that she talk to Kelly alone.

"I won't threaten her," Pammy said tightly.

"That's not what I meant," Val said. "If you showed up out of the blue to talk to me about some trauma in my past, I might slam the door on you. But maybe, if you can approach her in a way that would get her to help someone else…"

Eagle shifted slightly in the folding chair. It creaked, and she felt a surge of irritation.

That was what they were doing with Val. They were bringing her in, getting her to help someone else, even as she was helping herself. Was she so self-aware that she knew this was going on? Or was this just a side comment without any awareness at all?

Pammy did not look at Eagle. Maybe Pammy hadn't made the connection, or maybe she was still struggling with losing control of the conversation.

"I can handle this," Pammy said again, her tone just as irritated as it had been before.

"I know," Val said. "I just find myself worried about this girl. If she was raped or traumatized somehow, then she's probably pretty fragile. That's why I think it's really great you're going to see her. Maybe you can get her to sign up for a class. Even if she can't help us, she might benefit from it. Because just the handful of details that we have point toward something awful in her recent past."

Compassion. Eagle hadn't expected that. Sometimes Eagle felt like she had lost the ability to show compassion. She faked it good, but her heart wasn't in it.

Val's clearly was.

Pammy's expression had softened. Somewhere she realized that Val hadn't been insulting her or trying to take over the conversation. Val was worried about the other woman, a woman none of them had met yet.

Pammy probably liked that. Pammy worried about other people too much. It was one of the things that irritated the hell out of Eagle. It was one of the reasons for situations like the one last night.

"I'll talk to her," Pammy said softly.

"Today," Eagle said firmly. "Maybe if we can figure out what's going on, we can still find the woman I saw."

Or, at least, find her alive.

Although Eagle doubted it. If this guy was kidnapping women—people?—and carting them off somewhere, maybe Mount Diablo, maybe somewhere else, he clearly wasn't keeping them forever. He was hurting them for his own sick reasons and then dumping them.

"I don't have a lot of classes today," Pammy said. "I'll head over to Stern and see if I can catch her. I'll make sure Jill's prepared to take my late afternoon class if need be."

"Thank you," Eagle said. She looked at Val. "What were the names of those cops with that jurisdictional case?"

"I just have last names." Val checked her list. "Fleenan and Ruffner."

"Not the men who came to see me, then," Eagle said. "I think I'll talk to those two, remind them of the jurisdictional case. Maybe they didn't even know."

"You might want to ask them about the girl in the park," Pammy said.

Eagle raised her head. Val looked over at Pammy as well.

"What girl in the park?" Eagle asked.

Pammy nodded. "Someone found a body in Tilden Park yesterday. Not your girl, Eagle. She'd been dead longer than Sunday."

Something in Pammy's manner seemed off, almost like she didn't want to tell them about the dead body at all.

"Was she in a blanket?" Val asked. "Bound?"

"I don't know," Pammy said. "She'd been there a while, and I didn't get all the details. The police don't know who she is, though."

"Where did you hear this?" Val asked. "Was it on the news? Because I missed it."

"The admissions office," Pammy said tightly. "They think she was one of my students."

"Why would they think that if they don't know who she is?" Eagle asked.

"She fought back," Pammy said quietly.

That sentence made no sense to Eagle. What did fighting back have to do with Pammy?

"Oh, for God's sake," Val said. "Just because a victim fights back doesn't mean she was trained to. I fought—"

She cut herself off, but not before Pammy looked at her sharply.

Eagle clamped her lips together. Val's body language was closed. This wasn't the time to ask what Val had fought. Or who.

Then Val opened her hands a little, then shook her head as if she couldn't believe she had just said that.

"I fought back," she said softly. "I just had no idea what I was doing. It didn't work. My fault. I didn't know what I was doing."

The "my fault" caught Eagle. It was said so softly, so gingerly.

"Not your fault at all," Pammy said. "Someone hurt you. You can't take the blame for that on yourself."

"I know." Val looked down. "It's just—Truman, you know. He always told me I should learn how to fight. I might need it. And I thought he was—well, he *was*—but I thought it was just part of him being overprotective, you know? I didn't think anyone would ever hurt me."

"If we constantly thought people were here to hurt us, we couldn't walk through the world," Pammy said.

It was one of those cliché things that Pammy said, without thinking. Pammy, who had led a pretty damn good life, all things considered.

"Oh, bullshit," Eagle said. "I thought you taught people how to survive in a hostile environment."

She was a bit startled at how angry she sounded.

"We have to be realistic," Pammy said. "I think part of being realistic is having the same skills as the men around us. We're human. We can be prepared for the good and the bad. Most women just aren't prepared for the bad."

Eagle snorted. "The world is a terrible place. Your husband, Val, he wanted to protect you, and he couldn't be there all the time. He—"

"He couldn't even protect himself, even with all of his skills. He died…" Val cut off half a word that Eagle couldn't quite make out. "He died on the job."

Eagle didn't want to deal with the emotion that was bubbling up. Not yet. Besides, anger was easier.

Much easier.

Eagle looked at Pammy. "What you learn out there in the real world is that there are just some kiss-your-ass-goodbye moments. You can't solve them. You can't fight your way out of them. You can't outthink them."

"But there are other moments that you can solve and you can outthink and you can fight," Pammy said. "With the right training. You can do it."

Val took a shaky breath. Eagle felt momentarily guilty. She'd been talking about Val's pain as if it were theoretical. Or maybe, Eagle had been talking about her own pain. Sometimes punching things solved nothing at all. It didn't even make you feel better. It just made your hands hurt.

"Well, Pammy," Eagle said drily. "Go ahead. Tell all those platitudes to this Kelly girl, and maybe along the way, you can find out what happened to her. Maybe that'll get us one step closer to saving another woman."

Eagle knew she wasn't making any friends at the moment, but she wasn't really trying. She wasn't quite sure why she was so angry either. Maybe because there were no easy answers.

Maybe because she felt so goddamn helpless.

She wasn't good at helpless.

She never had been.

Pammy raised her chin slightly. "Have you thought about how we're going to 'save' this woman once we find out who has her? Because I can't come up with anything."

"Maybe the police will help," Val said. "I spoke to at least one detective who wants to catch this man."

"Maybe," Pammy said. "If we don't present this as a Berkeley thing."

But she sounded like she didn't believe they would get any help at all.

"We'll figure that out when we get there," Eagle said. "Right now, we know that there's a guy out there, hurting people, and he drives a truck. That's pretty much all we know."

"Which is more than we knew yesterday," Val said.

"We knew it," Pammy said.

"We *suspected* it," Val said. "And we didn't know the extent."

She sounded stronger now. That woman who had spoken softly, who had spoken of pain and hurt and blame, seemed to have disappeared.

"We're actually moving forward on this, faster than I would have expected." Val clearly said that second part for Eagle.

Val met the gazes of both Pammy and Eagle as if she were in charge. Eagle was beginning to get used to that, and it had only taken one conversation.

"I tell you what," Val said, "let's meet for dinner and see if we have anything new. That'll give Pammy a chance to talk with Kelly and find out what happened."

Eagle would drive herself to the precinct, see if she could talk to the detectives that visited her. That news from Walnut Creek might actually help.

"What are you going to do this afternoon?" Eagle asked Val, hoping they could have lunch again. Hoping they could find some quality time together.

Val smiled sheepishly. "Pammy's been kicking my butt. I'm exhausted. Plus, I hardly slept last night. What I really need right now is a nap. Then I'll figure out how I can continue to contribute to this investigation."

She sounded so reasonable, but she stood as she spoke, and her movements were slow—the movements of an old woman.

"If you don't mind, that is." Val said that last to Pammy, not to Eagle.

Pammy waved a hand, not quite dismissively. "Rest is an essential part of getting into shape. Don't I say that as part of the instructions?"

She sounded just a tad defensive.

"You do," Val said. "Dinner?"

"Yes," Pammy said. "Let's just meet here. My class ends at six, students will be gone by seven. I can find someone to watch the gym for an hour at least."

"Or maybe we should get take-out," Eagle said, "considering what we'll be talking about."

"All right then," Pammy said. Her tone was getting harsher and harsher. "You're in charge of the eats."

She stood too, but her movements were easy. Fluid. She was used to the exercise.

Eagle had no choice but to stand up. Apparently, this meeting was over.

"I'll see you both in a while." Val grabbed her purse. She smiled at Eagle, waved her fingers at Pammy, and left the office quickly.

Either she *was* tired, or she needed to get out of the room. Maybe a little of both.

Pammy held up one finger. She tilted her head slightly, as if she were listening. Eagle couldn't hear much beyond the hum of the fluorescent light overhead.

Finally, Pammy put her hand down.

"Do you like her?" Pammy asked.

Eagle's face warmed. Was it that obvious? Had her crush become something other people could recognize?

"Because she seems a little pushy," Pammy said.

Oh. Eagle let out a small breath. *That* was what Pammy meant.

"She's helped a lot," Eagle said. "She found out a great deal more than either of us."

Pammy let out a big sigh. "I know. I'm just…not used to someone else taking charge like that, I guess."

Eagle smiled. "I know."

Pammy raised her eyebrows. "You—?"

"She doesn't even know she's doing it," Eagle said. "She's clearly used to being the smartest person in the room."

Eagle was beginning to think that maybe Val *was* the smartest person in the room. At least, the smartest person in *this* room.

But Eagle wasn't going to say that to Pammy.

"Well," Pammy said in a little softer tone, "I guess that's something I can understand."

She sat back down, and nodded toward Eagle as if she expected Eagle to do the same.

Eagle sat.

Pammy extended her arms over the desktop, half covering those lists. "Do you think I'm doing the right thing?"

She sounded uncertain. Pammy *never* sounded uncertain.

"About seeing Kelly?" Eagle asked. "I think Val is right; I think you're our best—"

"About this place. Teaching women how to defend themselves. Do you think I'm doing the right thing?"

Eagle leaned back. She had heard Pammy vigorously defend the gym against anyone who suggested that Pammy was doing something wrong. The fact that Pammy was asking Eagle herself was a surprise. Because Eagle was often one of those people Pammy was defending this place against.

"Do I think you got that girl killed?" Eagle asked. "There's no evidence that she was even here—"

"I know all of that," Pammy snapped. "That's not what I asked you."

Eagle straightened. The metal folding chair was digging into the back of her legs.

"Are you doing the right thing," she mused. "Teaching these women how to use their fists? How to fight back?"

Images filled her mind before she could stop them. Small Vietnamese women lifted above the heads of American G.I.s, as the men laughed and the women hung their heads in panic and humiliation; children tossing infants in a nightmarish dream—

"Yes," Eagle said, as much to make the images go away as to answer the question. "Yes, I think you're doing the right thing."

Pammy looked at her, shocked. Eagle had never said that before.

Eagle continued, "You were right with what you said to Val a few minutes ago. In some situations, it pays to fight back. And it pays to have every single ability you can at your fingertips. Me, I'd rather not get into the situation, but I know I can survive the survivable ones. I have a brain, I know how to use a gun, and I know how to fight dirty. That's enough."

"And medical training," Pammy said.

"Well, that'll help other people," Eagle said. "It might help me in a situation, and it might not. I have to be conscious, clear-headed, and able to communicate. That's a tall order in a crisis."

Pammy nodded. She ran her hands through her short hair.

"It's not like you to doubt," Eagle said, before she could stop herself.

"It's just..." Pammy's voice trailed off. Then she squared her shoulders. "I thought I was helping a particular group of women."

Eagle frowned at her.

"I don't mean consciously," Pammy said. "But it turned out that way. Women like me, you know, women of a certain age and socioeconomic status. Women who had some means, but who usually married or when they were younger, got involved with the wrong men. Women who sometimes found themselves in a bad neighborhood. Women whose problems were mostly middle-class."

"Violence happens at all levels," Eagle said.

"I'm realizing that," Pammy said. "It's becoming clearer and clearer to me. Every time I think I've seen it all, a new rock moves, and something even more horrible climbs out from underneath it."

"Like this man in the truck," Eagle said.

"If I didn't know you, I wouldn't have heard of him. If I hadn't had the classes here, I wouldn't know he hurt more than one person. If Val hadn't made her calls, we wouldn't know about the dead bodies wrapped in blankets and dropped off trucks." Pammy threaded her hands together and pressed them against her mouth. "I'm a cop's daughter. I know that things can get bad. I guess I was a cop's *sheltered* daughter, because I didn't know how bad. I'm just beginning to realize how bad."

"That baby...?" Eagle asked.

Pammy's eyes widened. "God, the baby. That seems like weeks ago. Yes, the baby. And people like that. If I'm not careful, Eagle, I'll only see the bad stuff. I was getting to the point where I was doubting Val because I don't know her well."

"You didn't know me well when I came here," Eagle said. She didn't add that Pammy *still* didn't know her well.

"I know," Pammy said. "But I was a lot more naïve when I met you."

Eagle tilted her head slightly. That was true. Pammy was just beginning to realize it.

Eagle stood. "The gym's worthwhile," she said. "I didn't think so at first. I think so now. It's been two years. You're building a community. The community helps its members out. You're building resources."

"We might not be able to save that woman you saw," Pammy said.

"I know," Eagle said. "But think about this: what would have happened if there was no gym? I would have called the police, the detectives would have come out, and they would have treated me the same.

And then…what? I keep hounding them? I try to write it off? I certainly wouldn't investigate on my own."

She didn't add that she might have slipped all the way down, hidden in her bong and some beer until they threw her out of her apartment. Given up on everything.

That woman, that man in the truck, that night, it might have been the very last straw.

"Your instincts are good, Pammy," Eagle said. "Trust them. I do."

And then, because she didn't want to continue this conversation any longer, she shifted. If she didn't get out of the room, she would confess to things she didn't want to admit.

Pammy didn't need to know how close to the edge Eagle had been. How close Eagle *still* was.

Eagle hadn't thought of it that way before, the fact that the gym had probably saved her too. Goddammit. She didn't like being that woman, the woman who needed other people.

But she was.

They all were.

They needed each other.

And it was time they all realized it.

VAL

I was so exhausted, I wasn't sure I was going to make it home. My legs shook as I walked, and my eyes burned as if someone had blown cigarette smoke into them. I barely noticed the other people on the street. They all seemed busy with something important.

I felt like I was wrapped in gauze and launched into a world I didn't quite understand. The cloudy day had turned into the kind of grayness that made the edges of everything, from buildings to signs to cars, indistinct. Finally, the day matched my mood.

Telling Pammy that I had been attacked—my cheeks got warm just thinking of it. I hadn't meant to. I hadn't wanted to. But both Pammy and Eagle needed to understand that fighting back wasn't the same as *successfully* fighting back.

It wasn't the same at all.

I had trouble keeping my balance. I was walking like a drunk, not quite in control of my movements, and a few people looked at me sideways, probably judging me.

Hell, I would have been judging me.

When I couldn't take it anymore, I went into the next sandwich shop I saw and realized, from the smell of corned beef mixed with

357

the tang of sauerkraut, that I was in an actual deli—a different one from the day before. I didn't even know the name of it, just that my stomach rumbled.

I ordered a corned beef on rye to go, and watched as the thick-armed man in the butcher's apron expertly stacked the meat, the Swiss cheese, and the thin cabbage on dark rye. The sandwich looked too big to put in my mouth, but I didn't say anything.

He pressed it down, wrapped it in wax paper, cut it with a sharp knife, then wrapped the individual pieces in butcher's paper. A real deli, and I had somehow missed it in all of my travels around this area of town.

He bagged the sandwich, offered me a pickle, which I refused, and took my money, almost in one movement. He didn't have a tip jar, and when I asked, he looked past me, and shouted, "Next!" as if he hadn't heard me at all.

The flush in my face grew warmer, and I wanted to get small.

I was tired. I was just tired. I got this kind of insecure when I was tired.

I walked outside clutching the bag and forced myself to look at the window of the deli. I then looked at the neighborhood, and the cross streets, making myself remember.

Too often in the past several months, I had stayed away from places after I had embarrassed myself like I had done here, things that would have made the me before I ended up on the other side of the crevasse shake her head in confusion.

Maybe I should be the one to talk with Kelly MacGivers. I at least would understand the aftermath of an attack. I would know how hard it was to go through life again.

Although that wasn't fair. I had no idea what had prompted Pammy to set up the gym or Eagle to work at it. For all I knew, their histories were as dark as mine. Or darker.

I was too self-centered, too self-focused.

I tried to recapture the feeling I had had in the middle of the night, when I had been *doing* something for someone else, when it felt like I was making progress.

I was tired, that was all. I defaulted to this depressed, scared woman when I was tired.

Somehow I made it to my street. The short walk to the house seemed like a slog. Too late, I remembered to be vigilant. I didn't want to stop and scan the entire street, but I did look, moving my eyes slightly, and glancing behind me to see if someone had followed me.

I had no idea how I would know if someone had, because I hadn't been keeping an eye on anyone.

The hairs on the back of my neck had not risen, though, and I didn't feel like I was being followed. That feeling was something I had gotten used to after the Queen Nefertiti Ball, and I had tried to dismiss the feeling back then.

I had been wrong.

He had been following me. Armand Vitel, police officer, colleague of Truman's. A horrid, horrid man, who apparently had been admiring me from afar.

There. I named him. Armand Vitel, the bastard.

There had been no way to stop him. The police wouldn't believe me. Truman would have killed him if he had known.

Instead, he ended up involved somehow in Truman's death. And after I had nearly died, a friend of Marvella's, a man named Smokey, had gotten involved. While I was in the hospital, Armand Vitel had died. Gang shooting they said, but something in Smokey's eyes, something in Marvella's stance made me think that wasn't the entire story.

I stood under the weeping willow tree in the front yard of the house where my apartment was now, and realized I hadn't thought that clearly about the attack and aftermath ever.

Maybe I was getting better.

I actually looked at the stairs leading up to the small porch, the tiny entry, which would *not* have fit a man bent on attacking a woman, and hadn't been thinking about running through it, about getting past it because I might end up a victim, again.

I had been thinking about the attack as if it happened in the past.

It *had* happened in the past.

And the only person keeping the past alive was me.

I swallowed hard, squared my shoulders, and moved forward. I climbed the stairs, and felt somewhat secure, which was better than feeling like someone was about to jump me.

I unlocked the front door without looking to see if anyone was behind me, ready to push his way inside the building. Inside me.

I slid through the door, closed it, and heard the snick of the automatic lock. Then I walked up the wooden stairs to my apartment.

Halfway up, someone's phone started ringing, insistent and loud. It wasn't until I unlocked my own door that I realized the phone was mine.

No one called me. No one had my number.

My heart started pounding hard. All that fear I had been so proud of avoiding, filled me.

Possibilities went through my mind.

Wrong number. Or my landlord—he had the phone number. So did the phone company. The utility company.

And Pammy. I had put the phone number on my application form for the gym.

I sprinted down the narrow hallway to the kitchen, scurried across the old linoleum, dropped my lunch on the counter, and picked up the phone mid-ring.

"Yes?" I said, then realized I sounded both panicked and breathless. "Hello?"

"Um, hi." The female voice on the other end was wobbly. "Is this…Paulette?"

I was about to say, *No, Paulette is my cousin,* when I remembered I had used the name Paulette when I visited Darla's roommate, Lucy.

And I had given Lucy my number too, on that note, because I had felt guilty.

"This is Lucy Sanders," the woman said. "You know, from the apartment. Sublet, you know, yesterday? Darla's…"

Lucy's voice trailed off.

"Yeah," I said, faking enthusiasm. "Hi. I didn't think I'd talk to you so soon."

"Me, either." Lucy cleared her throat. "Sorry. Didn't think. I mean. You heard, right?"

I tensed. "No. Heard what?"

"That girl they found, you know, you heard that right? The one in Tilden Park?"

The one Pammy had mentioned? Hadn't she said the body wasn't unidentified? I didn't ask Lucy, though. I had to remember that Paulette was someone else, someone a bit more timid that I was, even at my worst.

"No," I said, rather surprised at how innocent I sounded. I had more acting chops than I ever thought. "I hadn't heard anything. What girl?"

"They found…a body…I guess, someone—Darla's dad, I guess—someone, anyway, first, then they, well it was a Jane Doe until, like an hour or two ago…"

Lucy's voice wobbled again.

"Anyway," she said, "the apartment. We're officially available for another renter."

I blinked, trying to process this. Was she saying that they had identified the body as Darla's or that Darla's father had grown scared because of the body, and decided to cancel his daughter's lease?

"A sublet?" I asked, letting my confusion into my voice. "You talked to Darla?"

"*No!*" Lucy's voice broke. "No. I'm sorry. No. She's…that body, they identified it. I shouldn't have called…."

My breath caught. "Are you saying that body was Darla?"

"Yeah," Lucy said. "It's only been an hour and I thought I was okay, but I'm—I thought, well, I need to call the others, but I thought if I called them and said someone was going to take the room, then they'd feel better, you know?"

God. What a position to put some stranger in. I grabbed one of the kitchen chairs and sat down.

Darla Newsome was dead, found beaten in Tilden Park. Apparently, she had been there for weeks. She had fought back, that's what Pammy had said.

I was so tired. I couldn't remember part of that conversation. Only the blame. Girls who fought back were automatically at fault. Hadn't someone said that to Pammy?

"Oh," I said, realizing that Lucy was waiting for me to respond, not just to the offer of the room, but to Darla's death. Maybe Lucy had called me because I had shown some sympathy. Or maybe she had called because she knew I hadn't spent a lot of time with Darla, and I would be sympathetic, but not necessarily as upset as the other roommates. "I'm so sorry."

"Yeah," she said, and this time her voice didn't break. "I—God, I shouldn't have called. It was the first thing I thought of."

"Are you all right?" I asked, almost wishing I couldn't. But I had to. Because I didn't want to leave her alone with the news.

"I'm…yeah. I called my dad, and I'm going home for a few days, but I have to call the others, and I thought…"

She was repeating herself, and she clearly stopped herself when she realized it.

"I…um…I'm leaving shortly, and thought, you know…"

"I know," I said. "I'm sorry. God, bad news on bad news."

"What do you mean?"

"I mean, after we talked, I talked to my boyfriend, and mentioned how I might have this place, and he asked me to move in, rent-free. I'm sorry. I would normally say yes, but…"

"Oh," she said, her voice even tighter. "Oh, of course. And yeah, that sounds great. Congratulations. I didn't know. I'm…well, I'm just a mess of stupidity right now. I'm going to go downstairs and wait for my dad to pick me up. Sorry. And if it doesn't work out—oh, wait, that's stupid too. Congratulations."

And then she hung up.

I put my hand to my cheek. It was warm. I was terminally blushing. What a liar I was. I had really upset this poor girl, who was upset enough.

I hung up slowly. So the body in the park belonged to Darla Newsome. She was dead. And she had been beaten. But I didn't know if she had been tied up. She wasn't wrapped in a blanket or someone would have mentioned that.

I ran a hand through my hair, then glanced at the bag holding my lunch. My stomach growled. How traitorous the body was. I had just heard of a woman's death, and my stomach responded by declaring that it hadn't had lunch.

I took a deep breath, then wondered what else I had neglected in my haste. Had I closed the apartment door?

Adrenaline shot through me again, filled with that familiar fear. If I hadn't, then someone could be in the apartment. I would have to search top to bottom to see if *he* was hiding.

I stood, clenched my fists, and unclenched them. Stupid, stupid, stupid. No one had followed me. I had locked the front door when I came in. No one else had come up the stairs—I would have heard them.

I made myself walk into the hallway. The door was closed, the lock on the doorknob pushed in. Apparently I did that sort of thing automatically.

I let out a small breath, then walked to the door, turned the deadbolt, and put on the chain.

I wouldn't have to search the apartment after all. Then a little trickle of worry filled me. Or would I?

I took another deep breath. It was a compulsion, this searching, and it wasn't based in reality. I had come home for lunch and a nap, and now I had just gotten some upsetting news. I was coping by jumping back into that scared woman I had become.

I didn't want to be her.

Pammy was teaching me how to banish her, or conquer her, or maybe just to live with her.

Pammy. I had to tell her.

I went back into the kitchen, grabbed the phone book, and searched for the listing for a Gym of Her Own.

I dialed, and the phone rang only twice before someone answered. A voice I didn't recognize stated the name of the business.

"Hi," I said, sounding even more breathless than I felt. "May I speak to Pammy?"

"She stepped out for the afternoon," the voice said. "This is Opal. How may I help you?"

I remembered Opal from that first Sunday. She'd been warm and manipulative, the kind of woman who seemed friendly, but might be a bit too controlling in the long run.

Not someone I wanted to confide in.

"Is Eagle still there?" I asked.

"I didn't know she had been here at all," Opal said. "So I guess that's a no. Would you like to leave a message?"

I thought about it, something in code—something about Darla or the park or something. And then I realized that was just cruel.

"No," I said. "No message. Thank you."

I hung up, and stood for a moment with my hand on the receiver. Sadly, the fact that Darla was dead wasn't really an emergency. It was just another piece of information.

I was startling myself, with the way that my brain was responding to all of this. Like I was putting a puzzle together, rather than dealing with other people's lives.

Besides, I think I had known about Darla's death all along. Not consciously. Deep down. The scholarship student who had left her favorite stuffed dog in the middle of her bed. The girl who had come into money somehow, when she really shouldn't have. The girl who had fought with her parents but who still dutifully called her mother.

That girl wouldn't have gone silent for more than a month.

Her father, that burly man in a plaid shirt, even though he had given me the stink-eye, I had still felt empathy for him. He had seemed so distraught.

He had known too. Maybe I had known from that moment. When a man like that left his comfortable environment to find his child, humiliating himself by going door to door with flyers, he knew something was horribly, terribly wrong.

I swallowed hard. Attacks—they were like a swarm of bees, all fists and fear and sensation. Swatting did no good, fleeing was often impossible, enduring took forever, and even though the fists stopped and the fighting ended, the effects remained.

If you survived.

I leaned my forehead against the back of my hand, the receiver moving slightly under the pressure from my fingers.

That was why I had felt nothing right away. Puzzle pieces were so much easier than empathy. Than identifying with the victim.

Than remembering.

I made myself raise my head. I grabbed a plate from the cupboard and made a production of unwrapping half of my sandwich. I put the other half in the refrigerator.

Then I filled a glass from the dish drainer with water and sat down at the kitchen table with my meal.

Darla was dead. I had never met her. I didn't know her. She had died horribly, and her death had upset her father, and Lucy, and would upset Pammy too, probably, and maybe even Eagle.

It had upset me.

But I was still alive. I needed lunch. I needed a nap. Then I needed to talk with my new friends, share this new information.

We would figure out what to do. If there was anything to do.

Anything at all.

PAMMY

Pammy had no way of knowing if Kelly MacGivers was at Stern Hall in the middle of the afternoon. Pammy thought of calling, but calling a dorm was difficult at best. The phones were in the hallway, and someone might answer or someone might not.

Pammy had no idea if the House Ass, as the resident assistants at Stern Hall were called in her day, was even in the building during the summer. Pammy assumed so. Summer was a legitimate term, and the girls needed guidance—that was what the assistants were for, in theory. But Pammy didn't know the House Ass's number or even who she was.

So Pammy decided to drop in. She had a folder in one hand with half a dozen old flyers made for the self-defense classes inside. She didn't want Kelly MacGivers to think she had been selected at random, although Pammy still hadn't come up with a good story of how she knew about Kelly's attack.

The entrance to Stern Hall looked no different than it had when Pammy had lived there during her freshman year. Stern had been built fourteen years before Pammy had moved in so, back then, it had been considered one of the newer dorms. Since then, dorms had sprung up on the hillside behind Stern Hall, making that part of the landscape less familiar to her. Only the eucalyptus trees in front looked the same.

That and the "modern" overhang, with the concrete walls on one side and the bricked walkway beneath. Everything in Stern was concrete, metal, and blond wood, designed in that Prairie Style that supposedly took in the landscape while keeping the interiors stark.

Pammy hadn't hated it, but she hadn't loved it either. She had heard, when she was living there, that Mrs. Stern had wanted the dorm to seem homey. Pammy had never been invited to Rosalie Meyer Stern's home, but Pammy couldn't imagine any place with lacquered concrete floors and painted concrete walls to be "homey." Not even with the large fireplace in the living area.

As she stepped inside, she noted the familiar smell of boiled potatoes and brown gravy seeping in from the dining hall. It was summer, so no one was using the fireplace. Indeed, no one was sitting on the blond and cinnamon couches or chairs, which had to be the same ones Pammy used fourteen years before. The ugly cowhide rugs still dominated the lacquered floors and took the view away from the windows.

She shook her head slightly, then ducked into the library. No one was in there either. She glanced at the Beau Room, where, in her day, male visitors had to wait to see any women, and noted that it was empty too.

The entire dorm felt empty, which shouldn't have surprised her, given it was the middle of the day and the middle of the summer. There were better places to study, even though the afternoon was overcast. It wasn't that cold outside, so students could sit on benches or outside of cafes and watch the world go by.

Pammy swallowed hard, hoping her gamble would pay off. If Kelly MacGivers wasn't in her room, then Pammy would come back down here and ask if the college students on the kitchen staff knew where she was.

Pammy went to the Stair Tower, which was her favorite part of Stern Hall. The glazed windows brought in a lot of light, and used to bring up her mood on the tough days of her very first year. She walked up the red concrete stairs to the blue second floor landing and looked at the glazed double doors, with *Residents Only* painted in black.

Well, she had been a resident once. Technically, then, that word still applied to her.

She shoved open the doors and almost turned down her old hallway. She had lived in a double, with Linda Kaputo. Barbara Springer had roomed right next door, with Sue Ellen Gerry. Sad to think that of the four of them, thick as thieves from the day they met, only Pammy survived.

Tears pricked her eyes. She wasn't that old. She shouldn't have lost three friends to violence.

That thought made her square her shoulders and pivot away from the one room that had been home for her for her first year in college. Instead she went down the hall where Kelly MacGivers lived, a hall Pammy almost never had ventured down in the past,.

As Pammy followed the numbered blond doors, she realized that Kelly had a prized single room. In Pammy's year, the girls who had had the single rooms were either quite wealthy or socially connected, or they were upperclassmen who didn't want to live off-campus. Freshman could only dream of having such privacy.

Kelly's room was at the very end of the hall. Pammy tugged on her shirt, straightening it, clutched the folder to her chest, and knocked. The door rattled. It was slightly off plumb.

Someone let out a small shriek from inside.

The shriek made Pammy's heart pound even though she knew all it meant was that she had startled the person inside the room.

No one responded to the knock.

Pammy brought her hand up again, about to knock a second time, then rethought that decision, and said, "Hello? Kelly MacGivers?"

Something rustled, followed by the scuffing sound of slippered feet against concrete—a sound Pammy had forgotten until now.

The door opened a half inch, and the sliver of a face with a greenish-brown eye gazed at her.

"Who are you?" Kelly MacGivers had a mid-range voice, but she pitched it deliberately low so that it had more weight.

"My name is Pamela Griffin. I used to live in Stern Hall."

"Bully for you," Kelly said. "If you had the room before me, I am not giving you a tour. I am accepting your apology for the keyed grooves in the closet door. Now go away."

Pammy felt her cheeks warm. She had started wrong. She had thought the fact that she had roomed here would help her bond with Kelly. Clearly, Pammy had been wrong.

"I'm not here as a former resident," Pammy said. "I was given your name. I'd like to talk with you in private for a few minutes."

The door did not budge, and neither did Kelly. "Who gave you my name?"

Pammy wasn't going to mention the admissions office. This girl was too defensive, and she actually might confront someone there.

"A woman I work with spoke to your mother," Pammy said, deliberately implying that she had gotten Kelly's name from her mother.

"My *mother?*" The words dripped with contempt. "Really?"

"Yes," Pammy said.

"I suppose she said she was *worried* about me." The contempt grew deeper.

"Not in so many words," Pammy said.

Kelly blew out a puff of air, a sound of disgust. "Well, you can tell my *mother* that I'm just fine, and she doesn't need to *worry* about me. I'm following the rules. And you can say that in as many words as you want."

She started to close the door, but Pammy slid the folder in the small opening between the door frame and the door.

"Wait," Pammy said. "Just give me five minutes."

"No," Kelly said. "And get that thing out of my door."

Pammy didn't move the folder but she did look both ways down the hall. "Is anyone nearby?"

"How the hell would I know?" Kelly asked.

"Because, Kelly," Pammy said. "I want to talk about March."

Kelly stepped away from the door as if Pammy had reached inside and hit her. The door inched open, since Kelly's hand no longer held it in place, revealing Kelly herself.

She was pale, with deep shadows under her eyes. She was too thin and her dark hair hung lankly around her face.

The room smelled of unwashed sheets and barely clean girl.

Pammy had seen this before. Too many times, in fact.

"May I come in?" she asked, not wanting to violate Kelly's privacy any more than she already had.

Kelly waved a hand. It didn't quite beckon Pammy inside, and it didn't indicate she should leave either. The confusion in the gesture probably mirrored the confusion inside Kelly.

Pammy had to tread carefully. Kelly was not strong, even though her voice had been. And getting her some help was much more important than finding out information on a case no one had asked Pammy, Val, and Eagle to solve.

Pammy took a tentative step inside. Kelly glared at her, then whirled and walked to the unmade bed. She sat down with a heavy thump.

Very slowly, Pammy eased the door closed, giving Kelly every chance to change her mind. Kelly just watched her, saying nothing.

Once the door snicked shut, Pammy walked to the desk, pulled back the blond wood chair, and turned it toward Kelly before sitting down.

A breeze came through the double-hung window, smelling faintly of eucalyptus. The breeze probably kept the stench in the room from being overwhelming, particularly since the garbage can under the desk was filled with banana peels, apple cores, and bread crusts.

Kelly didn't say a word. She waited.

Pammy had never had to do all of the heavy lifting in one of these conversations before. She wasn't exactly sure where to begin.

She put the folder on her lap.

"I…know about your trip to San Francisco General," Pammy said.

Kelly closed her eyes.

"I know how badly you were hurt."

Kelly was sitting so still she looked like the statue of a girl. She hadn't opened her eyes.

"I teach classes, some of them connected to the university," Pammy said. "I own a gym for women only called A Gym of Her Own. One of the classes is self-defense—"

"My *mother* sent you?" Kelly's eyes had flown open as she spoke, her face suddenly beet-red. "My *mother?*"

"I didn't say that exactly—"

"Fucking hypocritical bitch," Kelly said.

Pammy's breath caught. She hadn't expected name-calling from Kelly—at least, not so soon.

But Kelly didn't stop. She said, "My *mother* sent you? That's so rich it's pathetic."

Apparently the fucking hypocritical bitch wasn't Pammy. It was Kelly's mother. Pammy stiffened, not sure what she had stumbled into.

"Did my *mother* also tell you that she hired the son of a bitch? She's the one who sicced him on me. Her and my dad. God." Kelly pounded the mattress with one hand, but the rest of her body didn't move at all. "And now she wants me to take a defense class? So that I can defend myself against who? Is she sending another asshole my way? Is she going to let someone nearly kill me again? I'm doing exactly what she wants now. I can't even leave this room, most of the time, but somehow I drag myself to class. And my *mother* wants me to go learn how to protect myself from the people she hires to force me to do what she wants? I suppose she told you that my *father* hired him. That this is all my *father's* fault. Didn't she?"

Pammy was trying to follow the torrent of words. They had shocked her to her core. They weren't at all what she had expected.

"*Didn't* she?" Kelly leaned forward, both hands fists now, both hands resting on the mattress as if she could launch herself off of it, using just the strength of her arms.

Pammy had screwed this up worse than she had ever thought possible.

"No, that's not what—"

"Tell my *mother*," Kelly said, "I can take care of myself, thank you. Now get the hell out of my room."

Pammy didn't move. It took all of her strength to remain in place. Her face was probably as red as Kelly's.

"Okay," Pammy said, working very hard to keep her own voice calm. "Let me be clear. *I* didn't speak to your parents."

"You *said*—"

"No," Pammy said. "I *implied*. A friend of mine did talk to your mother. Your mother wouldn't say where you were or what you were doing. I just—"

The color drained from Kelly's face. Pammy could feel Kelly switch from anger to fear as if it were a live thing.

"You *lied?*"

"Yes," Pammy said.

"What the hell do you want? I'm not taking some stupid class. I'm not giving you money for *anything*," Kelly said.

"I understand," Pammy said. "I screwed this up. I'm sorry."

"Then get out," Kelly said.

Pammy shook her head. "I wanted to talk to you in private. I need to talk to you, because I need your help."

"That's rich," Kelly said. "You come in here, you lie to me, you say you know something about me, and now you want my *help?* Get out."

She wasn't getting up to enforce her command to leave, so Pammy wasn't going to stand either.

"I don't even know where to begin," Pammy said. "That's part of the problem."

"I don't care," Kelly said, but her words had a little less force behind them.

"I run a gym—"

"We established that. And I don't want another goddamn class. I can barely handle the ones I've got. Now get out."

"—it's off Telegraph," Pammy said. "We've been seeing some disturbing things."

"I'll bet," Kelly said. "You old people find *everything* young people do disturbing."

Pammy squared her shoulders.

"A number of people have gone missing," Pammy said, soldiering forward. "Activists, people in the Movement."

She deliberately used Strawberry's phrase.

Kelly's chin had gone up. Her face was turned slightly, as if she were both fascinated and frightened. She no longer seemed to want to look at Pammy head-on.

"On Saturday night," Pammy said, "a friend of mine saw a man in a one-ton pickup truck slam a woman's head against the truck and toss her into the truck's bed."

What color remaining in Kelly's face drained away. She looked greenish and sick.

"And my friend, who is very competent, tried to stop the truck, but couldn't. She got the license plate, and reported it, but the police never came."

"Yeah," Kelly said, but it sounded like the word had slipped out, like she hadn't planned to speak at all.

"We're hoping to find the woman, but while we've been looking, we've discovered all these other missing people."

"And you're doing this…because…why? Because you're nice?" Kelly's words were sharp but she looked even queasier than she had a moment before.

"My friend—none of us, really—can sit idly by. If the police won't look, we have to. That's why I opened the gym. It's for women only—"

"Oh, here's the pitch," Kelly said.

"No," Pammy said hastily. "That's not it at all. I've lost too many friends to violence that the police won't investigate. I'm doing my bit to stop that from happening."

"Altruism at its best," Kelly said.

Pammy flushed. This girl was trying to get under her skin, and damn if she wasn't succeeding.

"My roommate from my freshman year, my roommate *here* in Stern Hall, she was beaten to death by her husband. We all knew it was coming," Pammy said. "The police wouldn't do anything because her husband had friends in the department. He was *important*. And no one ever charged him with murder because he claimed it was an accident, and no one investigated. She had a lot of accidents. She fell down the stairs and walked into doors and got her arm twisted in the strangest ways. And being accident-prone killed her."

The color was starting to come back to Kelly MacGivers' face. She was looking up, watching through her eyelashes as if she couldn't quite handle what Pammy was saying, but she couldn't look away either.

Pammy was working to keep her voice level, but emotion was creeping into it anyway. She didn't want to sound as charged as Kelly was.

"I kept telling her to leave him," Pammy said, "but she wouldn't. And then, just before she died, our friend Barbara was attacked near the Presidio. She had gone down there for some event. And she was dressed wrong or she was alone or something. Anyway, she was attacked, and killed, and maybe, just maybe, if my two friends—my *best* friends from my freshman year—maybe if they had known how to fight back, maybe I wouldn't be talking to you. Maybe I'd be drinking tea at some society function, happily oblivious to the darker side of my town. Maybe you could be alone like you claim you want to be."

Pammy was probably being too harsh, but she couldn't stop now. The memories of the good times here at Stern, and the way everything had turned dark, got to her, along with Kelly's constant ping-ponging between terror and anger. Pammy had seen that before in someone who had been attacked.

Kelly had raised her head all the way and was looking at her directly as if Pammy were something she had never seen before.

Pammy wanted to clear her throat, make the growing lump go away, but she didn't. The emotion was reaching Kelly, maybe as much as the words.

"You were one of the people that other students had said disappeared," Pammy said. "My list says you were active in some women's issues causes and you participated in some anti-Vietnam rallies. Then everyone says you disappeared. So my friend—the same one who saw the woman kidnapped—she called hospitals trying to trace the people who were injured, and she found out about you."

"They told her?" Kelly's voice rose slightly in panic.

Pammy sighed. The pain in Kelly's question deflated some of Pammy's anger.

"They told her very little," Pammy said gently. "Just enough to let us know you had been beaten, and your parents acted strange."

"No shit," Kelly said, but there was no power behind the words. "My parents are strange."

"I was hoping you could tell us if you knew anything about the man in the truck," Pammy said. "If there was a man in the truck. If we're not misreading what happened."

She wanted to add, *If we are, then please talk to me. Tell me what happened with your parents so I can help.*

But she didn't. Kelly was defensive enough.

Kelly had frozen in place. Her expressive face had gone pale again. "You're not misreading."

"You were taken by a man in a one-ton pickup?" Pammy asked.

Kelly nodded.

"He beat you and tossed you away like you meant nothing to him?" Pammy asked.

Kelly's mouth twisted in a bitter smile. "Oh, I meant something to him," she said softly. "I meant money."

"He blackmailed your parents?" Pammy asked. Maybe they hadn't paid quickly enough. Maybe they had not believed the man.

"No, he didn't blackmail my parents." Kelly's voice had become so soft that Pammy had to lean forward to hear her. "My parents hired him. And so far, they're really happy with the work he's done."

EAGLE

Eagle parked her truck as close to Grove Street as she could get. She didn't like to park near government buildings. There were too many rules and regulations. So she parked on Addison, and walked the few blocks to the building, tugging on her outfit the entire time.

After meeting with Pammy and Val, Eagle had gone home and dressed like a real person. She figured it would get her traction with the cops if she looked her age, instead of like an adult college student who liked to get high.

Her look and her address had hurt her the first time she had seen these cops. She wanted just a little credibility the second time.

So she was wearing the only dress she had. It was a white sleeveless cotton number that almost made her look like she should be on her way to first communion or something—if she were eight, which she most decidedly was not. She paired it with white pumps that made her feet hurt, particularly on the walk to the precinct.

She had draped a blue sweater over her shoulders to ward off the day's chill. And, God save her, she carried a clutch purse. She was a bit startled she still owned one—and she'd had to wipe off the vinyl sides so that it at least looked slightly white.

She had drawn the line at makeup though. She had never known how to put on the real stuff—eyeliner, rouge—and she used to use a little lipstick, but the tube she'd found had caked into some kind of sweet-smelling red mass. She had tossed it away.

Her ensemble, much as she hated it, had gotten her past the entry, past some woman who wanted to take her police report, and had actually gotten her to the desk sergeant.

He was a beefy, ruddy-faced man in blue, with watery eyes and broken capillaries in his nose. Eagle recognized the alcohol-induced redness. She would go the same direction if she weren't careful.

The desk was built deliberately high so that no one could launch themselves across it. The heels made her five-ten, five-eleven, and still the desk came up to her shoulders.

"I'm here for Detective Brunsan," she said, deliberately keeping her voice soft and nonthreatening. "I have information on something I reported on Sunday."

She had opted to see the older detective, the one who was blunt and slightly mean. The younger one hadn't listened to her, despite their shared military service. She doubted he would listen to her now.

"You shoulda called, ma'am," the desk sergeant said. "Our detectives, they don't normally sit at a desk."

"I know," she said, already feeling some disappointment. "But I was in the neighborhood and I figured this was easier than having him come to my home."

She said it in such a way that it implied she—the middle-class woman the desk sergeant had just called ma'am—didn't want her neighbors to see the police.

"I'll see if he's here." The desk sergeant looked around. One of the nearby chairs had a sleeping long-hair in it. Another had a black man, head bowed, arms folded. "Just stand to one side, okay?"

Clearly, he didn't want this "lady" that Eagle was pretending to be to sit near either man.

Eagle stepped back. She held her purse in both hands, remembering why she hated a clutch. You had to *clutch* the damn thing. You couldn't hang it over your shoulder like something useful. You had to hold it, even if you didn't want it. Although she could probably stuff it under one arm, like so many women did. She found that even more uncomfortable.

"Can I help you?"

She looked to her right. Brunsan stood there. He seemed even shorter than he had when he came to her apartment. The stink of a fresh cigar clung to him like body odor.

"Hey, I know you," he said, frowning. He was trying to place her. That was proof enough at how different she looked.

"Is there somewhere we can talk, Detective?" she asked in her best "handle the brass" voice.

"Yeah, sure, come with me."

He led her through a pale yellow door, covered with dirty fingerprints at chest level. He stepped into a large square room filled with mismatched desks. Each desk had one phone on it, a blotter, and too many files.

She wondered which desk was his.

But she didn't get an answer. Just past the desks was a small room with windows that overlooked the detectives' area. A single table fit in there, with only two chairs. It wasn't an interrogation room, but it wasn't comfortable either.

"Private," he said, and stood until she entered. She waved her purse, as if to ask which side he wanted her on. "Sit anywhere."

As if she had a lot of choice. She sat in the nearest chair, regretting the white dress. She wondered how much filth was now covering her back end.

She placed the purse on her lap, and folded her hands over it, deciding not to touch the table, which was stained with coffee rings.

"So, you know who I am," Brunsan said as he sat across from her. "I'm sorry to ask, but who're you again?"

"Captain June Eagleton," Eagle said. "We met on Sunday."

"Jesus, yeah, the military lady. I didn't recognize you. You clean up nice." He meant it as a compliment.

She made herself smile. "Thank you. I was wondering if you found the man yet? Because I have more information."

"The man you called us about?" Brunsan asked. "The one who hit that girl and tossed her in his truck?"

"Yes." Eagle was pleased he remembered so easily. She hadn't expected it. She had expected more of a dance, like they had had on Sunday.

"Yeah, that guy," Brunsan said. "We found him."

She blinked in surprise. She hadn't expected that answer. She also hadn't expected the relief that flooded through her.

"You found him," she said, letting some of that relief out. "And the woman?"

"He didn't have no girl with him, and I'll be honest with you, Captain, I looked. I looked hard." He wasn't belligerent like he had been on Sunday. He was treating her with respect. That surprised her too.

But the relief had vanished. "No girl."

"Yeah, here's the thing, he had her." Brunsan crossed his arms and leaned back. "But he'd already gotten rid of her."

Eagle felt like she had whiplash. Found the man, but didn't find the girl. Had the girl, had gotten rid of her.

She didn't like that wording. He had killed her, and Brunsan couldn't find the body.

"What do you mean, 'gotten rid of'?" she asked.

"Not quite what you're thinking," Brunsan said. "Here's the thing. This guy, he's legit."

Eagle frowned. "What?"

Brunsan shrugged. "I don't like what he does, but he can do it. He's got papers and everything, and there's nothing on the books that—"

"He can hit women and throw them around?"

"Well, that, no, technically he can't do that." Brunsan sighed. "And frankly, that's your word against his since I can't legally get the name of the girl from that night."

Eagle shook her head. She felt like she had slipped into a *Twilight Zone* episode. "What do you mean you can't *legally* get her name? That woman was screaming for help. He knocked her unconscious and tossed her in his truck. How is that possible? How is that *legal*?"

Brunsan uncrossed his arms, and held up his hands, palms facing Eagle, as if he were trying to placate her.

"Lemme tell you what we found first, and then you can bitch all you want, because I did too. I even talked to my captain, okay?" He sounded frustrated. And open. She hadn't expected him to be open.

Eagle wrapped her fingers around that stupid purse so that she would have something to focus on.

"All right," she said.

"Okay." Brunsan took a deep breath, and scooted his chair forward. "I was kinda hoping I wouldn't have to talk to you, because you know, in twenty years of doing this job, this is new to me. But, rich people, you know?"

"The guy in the truck is rich?" Eagle asked.

"Captain," Brunsan said, chiding her, "you said you would let me tell you what I found."

"Okay, right." Eagle ran her thumb on the clasp of the purse. The metal dug into the skin just underneath her stubby nail.

"This guy, whose name is, um, LaSalle, Laventer, something—I'll get it for you, because while he might be legal, I don't like him."

"Thank you," she said, not sure where this was going. Why would Brunsan want her to have the name?

"This guy LaCross or whatever, he, um, he's a licensed bounty hunter from Louisiana."

"I'm sorry?" Eagle asked. She didn't understand. Bounty hunter? "That girl was a fugitive?"

"No," Brunsan said. "If she was, I'd've told you and we'd be having a different conversation. Let me talk, Captain, okay?"

"Okay." Eagle tucked her thumb under the purse, and focused on Brunsan.

"Okay," Brunsan said. "This Levenser, he's a licensed bounty hunter, but somehow, he's combined it now with detecting. He's a private investigator too, but he specializes in finding people."

"Finding people," Eagle muttered.

"Yep," Brunsan said. "He hires out—expensive rates too—mostly to rich people. Started in the so-called Summer of Love, you know what I'm saying?"

"Not exactly," Eagle said.

"All them kids, coming here, wearing flowers in their hair like that song. Most of them kids are missing, at least as far as their parents are concerned. Most of them kids are middle class, and they're gonna stay missing. But some, they come from money, and money, it tends to get what it wants."

Eagle was still having trouble following this. "He's hunting kids?"

"Not children," Brunsan said. "Teenagers. Not quite twenty-one. If they're not twenty-one, Mommy and Daddy are still responsible for them, and they don't got any rights. They can be dragged back home any which way, you getting me now?"

She was beginning to. The teenagers, the twenty-year-olds, would leave home and lose touch with their parents, and their parents would hire the man in the truck to find them.

She frowned, combing her memory of Saturday night. It was dark, but that man wasn't holding a girl. Eagle had gone over it and over it. He had been fighting with a woman.

"That woman I saw? She was under twenty-one?"

"Yep," Brunsan said. "And I'm not telling you who she is. I talked to her parents. They wouldn't let me see her, said she was upset as all get out and would say some stuff about cops that I didn't need to hear. I didn't press the point, not that I could, really. But they assured me she was okay."

"She needed medical attention," Eagle said. "I can guarantee that."

"And I remembered that. I said the very same to them, and they assured me they'd taken her to see their family doctor, and she's a bit bruised up, but she'll be fine. Absent a warrant, I couldn't barge in, and I didn't have cause." Brunsan's florid face seemed even darker.

"Are you sure she's the woman I saw?" Eagle asked.

"Pretty sure," Brunsan said. "She was staying in an apartment about three doors down from yours when he grabbed her. The parents told me that she got home yesterday morning, so the timing works."

Eagle's frown grew deeper. How would she know if that was the woman? How would he? Absent finding the woman in that truck or in that man's hands, the timing was all they had.

Her stomach was churning. She went over everything Brunsan had just said.

"Let me get this straight," she said. "Parents hire this man to find their missing children?"

"Yep," Brunsan said.

"And they don't care if he beats them?" Eagle asked.

"C'mon, Captain, you know it's never as simple as that, specially now." He ran a hand over his chin. "Those kids take all kinds of crap. They get wild. Drugged-out. I can tell you some stories—"

"I can tell you the same," Eagle said.

He looked at her, and frowned a little.

"I'm a nurse," she said.

"Oh, yeah, I remember," he said. "I been thinking of that since we found the guy. I wished I could use your words to get a warrant, but I can't. The parents won't let me in, and they got custody of her right now."

What a nightmare. Eagle bent the clutch purse ever so slightly.

"I'll be honest with you, Detective," she said. "That woman didn't strike me as an out-of-control drug addict. She seemed like a woman screaming for her life."

"I get that," Brunsan said. "I trusted that. I did. And I did what I could. I looked at his truck, which, by the way, he'd cleaned pretty damn good—something I find suspicious right there. I *called* on his license, and yep, it's valid in Louisiana, which means we gotta honor it here. *Both* of his licenses, because he's a cross-your-i's and dot-your-t's kinda guy—"

Eagle didn't even smile that Brunsan had gotten that wrong. She was too upset.

"—he's got a detective license, even though he don't need one of those with his bounty hunter's thing. Anyway, he's legit. He had a hotel room, which was damn near as clean as the truck, which I didn't like either, but he told me he didn't use it on Sunday night. He took the girl somewhere, he couldn't remember where, got her coffee, calmed her down, and then drove her to the parents, who paid him in cash, even though they'd paid him with a check for the first half, and he was done."

Eagle tapped the clutch purse with her forefinger. Every muscle her body was taut. "How can this be legal? Isn't it kidnapping?"

"If she was twenty-one, yeah, probably. If he did more than just toss her in his truck *and we can prove it*, yeah, probably. But we can't prove nothing, the parents say they're happy, and they're not letting the girl say nothing either. He didn't have scrapes or scratches, and both parties say the girl is fine too. Even if I knew who the family doctor was, and I don't, he has no legal obligation to talk to me. I don't got jurisdiction over the daughter. The family's in Marin."

Eagle hated this jurisdictional stuff, not that it was the entire problem. But it was part of the problem.

She just couldn't believe that the girl was all right.

"She should have gone to the hospital," Eagle said. "She probably had a concussion from the way he slammed her into that truck."

Brunsan opened his hands, as if to say he had nothing to do with that.

"There's got to be a way to see her," Eagle said, more to herself than to him.

"Nope," Brunsan said. "We don't have cause."

Cause. One of those legal wiggly words. She hated those. Maybe she could come up with *cause.*

"Was he blackmailing the parents?" Eagle asked. "That would explain the cash."

"It would, wouldn't it?" Brunsan asked. "But I told you, I was thorough on this."

She believed him. He wasn't talking to her today like she was some dumb college student. He was talking to her like another adult. He truly must have been bothered by this.

He said, "I talked to the bank. I saw the canceled check from the front part of this month. Bank hasn't sent it as part of the statement yet. They paid him a buttload of money. Pardon my mouth, but you shoulda seen that check. It was for a lot. I could've bought a house with that money. But that check, it was made out to this Levenger's business, his *bounty hunter* business. And if I was blackmailing rich people, I wouldn't have no check written to my legal business, at least not after the first time, and I know this wasn't his first rodeo."

"How do you know that?" Eagle asked.

Brunsan shook his index finger at the air, and raised his eyebrows, as if rewarding himself for being clever.

"Parents," he said. "They got LaVally or whatever's name from some other parents. There's a whole network of these people, trying to get their kids back."

"Back from where?" Eagle asked.

"That I didn't get. I'm thinking drugs or something, but they didn't say. Just 'bad influences,' which could mean anything. Bad boyfriends, bad drugs, anything."

Eagle nodded. That she did understand. Whenever she thought about those kids, particularly the Mini Mob on Telegraph, she wondered where the parents were. Maybe they were searching for the kids in the Mini Mob as well.

"So," she said slowly, "you have no proof of anything."

"Nope," he said. "That license plate number brought us to LaSalle, or whatever, and his shady little business, but it didn't bring us anything truly illegal."

Eagle swallowed. She liked this version of Brunsan better than the man who had called her Annie Oakley, but she was still wary.

Wariness, however, wouldn't help all those kids who were disappearing.

"What if I can get you something illegal?" she asked.

"Honey," he said, immediately reverting to the Blue Meanie who had come to her apartment, "you're not supposed to get me anything. You can't get involved."

She wanted to throw the clutch purse at him for the word *honey* alone. Instead, she just gripped the purse as tightly as she could.

"I already have something," she said.

"You didn't go off half-cocked with that gun of yours, did you?" he asked.

She gave him her most withering look. He met her gaze for a moment, then smiled just a little.

"I should know better, right?" he asked. "You're not that dumb."

"I'm not dumb at all," she said coldly.

He nodded, not chastened, exactly, but a little subdued. "Then how did you get something?"

"I was talking to a friend. I was telling her about what happened, and how upset I was." Eagle was laying it on a little thick, but she needed to. "And she told me about a conversation she had with someone in Walnut Creek."

"Gossip isn't something," he said.

"This is more than gossip," Eagle said. "It seems that the truck pulled into the Enco station there, with a girl screaming in the back—"

"On Saturday night?" Brunsan asked.

"In June," Eagle said.

"How do we know it's our truck?"

Eagle opened her mouth, nearly telling him about the license plate number that was off by one, then realized there was no way she would have that information.

"The descriptions match," she said. "The girl was wrapped in a blanket, bound, and screaming. The gas station attendant called the police."

"Good for him. They do anything with the truck driver?"

"No," Eagle said. "By the time they showed, the truck driver and the girl were gone. The driver had tossed the gas station attendant around like he was made of straw, and then had poured gasoline on him and threatened to toss a match on him."

Brunsan's eyes lit up. "Really?"

"Yes, really," she said, buoyed up by his interest. They both knew the gasoline incident was something he could use. "And one more thing. Apparently, they've found some bodies near Mount Diablo, wrapped in blankets."

The light faded. "That's jurisdiction again. They're not going to want us to mess with their cases."

"You can talk to them, though," she said.

He shook his head. "I don't got a reason to right now. We don't have any active cases that pertain to theirs."

She wanted to scream with frustration. It wasn't about jurisdiction. It was about stopping the man with the truck.

"What about that dead girl that you and Oakland have been fighting over?" The words were out of her mouth before she thought to couch them in something else.

"What dead girl?" Brunsan peered at her.

"A different friend," Eagle said, constructing the lie hastily, hoping it would hold up. She shrugged, pretending to be all girly and concerned. "I needed to talk to people."

"A different friend what?" Brunsan growled.

"She works near 61st and Dover. She says a body was dumped there, and no one's investigating it. She's been scared ever since."

"When was that?" he asked.

"I don't know," Eagle said. "I just think there might be more than the one thing I saw, given how many people are seeing things."

He grunted, frowning. "Sounds like you're investigating."

She shook her head. "If I were investigating," she lied, "I wouldn't be talking to you. I know how this works, Detective."

He grunted again. He clearly didn't believe her. "I warned you to stay out of police business."

"You did, and I did," she said. "I've been pretty upset. I know a lot of people, and frankly, you were right. I shouldn't have said anything."

Girly again—or the best she could do which, compared to Pammy and her friends, was piss poor.

"You'd be surprised, Detective," Eagle said softly. "It seems everybody has a horror story."

Brunsan tilted his head as if he didn't know what to make of her. "Like what?"

"The blanket thing," Eagle said. "*Twice.*"

"Yeah, I got that," he said, his tone a lot less conversational. "What else?"

She might as well go for broke. "The girl they found in Tilden Park yesterday."

"How do you know about that?" he snapped. "We haven't released it yet."

"I know someone at the university," Eagle said, which was kind of true. Not entirely true, but close enough. "She had to see the pictures. I guess some detectives needed help with ID…?"

"That girl was not wrapped in a blanket," he said.

"I didn't know," Eagle said. "I just heard she died defending herself."

He looked down, then shook his head. "Someone was pretty angry at her."

"Are you on the investigation for that one?" Eagle asked, hoping she seemed even more girly.

"No, thank God," he said. "Kids like that, you don't want to see them."

"Another college student?" Eagle asked.

Brunsan raised his index finger again, this time to request silence. "I said too much. Don't you go off repeating that."

"I won't," Eagle said. "If you just call the police department in Walnut Creek."

"I can't get a warrant for a family in Marin because of information from Walnut Creek," he said.

"But maybe Walnut Creek can go after the man with the truck, once you give them the information," Eagle said.

Brunsan studied her, his expression flat. She had no idea if police departments were competitive with each other, if they held their cases tight the way some doctors did.

She hoped not, for that girl's sake.

"Okay," Brunsan said. "You don't say nothing about the Tilden Park girl, and I will talk to Walnut Creek about their gasoline nut job."

She smiled at him, not girly at all this time. She let out a small breath. The relief wasn't as strong as it had been when she thought he had solved the case, but it was there nonetheless.

"Deal," she said.

He started to stand, but she didn't move.

"You promised me something at the beginning of this conversation," she said.

He glared at her. "I'm not giving you LaSalle's real name," he said. "You been investigating, and I don't want you going off half-cocked."

Naw, she wanted to say, *if I went off, it would be fully cocked. Loaded for bear. Whatever damn cliché you wanted.*

"I'm not going to do anything," she said. "Except, warn people like you had suggested earlier. I'll have them call you if this man shows up around them or their friends. How's that?"

He squinted at her. Then he nodded.

"Fair enough. I don't like this LaFarge character. I want him to go back to Louisiana where he belongs. Maybe if we can cut off his gravy train, we can get him the hell out of here." He slapped a hand on the table. "I'll be right back with the name."

"Thank you, Detective," Eagle said.

He was almost to the door. He stopped and pointed at her.

"Don't make me regret this," he said.

"Believe me, Detective," she said as demurely as she could. "I won't."

PAMMY

The words seemed to echo in Kelly MacGivers' private dorm room. *My parents hired him. So far, they're happy...*

Pammy shook her head. The words didn't quite go together for her. But they explained Kelly's extreme anger when Pammy said she was teaching a self-defense class. Of course, Kelly's parents wouldn't want her to take self-defense if they hired someone to hurt their daughter on a routine basis.

The light from the gray sky filtered into the room. The smell of eucalyptus was fading, replaced by the stench of unwashed sheets. No wonder Kelly wasn't taking care of herself. She had been attacked and she wasn't getting any help, at home or here.

Pammy wanted to reach out to her, but knew better.

"Shocked you, didn't I?" Kelly said. "Now, you can leave."

Pammy shook her head, then licked her lips, trying to find words. She started to speak twice before something actually came out.

"Please help me understand what's going on," Pammy said.

"Why?" Kelly asked.

"Because," Pammy said quietly, "no one should beat another person the way you got beaten."

Kelly's eyes filled with tears. Rather than wipe them away or acknowledge them in any way, she didn't blink. One slipped out of her left eye, ran down her cheek, and hung on her chin for a moment before dripping on her bare leg.

She didn't seem to notice.

"And one's parents," Pammy said, "should never authorize it."

Kelly's lower lip trembled. She finally blinked, and tears cascaded down her face. She let out a little sob, then wiped at her face.

"Sorry," she said. "Sorry."

"Don't be," Pammy said. "It sounds like you're in some kind of weird hell."

Kelly nodded, dislodging more tears. Another sob shook her. She leaned over, grabbed a blouse that had been half under her bed, and wiped her face with a sleeve.

Pammy wanted to hug Kelly, but knew better than to just presume. The women Pammy had been working with often didn't want to be touched. Touch frightened them almost as much as the original attack had.

"Please," Pammy said, "tell me about it."

Kelly shook her head, then wiped her face again, this time using the entire blouse. Pammy wanted to find some tissues, but she knew better than to take her gaze off Kelly.

"I...can't," Kelly said.

"Can't because someone has said you can't?" Pammy asked.

Kelly's face screwed up at the question, her gaze not meeting Pammy's.

"Or because it's hard to talk about?" Pammy asked, keeping her tone gentle.

Kelly bit her lower lip. She balled up the wet blouse and held it against her stomach, then looked out the window.

"I haven't told anyone," she whispered.

"Tell me," Pammy said. "I'll listen. I won't judge."

Kelly reached over to the nightstand and grabbed her alarm clock. "I'm supposed to be in the library. Study group."

Pammy knew better than to argue. She'd learned that telling women what to do in this circumstance was often the wrong thing.

"If you need to leave, then go ahead," Pammy said. "But I do want to learn about this man. I want to stop him from harming other people."

Kelly closed her eyes. More tears fell, but she didn't wipe off her face with the blouse. Instead, she clung to the alarm clock with one hand and kept pressing the blouse against her stomach with the other.

Pammy thought of a dozen things to say. Encouraging Kelly to talk, so Pammy could help others. Empathizing with Kelly over the attack. Asking for an explanation.

In the past, though, when Pammy had done those things with other women, they had gotten angry. The pressure from Pammy had proven too much, and they had moved on as if they couldn't deal with anything, not even friendly inquiries.

"It's my fault," Kelly whispered.

Pammy almost didn't hear her. In fact, Pammy wouldn't have heard her if she hadn't seen her lips move.

"What is?" Pammy asked.

Kelly swallowed hard. "All of it."

Linda used to say that. Her husband would beat her within an inch of her life, and she would take all of the blame. She'd burned dinner. She had mixed his martini without enough vodka. She had failed to wash his favorite shirt.

Pammy knew better than to argue with the "fault" statement too.

"How is it your fault?" she asked.

"I..." Kelly squeezed her eyes, releasing more tears, then she opened them. Her eyelashes were wet and spikey, the green in her eyes brighter than it had been a moment before, as if the tears had washed the brown from her irises.

She swallowed hard again.

"I...thought...I was grown up," she said. "I forgot...they still own me."

Pammy frowned ever so slightly, before catching herself. "Own" was not a concept she associated with parents and children. Her parents would never have used that word. Not once.

It took a moment to figure out how to phrase a neutral question.

"How did you forget?" Pammy asked.

Kelly pressed her lips together. Her cheeks were flushing again. There was a rage behind her tears, a rage she didn't seem to want to acknowledge.

"I moved out of the dorms. I got a job and an apartment. We couldn't afford a phone, and…." She shook her head, as if she couldn't believe her own stupidity. "…I didn't tell them. I figured I was old enough to be on my own. They didn't need to know. I'd call them now and then. They weren't paying for school anymore. I had scholarships, and my allowance all saved up, and I had more than enough money."

Pammy nodded, even though she had no idea where this was going.

"I didn't know they were getting mad," Kelly said.

Pammy started to shake her head in wonderment, then stopped. She had promised she wouldn't be judgmental. But for heaven's sake, weren't parents supposed to be happy when their children became self-sufficient?

"Then I made the mistake of telling Daddy that I had gone to a rally. He got really mad and asked what else I was doing. I lied, then, and said nothing, really, and it would've worked if my picture wasn't in the *San Francisco Chronicle* last October, at the GIs for Peace Rally. I didn't do anything there, I swear. I was just there for support. I mean, can't people see that the war is wrong if the guys who *fought* it are protesting it?"

Her voice rose to a wail, almost as if she were recreating the argument she'd had with her father in front of Pammy.

Pammy wasn't going to argue the war. It was a minefield, even among people who agreed with each other.

"Your father saw the photograph?" Pammy asked.

"And he said something the next time I called. He said he would come and get me because I clearly wasn't getting an education, and I said what I did was none of his business, and I hung up on him." Kelly ran a hand over her face, then wiped the hand on the wet blouse.

She sniffled, set the alarm clock back on the nightstand, opened a drawer, and found a pack of tissues. Then she blew her nose. Talking was calming the tears.

"I called at the beginning of November, and my dad started yelling again, so I hung up again. I didn't go home for Thanksgiving. I sent a note, saying I was going to take a break from the fighting. No holidays, period. I was going to do them with my friends."

She blew her nose again, then took a shaky breath.

Pammy was feeling shaky too. "Did you?"

"Oh, yeah," Kelly said. "It was fun. We cooked really bad turkey on Thanksgiving and we marched against the war on Christmas, but no one noticed. We didn't care. And New Year's was a blast. It was...I...I don't know. I felt like me—"

She let out a weird sigh, half deprecating and half sad. Pammy wanted to take her hand.

"I don't anymore," Kelly said, voice breaking. "I'm just going through the motions, you know?"

"I do," Pammy said quietly.

She let the conversation lag for a moment. She wanted Kelly to tell this at her own pace, in her own time.

Kelly squeezed her eyes closed for just a moment, then shuddered. She shook her head, a loose tear flying through the air and landing on the unmade sheets.

She shoved the blouse even deeper into her stomach, then opened her eyes.

"The guy in the truck," she said, her voice stronger than it had been before. "I don't know his name. He never told me."

Pammy tried not to let the disappointment show on her face.

"In February, he starts showing up at the weirdest places. The classes I went to, my favorite study spot, he even showed up at Si's Charbroiler at lunch because I liked the hamburgers there." She made a face. "I can't even go near it now."

Pammy nodded, mostly to keep her talking. But Kelly didn't say anything, just continued to push on the blouse. It was as if she had gotten lost in the memories.

"Anyway," Kelly finally said, "he kept saying my parents wanted to see me. I thought it was a line, you know? Like he was trying to pick me up. My roommate Dave, he started going everywhere with me because he thought the guy in the truck was going to do something. My roommate Marsha, she thought we should call the cops, but what could we say, really? Besides, half the house voted against calling them. The pigs, what could they do?"

Pammy stiffened just a bit, remembering Eagle's experience. "House?"

"Yeah, I was living off Ashby in this big house with a lot of other kids. It was divided up into, like, three apartments, with a big room in the middle, but we just went back and forth between them." She shrugged. "I don't know if everyone's still there. I promised I wouldn't talk to any of them again."

Her eyes filled with tears again. She sniffled. Pammy wanted to take her hand, but instead, clung to the folder.

"Anyway," Kelly said, using what was clearly a rhetorical tick for her, "the guy in the truck. Half the house went away for spring break, and I didn't because I didn't want to go home, so there were times I went places by myself."

She raised a hand. It was shaking.

"And see? It's my fault. If I had listened to Dave or Marsha, if I had just asked someone, he wouldn't have, they wouldn't have, I wouldn't be here."

Here ended in a sob. She took a gasping breath, then wiped her face with the blouse again.

"Sorry," she said.

"I'm sorry," Pammy said. "I'm so sorry this happened to you."

Kelly looked up, startled, and for a half second, Pammy wondered if she had spoken out of turn.

Then Kelly nodded, as if she were agreeing with Pammy.

"Yeah, me too," Kelly said. "I'm sorry it happened too."

For a moment, Pammy couldn't tell if Kelly was done talking. Pammy tried to figure out what to say next, to get her going again, but couldn't think of anything. A question might seem too intrusive, but the statements seemed to be just as intrusive.

Kelly took a deep breath.

"On March fifth—it was a Wednesday night—I had just gotten a job at Si's. I guess it paid being a regular, you know? Anyway, I was leaving. I hadn't asked anyone to walk me to the house. I didn't have far to go, I figured I'd be okay and then he...and then he..."

She shook her head again, as if trying to get the memories out of it.

"It's okay," Pammy said. "I don't need all of the details."

"No," Kelly said in that angry tone, the one that had been missing for the past twenty minutes. "You asked. He grabbed me. He put his hand over my mouth. He stank of sweat and onions and beer and he told me that I couldn't scream, because if I screamed, he would snap my neck."

Pammy had never heard of anyone doing that before.

"I can't smell beer or onions without getting ill," Kelly said. Her lips pursed in disgust. "He lifted me up, kept his hand over my mouth and lifted me up with one arm, and he carried me to his truck, and he told me if I didn't—if I didn't cooperate, he would hurt me. Then he shoved me up against the cab, and grabbed my hands, and yanked them behind my back, but I screamed anyway—I figured I'd rather die than not try to get away—and I screamed, and he picked me up by my wrists and Jesus, you have no idea how much that hurt—"

Actually, Pammy did. She'd learned that trick at Mountain Phillip's gym, as a self-defense maneuver. It pulled on the shoulders and made the arms feel like they were going to come out of their sockets.

"—so I started kicking him. He didn't say anything, except once. I made him grunt. I think I hit his balls, but I don't know." Kelly sounded almost proud of herself for that. "I kept screaming and no one came and then he let go of my wrists and I was thinking I could get away, but he grabbed my hair and pushed my head into the truck. Like, a dozen times, I don't know."

She touched the left side of her face.

"He broke my nose. And that bone, just above your eye?" Her fingers flitted over the edge of her left eyebrow. "He fractured that. If it had broke all the way, I might've gone blind."

Pammy let out a breath that she hadn't even realized she'd been holding.

"I think I passed out, because the next thing I remember, I was in the back of his truck, and my arms were tied behind my back and so were my ankles, and then they were tied together. I was wrapped in a blanket, and I couldn't breathe real well. He put some kind of rag in my mouth, and taped it there or something, I don't know."

She wiped her mouth as if the gag were still there. Her gaze met Pammy's. Kelly's eyes were defiant, as if to say, *You asked. You wanted to know.*

"I bounced around back there for what seemed like hours, and stuff fell on me, and it hurt, and sometimes, I couldn't breathe at all. If my legs pulled or my arms pulled and my head jerked back, I think there was a rope around my neck too, but I don't know. Because I passed out again at one point."

She took a deep breath, and looked down.

"We stopped at this motel, and he made me take a shower. He watched."

Pammy stiffened.

"And before you ask, that was all. He just watched. And he handed me my own clothes, from my parents' house, stuff I left behind, and told me to get dressed. He watched when I did that too. And then he tied me up in the bathroom, and locked the door, but I heard him in the other room. He made a phone call, and he said, 'I have her. I'll bring her at nine. You better be home.' And that was all he said the rest of the night."

"The night?" Pammy asked, before she could stop herself.

Kelly nodded. "I slept, kinda, in that bathroom. He left enough give in the rope that I could use the toilet, and I was wearing a dress with no underwear so, you know..." She waved a hand over her thighs. "...air dry. And the next morning, he tied me at the ankles and wrists, but he didn't tie them together, and then he put that gag back on, and he wrapped me in that blanket, and we bounced around and around, and..."

She let out a small sound. Pammy wasn't sure exactly what it was.

"...we stopped and he picked me up and carried me over his shoulder and I couldn't fight anymore. I should've kicked him, but I didn't. He just carried me, and then he knocked on a door, and my dad answered, and the truck guy, he asked for the rest of the money, and my mom told him, 'Here, here it is, just give me my baby,' and he threw me at her, really hard. I hit my head again, and the next thing I know, I'm at San Francisco General, and the nurse is telling me how lucky I was I didn't die because I had all kinds of bruises and injuries and they had to operate on some stuff, but they were afraid to because I'd hit my head and..."

She rubbed her mouth again.

Pammy felt cold. Very, very cold. She'd heard a lot of bad things, but never anything like this.

"And then my parents came in and I asked what happened, and they said they'd tell me later, and my mom, she apologized kinda, like you know, saying she had no idea he would hurt me, and my dad told her to shut up, and that was it."

"They didn't say anything else?" Pammy asked.

Kelly looked at her. The tears were gone now. She was sitting very straight, her arms no longer cradling the wet blouse.

"They did. Or my dad did. He came to my room a few weeks later. I wouldn't leave it, and he told me, he said that I brought this on myself by becoming a degenerate. He'd sent me to college for an education, and I had pissed all over it, and he was going to give up on me, but my mother convinced him to give me a second chance."

Pammy's heart was pounding. She wanted to hurt those parents the same way they had hurt Kelly.

"So, here was the deal, he said. He said I had to come back to school, and I had to get straight As and he would pay for everything, if I stayed in the dorms and dumped my old friends, and took the classes he said I should take, and I am. I'm doing that, but not because I want the education."

Her hands had become fists again. She was grinding them into the mattress.

"It was the only way to get out of the house," she said. "And once I turn twenty-one, I can leave for good. If I can, you know, manage to stay outside long enough. It's hard to go to class. You have no idea. I practically run, and I sit with my back to the wall in each class, and I watch the door more than I watch the professor, and I always make sure I leave in the middle of a crowd."

She leaned forward, just a little.

"If I don't get good grades, he'll come back," she said. "And if he comes back—God, I'll die. I'll just die."

Or wish she had, Pammy thought. This poor girl had been terrorized, and she was barely holding it together.

"Then help me catch him," Pammy said.

"Why?" Kelly asked. "Daddy'll just hire someone else."

Pammy shook her head. "I can't imagine that a lot of people are doing this job."

"Did you know that *anyone* did this?" Kelly asked.

"No," Pammy said, and frowned. "Do you think you can find out who this man is?"

"*No,*" Kelly said with great emphasis. "I'm never talking to my dad again."

Pammy nodded. She had some ideas already.

"I don't want to help you, either," Kelly said. "If my dad finds out—"

"He won't," Pammy said. "I won't say anything, if you won't."

"What about your friends?" Kelly asked.

"I'll tell them what I know," Pammy said. "We found you together."

She bent a corner of the folder with one finger, thinking for a moment.

"This man who took you," she said, "we've had reports from other jurisdictions of people—not just girls—who died wrapped in blankets. Do you think he's done this before?"

"You said your friend saw him. He's still doing it," Kelly said.

"But before you?" Pammy asked.

"Yes," she said. "He didn't get that motel room that night. He had it already. There wasn't a window in the bathroom. It was ready for me. He'd used it before."

The anger was back, strengthening her voice.

"Anything you can think of that would identify him?"

"I know what he looks like," she said. "As if that'll do you any good. Because I can't draw worth a damn."

The police had sketch artists, though. If they could get one to talk with Kelly, that would help.

But Pammy wasn't going to ask for that right now.

"Do you know how he found you?" Pammy asked.

Kelly stiffened again. "What do you mean?"

"You had no phone number. Your parents couldn't reach you. You were living some place that they didn't know existed, right?" Pammy asked.

Kelly nodded slowly.

"How did he find you?"

She swallowed hard. "I didn't ask. I didn't think of it until just now. That means he can still—" Then she let out a self-deprecating sigh. "Well, of course he can still find me. I'm in the damn dorm, and I call my parents every Sunday to report in. Or my mother, actually. I call, I say my name, I say I've been to all my classes, I'm doing fine, and then I hang up."

"They don't check up on you?" Pammy asked.

"I'm sure they're talking to the House Ass," Kelly said. "But that's it. They don't come here."

"Good." Pammy pulled the flyer out of the folder.

"Oh, God," Kelly said. "You are doing a pitch."

"Nope," Pammy said. "If you don't tell anyone, I'll give you the class for free. Because you need someone in your corner, Kelly. I want to be that person."

Kelly took the flyer. Her hands shook. "Why? Because of your friends?"

"Maybe in the beginning, yes," Pammy said. "But no one should have to go through what you're going through. No one. Let me help."

"I don't know how you can," Kelly said.

"Come to my gym," Pammy said, "and you'll find out."

EAGLE

E agle went home and changed clothes after her meeting with Brunsan. In a pair of faded jeans and a long-sleeved shirt, she felt more like herself than she had in that summer dress, which was now scuffed along the back—although if she were honest, she had no idea if the scuff marks were from the bench seat in her truck or from the dirty chair in that room at the Berkeley Police Department.

Her mood kept switching from upbeat to angry. She was happy to have the name of the man in the truck, but furious that BPD had let the bastard go without actually eyeballing that girl.

Eagle hadn't been able to ask for the girl's name again, either. Brunsan had handed her the slip of paper with the man's name on it and said, *This better not come back to bite me*, and walked away before she could promise, again, that it wouldn't.

Even though she didn't quite know what she was promising. Even though she didn't know what she could do.

She thought about it as she cut across campus. She had to get dinner for herself, Val, and Pammy. Eagle opted for the best take-out in the area, because she needed it. The Dynasty Restaurant on Euclid had actual Chinese food, not American Chinese. She didn't want to see what the kitchen was like but she knew the results were spectacular.

She hadn't even called ahead, and she hadn't driven her truck. Parking was too difficult, even in the summer.

Besides, she needed to clear her head.

The woman that she had seen was, in theory, safe. If Eagle believed Brunsan, and she did. He seemed as frustrated as she felt.

The Dynasty was small, and smelled of garlic and shrimp. Usually those smells calmed her. Her stomach did growl—somehow she had missed lunch—but the smells didn't make her feel better. If anything, her confusion grew while she waited for the three large meals she had ordered.

It hadn't taken long. The restaurant wasn't that busy on a Tuesday night. Most of the students who had come in had picked up take-out as well, but unlike her, they had called ahead.

She eyeballed all of them, boys and girls, involved in their own lives, some of them discussing the moon landing, others their classes, and still others revealing way too much about their sex lives. All of those kids seemed oblivious to any danger that they might have been in. They were self-absorbed and focused.

Eagle couldn't remember if she had been that way in college or not. She had probably been too self-absorbed and focused to consider what she looked like to people other than herself.

She paid cash, asked for a large brown paper bag to make carrying all the food easier, realized she had forgotten to order drinks, and then decided she didn't care.

She had to make it all the way across campus before the food got cold, the only downside of her plan.

So she scurried away, not realizing until she got to Observatory Hill that she hadn't been watching for a guy in a truck either. Or anyone else, for that matter. Someone could have followed her from the restaurant without even trying hard, and she hadn't noticed.

All that self-absorption among the college students, all that focus, and they wouldn't have noticed at all.

A chill ran down her spine. It had been easy pickings for that man— once he had found the students.

But she had no idea how he had found the students. Maybe the way that he found the students could provide the illegal entry point for Brunsan.

She walked a little faster on the way back, and from Observatory Hill on, she watched everyone around her as if they were following her.

She supposed the man in the truck—Justin Lavassier, his name was—could have somehow gotten records from the school and waited near the classes to find out where the students were.

But parents could have hired a regular private detective for that. This man combined his detecting skills with his bounty hunter skills, located the kids, and then took them back to their parents by whatever means necessary.

She had reached Sather Road by the time she realized she had missed one important point: What about the students who had dropped out? How had he found them? It couldn't have been easy.

So many questions, things she hadn't thought of when she was talking to Brunsan. She hadn't even thought to ask if Lavassier was working alone. She had just assumed he was, because he was a bounty hunter. Generally, they worked alone.

At least, she thought they did. She wasn't even certain she had met one, or knew of one who operated anywhere near her.

She turned down Bancroft rather than taking Telegraph on her way back to the gym. She didn't want to see the Mini Mob or the gaggle of hippies who gathered on Telegraph's sidewalks. She had enough distractions on this cool evening. She didn't want to look at all of those dirty, drugged-out people who sold ugly tchotchkes on the sidewalk day after day so they could pay for their high. She didn't want to think about how many of them were missing.

She had learned the hard way that helping people like that was not her thing. One week at the Berkeley Free Clinic after she returned had made her decide that nothing was worth the aggravation of dealing with the filth and the starving children of the addicts and the problems that came from sharing needles.

She had known she couldn't explain the dangers to the people she was seeing in a way they could understand. Or, better, in a way they wanted to understand.

She had left, deciding that whatever advanced degree she got with her GI Bill, it wouldn't have anything to do with medicine.

And then, of course, she had ended up volunteering—albeit reluctantly—at the gym.

She arrived at the alley faster than she expected, realized that once again, she hadn't been paying attention, and felt another shiver. She looked both ways before ducking into the alley. She wasn't even sure what she was looking for. She knew that Lavassier had no idea who she was and wouldn't be coming after her for any reason.

Yet.

She wasn't quite sure where that *yet* had come from. But it had been firm and a bit angry. She hated this man, and she had only seen him once. He had seen her too, but he wouldn't recognize her. He had been busy—beating a young woman into unconsciousness.

Whatever he had told Brunsan, it was a lie. Brunsan, to his credit, had known that. He had just run into that horrid place where justice and the law intersected and completely ruled out any kind of real resolution.

A place that Eagle couldn't live with.

She let herself in through the gym's back entrance. She didn't hear any conversation in the kitchen. Val and Pammy were standing on opposite sides of the kitchen, both looking in Eagle's direction.

"Glad it's you," Pammy said. She looked even more tired than she had earlier, if that were possible.

Val still had deep circles under her eyes as well. "Jill is still out front."

Eagle couldn't tell if they had been talking or not. They seemed incredibly tense.

"I'm going to tell her we have a meeting," Pammy said. "I'd like to eat in here, but I think she'll bother us."

"How about I put out the food," Eagle said, "then we serve ourselves and go into the office, and Jill can have some if she wants."

"Sounds good." Pammy pushed open the door. "I'll tell her."

She left.

Eagle set the large bag on the table. Val got dishes out of the cabinet while Eagle unpacked the Szechuan chicken, the house special chow yuk, the beef and tomatoes, and the vegetable stir-fry that she particularly loved. She also set fortune cookies on the counter and the three containers of rice.

No wonder the bag had felt heavy. She had carried a lot of food.

She grabbed serving spoons from the drawer and shoved them into the food. Then she grabbed forks.

"No chopsticks?" Val asked.

Eagle shuddered a little. That was one of the things she had promised herself when she returned from Southeast Asia, that she would never have to use chopsticks again. She had gotten good with them, but she had seen them misused as instruments of torture more than she had ever seen forks misused in the same way.

"Forgot," she lied.

"Too bad," Val said. "I prefer them."

La-di-da, Eagle thought, then caught herself. She hadn't had that kind of sarcastic thought directed at Val before.

"Get your nap?" Eagle asked.

"A little," Val said. "I got some news."

"Did you tell Pammy?" Eagle was surprised at how quickly the question came out, at the tinge of jealousy behind it.

"Not yet," Val said. "We both decided to wait for you."

No wonder they had just been standing, staring at each other.

The food still steamed from their little containers, which was good, since Eagle wasn't sure there were enough pans here to quickly reheat everything.

She helped herself to rice, the vegetables, and the chow yuk, just as Pammy came back in, followed by Jill.

"Strange group meeting," Jill said, clearly feeling left out.

"Yeah, well, we have some things to discuss," Eagle said flatly. "The food initially wasn't even meant for you."

"Eagle," Val said, and everyone looked at her. She shrugged. She had already served herself some of the chicken and a little of the veggie dish as well.

"That's okay," Jill said, grabbing the plate that Val had clearly pulled down for Pammy. "I'm used to it. Eagle and I should really call a truce someday."

Eagle didn't respond to that. The last thing she wanted was to acknowledge anything that Jill said.

Pammy didn't jump into the conversation at all, which was odd. There was silence while Jill filled her plate. She grabbed a napkin, some silverware, and a glass of water.

"Use the kitchen," she said. "I'll make sure no one bothers you."

Then she let herself out.

"Why don't you like her?" Val asked.

"Because." Eagle sat down in the chair closest to her, then cursed. "I forgot beverages."

"I made hot water for tea," Val said. "I couldn't find a teapot, though."

"We're coffee people here," Pammy said.

"I'll take tea," Eagle said at the same time.

Val found some Lipton teabags and some larger cups. She poured hot water from the kettle into two of the cups and set them down by Eagle and in front of another place.

Pammy poured the last of the old coffee into another cup, then took a plate from the cabinet.

With her back to everyone, she said, "This has been a *shit* day."

Eagle looked at her in surprise. Random cuss words were Eagle's department, not Pammy's.

"What happened?" Val asked.

"You found Kelly MacGivers," Eagle said.

"Yeah." Pammy braced her hands on the countertop. "And I almost wish I hadn't."

PAMMY

ammy told them everything. How odd it felt to be in Stern Hall. How she had been thinking of Linda, Sue Ellen, and Barbara. How she had found Kelly, and how alone that poor girl had been.

At first, Pammy could only talk with her back to Eagle and Val. She didn't want them to see how close to the edge she was. She kept her hands flat on the countertop, the smell of garlic and soy sauce turning her stomach.

As she talked, she managed to turn around. Someone had already filled her plate with some kind of chicken dish, and something that had those mini corn things as well as bamboo shoots. She added more rice to sop up the sauce, then sat down, happy that her hands weren't shaking.

Maybe they weren't because she was getting the story out. Or maybe they weren't because she had finally felt the anger underneath.

She wanted to take those parents and slam them against the wall, maybe toss *them* into the back of a truck. Or bring them here, have them fight bare-knuckled against a more savvy opponent, let them feel how badly punches and kicks could hurt.

Eagle didn't say anything as Pammy spoke, but her eyes didn't move from Pammy's face. Val looked down, almost folded in on herself, as if Pammy's words were personal.

Finally, she finished. Finally, there was no more to tell.

Val looked up from her plate. Her brown eyes seemed wider than they had before, her face lined with exhaustion.

"Is she going to come to the gym?" Val asked.

And that question, that simple question, more concerned with Kelly's health than with all of the ins and outs of the man with the truck, of the horrid parents, of those awful events, made Pammy tear up.

She blinked hard.

"She needs a community," Val said. "I don't know how to provide it for her, and it might be too soon, but it sounds clear. Because she's in a bad place."

Those last two words were soft. Eagle, frowning slightly, looked over at Val as if hearing something deeper there as well.

"I don't know if she's going to come here," Pammy said. "I asked her to. I told her—"

Well, Val didn't need to know that Pammy had offered the classes for free. Eagle didn't either. Eagle would probably yell at her for forgetting this was a for-profit business.

"—that, um, we had a community here. That we would understand."

Val nodded. Eagle was still watching her.

"Poor girl," Val said.

"She's not alone," Eagle said drily.

Val glanced at her, startled.

"I talked to one of the detectives," Eagle said.

Pammy looked at Eagle so quickly that she made herself dizzy. She had to remember to breathe.

"And, surprise surprise," Eagle said, "he actually tracked down the license plate of that truck."

"Oh, thank God," Val said.

"Don't thank your erstwhile deity yet," Eagle said. "Because this doesn't end well."

She told them exactly what Brunsan had told her—that the man in the truck was running what seemed like a legitimate business, and that Brunsan believed the woman Eagle had seen was still alive.

"I doubt that she's well," Eagle said. "Particularly after everything that Pammy told us."

Pammy threaded her fingers together. "I love how this man told the police that he 'calmed her down.' In a different motel room, where he terrorized her."

"Yeah," Eagle said. "I didn't like that part either, and that was before I heard your girl's story."

Pammy's girl. She supposed that was true. She had acquired another person to worry about, even if she never saw Kelly MacGivers again.

"This man should be arrested," Val said, her voice thrumming with passion.

"I agree," Eagle said. "The thing is, Detective Brunsan agrees too. He wants this guy, but he can't find any legal way to get him."

"Call him," Val said. "Tell him about Walnut Creek."

"I did already," Eagle said. "He's going to contact the department in Walnut Creek. I also told him to investigate the jurisdictional thing you found."

"That poor woman, found on 61st and Dover?" Val asked.

"Yes," Eagle said. "It's not Brunsan's case. I'm not sure he even heard of it."

Pammy's fingernails dug into the palms of her hands. "Do you think he'll actually do anything?"

"He was polite to me this time," Eagle said. "He found out I was right. He doesn't like this man, and he really didn't like those parents. He wanted to see the girl, although he couldn't figure out how to do it."

Val nodded. "Sometimes cases get to some cops."

Pammy looked at her sideways. Her father always had one or two cases that he couldn't let go of. Apparently, Val's late husband had had some too.

"Brunsan said there was a lot of money involved," Eagle said.

That got Pammy's attention. "How much?"

"Enough to buy a house," Eagle said. "What would that be?"

"I don't know about here," Val said, "but in Chicago, that would be at least ten thousand dollars."

Pammy nodded. She had purchased her house for less than that, but it had been years ago now. Still, that was pretty expensive.

"The thing to remember," Eagle said, "is that's just the initial payment. They paid the rest in cash."

Val let out a small whistle. "He's making a fortune."

"I think the correct term is 'killing.'" Pammy's tone was even more biting aloud than it had been in her head. "Kelly will never be the same girl again. That much was clear. I'm amazed she's even making it to class."

Val's gaze met Pammy's.

"Me, too," Val said quietly.

Eagle crossed her arms, and leaned back in her chair. "Brunsan's going to do what he can, but he won't be able to do much."

"If he gets ahold of Albert Jessup in Walnut Creek," Val said, "they should be able to do something. I think that attack at the gas station might get the truck guy put away."

"That's the thing," Eagle said. "Brunsan gave me the guy's name."

Pammy inhaled sharply. "What?"

"He told me who we're looking for," Eagle said.

"Why would he do that?" Pammy asked, unable to fathom it. "He didn't trust you on Sunday."

"He still doesn't," Eagle said. "He just wants me to warn people."

"He also knows you have a gun," Val said quietly.

Eagle looked at her. So did Pammy. Val's face had gone slightly gray. Her eyes glittered. She was serious.

"He wouldn't tell me to kill someone," Eagle said.

"You sure of that?" Val asked.

"This is *not* Chicago," Pammy said, a warm flush running from her cheeks to her torso. She couldn't believe someone suggested murder in her kitchen.

Val faced her, a small frown forming above her nose. "What does *that* mean?"

"We don't go around sanctioning murder here," Pammy said.

"No one said anything about sanctioning murder, Pamela," Eagle said. "Calm down."

"No one sanctions murder in Chicago either," Val said, but something in her tone suggested otherwise. If Pammy had been defending her city, she would have defended it with more force.

"*I* certainly wasn't saying Eagle should go out and kill the guy." Val looked at Eagle, who nodded just a little. "I did suggest that the cop knew

Eagle had a gun. He might have wanted her to use it, maybe in defense of someone."

Then Val sighed. Pammy was still tense.

"Ah hell," Val said. "It did cross my mind that he wanted Eagle to go after this guy. Sometimes cops do that, you know? Sometimes they look the other way."

Eagle leaned back in her chair, her gaze not leaving Val's face.

Pammy was trembling. Her father would never have sanctioned murder. "I never knew of a cop who—"

"Pammy," Eagle said, "your knowledge of cops comes from growing up in a cop's family. Val married into one."

"Oh, she was an adult, so she knew things I didn't?" Pammy snapped. "I don't think so. Cops wouldn't—"

"Give it a rest," Val snapped. "You're arguing for the sake of argument's sake. I've been hearing about your People's Park since I got here, and it seems to me your *governor* sanctioned murder not six months ago—"

"It's not the same," Pammy said.

"Pammy, calm down," Eagle said.

Pammy glared at her, feeling betrayed.

"It is *not* the same," Pammy said. "That's the governor talking about how to deal with rioters. That's not one cop telling a civilian to use her gun."

"Pamela," Eagle said. "Think it through."

Pammy looked at her. Eagle's expression was neutral, the same way she looked at some of the women who had hurt themselves by punching something wrong.

"You were gassed in May, on that governor's orders," Eagle said. "I don't think anyone in Chicago has been gassed like that."

Val let out a small snort. "That's because the people who get covered with tear gas in Chicago live on the South Side. They're not worthy of the national news."

Pammy looked at her. What was she arguing? That the three of them go rogue? That they become lawless? Or that the whole world was already lawless?

"There was tear gassing on the national news from Chicago," she said, not quite willing to let the argument go. "The whole world watched the Democratic National Convention. Kids got gassed there too."

Val raised her chin defiantly. Her brown eyes flashed with anger. She was about to speak when Eagle cut in.

"But no white kids died at that convention," Eagle said. "One did die here in May."

She had spoken softly. Somehow that was much more devastating than if she had shouted the words.

Because she was right.

Pammy stood up, and realized she was shaking. "I mean what I said earlier. I don't want to sanction murder in my kitchen."

"We're not talking about murder, Pammy," Eagle said. "I'm reporting what one cop said to me. We can speculate all we want about his motives, but the only way to know those motives is to ask him. And I don't plan to."

Val moved her hands up and down in a small, placating gesture. It seemed to mean calm down. *Sit* down.

Pammy wasn't ready to, though. Not yet.

"I would rather have the police handle things, no matter what they've done in the past," Val said in a completely different tone, one not as charged with anger. "This man sounds dangerous."

Eagle looked up at Pammy but answered Val. "He does sound dangerous. But I'm pretty convinced the police won't handle anything."

"Not even Walnut Creek?" Pammy sat down slowly. Her heart was pounding hard. She was still shaken, but she wasn't sure what had her so upset, at least from this conversation. Maybe she was still upset from talking to Kelly. Scratch that. Pammy *was* still upset from talking to Kelly.

"I don't know what kind of information the police have," Val said. "It sounds like this man can talk his way out of things."

It did sound that way. And of course he could. He was *licensed*. An authority of some kind. A man used to getting what he wanted.

Pammy had met men like him, men that seemed reasonable on the surface and were so very horrid underneath.

"Maybe that body wrapped in a blanket on 61st might help," Pammy said. "Not to mention the poor girl who died in Tilden Park. Did you mention that to him?"

Eagle nodded, but Val held up a hand before Eagle could speak. Val's cheeks were flushed, and she spoke quickly.

"That girl in Tilden Park," Val said. "I know who she is."

The conversation stopped cold. Both Eagle and Pammy looked at Val. Val's tired face seemed even more drawn, as if the news she was about to impart pained her greatly.

"The body belongs to Darla Newsome," Val said. "I got a call from her roommate, offering me the apartment."

"Offering you the apartment?" Eagle asked. "That's cold."

"No, it wasn't," Val said. "She wanted a friend, I think. It was her excuse to call me."

Pammy pushed her plate away. Food had been a good idea, but it wasn't the kind of idea she could contemplate at the moment, not with her stomach tied in knots and the gigantic lump in her throat.

She had been hoping that Darla Newsome was alive. Part of her had been counting on it.

She had really wanted Jill to be right—she had wanted Darla Newsome to have gone somewhere else, on some "Movement" business, hiding from her parents and living her life elsewhere.

And now the poor girl was dead.

After defending herself against someone.

"Did this man kill her?" Pammy asked Val.

If this horrid man had killed her, maybe something could come out of Darla Newsome's death. Maybe they would end up with something to give to the cops, something to allow them to take the entire investigation and actually do something right.

The cops could save some lives down here, instead of terrifying everyone.

"Brunsan said no," Eagle said.

Pammy hadn't expected that. "You asked already?"

"I was grasping for straws, trying to get him to work the case," Eagle said. "He was pretty shocked I even knew about it. They hadn't released the information yet. So I'm shocked the roommate did too."

"I think Lucy—that's the roommate—called me right after she heard," Val said.

Pammy frowned. She didn't care about the roommate. And she didn't want to think about the father. The man had been devastated before he had walked into the gym, when he thought his daughter was missing.

He would be destroyed now.

"How can your detective know that the cases aren't related?" Pammy asked Eagle.

"I don't know exactly," Eagle said, "although he did say she wasn't wrapped in a blanket."

"Too bad," Val said, and Pammy glared at her. Did she want Darla Newsome to die a horrid death?

Then Pammy realized how ridiculous that thought had been. Darla Newsome *had* died a horrid death, and Val was right. It was too bad that there were no obvious ties.

"So I don't understand," Val said. "He told you that Darla's death was unrelated. He told you he couldn't do anything with the information he had, and *then* he gave you the guy's name? If Pammy's right, and he didn't want you to go rogue on this case, why would this detective give you the man's name?"

It was a good question. In fact, it was the most pertinent question that any of them had asked.

Pammy nodded to show that she wanted the question answered too. She didn't trust her voice or she would have said that aloud.

"I've been thinking about it since he did it," Eagle said. "I don't think Detective Brunsan gave me that name lightly. And I don't see it as a trust thing. I think he had a motive in mind."

Pammy forced herself to speak quietly. "What motive?"

"I think he gave me the name to warn everyone," Eagle said. "He believes—and he's clearly right—that this man is dangerous. And we need to keep as many people away from him as possible."

"Are you planning to share the name?" Val asked.

"His name is Justin Lavassier," Eagle said. "And he has no fixed address. Just a hotel room."

Pammy frowned. "You said he has a California license plate. How did he get that without a fixed address?"

Eagle shrugged one shoulder. "According to Brunsan, he moved out of an apartment and into a hotel."

"Did Brunsan check this?" Val asked.

"Yeah," Eagle said. "The address traced back to an empty building. It had an office on the first floor and an apartment on the second."

Pammy knew that tone. There was something in it, something else Eagle wasn't saying.

"And?" Pammy asked.

"Brunsan said he talked to some of the neighboring businesses. The building's been empty for more than a year."

Val shifted in her seat and looked at Eagle. "Brunsan doesn't find that suspicious?"

"Brunsan finds it all suspicious. It's just something he can't prove," Eagle said.

Pammy shook her head. Maybe she had too much information in it, or maybe the world was shifting on her. Maybe she was just too upset to think clearly.

"I'm not following," she said.

"I didn't either at first, until Brunsan told me the last known business in the downstairs space," Eagle said. "It was a two-room operation, a secretary and a back office. And it was called Finders, Inc."

"Finders?" Val asked.

Eagle nodded. "The name of Lavassier's business is Finders, Inc."

Pammy shook her head again. This wasn't making sense. "Why would he close his office if he was still running the business?"

"According to Brunsan, Lavassier said he couldn't afford the rent or the secretary any more. And that makes no sense, considering this man is earning at least twenty grand per job."

"Twenty thousand dollars," Pammy breathed. If her business brought in twenty thousand dollars in one month, she'd be rich. She made eight thousand dollars last year, and barely broke even.

"Did you mention the illogic of that to Brunsan?" Val asked.

"I didn't have to," Eagle said. "He asked Lavassier about it. Lavassier said he wasn't making that much early on. Then he grinned and added that he had one expensive secretary."

"Brunsan saw that as suspicious, right?" Val asked.

"It's all suspicious," Eagle said. "It's just not illegal."

Pammy was turning this over and over in her head. He had an office that he got rid of. But the office, with the apartment above, established him. It allowed him to get a California driver's license. It also made him seem legitimate.

"If he doesn't have an office now," Pammy asked, "how do these parents find him?"

"Word of mouth," Eagle said. "Satisfied customers tell other prospectives about him."

"But how do they reach him?" Pammy asked.

"And how did Brunsan find him if he has no fixed address?" Val asked.

Eagle looked at Val, clearly planning to answer her first. "Brunsan said they found the truck at an A&W. They brought him in to the station. He cooperated."

Pammy didn't care about Brunsan. She wanted to know about the parents. If a man ran his business from his truck, there would be no way to reach him.

"Did he say how the clients reached him?" Pammy asked again, louder this time.

"I don't think Brunsan asked," Eagle said. Which meant that Eagle hadn't asked. She probably hadn't thought of it.

Pammy stood. She couldn't sit any longer. She walked to the counter, poured herself some cold coffee, and stood there for a moment.

"He has to have an answering service," she said, more to herself than to the other two.

"You're right," Eagle said. "That's the only thing that makes sense."

Val was nodding as well. "I worked for a lawyer who had an off-hours answering service. We called in first thing to make sure he had no messages overnight. He took emergency calls directly, but other messages waited for us."

"There are no emergencies in Lavassier's business," Eagle said. "Not like the ones lawyers and doctors would have."

"He doesn't need a fixed address now," Val said. "But he needed one to establish his business. He needed to give the answering service one, and he needed one for his California identification."

Pammy leaned on the counter, its lip biting into the skin above her back. "I don't like this. It's legal, but it's shady."

Eagle nodded. "That's why Brunsan wants us to get the word out."

"We need to do more than that," Val said quietly.

Pammy sighed. She knew she would regret asking this next question. But she couldn't keep it in, not after talking to Kelly MacGivers.

"What would you suggest?" she asked Val.

"We have to stop him," Val said. "We have to stop him right now."

VAL

I felt cold as I spoke. Cold and clear-headed.

But I also felt like someone else.

I set down my fork. Despite the conversation, I had managed to eat all of the rice, chicken, and veggies on my plate, and despite my nerves, none of that meal was threatening to return. My stomach wasn't even upset.

I should have been upset. Shouldn't I?

Eagle was watching me, a slight frown on her forehead. I couldn't really see Pammy. She was standing to my side, leaning against the counter, her hands gripping its edge.

I was rather relieved she couldn't see my face. She clearly didn't know what to make of me.

I could understand that. I didn't know what to make of myself these days.

But every time I thought of that statement I had just made, that clear, cogent, *We have to stop him*, which emerged from me without thought, just as if it were the easiest and the most logical thing in the world, I couldn't back away from it.

We had to stop him. No one else was going to.

"Why is it our responsibility to stop him?" Pammy asked.

I knew she would say that. Hell, I would have said that a year ago.

"It's not," Eagle said. "It's the police's responsibility. But they're not going to. Not without help."

"Help?" Pammy asked.

She had a good question. Even I didn't know what *help* meant in this context. Nor did I know exactly how we could stop this man.

I just knew that he couldn't be allowed to continue with what he was doing.

And I was glad I was having this discussion with Eagle and Pammy, not Marvella and Paulette. Because Marvella and Paulette would dismiss my comment, pointing out—rightly—that what this Lavassier was doing to those college kids echoed what Armand Vitel had done to me.

Everything was replaying, from the fact that Lavassier apparently followed them to learn their routine to the way he grabbed them off the street. He tied them up and delivered them, broken and bleeding, to their parents, unlike Vitel, who had taken what he wanted from me in the hallway of my apartment building, but the concept was the same.

These men hunted a person, taken something from that person, and left that person physically damaged. Badly damaged.

And in the case of Lavassier, maybe even killed some people, although we didn't know that for certain.

And now, as I learned through this discussion, the similarities continued. Eagle's frustration with the Berkeley Police detective mimicked my frustration with a private detective I had hired in February, to see if there was a way to stop *him*—Vitel, dammit, I would use his name now—from following me everywhere.

The language Eagle used to describe her conversation with Detective Brunsan echoed the language in the letter I had received from the private detective, a letter I had memorized because I had read it so many times:

Although Mr. Vitel's actions are invasive, they are not illegal. His unwanted advances simply make him a persistent suitor, something the law can do nothing about. Unless Mr. Vitel breaks the law in his contact with you, you cannot bring any authorities in to dissuade him from his behavior.

Given Mr. Vitel's profession, he probably knows this. We suggest that you continue to politely rebuff his attentions until he finds another target for his affections.

Affections, suitor—those words did not describe Lavassier. Of course, they hadn't described Vitel either. But the rest of that letter matched what Lavassier was doing. His actions were invasive, but not illegal. At least, not in any way that someone could prove.

So we needed to figure out how to prove that Vitel—I closed my eyes, and forced myself to start again, glad I hadn't spoken aloud.

We had to figure out how to prove that *Lavassier* was acting illegally, that he was causing extreme harm to these kids.

And we had to do it in a way that protected them.

Eagle was staring at me. She had a penetrating look, one that seemed to see all the way through to my soul.

"What are you thinking?" she asked softly.

I was thinking that I had to be careful. I had to make certain I wasn't reacting out of fear of Vitel or some kind of flashback.

But aside from that mental slip—Vitel's name for Lavassier's—I was clearheaded. I was calm, calmer than I had been in months.

Then I realized that Eagle wasn't asking what I was thinking about, the way a friend would. She was asking what kind of help I thought we could provide the police.

I picked up the cup of tea that Eagle had poured at the beginning of the meal. The cup was warm, but the tea had a small film over the surface. It had grown tepid.

"Does it seem to you that this Lavassier works alone?" I asked.

I had to know that—*we* had to know that—before we made any decisions. Because if we were dealing with an organized group of bounty hunter detectives, then we were out of our league.

We were probably out of our league with one as well, but I wasn't going to consider that. Not at the moment, anyway.

"If he has an answering service, then I'd say yes." Pammy pushed away from the counter and came back to the table, sitting gingerly. This conversation was making her uncomfortable, but to her credit, she wasn't backing out of it.

"Eagle?" I asked, looking at her.

"Brunsan seemed to think so," she said.

"I'm not asking Brunsan," I said. "I'm asking you."

She used her fork to mound the remaining food on one side of her plate. "I don't know much about bounty hunters. I have no idea if he's working alone."

"In larger cities," Pammy said, "there are bail bonds organizations that employ bounty hunters. But I don't think this is one of those organizations."

I sipped my tea. It was barely warm at all and pretty weak. I agreed with Pammy, but I wanted to hear her analysis.

"I mean, your detective friend—"

"He's not my friend," Eagle said sharply, as if Pammy had offended her.

"All right. The detective, Brunsan, he told you that this Lavassier is from Louisiana. That's where he's licensed. He went through some kind of elaborate scheme to get California plates and establish himself here." Pammy was holding a cup as well, only hers was filled with coffee. It looked as cold as my tea.

She looked at me, then at Eagle, before continuing.

"You don't do that if you have a big company behind you. And you don't move all the way from Louisiana to here by yourself. He has clearly rebuilt his business here. I wonder if he got in trouble in Louisiana." She said that more to herself than to us.

"Huh," Eagle said, as if all of that were new to her.

"If he got into trouble there," I said, "wouldn't they have told Detective Brunsan?"

"I don't know if they attach information like that to a detective license in Louisiana," Pammy said to me. "Besides, I doubt anyone cares if a bounty hunter roughs up someone who skipped bail."

Eagle looked at her sideways.

"There are a lot of people who can be roughed up without authorities taking notice," Eagle said. "Generally speaking, though, rich white college kids aren't those people."

"Except that the parents sanctioned this," Pammy said.

"And that's not entirely true," I said. "Pammy mentioned the Democratic National Convention last year as a scene of tear gas and violence. There's a lot of sentiment out in the rest of the country that these rich college kids are out of control."

"Nixon's Silent Majority certainly think so," Eagle said.

"And Nixon's Silent Majority," Pammy said with a bit more charge on the phrase than I would have expected, "happen to be primarily rich and white."

"Maybe," I said, "this Lavassier guy simply saw this as a money-making opportunity. You know, missing kids, distraught parents, the whole counterculture scene."

"He might've come out here to find someone's kid, got paid well, and decided to stay," Pammy said.

"Who cares why?" Eagle said. "Whatever prompted this behavior from him, the point is that he's doing it, and he's making a fortune at it."

"And he's destroying the kids," Pammy said softly.

"Those who survive his treatment," I said.

Both Pammy and Eagle looked at me. I shrugged. They hadn't talked to the police departments. I had. I thought there were too many coincidences.

"If only we had some proof," Pammy said.

"Why don't we get some?" I said.

"How would you propose we do that?" Eagle asked.

"Maybe we should hire him," I said.

"To do what?" Pammy asked.

"To find a kid," I said.

"But we don't have any kids," Eagle said, as if I didn't know that.

"I know," I said gently.

"And we're not putting the college students who come to the gym in jeopardy," Pammy said.

I almost smiled. I hadn't thought of that, but I wouldn't have allowed it, even if I had.

"I know," I said. "You two are being literal."

Pammy frowned at me. "You have a plan."

I shrugged. "It's not big enough to be a plan. It's more of an idea."

"What is it?" Eagle asked.

"We have to track him down, of course," I said. "And then we lie. We say one of the parents recommended him. Probably Kelly MacGivers' parents. He won't check, because we'll have the phone number."

"If it's unlisted," Eagle said.

"I'll wager it is," I said. "I'll wager it's word of mouth only."

"That's easy to check," Pammy said. She almost sounded eager to hear the rest, but I wasn't going to put that interpretation on her. I still hadn't quite figured her out entirely.

"We call him, and then what?" Eagle asked.

"We schedule a meeting with him at some public place with a parking lot," I said. "He goes inside, has the meeting with one of us—probably you, Pammy. Eagle waits at a different table. I'll search his truck."

"You would?" Eagle asked.

I shrug. "He's a white boy from Louisiana. He's used to dealing with rich white clients. I don't think he would talk to me very long."

"But I could search the truck," Eagle said.

"Yes, you could," I said, "but if someone sees me do it here, they won't be able to identify me."

Eagle thinned her lips and shook her head just a little. She understood.

But Pammy asked, "Why not?"

"Because, Pamela," Eagle said, "to white people, all black people look alike."

"That's not fair and you know it," Pammy said.

"And you know it's true," Eagle said.

Pammy scrunched her mouth as if she had eaten something that tasted bad. "It puts Val at risk."

"It puts us all at risk," I said. "I don't mind. We might find something in that truck, something your detective Brunsan could use."

"He's not mine," Eagle said, sounding annoyed.

Pammy was nodding. "You're right. We might get some names or something, something that could help with a real investigation."

"Or," I said, "it might be a bust. But it would be something."

"It won't stop him, though," Eagle said. "Even if the police do get something, it won't stop him. They're going to be very reluctant to act on this, because those rich white parents aren't complaining about him."

"We can't just let him continue to harm these kids," I said.

Eagle frowned. "Maybe we don't have to."

"What does that mean?" Pammy asked.

Eagle's frown deepened. For a moment, I thought she wasn't going to answer Pammy.

Then Eagle looked up.

"We take it one step farther," Eagle said.

"What does *that* mean?" Pammy asked, sounding hesitant.

Eagle sighed. "We have to find something in the truck that the police can use, right?"

I nodded. Pammy just stared at her.

"And," Eagle said, "something they can actually get their hands on."

Pammy was clutching her cup so hard that her knuckles had turned white. "There are all kinds of procedures that prevent them from just breaking into the truck."

"And what I discover in that truck won't get the police in there," I said. "We'd have to get him pulled over or something."

"And the vehicle searched," Pammy said.

Eagle was shaking her head as we talked.

"We set him up," she said.

"That's what we're talking about," Pammy said.

Eagle leaned forward. "We make sure the police find something. We use the stuff from the truck if we can, but if we can't, then we plant stuff."

My stomach twisted. "How would we do that? This guy sounds dangerous."

Eagle smiled, just a little. "I used to work in psychiatric clinics. There are drugs that can subdue very large violent people quickly."

Pammy was staring at her. "What are you saying?"

"She's saying we knock him out." I was frowning. "And then what? Put him in his truck?"

"No," Eagle said. "If the truck has something with the address for his motel room, the one that he kept Kelly in, then we use that motel room. We plant him there and we give him something else, maybe some LSD, something that'll make the cops think he had his guard down. Then we tie him to the bed, scatter incriminating stuff around the room, and one of us screams real loud. We flee the room, drive off, and call the cops from the nearest pay phone, saying he tried to hurt one of us, but not saying who we are. Then we make sure the cops show up."

"How do we do that?" Pammy asked before I could.

"We watch," Eagle said. "And if no patrol shows up, we call again. And again, until someone comes."

"Seems risky," Pammy said. "Subduing a man like that—"

"Isn't hard if he's not expecting it," Eagle said. "We get him from behind."

I pushed my plate aside. I was both fascinated with this plan and nervous about it. "The drugs concern me. You don't practice anymore, Eagle. How would you get them?"

She smiled. "I have friends."

"For the LSD, too?" Pammy asked, with a bit of an edge to her voice.

"It's still used clinically," Eagle said.

Pammy shook her head. "The authorities would catch us."

"Not if we wore gloves," I said. "All they would have to go on are fingerprints. We just make sure we don't leave any."

"But he'd see us. He'd be able to describe us," Pammy said.

"And who believes a man who has been hallucinating?" Eagle asked.

Her question stopped Pammy cold. The question made me smile. No one would believe a drug addict. No one. I had seen that a lot with Truman. Hell, I had used it to talk to the police just the night before.

"What if we don't find the motel?" Pammy asked.

"We get one here," I said, surprising myself. I looked at Eagle. "We rent a room ourselves and drag him into it."

"Not under our names," Pammy said.

"Under his name," I said. "It shouldn't be hard. And then we make sure your Detective Brunsan gets the case."

Eagle shook her head. "He would know it was me, then," she said.

"But he couldn't prove it," I said.

Eagle frowned at me.

Then I shrugged. "I could go to the precinct and ask for Brunsan, saying I was attacked."

"He'd figure out that we know each other," Eagle said.

"Not if I run off before he talks to me," I said. Then I smiled at her. "My description and yours don't match."

"We're assuming we can take him on," Pammy said. "We're assuming he won't hurt us."

I stiffened. I let her words roll around in my head.

"No," I said after a moment. "I don't know about the both of you, but I'm not making that assumption. I think he might hurt us. And I think that we can risk getting hurt fighting him, if it gets him off the street. At least, as far as I'm concerned."

Eagle's gaze met mine. "Do you mean that?"

I nodded. "I fought back in February. I lost. But I hold onto that. It's why I'm here. I fought back. I just didn't do it well."

"I tell people not to engage," Pammy said.

"You also tell them to avoid these situations," I said. "But sometimes you can't."

"And I've been trained that you step in when you see something go awry," Eagle said.

Pammy looked at both of us. "You're talking about a big risk."

"Yes," I said. "I'm willing to take it on. Are you?"

She bowed her head, then sighed. "It's been a *shit* day," she repeated.

Eagle was about to speak, but I put my hand up slightly, stopping her.

"You should've seen her," Pammy said. "Kelly. She's never going to be the same."

I knew that, without having seen her. I wasn't the same. Poor Kelly. She had found herself on the other side of that crevasse as suddenly and horribly as I had. Only she hadn't had family to help her through it.

Then Pammy nodded. She raised her head, her gaze meeting mine.

"Yes," she said. "I'm willing to take it on."

Eagle looked at both of us. "Me, too," she said.

I took a deep breath. Truman would not have approved. But I did. People had to step up sometimes.

"Then we have some planning to do," I said.

"We have to make sure we've got all the bases covered," Pammy said. "Preparation is the key. We need clearly defined roles, back-up plans, and bail-out options. We need code words so that we know if we have to run away."

"Run away?" Eagle asked.

Pammy sat up straight. "If this goes seriously south, we need to get out fast. I want a plan for that. Or I won't do this."

Eagle looked at me as if I could talk sense into her. But Pammy's requirement sounded right to me.

"I agree," I said. "We need to plan for everything we can think of."

Eagle took a deep breath. "All right then," she said. "But I'd like to do this fast."

I understood why. "Because of the woman you saw?" I asked.

"Yeah," she said, sounding a little uncertain. "But more than that. If Brunsan's right, and she's home with her parents, Lavassier's looking for a new payday. We have an opportunity right now. If we can find him."

"We'll find him," Pammy said with more determination than I expected from her. "No matter what it takes."

EAGLE

They figured it would take two full days to prepare. Eagle convinced them to add a half day as well. She wanted this plan to be implemented on a Friday night. It added credibility.

That meant Pammy had to close the gym on Friday night. She usually kept it open, even though she didn't hold a class. Eagle wanted no distractions. She also wanted no one near the gym. She was particularly worried about Jill.

Eagle didn't believe she, Pammy, or Val would end up anywhere close to the gym, but just in case, she wanted the gym clear.

She wanted all of them clear. She went over and over the plan with them, but she also had to trust them, something she really wasn't good at.

Because she was the one who had tweaked Val's plan, she became the person in charge. She was okay with that. It meant she didn't have to tell everyone everything.

She had two contingency plans of her own, plans she would never tell Val or Pammy about. If they couldn't gather enough evidence to convict Lavassier or, if Eagle believed that this man was so slippery, he would get out of everything, she would take extra measures.

Thanks to her training and the things she had seen in Pleiku, she knew what certain drugs did in large quantities. She could make him overdose, if need be. Or she could guarantee that Lavassier would live, but never hurt anyone again.

She wasn't sure she wanted to be judge, jury, and executioner, though, even though she wouldn't execute him, even in the worst case scenario. She would guarantee that he couldn't walk again. Or couldn't use his hands.

Or couldn't think. She woke up on Tuesday night to find herself debating what would be better—leaving him a quadriplegic or just a mindless thing.

She had already ruled out a fatal overdose. She didn't want there to be any chance that she or her friends would go to jail for harming this man.

But she believed that she could hurt him permanently. All it would take would be one or two minutes alone with him, after Val and Pammy had exited the room. One shot between his toes, one tab under his tongue, and Lavassier would be damaged for good.

She decided to have the materials on hand but not make a decision as to what to do until she'd assessed the entire situation.

That need for flexibility left her with a lot of errands to run. She needed to get a large medical kit, and she needed to upgrade her medical supplies. She stashed a second bag in her truck, just in case.

She also cleaned her apartment again, this time removing all of the illegal drugs, from the marijuana she bought on Telegraph to the tabs of LSD she had acquired the past year to the back-up kit she'd brought back from Nam. A number of the soldiers she'd worked with had back-up kits, although they all called it something else—the security blanket, the exit strategy, the escape route.

She didn't need hers anymore. She wasn't going to end her life, no matter what kind of nightmares she had. She had proven that to herself over and over again. The kit was redundant, and here, in this apartment, it was also dangerous.

She never said anything to Pammy or Val, but part of her knew that she was preparing for the worst-case scenario. Worst case: Eagle couldn't return to the apartment. Someone else would have to clean it out.

Somewhere in the middle of all that planning and prep, she moved her pistol to the truck as well, making sure it stayed locked. She put the weapon in a small metal cash box, made sure the thing was locked with a tiny key, and had a combination lock on the front.

Someone had to be really determined to break into that. And they had to know something valuable was in it. Her truck was such a ratty vehicle that it looked like it could hold nothing valuable.

Still, she wrapped the cash box in a shirt and put it inside a woven pouch that someone had given her a long time ago. Then she stashed it on the floor—not under the seat. Anyone looking to steal something would look under the seat and consider whatever was in plain sight to be worthless.

She also monitored what Pammy and Val were doing.

Pammy was in charge of getting Finders Inc's phone number. There were only a handful of answering services in the Bay Area, and only a few of those had options that allowed someone to call in from any neighboring community.

Pammy had guessed that Lavassier would use one of those services and have multiple phone numbers for various areas in the Bay. She toyed with talking to Stella and asking Stella to contact the MacGivers, but Eagle had talked Pammy out of that.

Eagle didn't want anyone else to know that they were going to contact Lavassier. And that meant Stella—even though Pammy thought Stella trustworthy.

Eagle was beginning to think that Stella was trustworthy as well, but Eagle also knew that the fewer people involved in this the better. They were planning to do something not entirely legal—hell, completely illegal—and she didn't want word to get out that they were involved.

Val had little to do to prepare. Part of that was by design: Eagle wanted full control over this operation. Part of it, though, was that there wasn't much Val could do.

She didn't know the area. She didn't have a vehicle. And she had no physical skills although, as she kept saying, she was working on them.

She was, in many ways, the brains of the group. She put pieces together. So Eagle kept her informed about some of the important things. Eagle also had her check, by phone, on the names that Pammy had gotten from the admissions office.

First, Val called the students who were still in town, the ones who were still enrolled. Two of them spoke to her, seemed stunned that people thought they were missing, and laughed about it. All they had done, they told her, was drop out of the political activities they had been involved in.

Apparently, they had said (in different ways) that they were disillusioned by the presidential election the fall before, and they didn't see the point of activism any longer. One of them had cited all the assassinations, and that he had decided to keep his head down and pretend like nothing was going on in his world.

Val reported that she had refrained from wishing him good luck with that.

She couldn't reach the third student and wanted to visit the address, but Eagle discouraged her.

They were moving from information-gathering to action, and once they hit action, there was no turning back.

Besides, if they got caught riffling Lavassier's truck—truly the most dangerous part of the operation, in Eagle's opinion—then she didn't want anyone to tie them back to the information they'd gathered earlier in the week.

Thursday morning, Eagle had just finished with the reorganization of her apartment when she got a phone call from Pammy.

"I got his number," Pammy said, "and I don't want to contact him alone."

"Call Val," Eagle said. "I'll be right there."

"She's here for class. Remember, he'll have to call us back."

"I know," Eagle said.

"If we use the gym's number, I'll have to answer until we hear from him. We can't have someone say the name of the gym," Pammy said.

Eagle thought of letting Val and Pammy come to her apartment. But that meant someone would have to babysit the phone until he called back.

She glanced at the clock on the stove. It was 11:00. If he was between clients, he would probably check his messages during the noon break. She would.

"I think the gym number is fine," Eagle said. "One of the three of us can man it until he calls."

If he called. Her stomach twisted. She wanted him to call. She had no back-up plan if he didn't.

But they could delay their plan if they had to. They could wait until they heard from him.

Eagle grabbed her regular purse, checked for her wallet and keys, then let herself out of the apartment.

She hated that this part of the plan was in his control.

But she was excited that they were going to get underway.

She hadn't lost her resolve. She wanted to catch this man. She had wanted to catch him since she saw him slam that woman's head into his F-350.

"Game on, you son of a bitch," she whispered, and hurried down the stairs.

PAMMY

Pammy hung up the phone and pressed her hands over her mouth. This was her last chance to back out before they contacted Lavassier, before they took the step that crossed a line from which they could never return.

Her office was quiet, and it looked no different than it had two days before when they had come up with a plan that would get Lavassier out of Berkeley. It might even make him stop permanently.

Or it might destroy them all.

Thin sunlight trailed in from the only window, despite the fact that she had pulled the curtains. She had kept the overhead light off, almost as if she were hiding. On the yellow legal pad before her, she had doodled the numbers of the various answering services. Below them, she had written all five phone numbers for Finders, Inc. and had drawn a box around them.

Her heart was pounding, and she felt slightly sick. She could probably back out. Hand the phone numbers over to Val and Eagle, and just back away from all of this.

Then Pammy folded her hands together and tapped her thumbs against her lips. She had a feeling of impending doom. She had had it ever since she had started calling the answering services. She had it now.

And she knew why: she was choosing to cross a line.

In the past, she had crossed lines because someone had pushed her. Stella had brought injured friends here as a refuge. Pammy hadn't brought those injured women here, and she hadn't helped them. She had just given advice and found someone else to help them escape.

She had never before initiated action against someone.

She had never decided to actively stop someone.

She had never crossed that line between concerned citizen, acting in a tough situation of someone else's making, and becoming a vigilante.

Eagle's plan took them precariously close to vigilante. It maybe even crossed the line, depending on what happened after they searched Lavassier's truck.

She kept hearing her father, complaining about neighborhood protection groups deciding to stop crime on their own.

They always make it worse, her father had said. *They think they know what they're doing, and they don't.*

Pammy hated having his voice in her head. He had lived in a different time and in a different place. It wasn't a simpler time, but it was one that seemed simpler.

Or maybe, as Eagle had said, Pammy was looking at her father's wisdom on law and law enforcement from the perspective of a child who had a policeman father, not from the perspective of an adult woman who knew that there were areas where the law did not work.

Pammy pushed her chair back. She had called Eagle the moment she had the phone numbers. That had been Pammy's subconscious, making it impossible to change her mind.

Or rather, Pammy could change her mind. But, now, because Pammy had called her, because Pammy had told her the numbers existed, Eagle would take those numbers and continue with the plan. Val would help her.

Val really wanted to do this, for reasons Pammy could only guess at, reasons Pammy didn't really understand.

Both Val and Eagle needed Pammy. Neither Eagle nor Val were strong enough to fight Lavassier on their own. If he discovered Val inside his truck, looking for something, he would break her in half. She had no idea how to defend herself.

If Eagle pulled a gun on him, he would wrest it from her with a twist of the wrist.

And then he would beat them both nearly to death, like he had done with Kelly MacGivers. Pammy didn't need to hear the hospital report to know what he had done to Kelly MacGivers, what he had done to the others.

Just Eagle's description of how he had treated that last girl had convinced Pammy this man had to be stopped. It didn't take much to go from using the side of a truck to beat a girl into submission to hitting her so hard that he crushed her cranium and "accidentally" killed her.

This Lavassier was used to dealing with criminals. He hadn't moderated his behavior to deal with unathletic and possibly drug-addled college students.

Pammy could train wives and family members of violent men. She could teach people how to defend themselves.

But Pammy couldn't reach the students Lavassier would target in the future. She couldn't train them to fight back. They had no idea they were at risk, and if they were involved in the "Movement" as Strawberry called it, they weren't likely to go to a gym just off Telegraph. Strawberry was the exception, not the rule.

The police already knew about this man. They couldn't stop him. Any more than the police department that Pammy's father had worked for in Philadelphia had been able to stop all the killings ordered by organized crime.

There were holes and failures in the way that law enforcement worked, in any area. Pammy's father had never discussed those with his daughter.

She had no idea if he had taken extra-legal action to shut down some bad people. No one would confess something like that to a child.

But there was evidence that he was concerned about those lawless areas. He had trained her to defend herself, after all.

Sometimes, baby girl, he had said, *there's no one around to protect you. So at those times, you have to know how to protect yourself.*

That advice, which he had repeated after every time her mother had interrupted them, every time her mother had argued that the things he had taught Pammy weren't "ladylike," had been Pammy's guiding principle. She had repeated those words to some of her classes, had murmured them to frightened women afraid to clench a fist.

Her father had been right.

Pammy had been right.

But neither of them had gone far enough.

Men like Lavassier found loopholes in the law. They exploited those loopholes for personal gain.

Lavassier was getting rich off of desperate families and wayward teenagers.

The police wouldn't be able to stop him. Hell, some cops might even agree with what he was doing.

Pammy was a realist: She knew she would get no help from the police. She also knew that there were some cops, like this Brunsan who had investigated Lavassier, who were disturbed by the things Lavassier had done.

The best she could hope for was that they would look the other way.

Pammy put a piece of paper over those phone numbers. Her hand hovered for a moment.

Pammy had to get Val. Pammy also needed Jill to start the class, just in case this took longer than Pammy expected.

If Eagle got here before Pammy brought Val back, Eagle might make the phone call herself.

And Pammy didn't want that.

She grabbed the legal pad and put it in the top drawer. It would take Eagle a moment to find it, if she went searching, and a moment was all Pammy needed.

The knots in her stomach were untying. And weirdly, she felt better about this.

That memory of her father felt like a blessing.

His blessing.

He had trusted her to do what was right.

And now she was.

VAL

The gym was filling up early. Students from the class talked to each other now as if we were old friends. I smiled at Joan, who had found a t-shirt that fit, but I didn't go talk to her.

I didn't feel like talking to anyone.

During class the day before, I realized just how far I needed to go. I was the dead weight in the plan to find Lavassier. I could barely do a sit-up. I had no idea how I could fight a man three times my size.

I shuddered. I knew this was causing some flashbacks. Armand Vitel had not been a lot bigger than me, but he had been wiry and strong. After the night he raped me, I tried not to think about some of my injuries. But I couldn't stop staring at the bruises his fingers left on my arm, bruises that went so deep that they didn't disappear for weeks.

I had no idea how to shake someone like that off. And, like Vitel, Lavassier made a career of dealing with and beating up criminals. He knew how to hurt someone and do it effectively.

My mouth was dry. I looked at the mat, at the jump rope that Joan had so kindly pulled for me, and felt the aches all over my entire body.

Mentally, I knew what I wanted: I wanted to be able to be as fluid as Pammy. I wanted to be able to surprise someone larger than me by flinging him on his back. Using my weight and my strength as a surprise, not being afraid of them.

But I wasn't anywhere near that. I had just started this journey.

I was going to have to be very careful on Friday night. I didn't want to be the one weakness in this entire plan.

I needed to talk to the others about that, when we talked again.

Pammy strode out of the office area. She looked pale, and there were shadows under her eyes. She was reluctant to take on Lavassier, and part of me didn't blame her. We were doing something that she advocated avoiding in the self-defense class I listened in on the day before.

Your job is to suss out any situation you're in, she said to the assembled students, some of whom were from the university, *and if it looks bad, leave. That's the best defense you have. Walking away from any possible bad situation.*

She also knew that wasn't always possible and she led them into those scenarios too.

But she had looked at me as she had said the thing about walking away, and it felt like she was speaking directly to me. I clearly didn't belong with her and Eagle on this, even though the original plan had been my idea.

I should walk away.

But I didn't want to.

They needed a third person, and I could tell just from a few days that Jill wasn't that person. I hadn't met everyone in the gym yet, but none of the women I had met could be that third person.

That person had to be me.

Pammy stopped at the counter. Jill stood behind it, shuffling some papers. Pammy was explaining something to her.

"Did you watch the splashdown?" Joan had come up beside me. She was tugging on the t-shirt, as if she still wasn't used to wearing it.

The Apollo 11 crew had splashed into the ocean about an hour ago. I had watched it at home before I walked here.

"I did," I said. "I was glad they made it."

Joan smiled. "Me too."

"Hey!" Marilyn joined us. Her hair wasn't sprayed into submission today. Maybe she felt calmer about the class as well. "Did you hear about the Bay Bridge thing?"

"I'm new here," I said. "I didn't know there was a Bay Bridge."

My cheeks warmed as I said that. I felt even more insecure than I had a moment ago. Marilyn's comment made me realize just how new everything in Berkeley was to me.

"Oh." Marilyn's lips thinned. "I was hoping someone here knew something about it. This morning's paper says they voted to charge tolls on the Bay Bridge, and that's how I get here."

I looked closely at her for the first time. "You drive here from San Francisco?"

She nodded. "There's nothing like this anywhere else that I know of. How do you get here?"

"I walk," I said.

"Oh." She sounded surprised. "You live near here?"

As if only crazy people lived near the university. Maybe she was right. Maybe only crazy people did. Crazy people and students.

"Val!"

Saved from answering by Pammy. She was hurrying across the gym. Jill was right behind her, a slight frown on her face.

"I need to talk with you," Pammy said.

My heart started hammering. What had gone wrong?

"Excuse me a minute," I said to Joan and Marilyn. Then I walked to Pammy's side.

She had touched Jill's arm. "This shouldn't take long. Just do warm-ups if I'm not out in ten minutes."

"Sure," Jill said, not sounding sure at all.

Pammy put a hand on the small of my back, steering me toward the office. Her touch made my heart beat harder. The fact that her hand was on the small of my back, directing me, made me think of Vitel again.

Bastard. He needed to leave my brain.

"I have the phone numbers," Pammy said, once we were far enough away from Jill that she couldn't hear us. "I called Eagle. She should be here any minute."

"Okay," I said, oddly glad to be included. Pammy didn't have to bring me in for the initial phone call. She and Eagle could have handled it.

Hell, Pammy could have handled it on her own and then told us about it. Lavassier used an answering service, after all. None of us expected him to be on the other end of the phone.

Or maybe something had changed. Maybe Pammy found out that the service was hired for after-business hours.

I didn't dare ask her in the front area.

We headed toward the back. I half expected her to tell me that I could back out of this now, that we all could.

But she didn't. We walked silently down the narrow hallway. Eagle was standing just outside the office door.

She looked taller than she normally did. Her back was straight for the first time since I met her. Her eyes were clear.

"Well," she said, "it's now or never."

And damned if she wasn't right.

EAGLE

Eagle let Pammy unlock the office and walk through the door first. Pammy slid behind her desk. Surprisingly, the surface was clean, something Eagle wasn't sure she had ever seen before.

Val walked to the folding chair, the one Eagle had sat in when they concocted this plan, and Eagle took the chair nearest the door. Val and Pammy were dressed for class—Val in the Gym of One's Own t-shirt that Pammy had given her, and Pammy in her usual light blue summer shirt and comfortable shorts. Both of them wore sneakers.

So did Eagle, but she wore jeans and a sleeveless shirt that had felt good despite the day's unusual wind.

"I was right," Pammy said as she opened her top drawer. "He has several phone numbers through the answering service. You can contact him from anywhere in the Bay Area without paying for long distance."

"Let me call him," Eagle said.

Val shook her head.

"I'll call him," Pammy said.

"I'm the one he'll be seeing face to face," Eagle said. "He should hear my voice first."

"Well, we haven't decided if you're the person to meet with him face to face," Pammy said. "What if he recognizes you?"

"He won't." Eagle was confident of that now, thanks to Brunsan. He had spoken directly to her, and hadn't recognized her at all when she was dressed up.

Pammy frowned. "Well, he's not going to be some voice expert. He's not going to know if any one of the three of us makes the first contact."

"No," Eagle said. "I think we should be consistent—"

"I think we need a story first," Val said. "We talked about a story, but never confirmed it."

Pammy stopped just as she seemed about to interrupt Eagle. Eagle almost smiled.

Val had easily deflected the building argument. She was good.

"We need to figure out where we're going to meet him," Val said. "We never made a decision."

Eagle had thought about that ever since they decided to reserve a motel room in Berkeley. She didn't want them to get one close to the university. That left the motels near the East Shore Freeway. She had even driven past the one she thought was the best.

She didn't leave Pammy or Val a choice. She said, "We'll meet at the Golden Bear on San Pablo. There's a restaurant right near the motel. Our fictitious woman would use that."

One of them—Pammy or Eagle (and of course, Eagle preferred it be herself)—would pose as the mother of a college student at Berkeley. She would pretend to be in town, traveling with her husband on business, and she would be consulting with Lavassier at the advice of a friend.

"But she wouldn't be staying there," Pammy said. "If she had local knowledge and she had enough money to hire Lavassier, she would be staying at the Claremont."

Val frowned. She clearly had to trust them on this part.

"The Claremont is too upscale for what we're going to do," Eagle said. "That's why the Golden Bear. It's classy enough for an out-of-towner to stay at, but not too upscale."

"What's it like?" Val asked. "Can we rent a room and not bother other guests?"

Eagle nodded. "We can ask for privacy. I'm pretty sure, at this time of year, we'll get it."

"But," Pammy started, "a woman from out of town—"

"Would never meet a suspicious man near her hotel," Val said. "She'd take a cab to meet him. We're assuming she has a friend who tells her about Lavassier, so she knows how much his services will cost. She'll also know that he doesn't always bring the kids back in the best of shape, so she'll know he's dangerous. She would meet him elsewhere."

"If she really existed, she'd bring her husband," Pammy said.

Eagle had thought of that too. But a fake husband was unworkable.

"Know anyone who would be willing to play the husband?" Val asked Pammy.

"Not someone I'd trust with this," Eagle said, answering for her. Not even close. They were taking too many risks already.

"I'll pay for the room," Val said, "but we'll use cash. And in this instance, one of you would have to actually rent it. Someone would remember me."

She was right about that. Eagle nodded.

"So," Eagle said to Pammy. "The restaurant at the Golden Bear. It needs to be getting dark enough that we can search his truck. So...eight?"

"Sun doesn't go down until about eight-thirty," Val said.

"Nine seems late," Pammy said, "especially on a Friday."

"She could be on her way to meet someone," Val said. "Maybe her husband and another couple at a bar or something?"

"This seems awfully elaborate," Pammy said.

"If he asks," Val said, "we need to be prepared for any question."

Eagle looked at her. Val's hands were clasped together, and the muscles in her slender arms were taut. She was nervous.

But she was right. Their cover story couldn't be thin. It had to be deep enough that they weren't making up lies on the spot.

"That all sounds like a good start," Eagle said. "We can come up with more in the next twenty-four hours. Let's see if we can meet with him first."

Pammy took a deep breath. Her gaze met Val's and then Eagle's.

"I'm calling," Pammy said.

Eagle suppressed a sigh. She wasn't going to fight it.

They had a name for the fictitious woman. It was Dorothy Knight, from Lawrence, Kansas. Her husband was a graduate of UC Berkeley and wanted their daughter to attend, over Dorothy's objections. Which was why she was hiring Lavassier without her husband's help.

Pammy's eyes were bright, her cheeks flushed. She took a deep breath, then grabbed a pen and tapped it on the page.

"Okay," she said. "Here goes."

She put the black receiver against her ear and used one of the pens to dial a number off the legal pad.

The trill of the rings through the receiver were loud enough for Eagle to hear. Val rubbed her thumbs against each other. Eagle stopped looking at Val's hands and watched Pammy instead.

Pammy bit her lower lip. The phone rang three times, and Pammy opened her mouth, perhaps to call it off, when someone answered.

Eagle could hear the voice, but not the words.

Pammy smiled a fake smile—a phone smile, maybe—something that didn't reach her eyes.

"Hello," she said, her voice trembling just a little. "I'm calling for a Justin...Lav...Lavas...Lavas...sir?..."

Someone spoke on the other end.

"Oh," Pammy said, sounding a little embarrassed and relieved. She was good at this. "Lavass-ee-ay. I guess you can tell that I've never met him. I was given his name by a friend. May I speak to him, please? This is a matter of some delicacy."

Again, the voice on the other end spoke. Pammy didn't look at either of them. She set the pen down and wrapped the cord around the fingers of her left hand.

Val sat stiffly, not moving at all.

Eagle leaned forward, wishing she could hear the other half of the conversation.

"Um...I am only in town through the weekend," Pammy said, "and I don't have much free time to speak to Mr. Lavass-ee-ay. I was hoping to consult with him tomorrow?"

Eagle was holding her breath. She made herself exhale.

"All right, yes," Pammy said. "I don't want him to leave his name if my husband answers. But…gosh, that won't work either. Um…could you get him to call in the next few hours? Otherwise, give me a time, and I'll call him."

Eagle heard the voice this time, something about impossible, and sorry.

"Oh, um…All right. I'll try to stay close to the phone. My number here in Berkeley is…" Pammy rattled off the gym's phone number. She swallowed visibly, then her gaze met Eagle's.

Eagle nodded, encouragingly, she hoped.

Pammy took a deep breath, then said, "Thank you."

And hung up.

Now, Val leaned forward. "Well?"

"She says he sometimes calls in during the afternoon, but she has no other way to reach him," Pammy said.

"Damn," Eagle said. "I was hoping she had a phone number for a direct contact."

"He drives around in his truck, doing God knows what," Val said. "He probably doesn't stay in one place long."

"You'd think he'd give them some way to contact him," Eagle said.

"Like what?" Pammy said, not really expecting an answer. "He clearly doesn't, so we'll have to stay by the phone. I already told Jill not to answer it. I'll tell the others."

"I'll take the first phone shift," Eagle said. "You have a class to teach."

Pammy took a deep breath. "I thought maybe we'd just wait…"

"It might be hours," Eagle said. "Or he might never call. Just go on with your day. We'll man the phones until we hear from him."

Pammy looked at Val. "You're coming to class, right?"

"Yeah," Val said. "I don't like waiting either."

"All right," Pammy said. "When the phone rings, don't identify the gym."

Eagle smiled. She knew that already. But Pammy was clearly nervous.

"I'll make sure I sound like a housewife in over her head," Eagle said.

Val let out half a guffaw.

"What?" Eagle asked, pretending to be offended. "You don't think I can do it."

"I do," Val said. "It's just, the image…"

Pammy smiled too. This time, the smile was genuine. "Well, Mrs. Knight," she said to Eagle. "Good luck."

"Eight o'clock, the Golden Bear Restaurant on San Pablo tomorrow," Eagle said. "And that's all he needs to know."

"If he sounds…I don't know…too dangerous," Pammy said, "back out."

Eagle nodded, glad she was the one answering the phone. She had a different definition of dangerous than Pammy did.

"You can be sure of that," Eagle said, then stood. She had to move so that Val could leave the room.

Eagle stepped into the narrow hallway, surprised to realize she was more than a little nervous—and relieved at the same time.

The plan was under way—and she wasn't going to turn back, any time soon.

PAMMY

Pammy barely remembered teaching class. She spent most of her time glancing at the counter, willing the phone to ring.

Or maybe she didn't want it to ring. *She* wanted to answer it, not Eagle, even though she knew that Eagle should have been the one to do so. If Eagle met with him.

If any of them were to meet with him.

Val stood in her usual spot on the mat, but she too would occasionally glance over her shoulder toward the phone. She was getting a little more fluid on her exercises, but she wasn't even competent yet. Her friend Joan was doing better, occasionally squealing with delight as she managed a full push-up in perfect form.

Val was still fighting all of it, overthinking on some exercises, too weak to do others. Pammy worried about her, especially in the context of the thing they were planning, the thing she didn't quite have a name for.

She finished teaching, thanked everyone, and listened to the murmur of conversation start as the women helped each other, gathered the jump ropes, and moved off the mats.

She walked around everyone, not wanting to talk. She wanted to head to her office and relieve Eagle from phone-guard duty.

Jill caught her as she reached the counter. "They're going to show the splashdown again over the lunch hour," she said. "Did you want to see it?"

Pammy wished she had never had a group of women together to watch the moon landing. Apparently, Jill thought Pammy was truly interested.

She was glad the men hadn't died…yet, anyway. No one knew what kind of space microbes and germs they had brought back with them. Now, they had to go into quarantine, and who knew what would become of them? They might actually die of something they picked up on the moon.

She did her best not to snap at Jill about that. Jill was excited, and a bit confused about Pammy's behavior this morning.

"Thanks," Pammy said. "I'm sure they'll show it on the evening news."

"Pammy, it's important," Jill said, sounding surprised.

"I know," Pammy said, and she didn't add that what she was doing was important too. Just in a different way. One that she wasn't sure she believed in.

Val had come up beside her. Her face was flushed, and sweat beaded on her forehead and temples. "I'll clean up and maybe pick up some lunch…?"

"Probably a good idea," Pammy said.

"May I ask what's going on?" Jill said primly. Her mouth was narrow, as if she had swallowed something sour.

"Um," Pammy said, not sure how to respond. "It's—"

"Personal," Val said. "Pammy is helping me with something personal."

"Oh." Jill held up her hands and backed away. "Sorry. Usually I help with personal."

Val opened her mouth, clearly about to say something, and Pammy wasn't sure what. She didn't want a fight here.

"I know you do," Pammy said in her most soothing tone. "Val actually confided in Eagle, not me, and Eagle brought me in."

"You confided in *Eagle*?" Jill asked, then pressed her lips together, clearly shocked those words had come out of her mouth.

Val's entire face had gone flat. Pammy had seen her do that a few times before, but hadn't understood it until now.

Val was angry, but she didn't show her anger. In fact, if someone had described her appearance, they would have said she was calm.

"Yes," Val said, her tone as flat as her face. "I confided in Eagle. Now, if you'll excuse me."

She headed toward the locker room, joining Joan and a couple of the other women. They smiled at Val and she smiled back, then disappeared inside.

"I'm sorry," Jill said. "I didn't mean to be rude."

You never do, Pammy thought, but didn't say, because it would be rude. Instead, she shrugged.

"People make unexpected friendships here," Pammy said. "It's something I've had to get used to."

Just like she had to get used to the people who decided to help out, and the different personalities that she encountered as she taught. She hadn't really expected to manage people. She had expected to teach them, nothing more.

The phone rang. She hurried toward the counter before she remembered not to pick it up. She couldn't take the call out here.

"You want me to get that?" Jill asked, even though Pammy had told her not to answer the phone.

"No," Pammy said. "I'll get it in back."

The phone trilled again. Val came out of the locker room, her feet bare. She ran toward the office, and Pammy was right behind her.

There were footsteps behind her. Pammy turned. Jill.

"Thanks," Pammy said. "We've got this."

Then she stopped, and realized that Jill might actually listen to the call out here.

She came back, as the phone stopped mid-ring, and grabbed the phone off the counter. She didn't pick up the receiver. She merely put the phone underneath the counter, on the floor.

"I should have done that earlier," Pammy said. "This way, we're not tempted to use the phone out here."

"I don't understand what you're doing," Jill said.

"I know," Pammy said. "You're not supposed to."

Jill went pale. "I didn't mean—"

"It's all right," Pammy said, even though it wasn't. She wanted to be in back. She didn't want to miss this. "As Val said, this is private. You don't want to know about it. Really, you don't."

Jill bit her lower lip. "I'm good at keeping secrets."

"I know," Pammy said, in that placating tone. "But let's respect Val's wishes, shall we?"

She hoped she hadn't made this too intriguing, because if she had, Jill would pick up the phone and listen in. But if she made it a bit unpleasant, Jill would ignore it.

Marilyn Bakewell was standing near the counter. Her hair wasn't as stiff today, but it still hadn't gotten messed up during class. She had been listening to the conversation.

Her blue eyes met Pammy's for a moment, and then Marilyn pasted a frown on her face.

"Jill, I think I pulled something in my leg. Maybe I'm doing something wrong…?"

Jill glanced at Pammy, as if expecting Pammy to help.

Pammy pivoted and headed toward the office, relieved that Marilyn had deflected whatever Jill was going to do next.

Pammy hadn't expected it, and she would have to thank Marilyn later.

She hurried to the office, hoping she wasn't too late.

EAGLE

Eagle was nearly asleep when the phone rang. She snapped to attention, her heart pounding. It took her a moment to figure out where she was.

Pammy's chair. Behind the desk. Office at the gym.

Shit. Eagle hadn't realized she was so tired that she could doze that easily. If she had known, she would have read the already-outdated morning papers, with their speculative coverage on what might go wrong when Apollo 11 tried to land.

The phone rang again, and her heart rate rose. She was actually nervous. She hadn't expected to be nervous.

Before she dozed, she had scrawled notes on a back page of Pammy's yellow legal pad. Eagle turned to those notes now, skimmed them, cleared her throat, and picked up the receiver.

"Yes, hello," she said in her most cultured voice. It wasn't really put-on. It was the voice of her stepmother, whom she used to imitate to her friends years ago.

"I'm callin' for Mrs. Dorothy Knight?" The male voice on the other end was deep, with an accent she'd heard before. One of the doctors she served with had come from New Orleans, and he spoke with the same low tones, with the precision that came from someone who knew that his accent was different than the accent of the people around him.

"This is Mrs. Knight," Eagle said.

"Mrs. Knight," the voice continued, "my name is Justin Lavassier. You left a message with my girl, said it was urgent."

He pronounced Lavassier differently than Pammy had. It wasn't quite in the French manner. La-Voss-e-ah.

She wasn't sure why she found that fascinating, but she did.

"I did, with a message for you, Mr. Lavassier." She tried to pronounce his name the way he had, but knew she had failed.

The office door opened. Val started in. Eagle held up her index finger.

"Let me just move around the corner, here, to somewhere a bit more private. One moment." Then, pretending she was in a hotel room, she said to Val, "You can just leave that alone. Just close the closet door. That's a dear."

Val frowned at her, then smiled, finally understanding that Eagle was pretending she wasn't alone so that any noise Val made would be covered. She slipped past the first chair, banging the desk.

Pammy opened the door as well, glanced at both of them, and then eased the door closed. She sank quietly into the only remaining chair.

"I'm sorry, Mr. Lavassier," Eagle said. "That took a little longer than I thought, but I didn't want to be overheard. My husband doesn't know I'm contacting you."

Pammy glanced at Val, then looked at the legal pad, which only had Eagle's notes on it. Not getting any information from that, she simply leaned back in the chair.

Lavassier didn't say anything. He just waited for Eagle to continue. That had to unnerve his upper-class clients. It certainly made her uncomfortable.

"I got your number from some friends—"

"Who referred you, Mrs. Knight?" he asked. His tone wasn't quite curt, but it was very businesslike.

"Carla MacGivers. We went to school together long ago, and I try to see her whenever we come to California. She says you found their daughter." Eagle let her voice rise just a bit on that last bit, almost as if she were asking a question.

If Lavassier heard the question, he chose not to answer it.

"I…um…my daughter, Angela, she's…um…my husband, he says I shouldn't worry about it. She'll come around. She'll come back to us. But he doesn't know she dropped out last spring, and I've hidden the clippings from him."

"Clippings?" Lavassier asked.

"Of the protests during that horrid park incident? One of the girls putting daisies in the barrel of the guns, in those photos that went to various newspapers? That's my daughter."

Pammy smiled a little, but Val's eyes widened. Eagle's heart was beating hard. She might have taken this a bit too far. She could almost read Val's mind: maybe Lavassier knew who those kids were.

"Have you spoken to her?" Lavassier asked.

"That's the other problem, sir. She has moved. She has no forwarding address and she has sent no phone number. Carla tells me you can find my girl, and convince her to go back to school. She says it's expensive—"

"I don't discuss my business over the phone, Mrs. Knight." Lavassier's voice was softer now, less businesslike. Eagle got the sense that he believed her, that he thought he was dealing with some distraught housewife. "Where are you staying? I'll come talk to you."

"No," Eagle said, a little breathlessly.

Pammy frowned, as if she didn't understand what Eagle was saying no to. Val just folded her hands and watched.

"My husband could be back at any moment," Eagle said. "I have some free time tomorrow evening. There's a restaurant near the Golden Bear Motel…? I believe the restaurant's also called the Golden Bear. Can you meet me there, say, eight?"

"No," Lavassier said. "I have other plans tomorrow evening. Perhaps next week…?"

"We're only here until Monday. My husband has business in San Francisco, and I asked to come along this time, to meet up with Angela, I told him. He's too busy. So, next week isn't possible, and I have some wifely duties over the weekend, you understand, things for the spouses?"

Lavassier made a sound that was halfway between a disgruntled humph and a sigh. "Why don't I come to you while your husband is in meetings?"

"Forgive me, Mr. Lavassier, but if I start receiving strange gentlemen in my hotel room, someone will surely tell my husband, and right now, I would prefer not to tell him anything."

Pammy swallowed visibly. Val nodded her encouragement.

Eagle looked away from them, at the legal pad itself, because she needed to focus.

"Mrs. Knight, I know that your friend Mrs. MacGivers told you that my services are expensive, but she probably didn't tell you *how* expensive. If you want my help, then you'll have to involve your husband."

Eagle let out a trill of a laugh that made Pammy jump. She'd clearly never heard Eagle make that sound—and, quite frankly, Eagle had only made that sound in the past when she was mocking her stepmother.

"Mr. Lavassier, I have family money, which my husband has no access to. My father did not approve of the marriage, and that was his condition, you see. Carla did tell me that you charge a small fortune. I have resources, and I am prepared to pay a small fortune to find my daughter and get her away from those filthy hippie creatures she's living with."

Eagle spit out those last words, and that truly was her stepmother's voice. Only she had heard it discussing that filthy Indian girl her husband made her live with. Her stepmother had only said that to Eagle's father once, and he had told her to never say it again.

So she had never said it to him again. Just to her friends, and to Eagle herself. That tone, she knew very well.

"All right." Lavassier sounded reluctant. Eagle didn't know if that was a negotiating ploy or if he truly was reluctant. "How about this? We meet tonight at eight at the Golden Bear Restaurant on San Pablo. Will that work for you?"

"Tonight," she repeated, her gaze meeting Val's. That would mean moving up a few things that Eagle had planned to do over the next twenty-four hours, but from Eagle's perspective, it was possible.

Pammy had gone pale. She looked terrified.

Val looked terrified too, but she nodded. She could do it. And Eagle had already figured out how to make her plan work with just the two of them.

"I...I...I would have to rearrange some things," Eagle said. "But I believe it is possible. If you require some kind of deposit in cash, I would not be able to do that—"

"You're moving very quickly, Mrs. Knight," Lavassier said. "We do not know if you actually need my services. They're quite specialized."

"I had an extensive discussion with Carla," Eagle said. "I like your results."

"Nonetheless," Lavassier said. "I might not want to take on your daughter's case. We will talk tonight. If we decide to work together, we'll sign an agreement, and I will take a check for one-third to one-half of my fee."

"All right," Eagle said. "I will bring my checkbook."

"And at least one good photograph of your daughter," Lavassier said. "A recent one."

Eagle's breath caught. A photograph? She hadn't planned on that.

"I don't have a recent photo," Eagle said. "But that photograph in the newspaper—"

"Isn't enough. You'll understand if we decide to work together," he said.

"All right." Eagle made herself sound slightly confused and a little frightened. She would have to make the photograph thing work, somehow. "How will I recognize you?"

"I'll find you," he said, and hung up.

She sat for a moment with the receiver against her ear, mostly because she wanted to process what he had said before she answered any questions.

He was confident he could identify her without any description, which meant he felt confident in his powers of observation. Eagle had been counting on the fact that he wouldn't recognize her from their encounter earlier in the week.

Having her sit across the table from him would be a bigger risk than she thought. But she didn't want Pammy to meet with him, and if Val did, they would have to deal with the race issue—and take the risk that he would not work for a black family.

Not to mention having to explain how someone like Carla MacGivers would have a close friend like Valentina Wilson.

Eagle put the phone down slowly.

"Tonight?" Pammy asked. "We can't do this tonight. We're not ready."

Eagle smoothed her hands over the legal paper, thinking how to answer Pammy, trying to figure out how, exactly to handle what would come next.

"What's he like?" Val asked.

That was a better question than Pammy's. Eagle raised her head. Pammy was flushed, her eyes too bright. But Val leaned forward, eager. Intent.

Eagle let out a breath. She had been a lot more nervous than she even realized.

"He likes to be in control," she said slowly.

"You got that from a phone call?" Pammy asked.

Eagle nodded.

"That's why he changed the meeting time?" Val asked.

"I don't know that for certain," Eagle said, "but it seemed that way. It was just a sense, though. Nothing I can put words on."

"He believed you about the MacGivers," Pammy said.

Eagle nodded. "He seemed to relax when I had a name, one that he recognized."

"You'd think he would have done some kind of background on the family," Pammy said.

"He probably had," Val said. "But who checks school companions?"

"You were lucky you didn't mention which school," Pammy said.

"I thought of that as I was saying it." Eagle ran her hands over the pad again. "If I listed a school and I was wrong, he might have known. I have the sense he did know."

"Do you think he'll investigate Dorothy Knight?" Val asked.

"I didn't give him enough to go on," Eagle said. "I didn't tell him what hotel, and I didn't tell him my 'husband's' name. I made it sound like we were in San Francisco, not Berkeley."

"But you did give him the name of the daughter," Pammy said.

"And unless he knows someone in admissions here," Eagle said, "he's not going to be able to find out if she's a student by tonight."

"I worried when you mentioned those photographs in the paper," Val said.

"Yeah," Eagle said. "I noticed. I figure if he brings the papers and points out some identification, I'll say that I was referring to a different photograph."

"You don't think he would do that, do you?" Pammy asked.

"I have no idea what he does with his new clients," Eagle said. "I can tell you this. He wasn't happy about having to deal with the wife. He would have preferred a couple or the husband."

"How are you supposed to know who he is at the restaurant tonight?" Val asked.

"Eagle will recognize him," Pammy said.

"I probably will, yes," Eagle said. "But he seems to think he'll recognize Dorothy Knight."

Val tilted her head to the side, as if she were considering all of the possibilities of that.

"Then you can't be Dorothy Knight," Pammy said. "I'll have to do it."

Eagle shook her head slowly. "We've been through this. I think we'll be all right."

Val put an arm across her stomach, then rested the elbow of her other arm on top of her wrist. It was a protective gesture, one that covered most of her torso. She probably hadn't even realized she was making it.

"He thought he'd recognize Dorothy Knight," she said, with great emphasis on the name. "There's a type he's used to dealing with, and that type doesn't fit into the Golden Bear Restaurant."

"Maybe," Eagle said. "I thought he'd key into the nerves instead. This isn't something most upper-middle-class people do."

"Maybe," Val said.

"I'll be nervous enough to take this," Pammy said.

Eagle shook her head. "The key is to *seem* nervous, not be nervous."

Val was still studying her. "Do you have any expensive clothing?"

Eagle let out a small laugh. Expensive clothing? She had the clothes she wore before she enlisted—or some of them—and her uniforms, plus the jeans and shirts she had picked up at the junky shops off Telegraph.

"I have a sleeveless white dress I was going to wear," she said. It would probably get ruined, but she was willing to pay that price.

"I've seen that dress," Pammy said. "It's dated."

"You'll need something new and stylish," Val said. "Forgive me for being blunt, but can you afford something upscale?"

"I can't even afford something downscale," Eagle said.

"Then I'll go with you," Val said. "We'll get you something at one of the shops—"

"Roos-Atkins," Pammy said.

Eagle made a face. "I hate that pretentious place."

"Precisely," Pammy said. "Get something conservative that someone would wear in the Midwest."

"And makeup," Val said.

"And some faux pearls or something," Pammy said.

"Costume but no gemstones," Val said. "If you wear fake pearls or something, he'll wonder why you're wearing fakes and pretending to have money."

"Good point," Pammy said.

"And good shoes," Val said.

Eagle half-smiled. "Does this clothing discussion mean you've both accepted the fact that I'm meeting him?"

"I don't like it," Pammy said, "but I don't see how we have any other choice."

"All right then," Eagle said, standing up slowly. "We have a lot of errands to do before we get underway. Meet back here at six?"

"I'm coming shopping with you," Val said.

"No," Pammy said. "That would be memorable. Let me."

She reached over the desk and removed the cash box. From inside it, she removed five twenty-dollar bills and handed them to Eagle.

"A hundred dollars?" Eagle said with a gasp. "For one outfit?"

"And shoes and makeup," Pammy said. "Believe me, at Roos-Atkins, that might not be enough. Don't skimp. If you need more money, come back here and get it."

"I'm just going to end up ruining it tonight," Eagle said. "That's a waste of money."

Val stood too. "We're risking a lot tonight," she said. "I think we can risk ruining one expensive dress."

Eagle felt dizzy. She had never owned anything expensive, and now she was talking about ruining it. Still, she made herself take a deep breath. She needed to think clearly. There had been one other point she wanted to make before they left.

Pammy stood up as well. The cash box sat on the desk between them.

"He'll probably call back," Eagle said. "Maybe as a double check. Don't answer."

"All afternoon?" Pammy asked. "But—"

"He's wily," Eagle said. "If you use the business name, then we'll never see him again. If you answer and you're not me, he'll wonder what's going on. Just don't answer. It won't hurt for one afternoon."

Pammy took a deep breath. "What about Jill?"

"She's trouble," Eagle said. "Send her home."

Pammy looked uncertain. Eagle felt a surge of impatience.

"Do you want this to succeed or not?" Eagle asked.

"Yes," Pammy said. "Since we've decided to do this, we need to do it right."

Eagle didn't like how Pammy phrased that, but it was better than a flat-out no.

"Then send Jill home," Eagle said.

Pammy nodded. "I'll need to close tonight, then."

"Yes, you will," Eagle said. "Apologize, call the class if you have one. But you can't answer the phone here between now and nine o'clock tonight."

Pammy closed her eyes, and nodded again. "All right."

"Good thinking," Val said to Eagle. "I wouldn't have considered that."

"We need to consider a lot of things," Eagle said. "He's smarter than I want him to be."

"Why is that an issue?" Val asked. "I always thought he was smart."

"I thought we'd have surprise on our side," Eagle said. "We might not."

"He won't see us coming," Val said.

"No, he probably won't," Eagle said. "But he'll recover pretty damn fast. We have to be ready for that."

"God," Pammy said softly.

Eagle glared at her. "There's still time to back out."

Pammy swallowed. "You need me. You both do. I'm not backing out."

"Then be prepared," Eagle said. "Because it'll take all three of us. And we might not win."

"I don't think anyone wins here," Val said softly.

"Getting this son of a bitch off the street is a win," Eagle snapped. "And if you two don't agree, I'll do it myself."

She was surprised at her own vehemence. She hadn't realized how much she hated this man until right now. Amazing how that hatred could flare with one meeting, one slam of someone else's head against the side of a truck.

"We're in this together," Val said.

"And we'll get this man off the street," Pammy said. Her voice was stronger than it had been earlier. "No matter what it takes."

VAL

I leaned against the wall near the locker room, arms crossed. Jill was running an advanced exercise class—she called it *Exercise 3*—and everyone in it looked just like everyone in my class.

Except they could do the exercises.

They were jumping rope like old pros, doing sit-ups without groaning, and touching their noses to the mat when they did their push-ups without bending their knees or their back.

Someday, I might end up like them, but not right now.

God, I was so out of my league, and I knew it.

I had showered and changed into the clothes I had brought for the afternoon, but they wouldn't do for the evening. Before I went to the Golden Bear Motel, I would need to change into all black and get the gloves I had bought. I had planned to dye one of my baseball caps black, but I wouldn't be able to now, and since I had moved here in the summer, I had left all my stocking caps in Chicago.

Hell, I had left almost everything in Chicago.

I let out a small breath and tried to shake off the nerves.

Eagle had left first. She had been galvanized by the talk with Lavassier. Yeah, he made her nervous, but in a good way. It felt like she

459

had a weight slowly lifting off her shoulders.

It wasn't that easy for me or for Pammy. I would have admitted that to Pammy if she hadn't given me a look that warned me off. I got the sense she didn't want to think about what we were about to do.

Then I learned, that she had realized she too had errands to finish before we initiated our plan, errands she had planned to finish tomorrow or later tonight. But the timeline got switched and we were doing our best to be prepared for whatever hit us.

"Take the phones," Pammy said to me. "Try not to answer, but if you have to, then pretend to be Mrs. Knight's sister-in-law or something. And don't do it in front of Jill."

Pammy couldn't tell Jill what we were doing and she couldn't send Jill home. There were back-to-back classes all afternoon, and Jill was one of the few people who could teach them.

I had suggested to Pammy that I could supervise, if she gave me a list of what everyone should do, and she laughed. It was the first time I had heard her laugh in the last few days.

"It doesn't quite work like that," she had said to me. Then she had told Jill she would be back, and I would handle the phones, and she hurried out of the building.

Jill hadn't had time to ask me what Pammy was doing, but Jill kept looking at me over the heads of the exercising women. They were sweating, their shirts blotchy and wet, and they seemed to be enjoying themselves.

But Jill wasn't.

I knew I looked out of place, leaning up against the wall, but I didn't want to be in the office. If Lavassier called back, I didn't want to answer the phone too fast, but I didn't want Jill to get it either. If she was standing right next to the phone near the counter, then she would pick it up— hell, *I* would pick it up—and that might ruin everything.

A group of white college-age girls entered, carrying books. Two of the girls were wearing flowing tie-dye skirts, three were wearing shorts, and all of them wore t-shirts. One of the girls glared at me as she led the way into the locker room.

I recognized that intimidating stare. I'd grown up with it. But I was a different woman now. Now, I stared back.

They all passed me in a wave of incense. I walked over to the counter to look at the schedule.

The next class was an innocuously titled class called "strength-building." I had no idea what that was, but those girls clearly did.

A few other women were straggling in. Jill clapped her hands together, ending her class, and thanking everyone.

The gym was filled with women, entering, leaving, heading to the locker room, and studiously ignoring me.

All except for Jill. I had hoped she would stay in class rhythm, but of course she wasn't going to. She headed straight toward me.

I let out a small breath. She intimidated me. What did that say about this evening, if a tall, athletic white woman intimidated me? How would I do with a strong, muscular and violent white man?

Jill stopped in front of me. I could go into the locker room to avoid her or slip past down the hallway to the office, but if I tried to get around her, she would probably grab my arms.

Jill said, "I know you said whatever is going on is private, but today is just weird. I'm helping out. Can you tell *me* what's going on?"

We're going to take the law into our own hands and try to get a man put away for life. If we're lucky, we'll help the cops. If we're not lucky, we'll fail. And the ground in between, well, Eagle wants to make sure he never hurts someone again, and Pammy wants to make sure Eagle doesn't go to jail, and I'm not exactly sure how I fit in.

"Um," I said to cover what I was thinking, "it really is private."

"How about the Reader's Digest Condensed Version?" Jill asked.

I closed my eyes and sighed, trying to think without the pressure. She was right. She was helping. She was annoying and she was difficult and she was doing all of this for Pammy for free. And Jill was used to being in the know, and she might just act out if she wasn't.

I opened my eyes, and I was surprised to find tears in them. One of the women here for the next class came out of the locker room, and the door banged closed behind her.

I jumped.

Jill frowned, and some of the charge left her body. "I'm sorry," she said. "I didn't realize—"

"No, it's okay," I said as quietly as I could. No one was close. The conversations going on near the mats actually gave ours some cover.

Jill's stance had softened. She didn't seem as angry.

"I…um…was raped in Chicago." My voice was nearly a whisper. The part of me that always observed the world, the one in the back of my brain that commented on everything, noted how ironic it was that one of the first people I told about this would be a woman I didn't like much, a woman I wasn't sure saw me as her equal.

Jill's mouth opened in a small "oh."

"I nearly died," I said. "When I got better, I came here. And now, there's this man—"

Jill held up a hand, stopping me. "Eagle and Pammy are helping you with this man, right?"

I nodded. Thank God she was intelligent. I had hoped the implication would be enough, but I had expected to take it farther, whatever that meant.

Jill already leapt to the correct conclusion.

"They're good women," Jill said. "They do for others in ways I never could. Even Eagle."

Then she gave me a half-smile. "You can tell from my tone I wasn't sure about Eagle at the start. She's pretty angry."

"Yeah," I said, and decided to go for broke. "You weren't sure about me either."

Jill blushed. The blush was almost instantaneous, and it ran from her neck up to her forehead, coloring her skin a deep red.

"I'm beginning to realize I have issues I didn't think I had," she said. "If you had asked me—"

I mentally finished for her, *I would have said I have Negro friends, of course I do. They're good people.*

"I would have said that I like everyone," she finished, not quite going the way I thought. "But there's some training in my past that I didn't even realize was there. Some things my parents used to say about Indians and the Irish and, you know—"

"Blacks," I said.

"Yeah," she said. "I'm sorry."

462

I'd never had anyone say that to me before. They always lied or covered up how they felt or pretended it didn't exist. But Jill was blunt. It was one of the things I had noticed about her, and found a bit intimidating.

I guess it cut in all directions.

"Me, too," I said, because I didn't want to give her a pass.

She lightly touched my arm. "Pammy's a good woman. She'll do the right thing, whatever that is. And Eagle too."

"Thank you," I said.

"And I know Pammy left you here to guard me, to make sure I didn't answer the phone. I'm going to promise you here and now that I won't. I'll teach classes until Pammy gets back and I won't ask any more questions. And I won't tell anyone what you told me. You're right. That's yours to tell, which is why I asked you personally, and I won't let anyone else know either."

"Thank you," I said, not expecting her kindness.

"We all have crosses to bear, and sometimes they're not obvious right away. I understand that." Then she glanced at her watch, and sighed. "Those college girls are always running late. Excuse me."

She pushed open the locker room door. A waft of steam mixed with perfume and sweat emerged.

She raised her voice. "Five minutes. I start at the top of the hour, no matter who's on the mats or not."

Then she smiled at me—a real smile—and headed back toward the mats.

I leaned my head against the wall, and sighed. I was relieved that she hadn't pressed me about what was going on. But I also felt a little calmer.

The locker room door banged open and the college girls came out, hair pulled back into ponytails or held in place with a headband around the forehead, shorts instead of skirts, and in two cases, bikini tops. They were laughing and talking and ready to go to work.

And none of them—not even the first girl—gave me a second glance.

But Jill did. She nodded at me, then talked softly to the women lining up for the next class.

And, I realized, the phone hadn't rung at all since Lavassier called back. I hoped it wouldn't ring until Jill was gone.

If only we could be that lucky.

PAMMY

Pammy parked her grimy white Pontiac just off 10th near Cedar. The neighborhood was surprisingly residential, this close to the East Shore Highway, but the houses were small—bungalows, mostly. A lot of them were clustered near Franklin Primary School, a few blocks away.

She hadn't been to West Berkeley in a while, which was surprising, considering it was only two miles or so from her gym.

Sometimes two miles stretched across an entire world.

She got out of the car. The wind caught her hair and whipped it into her face. It was a surprisingly blustery day for July, and she hoped the wind would die down after dusk. Wind sometimes interfered with sound, and she wanted both herself and Val to listen carefully tonight.

Pammy turned into the wind, adjusted her short-sleeved shirt, and slung her purse over her shoulder. Before she had left the gym, she had changed into one of the outfits she had brought that morning in case she needed something more appropriate to the real world. She was now wearing a white blouse over black pants and sandals.

Her black purse matched. She went from a somewhat odd female gym owner to middle-aged housewife with just a change of costume.

464

She ducked her head and walked up the street to San Pablo Boulevard. The motel's white sides gleamed across the sidewalk.

She had never been to the Golden Bear Motel, although she had put friends up there when the Flamingo Inn didn't have room. Most of her friends from out of town couldn't afford the Claremont, which was where she would have preferred to put them and where, in her mind, the fictional Dorothy Knight was staying with her nameless husband.

The Golden Bear had an adobe exterior with brown shutters on every window, shutters decorated with tiny bears. The bear motif went across everything affiliated with the motel, including the restaurant.

She passed the restaurant first, on the way to the motel's office. The restaurant was in its own little building near the front of the Golden Bear complex's parking lot.

The motel itself was U-shaped. The part of the motel just behind the restaurant was two stories tall. The rest of the motel was on a single level.

As she passed the restaurant, she peered at it, looking for its hours sign. It wasn't in the two large windows across the front. So she looked in the tiny vestibule that housed the official entrance, the cigarette machine, and the pay phone.

There, the hours were printed in black on a white sign. Weekdays until 10:00 p.m. She had had a feeling that it wouldn't be open too late. She would have to tell Eagle about that. Although Eagle probably wasn't going to talk with Lavassier for two hours—or even one hour—they also didn't want to be the last ones in the restaurant. That would make them memorable.

The motel's office was across the parking lot from her, in a rounded area at the end of the single-story building. The parking lot was mostly empty. A Firebird in bad need of a new paint job was parked behind the restaurant, and a brand new LeMans was parked at the very center of the two-story building.

A woman, wearing a blue maid's uniform, sat on a bench outside the office, a purse over her shoulder and a cigarette in her mouth. She was clearly waiting for someone to pick her up.

Pammy nodded at her as she ducked into the office. It smelled of stale cigarettes and pine freshener.

The interior was perfectly square, which was odd, considering the rounded exterior wall. A brown couch sat beneath a map of California, with affiliated motels marked by pushpins. Ashtrays sat on both end tables. A bookshelf filled with some area guidebooks and pamphlets graced one wall. On top of it were several statues of bears, but only one of them was golden. A large stuffed bear wearing a UC Berkeley t-shirt rested on one corner of the counter. A hand-lettered sign leaned against its leg, telling people to hit the bell for service.

She had to look for the bell. It had fallen between the bear's arm and its shirt. She hit the tiny metal button on the top, and it made a surprisingly loud "ping."

Then Pammy held her breath. This was one of the moments she was worried about. She knew a lot of people from her activities in town, and it wouldn't surprise her to find out that she had made the acquaintance of someone who worked at the Golden Bear.

A woman came out of the back. Her bright red hair was piled in an elaborate beehive. Her face was naturally pale and covered with freckles. She was older than Pammy and looked worn out.

"Help you?" the woman asked as if helping someone was the last thing she ever wanted to do in her entire life.

"I need a room for a friend of my husband's." Pammy matched the woman's tone. Pammy wanted the woman to think that this favor was a reluctant one. "He's driving in late, and he wants to make sure he has a place to sleep tonight."

"We don't normally book up on Thursdays in July," the woman said. "He'll be okay."

"Still," Pammy said, "if I don't have a key, my husband will be upset."

"All right." The woman hauled out a leather bound book and flipped it open. "How long's he staying?"

"I have no idea," Pammy said flatly. "We'll cover one night, and he can figure out what he's doing after that."

The woman smiled a little, as if Pammy's exasperation reflected something in her own mood.

"He has this truck that he just loves," Pammy said. "So if there's somewhere you can put him where he can see the truck from the window, and where no one else'll be around him, that's probably for the best."

"He loud?" the woman asked.

"I have no idea," Pammy said. "But he's not staying at *my* house."

The woman chuckled. "He's really your husband's friend, isn't he?"

Pammy made a face and nodded. "I'm spending as little time with him as possible."

"What's this charmer's name?" the woman asked.

"Justin Lavassier," Pammy said. "Let me spell the last name."

She did, and the woman wrote it down carefully in her little book. Then she reached behind her and opened a cabinet built into the wall that Pammy hadn't even seen. Keys hung from hooks. The woman grabbed one.

"We'll put him in 116." She tapped the hand-drawn map of the complex pasted on the counter. "People don't usually like that part of the hotel. It's a bit of a walk to the restaurant and the office. On slow nights, we tend to put most people in the two-story building."

Pammy looked at the map. 116 was at the bottom of the U, not near anything except other rooms. On the back side were houses, probably, or maybe someone's yard. Not even close to the nearby streets. The closest units wouldn't have anyone in them, and the ones that might actually get residents were on the San Pablo Avenue side of the motel, which meant there would be traffic noise.

"Looks good," she said, and meant it. She pulled her wallet out of her purse. "How much?"

"Fifteen dollars should do it," she said, "since you're paying ahead, and you're local."

Pammy smiled and handed her a twenty. The woman opened a drawer and gave her back a grimy five.

"Do you have two keys?" Pammy asked. "Because I'd like one. My husband will give it to him, and that way you don't have to worry about a late arrival."

"Good," the woman said, "because the night guy hates having people show up after the eleven o'clock news."

"You have one to give him, though, if he shows up early, right?" Pammy asked.

"Oh, yes, we're covered both ways. That way you won't have to worry," the woman said, and smiled.

Pammy smiled back. Mostly she was pleased that there would be a "night guy" who didn't like to be disturbed. That would help.

The woman handed her a key attached to a brown plastic oval marked 116. Pammy shoved it in her purse, grateful that her hands weren't shaking.

She didn't ask for a receipt or anything else, because she didn't want the woman to ask her name.

But apparently, the woman was used to renting rooms to locals. Or maybe to women who didn't want their names to get out. For all this woman knew, Pammy was reserving a room for her own purposes later.

She thanked the woman, and let herself out of the door. The parking lot was deserted. The maid was gone, a crushed cigarette butt on the sidewalk the only indication she had been there.

The wind still blew strong, amplified by the corridor created by the parking lot and the entry from the restaurant. Pammy didn't even look at room 116. She'd probably get to know it better later.

Instead, she walked toward the restaurant in case the woman was watching. Pammy didn't want the woman to see that she had parked far away from the motel.

Her stomach was tied up in knots, but she vowed to ignore that. Instead, she walked down the sidewalk, hoping that the next twenty-four hours would go by quickly, and she could return to her regular life as if nothing had changed at all.

EAGLE

At 7:15, Eagle left her apartment and walked to the Hotel Durant. It was only a few blocks from where she lived. It was also the only place where she knew she could get a cab at any time of day or night.

She had already given the keys to her truck to Pammy, with the instruction that she and Val park away from the Golden Bear Motel. She didn't want anyone seeing them arrive. But the truck had to be close enough that they could make a quick escape if they needed to.

Eagle had a second set of keys tucked in her white purse, just in case something happened to the truck's regular keys. Given the neighborhood's proximity to the East Shore Highway and the nearby nightclubs, she had also instructed Pammy to make sure the truck was locked when they left it.

Eagle had given locking the truck some thought because she wanted it to be easy to get into, but she also knew there were too many important things in the truck's cab to leave unattended.

She wished she could drive her truck. But people would notice her, especially considering her outfit. Women dressed like she was right now did not drive trucks.

She spent most of the money Pammy had given her on a dress she hated. It wasn't like anything Eagle would ever wear—before or after. In theory, it wouldn't bother her to destroy it. In practice, it was the nicest thing she'd owned, maybe ever.

Made of gold, pink, and ivory seersucker, the dress's skirt belled outward from a tight bodice. The entire dress had thin vertical stripes, which were (sadly) flattering. The pink looked like a normal stripe from a distance, but in actuality was made up of little tiny hearts and flowers, which Eagle found damn near unforgivable.

She wore gold slippers with it, "like Cinderella," the in-store shoe salesman had said as he handled her feet, making her feel less like Cinderella and more like one of the wicked stepsisters. Eagle had forgotten to buy a matching purse, but she did pick up a matching gold headband that held her dark hair away from her face.

Then she'd spent the last hour plucking and applying makeup, thankful that she didn't usually live this way. She put a summer sweater over the whole ensemble and tucked her hands into proper white gloves. She had two cotton pairs in her purse, and some rubber gloves in the truck.

The Hotel Durant was as upscale as Berkeley got, at least near campus. The hotel was over forty years old and was starting to show its age. The weird fresco around the front door should have been ivory but had a greenish tint from the pollution and the salt air.

Eagle had come to this hotel before, mostly for the full-service bar, but the men she encountered there always thought she was there because she was lonely. Since she was there to drink, she found the attention annoying. Eventually, she stopped coming to the Hotel Durant at all and took to drinking at home, which, she knew, had not been the best solution.

She slipped inside the door to find the valet desk. It was the first test of her uncomfortable outfit.

The man behind the desk, wearing a blue suit and bellman's cap, pasted a smile on his face and told her it would be no trouble at all to hail her a cab.

He went outside, blew on a whistle, and within seconds, a cab she hadn't even seen pulled up alongside the curb. She walked out of the hotel and down the sidewalk as the valet opened the cab door.

"Where are you heading, ma'am?"

She smiled and pretended she hadn't heard the valet. She gave him a tip as she slid into the back seat. He shut the door and tapped on it.

The cab driver, a middle-age man with too much Brylcreem in his hair, said, "Where to, Missus?"

"The Golden Bear Restaurant on San Pablo," she said. "Do you know where that is?"

"I do, ma'am, although I must say, there are nicer restaurants in Berkeley."

"I know," she said, pretending once again to be her stepmother. "But I am meeting a dear friend, and this is where she said we would have the most privacy."

"I understand, ma'am," he said in a tone that made it sound like he didn't believe she was meeting a female friend at all.

He pulled away from the curb, heading east toward College Avenue. He was going to take Haste. She would have preferred going up Cedar, but she didn't want to sound like a local.

Instead, she clasped her hands together, resting her wrists on her damn purse, wondering what it was about this week that made her haul out that silly purse twice when she hadn't used it at all in the past year.

The cab driver didn't engage her in conversation, and she was grateful. She had a hunch she would be lying a lot later in the evening, and she didn't want to have to keep track of what she had told everyone.

That purse was barely big enough for everything it needed to hold. She had put her various pairs of gloves in the purse, some medication, two capped syringes, and her wallet.

She had also managed to put two Polaroids in there. She had taken them from that box she had discovered in the garbage behind her apartment the week before. On top of it all, she had placed her wristwatch.

She had initially worn the watch, but it was too downscale for her outfit. The watch gave her away as someone without money.

But it was the watch she needed now. She fumbled with the gold clasp on the purse, hating the gloves, but knowing they were part of her disguise. She pulled out the watch and glanced at its tiny face.

It had already taken fifteen minutes to go from the Hotel Durant, and they still had half the distance to go. It was now quarter to eight. She had wanted to arrive early, like any tense parent would, and it looked like she would arrive closer to on time.

She shoved the watch to the bottom of the purse, then glanced at one of the Polaroids. Eagle did not recognize the girl in the photo. If she had lived in Eagle's building, Eagle had never seen her.

In some ways, the girl looked like every other white middle-class teenage girl. She had brown hair, blotchy skin, and a round face. There were unique characteristics, though—a dimple in her chin, a long neck that spoke of future glamour.

Eagle hoped that Lavassier would ignore those things. Or better yet, that he would not have time to track down this particular girl.

Eagle had consoled herself when she put the photographs into her purse that he would have the wrong name in the first place, and if this went right this evening, he wouldn't be hunting teenagers again any time soon.

But she knew she was taking a risk, and with these photographs, she was taking a risk with someone she didn't know.

With luck, she wouldn't have to use the photographs at all.

She sighed and looked out the window.

The cab pulled into the parking lot beside the Golden Bear Restaurant. Eagle fumbled with her purse again to pay the cab driver, just the way that she figured a nervous middle-class woman from out of town would.

She paid and tipped him, privately noting that she had paid him with the last of the money Pammy had given her.

"You'll need a cab home, won't you, Missus?" he asked, putting a little too much emphasis on *Missus*, as if he were afraid that Eagle was forgetting herself.

"I will," Eagle lied. She wasn't planning to take any cab home.

The cab driver pulled a receipt off his clipboard. It had the cab company's name, address, and phone number. On top, he had scrawled his name and a number.

"You just ask for me, ma'am. I'll make sure you get home no problem," he said.

"Thank you." She made herself sound very grateful. Then she started to put the receipt in her purse, and stopped. She didn't want any evidence that she had been the woman who had taken this cab. She clutched the receipt in one hand and the purse in the other.

She slipped out of the cab. The parking lot was poorly lit. There were lights near the office door directly in front of her. Half of the lights above the motel's doors were on, but the others looked burned out. The reddish-clay tiled roof hung over the sidewalk to the rooms, absorbing half the light.

The only other lights in the parking lot came from San Pablo Avenue on one side, and from Cedar Street on the other. There wasn't even a good light behind the restaurant.

All of this relieved her immensely.

She did not look at room 116 to see if its overhead light was on.

The cab drove around the back of the restaurant so that it could take the other exit onto San Pablo.

She wanted to walk the same path the cab had taken, around the back of the restaurant to see if there were any doors or windows back there, or any kind of fenced-in trash containers, but she didn't. Because that would be strange, given the role she was playing.

Besides, she was barely on time as it was.

She walked up the slight incline to the sidewalk, then clutched her purse tightly against her side as she walked to the restaurant's main door. The door was on the side of the building, away from the sidewalk—an odd choice, she thought.

She did not look inside the restaurant as she passed its two big windows. She couldn't hear anything through them, not music or laughter or even the clink of silverware, the way that you sometimes could through single sheets of glass.

She reached the entry side of the restaurant, finally seeing why the cab hadn't deposited her there. Half a dozen cars were parked in the parking spaces nearby, at least two of them sticking out so far that it had been nearly impossible to turn in from San Pablo. The cab driver apparently thought he could negotiate his way out easier than he had been able to find his way in.

She was relieved that she hadn't seen her truck or Pammy or Val. They weren't supposed to be anywhere near the restaurant, and so far, they were sticking to the plan.

She pulled open the glass door and entered the anteroom, with its gigantic cigarette machine and the smaller pay phone hanging beside it. She tossed the receipt in the sand-covered ashcan.

Then she pushed open the plain brown door into the restaurant itself, immediately overwhelmed by the smells of roast beef, coffee, and baking bread. Her stomach growled. In all the running around she had done, she had forgotten to eat.

The sounds she had missed outside were here now. A low hum of conversation. The rattle of ice and soda machines. The sizzle of food on a grill. The clink of silverware on china plates.

There was a cash register directly in front of her, along with a tall table that vaguely resembled a podium. A large pile of thick menus rested on top. Waitresses, wearing brown with white aprons, scurried past.

Eagle had never eaten here before, and the interior was larger than she expected. It went deep into the back of the building, with various combinations of large and small tables, and booths running along the walls. Only in the very back was there a counter, with some stools and enough space for a handful of patrons.

But it was pretty clear that sitting back there was discouraged—at least at this time of day.

She didn't see any single men sitting alone, and certainly no one who looked like Lavassier. Despite her confident talk, she wasn't certain she would recognize him in the golden lights of a fairly nice restaurant.

A balding man wearing a wrinkled white shirt, a gravy-stained tie, and an ill-fitting suit coat over it, grabbed one of the menus. He was clearly the restaurant's manager.

"One tonight?" he asked and smiled tiredly at her.

"N-No," she said, making herself sound nervous. "I'm here to meet…" She couldn't call Lavassier a friend. She couldn't say this was business either. "…someone."

The man nodded and grabbed another menu. He started to lead her toward one of the windows, but she said, "Um, could we sit in the back?"

The man gave her a knowing glance, then nodded again, pivoted, and headed toward a booth across the restaurant. He set both menus down on the brown Formica tabletop.

"This okay?"

It was midway between the counter for singles in the very back, and the front with all the windows. There were a few windows that ran along the Cedar Avenue side, but they were smaller and farther away. It would be hard to see her from in here and, with the growing darkness, it was impossible to see out of them from this spot.

"Yes," she said.

"Coffee?" he asked, making it clear with that one word that they didn't serve alcohol here.

"Yes, please," she said. "Cream and sugar."

"Sugar's on the table," he said, and vanished deeper into the restaurant.

She slid into the booth, placing her purse on the leather seat close to the wall. She opened the menu, trying to think like her stepmother.

Never take a table at a restaurant without ordering something. But Eagle knew better than to order an actual meal. Even though she was hungry, she didn't want to be weighed down by what she had eaten.

She looked at the desserts on the back, seeing an array of pies, and figured she would have one of those. Then she set the menu aside and shifted in her seat so that she could see the door.

The manager came back carrying a coffeepot and a bowl filled with creamers. The packaged creamers disappointed her, not because she preferred real milk with her coffee, but because she was hoping for a little pitcher of milk like some restaurants served.

The manager poured coffee into the thick cup in front of her, then swung the pot toward the other waiting cup.

"Your friend going to want some?"

"I don't know," Eagle said. "Maybe some water, though."

"Your waitress will bring that," the manager said, and hurried away, the coffeepot held in front of him like a shield.

Eagle didn't see anyone who looked like Lavassier. Not yet. She opened her purse and shifted everything around, shoving her watch, wallet, and some of the gloves as close to the bottom as possible, and putting the photographs on top of the loosely closed small pill bottles she had brought with her. They contained various kinds of drugs, from muscle relaxants to potent sedatives.

She'd choose the best one after she met Lavassier.

She would need observation skills and dexterity. The dexterity she wasn't worried about. She'd administered a lot of different kinds of drugs to all kinds of patients, from those who had welcomed the drug to those who would fight anything she wanted to put in their bodies. She knew how to administer drugs quickly and she knew how to be sneaky about it.

Eagle had told Val and Pammy that they would only need the motel room in case of emergency.

Eagle had lied.

She was going to take this bastard off the street, one way or another. With or without help.

She wasn't going to let him hurt anyone ever again.

VAL

The moment we pulled up to the San Pablo neighborhood in the growing twilight, I realized I had made a mistake. Somehow I had expected the area to be suburban—or at least, a little more upscale than it was.

Instead, I found myself in a dying industrial neighborhood, with shops and music venues and more restaurants than I had expected. The clubs had weird names like the Freight and Salvage, the Lucky 13, and Tito's.

The neighborhood was in transition, and I wasn't as out of place as I had expected to be. In fact, in some ways, Eagle and her lovely new dress were much more unusual than I was. Women dressed like she was were slumming.

Pammy sat on the bench seat next to me, her feet outstretched over two black medical bags and some other things Eagle had crammed under the seat of her truck. Pammy had never driven a truck before, so it was up to me. Fortunately, I'd driven almost everything, even though reaching the pedals of this thing was a bit of a trick.

Parking it would be even more fun.

We drove past the Golden Bear, just so I could see it. The parking lot beside the restaurant was full. A clapboard sign in the middle of the motel's lot said *Parking for Motel Guests Only*. I doubted Lavassier would park there anyway. I knew he didn't want to call attention to himself.

We didn't either.

Pammy instructed me to turn off and start looking for a good place on the numbered streets behind the Golden Bear Motel. The houses back here were small bungalows, maybe one or two bedrooms, tiny windows (thank heavens), and postage-stamp yards. All seemed to have been built forty or fifty years before.

"I thought we were going to be in an upscale neighborhood," I said as I rounded a corner onto a narrow side street.

"Not this close to the Bay," Pammy said. "Although I remember it being nicer ten years ago."

Great. We were relying on her older memory for something that should have been more clearly thought-out.

But I didn't say that. We were already underway. I had left Eagle, with her truck keys in my hand, not an hour ago. She didn't look like the same woman. She looked older and almost conventionally pretty, with her dark hair pulled away from her face, and makeup that made her golden skin look like she was just tan.

She didn't seem nervous at all, even though I was jumping out of my skin. She just handed me the truck keys, made sure (once again) that I knew how to use a shift on the column, and told me she'd find us.

I didn't doubt her.

I did doubt me.

My heart was pounding hard as I drove, my hands damp on the rigid steering wheel. Both Pammy and I wore black. I made Pammy tuck her hair under a stocking cap, but that still didn't help how reflective her skin was.

I told her she needed to stay away from streetlights, but I'm not sure if she understood why.

We both had several pair of gloves, some stashed in the truck. Eagle had insisted. No prints anywhere. That would trip us up.

Pammy had brought the gloves, mostly black leather, curved from someone else's hands, although she had found some of those newer plastic cleaning gloves made for housewives. Eagle insisted on some of those.

Pammy had a grocery bag with her as well. She had filled it with items from the lost and found at the gym. Bras, panties, a few female personal items. She planned to put them in the motel room with Lavassier if we didn't have enough evidence against him.

I finally found a place to park near a dingy blue bungalow with a weed-infested yard. The place next door had a tumble-down fence and looked like it wasn't in much better shape. Both driveways were so cracked I wouldn't have parked Eagle's truck in them for fear of shredding a tire—not that I planned on parking the truck in a driveway in the first place.

I looked up, saw that we were only two blocks from the motel, and looked at Pammy.

"Ready?" I asked.

"As I'll ever be," she said, only this time, she didn't sound reluctant. There was a hint of excitement in her voice, which I hadn't expected.

She didn't grab any of the bags. We were instructed to lock the truck because of all of Eagle's medical supplies. So we were going to lock Pammy's stuff in here as well.

We'd get the stuff later, after we searched Lavassier's truck. We might end up driving it all the way to Walnut Creek, which I wasn't looking forward to. Then we'd have a little parade of trucks, heading out of town.

Pammy got out, locked her door, and slammed it shut.

I eased out as well, my shoulders aching from the tension. I locked the door and shoved the keys in my pocket. I took a large macramé purse and slung it over my shoulder. Inside, I had a wire coat hanger, my gloves, and just a little cash.

Pammy came up beside me. "You take the intersection near Hopkins and Cedar. It's not far from the New Orleans House. People will think you belong there."

"What's that?" I asked.

"Rock club," she said. "Here. Take these."

She offered me a thin pack of Virginia Slims and a lighter.

"I don't smoke," I said.

"You will if someone asks you what you're doing," she said. "I have one too."

I tucked the cigarette pack and lighter into my purse.

"Where will you be?" I asked.

"To start, I'm going to be right across from the Golden Bear. There's an apartment complex with a stupid little concrete fence and some stairs. I'm going to sit there and watch for him."

"I hope we recognize him," I said.

"Eagle thinks we will," Pammy said.

I'd expressed this worry before. Eagle had promised that if we missed him going in, we'd see him coming out. She was going to walk with him—or she planned to. If we hadn't found the truck yet, Pammy was supposed to come up to them, act drunk, and figure out how to engage.

I didn't like that plan at all. We had a half an hour to find the F-350, and judging by this neighborhood, we were in luck on one thing: that kind of truck would be unusual. Most of the cars here were tricked-out Volkswagens or sedate sedans.

In theory, either Pammy or I would see what direction he came to the restaurant from. We would then walk in that direction and search for the truck. If he parked in an obvious spot, it would be easy. If he didn't, it would take us a while.

I nodded. I wished we had walkie-talkies. I wished we had smoke-signals, for heaven's sake. I didn't like the initial part of the back-up plan—that whoever found the truck would fetch the other woman and bring her back to it. It seemed like a waste of precious time.

I had already made that argument, and I had lost.

"Good luck," I said.

Pammy looked somber. "To both of us," she said.

And, bless her, she didn't mention how much we would both need it.

PAMMY

Pammy left Val and walked the long way to the apartment complex. Pammy tucked the cigarettes in the pocket of her shirt front, the lighter in her pants pocket. Val had the burglar's tools. She was the one who was supposed to break into the truck and see if they could find anything they could use against this guy.

Pammy hoped they would, because she didn't like the look in Eagle's eyes. She was planning something, and she hadn't told Pammy the extent of it.

As Pammy rounded the corner onto Virginia, she glanced at her watch. Ten minutes to eight. She let out a small sigh.

Right on time.

She hurried up the block. The sun was low on the horizon, and the day's wind was dying down. Long shadows were starting to appear around the buildings across from her.

She thought she could hear the rush of cars on the freeway a few blocks away, but it might have been the traffic noise from San Pablo Avenue.

She reached San Pablo faster than she expected and waited at the intersection for cars to go by. She shifted from foot to foot.

There were a lot more pedestrians than she expected. Hippie kids from the university were heading toward the New Orleans House half a block away from her. Some stood outside, near vehicles that looked like they'd been parked in the small lot forever.

Some older adults were sitting outside a small restaurant across the street. A small group of tables had been clustered together near the sidewalk, almost a makeshift outdoor space.

Pammy turned her back on all of them and headed toward the apartment complex. She tracked the motel out of the corner of her eye. Most of the windows were closed, the curtains drawn. There didn't appear to be any lights on inside the rooms, but she couldn't really tell yet. The sun hadn't gone down far enough to give her a sense of whether or not the rooms were occupied.

When she reached the crumbling concrete stairs, she pulled the cigarette pack from her shirt front. She leaned against the concrete barrier, so that she wasn't quite sitting, and tapped the cigarette pack on her left thigh.

She figured tapping the pack would cover her own nervousness and give her an excuse for looking up and down the street as if she were waiting for a ride.

Val had found a car to lean on half a block away. She played with her macramé purse, as if she were looking for something lost inside it. Every now and then, she would glance up as if she were waiting for someone as well.

A couple other people were standing around on various parts of the street, and more than one person was outside smoking, staring at the setting sun.

Val was concentrating mostly on Cedar, but she would occasionally look farther down San Pablo than Pammy could see. There were more nightclubs in that direction. The parking lots there would probably be full as well, but they would suit a one-ton pickup better than the neighborhoods behind the motel.

Then, as if she had conjured it out of thin air, the truck drove by her. It was dark blue and shiny clean, as if someone had just washed and waxed it that morning. The truck was heading toward Virginia, away from both Pammy and Val.

Pammy squinted, catching just enough of the license plate to know she had seen the right truck.

She didn't want to look away from it and possibly lose it, but she needed to signal Val. Pammy glanced back toward Cedar.

Val was not leaning against the car anymore. Instead she was standing on her tiptoes, leaning into the street, looking about as conspicuous as anyone could.

Clearly, she had seen the truck.

Pammy stuck out her arm and waved her hand, pointing after the truck. Then she started to walk that way, keeping the cigarette pack in her hand.

The truck had disappeared from view when she'd been looking back at Val. Pammy hoped that meant he had parked it just out of her range of vision.

She walked faster, trying not to stare at everyone walking in the opposite direction. No trucks parked near her so far, but lots of small cars she couldn't identify, covered with smiley faces, peace signs, and bumper stickers that read *Hell No! We Won't Go!*

A couple of the people sitting outside that restaurant watched her walk past. She smiled at them and kept going.

She didn't see him. She didn't see the truck. Maybe he had parked on a side street after all.

Her heart was pounding hard. She glanced both ways when she reached Virginia—and then she saw him to her left, walking purposely down the sidewalk that intersected with hers.

He was taller than she expected, with rust-colored hair. It wasn't too long, but it wasn't military short either. It made him look hip, but not too hip. It simply gave him camouflage—he wouldn't stand out in counterculture Berkeley, but he would be all right in more conservative areas because, it could be argued, the length of his hair simply meant that he needed a haircut.

His clothes straddled the line between hip and square as well. He wore navy blue pants that did not look like they were part of a suit, and a white linen shirt that would have seemed dressy if paired with some kind of coat. His sleeves were rolled up, revealing tan arms that, even from this distance, looked like they were made of muscles.

She made herself look away, tapping the cigarette pack against her hand. She didn't want to seem like she was studying him.

But she was. She wanted to see his face. She wanted to commit it to memory.

When she looked west, he was nearly to the intersection. His gaze met hers and he nodded. She cursed silently. She hadn't wanted to make eye contact.

She couldn't make herself smile, but she did nod back.

Then she looked away as if he didn't concern her at all.

Out of the corner of her eye, she watched him cross the road. He stopped when he reached her.

Her heart was pounding. Did he know she had targeted him? Had he figured out what they were planning? How could he? He hadn't met any of them. He probably had forgotten all about Eagle by now.

He leaned toward Pammy just a little. Her mouth went dry.

"Looking for a light?" he asked, nodding toward her cigarette pack.

He was a half-step too close, the kind of man who used his physical presence to intimidate and charm. Right now, she figured, he was trying to charm.

And maybe it would have worked if she had no idea who he was.

She looked up at him. His face was square and long, his eyes a greenish-gray. He had a small scar on the side of his mouth, which was twisted into smile. If she hadn't known it, she never would have thought of him as a man who had grabbed a woman by the hair and slammed her head into his truck.

He clearly expected an answer.

She couldn't smile in return, so she went full jittery and a little cold.

"Thank you, no. I'm trying to quit. Just bought these and I'm trying to change my mind." She held the pack up, almost like a shield between them. "You want them?"

His gaze flicked down at them. His smile grew wider. Full-on charm, and yet that smile chilled her.

"Thank you, no," he said, repeating her phrase, inflection and all. It wiped out all of the South that had been in his voice, an accent she hadn't even realized he had until now. "Not my brand."

She let out a nervous giggle. She would like to think she had planned it—she hadn't giggled in years—but she hadn't. He made her that uncomfortable.

"I'm not sure they're anyone's brand," she said. "I don't like them much. My concession to trying to quit."

He touched her shoulder lightly, in a manner she would have thought both flirtatious and comforting in another context.

"Quitting's overrated," he said, and walked past her.

She waited until she heard his footsteps recede, then she let out a slow breath of air, as quietly as she could.

Son of a bitch. She hadn't expected him to actually *see* her or notice her or talk to her.

On some level, she hadn't expected him to be real.

She didn't let herself turn around. She didn't want him to see her gaze following him. If he had no idea who she was (and how could he?) then he would think her some foolish woman, intrigued by a passing flirtation.

Instead, she looked east, as if she were still waiting for someone. She grabbed the lighter out of her pocket. It was silver and heavy. She turned it over and over in her fingers, then tapped the cigarette pack against the back of her hand.

As she did that, she looked west.

And saw the truck.

It was parked halfway down the block, in the lot reserved for the Franklin Elementary School. He knew the neighborhood better than she did. On a weekday night in July, that was a great place to park. No one would notice the vehicle. If she had been thinking, she would have had Val park there as well.

Pammy was glad she hadn't. He would have seen Eagle's truck. He might have made some kind of connection.

Pammy finally turned around in time to see him cut across San Pablo Avenue in front of the Golden Bear Restaurant. Her stomach tightened. She couldn't see where Eagle was from here. Pammy couldn't see the front door or the main windows.

And she couldn't have him see her watching either.

She took one quick glance at the sidewalk behind her and didn't see Val. Had he talked to Val as well? Or had she hidden from him?

It didn't matter.

They knew where the truck was—or Pammy did—and he was going inside the restaurant.

They were on the clock now. Thirty minutes, if they needed that. He had given them a gift by parking far away from the restaurant. He couldn't interrupt them, and he couldn't see from inside.

Yes, he had seen her, but he wouldn't remember her. And even if he did, he wouldn't think of her as the person who broke into his truck.

Pammy let out another long breath and tucked the lighter back in her pants pocket. She kept playing with the cigarette pack, though, as she moved a little farther down the street.

Val would come to her. That was the agreement. Then Pammy would point out the truck, and they could begin.

EAGLE

Ashadow went by one of the large plate-glass windows in the front of the restaurant. The shadow shouldn't have caught her eye, but it did.

Eagle felt an incredible calm come over her. She hadn't felt like this in months, not since she went onto the street during the People's Park melee, wearing her Army-issued gas mask and helping whomever she could find.

She had had a purpose that day; she had a purpose now.

She removed her gloves and set them on the table. Not quite the way that a well-dressed society matron would behave, but this wasn't a restaurant that a society matron would frequent, at least, not without her husband and family. Eagle stirred her coffee, even though she had put nothing in it, and set the spoon on the saucer. Her fingers tapped the laminate covering the menu.

The manager walked past the doorway, stopped, and then went behind his little podium, grabbing menus as he did so. A waitress hurried by with a tray balanced on one hand, the smell of turkey and gravy trailing behind her.

Once the waitress had gone past, Eagle had a clear view of the door. She feigned a nervousness she no longer felt, letting her fingers fidget with the spoon and the menu itself.

The door opened, and the manager moved slightly, clutching the menus. A man entered, scouting the room. He was tall, with russet-colored hair and a long face. Eagle's heart sped up.

Lavassier.

His gaze met Eagle's.

Eagle's back remained rigid. She picked up her gloves, then flapped them just a little so that he could see they existed, then set them on the other side of her coffee cup. Then she picked up her spoon again and stirred the coffee once more.

He broke the eye contact, turned, and grinned at the manager. They spoke to each other quietly. Eagle hadn't realized that Lavassier was quite that tall. He had looked large on Saturday night, but she hadn't registered him as over six feet, which he clearly was.

His linen shirt pulled over his broad shoulders and muscular arms. His hair needed a trim, but he probably kept it that way on purpose. He wasn't wearing jeans, but his slacks were casual, without the usual crease that a businessman would have.

He nodded to the manager, then rounded one of the tables in the center of the room and headed directly for Eagle.

It only took him a moment to reach her.

He stopped in front of the table, dipped his head slightly, and for one dizzying second, she thought he was going to extend a hand and ask her to dance.

"Mrs. Knight?"

"Yes," she said, and made herself swallow visibly.

"I'm Justin Lavassier."

She picked up her gloves as if she were going to put them on. Instead, she waved them at the seat opposite her.

"Please," she said, "join me."

He nodded, then slipped into the booth. "I still held hopes that you would bring your husband."

Eagle shook her head slightly. "He doesn't know about any of this."

"He's going to have to know," Lavassier said. "I can't do business with only one parent. Unless you're getting a divorce...?"

Eagle's eyes narrowed. A society matron would be insulted by that question, but she didn't want to overplay her reaction.

"No, of course not," she said. "And I do not understand why my husband needs to be involved."

A waitress stopped in front of their table. Her white apron had a large coffee stain over one breast, and the pouch where she kept her pens and order pad looked a little greasy on the edges.

"What can I get you, hon?" she asked Lavassier, as if Eagle didn't even exist.

"Coffee," he said.

"And water?" Eagle asked, but the waitress scurried off as if she hadn't even heard.

Eagle sighed and let some of her real exasperation show.

"I've asked three times now," she said.

Lavassier shoved his silverware to one side and moved the coffee cup directly in front of him. Eagle tried not to look at it. She had planned to slip a sedative into it when he wasn't looking, but now she would have to reach all the way across the table.

He would notice that.

"What did Mrs. MacGivers tell you?" he asked.

"Only that you were expensive, but good," Eagle said. "She said you gave them their daughter back. I understand she's studying again."

"Good to hear," Lavassier said, although his tone suggested that he really didn't care.

"I would like my Angela back," Eagle said.

"I'm sure you would," Lavassier said, "but I don't take every case presented to me."

Eagle's lips thinned. Had she blown this already by not having a fake husband here at the table?

"I do a lot of preparation," Lavassier said. "I study the child, find out who she is, what her interests are, and where she went wrong. It's valuable to speak to both parents about this, as well as some friends."

"Some of that will be difficult. We're not going to be in San Francisco long." Eagle deliberately got the name of the community wrong. "I don't know most of my daughter's friends. That's the problem. Her high school friends are scattered all over the country. My husband—"

"Let me finish," Lavassier said. "I—"

He stopped as the waitress approached. She was holding the coffeepot. She reached for his cup and saucer, but he intercepted her and handed it to her. She set the cup and saucer down on the edge of the table and poured coffee in the cup without sloshing.

He lifted it back to the same position.

Eagle had pegged him correctly. He liked to be in control of everything.

Which was going to make sedating him hard.

He waited until the waitress left.

"I charge a lot of money," Lavassier said. "I do *not* guarantee my work, nor do I offer a refund."

Eagle opened her mouth, wondering if normal society matrons protested here. Then she closed her mouth again.

"I do, however, take payments in installments," Lavassier said. "Since you live outside of California, I would take three installments. The first is half of my normal fee. The second installment would be my travel expenses should I have to bring the child—"

"Angela," Eagle murmured, partly to irritate him, and partly to play her role.

"Should I bring the child," he said a little stronger, "back to …?"

"Lawrence," she said. "Kansas."

"That's some distance, and transporting her will be difficult. We might have to meet here, in California. Nonetheless, we're still talking about a second installment of expenses, which might work out to as much as a quarter of the overall fee."

Eagle pulled her purse onto her lap. He watched the movement. It didn't seem like he missed anything.

"Are the expenses included in the fee?" Eagle asked.

"No," he said. "As you'll discover if we decide to work together, I take a lot of risks. I need to be compensated for them."

"But you don't guarantee your work…" she said, letting her voice trail off.

"Of course not. I deal with human beings, not objets d'art."

His pronunciation of the French phrase was more Louisiana than Paris.

"I can't guarantee that I'll bring your child back because I can't guarantee that I'll find her. If I do find her, I'll bring her to you, but I can't guarantee that she'll listen to any of my persuading."

Your beatings, you mean, Eagle thought but didn't say.

"So, we're taking all the risk here," Eagle said, running her fingers along the side of her purse. Maybe she would ease it open. Maybe she would be able to palm some of the pills. But getting them to his cup was another matter. And he still hadn't touched his coffee.

He gave her a cold smile. "You're not taking any risks at all, Mrs. Knight. I am. I've been bitten, kicked, tossed out of reputable places, had knives thrown at me, and been threatened with guns. Just because these kids are college-age doesn't mean they're running with a good crowd. Depending on what your daughter has gotten involved in, I can end up in a lot of danger."

"I meant financial risk," Eagle said. "It seems there aren't any guarantees."

"You seem awfully worried about money, Mrs. Knight," Lavassier said. "I suspect we might not be able to work together."

She didn't want to lose him. She needed to keep him here long enough to let Val and Pammy search his truck.

"What do you charge?" she asked.

"For this kind of job, with a kid who is an out-of-state college student? The job starts at fifteen thousand dollars and goes up dramatically if I believe that it'll take additional work."

Eagle ran her thumb over the clasp on her purse. "So the price changes as the job continues?"

"It has to," he said. "If your child is involved in gang activity, I'm taking on great risk."

"She wouldn't," Eagle said.

"If she's taking drugs, guaranteed there are gangs involved," he said. "Someone supplies the goods. And if she's selling drugs—"

"She *wouldn't*," Eagle said, partly because parents would say that, and partly because it felt like a sidetrack.

"You don't know what she's doing," Lavassier said. "That's why you want to hire me. You've lost track of your daughter, and you need me to get her. Tell me, how old is she exactly?"

Eagle was prepared for this question. "Nineteen. Her birthday was in February."

"Then we have eighteen months to find her and bring her back," he said.

"Eighteen months?" Eagle was legitimately confused.

"There are things I can do for you as the underage child's parent that I cannot do for you when she's considered a full-fledged adult under the law," he said.

His words sent a chill through Eagle. The parents weren't going to complain about Lavassier. They were complicit in his hire. And the underage college student had no legal recourse.

"That's why," Lavassier said, clearly sensing the surprise in her hesitation, "you and I will have a contract that will bind us. It will be completed with the check. And that's why we need your husband, Mrs. Knight. In California, I will need the consent of the custodial parent to do this."

"We don't live in California," she said, feeling stunned. She had forgotten that some states did not allow wives to sign legal documents for issues that concerned the family.

"It doesn't matter," Lavassier said. "I'll start my work here and, I hope, find your daughter here. I want a legally binding contract that will hold up in *this* state, not in your state."

Eagle bit her lower lip. This was something she hadn't expected at all. She wasn't even sure how to finesse it.

"So," Lavassier said. "Let's get your husband on board, shall we? And then you and I can talk."

He started to slide out of the booth.

"Wait," she said. "Don't you want my daughter's picture? Don't you want to know what I know about her, maybe so we can set some kind of price?"

He gave her one of those patronizing smiles new doctors in Pleiku used to give her, before they realized just how much she knew and how much they needed her.

"I'd prefer to have this conversation with your husband, Mrs. Knight," Lavassier said. "Call me when you convince him to help your daughter. Otherwise, we won't be doing business together."

He got out of the booth and was heading down the aisle before she could say another word. He walked fast.

Eagle's mouth had gone dry. She opened her purse and checked her watch.

It was ten after eight. She had promised Val and Pammy half an hour. In fact, she had thought half an hour would be easy. And she thought there was a good chance he would be feeling the effects of a powerful narcotic by the time he reached the truck.

None of that had happened.

She opened her purse, grabbed three one-dollar bills, and tossed them on the table. Then she grabbed one of the hypodermic needles she had brought, this one filled with a drug cocktail she designed herself back in Nam. It subdued patients quickly, turning their limbs into rubber before they lost consciousness.

The problem was, she had underestimated how big Lavassier was. She probably had a smaller dosage than would be effective.

But she couldn't worry about that right now.

She moved the hypo to the top of her purse so that when she got close, she could just grab it. She didn't want to run with it in her hand. That was too dangerous. She'd seen more than one nurse stab herself with the hypo trying to subdue a patient.

Eagle had it down to a science, but even her method held room for error.

He was already out the door.

If she didn't hurry, she wouldn't be able to follow him. She wouldn't find his truck.

She wouldn't get to Val and Pammy in time.

VAL

The cinderblock wobbled beneath my feet. I leaned on the driver's door of Lavassier's truck, my arms bent above my head, my purse slung over my back, and my hands holding the edge of the coat hanger tightly. Pammy stood behind a crumbling concrete wall, which gave her a partial view of Virginia Street.

Lavassier had parked in an area that served as a partial loading dock for the school. The greenish gold overhang had seen better days. Someone had cleaned the area underneath it, but the trash cans smelled like someone else had been using them during the summer months.

Lavassier had parked the truck with its nose pointed toward the back of the building, not sideways the way the painted lines indicated. That was why Pammy had been able to see it from the street.

But she had only been able to see it because she was looking for it. Fortunately, I had seen her turn left on Virginia or I wouldn't have known where she was going at all. I kept looking for evidence of the truck against the curbs, with the VW Beetles, the dented sedans, and the one or two new cars, parked in driveways half a block away.

When I arrived, Pammy was already walking around the truck, looking for entry. She had her gloves on, and she was trying the passenger door. It was locked. The entire truck was locked.

But that didn't stop us from looking into the bed. It had been recently cleaned, but it was still a horror show. All along the frame, Lavassier had attached hooks.

Pammy and I had looked at each other when we had seen that, but neither of us said anything. There was no reason to. We knew what he had used those for. He had tied the ropes to the hooks and then wrapped the ropes around his victims. That way, they couldn't wiggle out of the back of the truck.

They couldn't untie themselves either.

The inside of the cab, on the other hand, was filthy. Papers and food wrappings were strewn everywhere, along with some hats and tools. There appeared to be boxes stashed underneath the dashboard on the passenger side, but we wouldn't know until we got inside, and that was up to me.

Pammy had never unlocked a car with a coat hanger. I'd become skilled at it, mostly because when I was in law school, I was always distracted—an airhead of the first order, Marvella used to call me. I often locked my keys in the car, particularly in the winter, when it wasn't wise to do so. Truman and I were married by then, and he had bought the car used, just for me. I never wanted him to know how often I locked myself out, so I carried a coat hanger in my backpack instead.

And, since I had done this a lot in the winter, I was adept at using a coat hanger while wearing thick gloves. The gloves I had on now weren't thick at all. I could feel the thin metal through the cotton.

But that old car was easier to break into than this truck was. The car was lower, for one thing. I could reach the top of the window by standing on the ground. I'd had to climb on a cinderblock so that I could see what I was doing here.

And the truck was newer and built better than my old car, so it was harder to squeeze the straightened coat hanger through the space between the top of the window and the arch of the cab.

I had to get the right angle. It looked like I would have no trouble once I did, because the button was a little wider on the top, like a tiny mushroom. All I had to do was snag that.

But once the hanger was inside, I had to stand on my tiptoes to move the wire around. My shoulders and upper arms ached, and the cinderblock kept shifting position every time I shifted my weight.

Pammy kept looking over her shoulder at me instead of watching the street for Lavassier's return.

"Got it?" she asked.

"Almost," I said. "Don't watch me, okay?"

She turned back toward the parking lot, Virginia Street, and Curtis. It was getting dark, too, which was helpful. I doubted anyone could see us. If it got too much darker, though, I wouldn't be able to see inside the truck. I had a flashlight in my purse, but I would have needed an extra hand to use it while I was manipulating the coat hanger.

Finally the lock clicked open. I didn't trust it though. I stayed on the cinderblock and pulled the door handle.

It moved this time.

So I jumped off the cinderblock and landed on the cracked concrete.

"Bingo," I said.

Pammy turned around and started to come toward the truck, but I held up a hand.

"Wait until I get the other door," I said. "And double-check your gloves."

She frowned, then turned her back on me so that she could monitor the street again. The streetlights hadn't come on yet. I hoped that the timer they were on was set for full dark, which would be about 9:00 p.m. I wanted that forty minutes or so of twilight to be ours.

I slid the coat hanger into my purse and grabbed the flashlight. Then I shoved the cinderblock aside and pulled open the driver's door. A waft of Old Spice mixed with cigarettes and old greasy food bags made my eyes water.

I had to leverage myself into the cab. This truck really wasn't built for a woman of my size. Once I had a knee on the seat, I reached up and unscrewed the dome light. Then I crawled across the seat to the passenger side and unlocked the door.

I rapped on the window to get Pammy's attention. She jumped as she whirled, cheeks flushed with panic. I waved at her.

Then I turned on the flashlight. I wanted that box first.

Papers were strewn all over the floor on the passenger side. Many of them were receipts from various stores and restaurants around Berkeley. A small open bag had coins inside as well as matchbooks from all over the county. For a man who made as much money as he did from each job, he was frugal about strange things.

The handful of matchbooks on top were from the same motel, a place near Mount Diablo in Walnut Creek. I felt the hair rise on the back of my neck. We'd been hoping for a Walnut Creek connection. Now we had one.

Pammy opened the passenger door just as I grabbed the box and pulled it forward.

I wanted to see what was in that thing. I didn't want her to look. I knew more about the things Lavassier had done than she did.

"Take the driver's side," I said. "I'll scooch over here."

"Okay." She closed the door before I could tell her to leave it open. I wanted some fresh air to clear the smell out of the cab.

I moved my legs forward, got off my stomach, and shoved some of the papers off the seat. Then I opened the box.

Files and notes, and not all of them in the same hand. There were file folders, each with a different name written in black on the side. I opened the top one.

Polaroids, high school pictures, notes, and in the back, a contract with a name I didn't recognize written along it. There was a ledger sheet as well, with the first payment noted along with a check number, but no second payment.

I grabbed another folder from farther down and saw a similar set-up. Only this one had notes in another hand.

...she spends most of her time at V.D.C. headquarters, stuffing envelopes and typing addresses. I think she lives nearby, but I haven't been in the position to ask her for an address yet. She thinks I'm one of the V.D.C. hangers-on, interested in the men, so she sort of sees me as competition. I'm thinking coffee might change her opinion, and give you a chance to maybe follow her? Once I set it up, I'll leave you a message on the answering service.

—Darla

I gasped.

"What?" Pammy asked.

I handed her the page of notes I had just read.

"Her roommate Lucy told me Darla was making a lot of money," I said, "but Lucy didn't know how."

"You think this is the same Darla?" Pammy asked as she handed the note back to me. I put it back in the folder.

"It wouldn't surprise me," I said, "since she ended up dead, too."

I shivered. We had more than enough here. We needed to get him in that motel room, drugged to a stupor, and call the police. We could bring the files inside, along with the matchbooks, and let the cops connect the dots. We wouldn't have to drive to Walnut Creek after all.

But, to make sure that Lavassier got caught, I would call Detective Jessup in the Walnut Creek police department when I got home tonight and pretend to be Carol Anne Houk again. I'd give him a head's up about the truck's location (which, at that point, would be the Golden Bear), the matches, and the Mount Diablo connection.

That would guarantee that someone would charge Lavassier with something and get him off the streets of Berkeley.

"How much time do we have?" I asked.

"About twenty minutes," Pammy said. "I think we're okay."

The faster we got out of the truck, the better. But I wanted to see if we could find a connection to any of the missing kids. I thumbed through the file folders, looking at names, while Pammy dug through the mess on the driver's side.

"He lives in his truck," she said.

"No wonder he parked it away from everything else," I said.

Then my breath caught. He probably had weapons hidden in here. We needed to find them.

"Pammy," I said, "make sure you look under the seat for weapons."

"Already thought of that," she said.

I pushed on the glove box. It didn't open. It was locked.

Pammy and I looked at each other. Did we waste the next ten minutes trying to open that or did we worry about it later? If we locked up the truck before he got back here, he would have to go through two different locks to get to any weapon he might have stashed.

And by then, if Eagle had done her job, he would be too impaired to do much.

"I don't suppose you know how to pick a lock," Pammy said.

"Not that one," I said.

"Then let's figure out what we need here so we don't have to spend a lot more time around the truck when we're in the Golden Bear parking lot," she said.

"Yeah," I said. Because we both knew the faster we finished, the better off we would be.

EAGLE

Eagle pushed open the outer door of the restaurant. She clung to her purse and looked both ways. Lavassier was on this side of the street, heading north.

She pivoted and started to run after him, cursing the stupid new shoes pinching her feet. She made it to the driveway into the Golden Bear Motel when she heard a man yelling.

"Ma'am! Ma'am! *Ma'am!*"

She glanced over her shoulder, saw the manager of the restaurant standing just outside the door, shaking something at her.

Her damn gloves.

She looked away, saw Lavassier had stopped, and was watching her and the manager. Goddamn it. She didn't want Lavassier to know she had followed him.

Although right now, he would think she was coming after him to get him to change his mind about finding her made-up daughter. But if she ran after him, what would he think then?

And her brain wasn't working well enough to come up with a plausible lie for stopping him in the street. He wouldn't want her to anyway. He had already made himself clear. He didn't want to do business with her.

If she followed him, he would speed up to get away from her, and that was the last thing she wanted.

She pivoted and walked back to the manager who, asshole that he was, didn't hurry toward her. He actually made her come to him.

He held out the gloves, and smiled as if he expected another tip. She had already overpaid for the coffee, by probably two dollars and fifty cents, but he wanted more money for doing something nice and friendly.

Bastard.

Or maybe he didn't want anything except a thank-you.

So she said, "Thank you," and snatched the gloves out of his hand.

When she turned around, Lavassier was gone. She couldn't see him anywhere.

This time, she did run. The motel covered most of San Pablo on this side of the street. There was nowhere for him to duck in. Which meant he had probably turned right on Virginia or had gone into a nearby house.

She had no idea why he would go into a house.

She reached the intersection faster than she expected, but at a cost. Blisters had formed on the heels of both feet.

She looked right, expecting to see him or the truck alongside the bungalows lining both sides of Virginia. But he wasn't there. And the truck wasn't there, not that she could see anyway.

She whirled, and as she did, she caught movement on the other side of the road, near Franklin Elementary.

Jesus, he had parked behind the school.

She started to cross the street, but a car nearly hit her, honking and swerving. Two other cars passed behind it, as well as cars in the opposite lane.

She had no idea where the traffic had come from, only that there was some. She had been so focused on Lavassier that she hadn't seen it.

She took the few seconds she was trapped on the east side of San Pablo to slip on the gloves. Then she removed the hypodermic from her purse. She'd still have to get the cap off the needle end, but that would only take a second.

Her heart was pounding.

The traffic light one block south changed to red, and the traffic coming toward her stopped. Three more cars went by on the far side of the street before there was a break in traffic.

She hurried across San Pablo. People were sitting at tables outside a small restaurant. She didn't want to yell a warning to Pammy and Val. Eagle didn't want to call attention to herself any more than she already had.

The restaurant patrons were watching her, some society matron, running in her Cinderella slippers while wearing gloves. They would remember her.

But what they would remember was the gold, ivory, and pink striped dress, the shoes, the headband, and the gloves, not her face.

Please, God, she didn't want them to remember her face.

She kept it turned slightly away from them as she passed them. She didn't see Lavassier. She hadn't seen him cross the street, she hadn't seen him go behind the school.

She didn't know for certain if that was where he parked. Maybe he had parked on a side street.

And it was getting just dark enough that everything had that twilight haze. The edges of buildings and trees looked fuzzy, as if she needed glasses.

At least there was no one else on this part of the street.

She hurried and finally saw the back end of the truck, barely visible behind the Franklin School.

"Oh, thank God," she said, surprising herself by speaking out loud. "Oh, thank fucking God."

EAGLE

W hat the hell are you doing in my truck?"

Pammy looked up. Val was sitting in the passenger seat, file folders spread across her lap. She looked out the window as if she had seen a ghost.

Pammy eased the driver's door open and slid out. "Come on, Val," she whispered, but as she did, the sound of the passenger door opening covered her voice.

The passenger door yanked back, and the entire truck shook.

"I asked you a question, bitch! What are you doing in my truck?"

Pammy couldn't quite see him, but she knew who it was. Lavassier. He grabbed Val and pulled her toward him, the file folders slipping to the ground. She braced her hands on the inside of the door frame, but she wasn't large enough to hold that position.

He yanked again, and she fell to the pavement with a sickening thud.

Pammy wished now that she had found a weapon underneath the seat. But she hadn't brought a gun. Pammy had always said that she thought guns caused more problems than they solved.

Maybe she was wrong.

"Who the hell are you?" he said, and at that moment, Pammy realized he wasn't yelling. He was in control. Complete control.

He knew how to hurt people, and he was a big man.

Val had had no training at all, and he had probably just knocked the wind out of her.

But, as far as Pammy could tell, he hadn't seen her. She cast about the parking area for a weapon, but she didn't see anything she could use. And the bastard hadn't even had a tire iron in the truck. Nothing. He probably kept it clean of make-shift weapons so his teenage prisoners had nothing to use to free themselves.

Bastard.

"Ouch!" Now, he sounded angry. "You bit me, you fucking bitch!"

Val was defending herself. But she had to get away.

Pammy tried to send Val a telepathic message. *Run! Run! First rule of defense. Get the hell out of here.*

Not that Pammy could follow that rule. She was trapped by the truck itself. If she tried to leave, he would see her, depending on how he was standing.

Second rule of defense against a larger opponent: *Use everything, and do not fight fair.*

Everything.

There weren't even rocks on this side of the truck. Just the cinder-block, which she grabbed. It weighed nothing—and that was when she realized that her adrenaline was pumping.

She had always told her students to use the power adrenaline gave them.

There was a loud bang, and the entire truck shook. Shit! Pammy suddenly realized that he was using the same technique to subdue Val that he had used to subdue the woman Eagle had seen.

He was slamming Val's head into the truck. That could kill her.

Pammy had to stop him.

The shortest distance between him and her was around the front of the truck. If he saw her, so be it.

She snuck around and winced as the bang sounded again, followed by a moan. The truck shook.

Pammy crouched so that she was half hidden as she made it to the passenger side of the truck. She ducked behind the door, then stepped around it.

He was half turned away from Pammy, but his head was bent slightly because he was focused on Val. His left hand was gripping the top of her skull, his right arm was wrapped around her torso, lifting her off the ground.

She was still alive, and not entirely knocked senseless, because she was kicking. She wasn't connecting, but she was kicking.

He whipped his entire body toward the truck, and as he did, Pammy stepped out from behind the door. She mimicked his movement, swinging the cinderblock, the pointed end aimed for the back of his head.

Hit hard, Pammy Girl, her father's voice instructed her, *because you'll probably only get one shot at this.*

She used her entire body, all the power she had ever had, to slam that cinderblock into Lavassier's skull.

The block hit as he moved toward the truck. She didn't connect with the back of his head, but the side of it, the pointed end of the cinderblock slamming into his temple.

He staggered sideways, letting go of Val, who crumpled to the ground.

Pammy ignored her for the moment, instead stepping forward and bringing down the block again, this time hitting the side of his face so hard that she heard the cracking of bones.

She lifted the block again, swinging it like a hammer, and slamming it into him a third time.

"Pammy. That's enough."

It took a half second for the voice to register.

She looked up. Eagle stood next to the crumbling concrete wall, looking like she had just come from a summer party.

"Set it down," Eagle said. "You've done enough."

EAGLE

He was obviously dead. Pammy had crushed his skull—and she had done so mostly silently.

That was the part that had impressed Eagle. There had been no screaming, not from Pammy, not from Val. All Eagle had heard as she ran toward the truck was the bang of Val's head against the metal and then the sound of crunching bone.

At first, Eagle had thought that was the sound of Val's head breaking against the truck—although she hadn't known it was Val, not right away. It could have been Pammy.

Then Eagle rounded the concrete wall, and saw Pammy hit Lavassier with the block while he was already on the ground. She had picked up that block like it didn't weigh a thing, and was prepared to hit him again, when Eagle spoke up.

Now, Pammy had stopped, her face speckled with blood, her eyes wild.

"Set the block down," Eagle said gently. She put the hypo back into her purse, then pulled off the gloves. She didn't want Lavassier's blood on anything she owned if she could avoid it.

Fortunately, she didn't have to touch him. No one had half a skull, lost that much blood, and lived.

The blood was flowing toward the street, away from Val, away from Pammy's shoes—at least at the moment.

Eagle stepped over Lavassier's body. Val was crumpled beside him. The back of her neck and part of her shirt was damp with blood, but whose Eagle couldn't tell.

Val blinked at her. "I'm all right."

"You're not," Eagle said.

Val's face was swelling and already bruising. Still, she gave Eagle a real smile. "I'll have a headache. But I'll be all right."

Eagle would test that as soon as they got out of here.

"We have him," Val said. "He kept notes. They're in the truck."

Eagle let out a breath. "Contracts," she said, more to herself than Val.

"Exactly." Val sat up, put a hand to the side of her face, and moaned. "Okay, Jesus, that hurts. That's good, right?"

Eagle had no idea. But she had to do something.

Pammy was still standing over Lavassier, staring down at him. She had left the block beside his head.

"Can you stand?" Eagle asked Val.

She put a hand on the side of the truck. Eagle looked at her, hoping for—and seeing—gloves. Val used the truck's side as a brace and got to her feet, swaying slightly.

"I bit him," she said.

Great, Eagle thought. They had to get out of here, then. Police could compare bite marks to someone's dental records, if they had the records.

"I don't think that killed him," Eagle said.

"He's dead?" Val turned, nearly fell over, and caught herself against the truck. "Jesus, he's dead. Pammy, he's dead."

"I know." Pammy's voice was flat.

"We have to get out of here," Eagle said. "Right now."

"We have the motel room," Pammy said. "I think I can pick him up."

"We don't need to," Eagle said. "Let's go."

"No," Val said. "We have to lock the truck."

"What?" Eagle asked. "Forget the truck. We have to go."

"*No*," Val said. "There's enough evidence in this truck to convict this asshole of at least one murder and maybe more."

"No one's convicting him of anything," Eagle said. "He's dead, Val."

"I know." She still had a hand on the side of the truck. "But no one will care who killed him if they figure out that he's been murdering college students for money."

She was right. Holy Jesus, she was right. If they got out of here now, and somehow left the truck intact, all the police would think was that one of his victims had killed him and then run away.

"Okay." Eagle glanced at Pammy's hands. She was still wearing gloves as well. "Pamela! I need you to pay attention."

Pammy looked up, eyes glassy with shock.

"You are going to walk to the driver's side of this truck, lock the door, and close it. Do you got that?"

"Why not you?" Pammy asked. She probably wasn't thinking clearly, but it seemed like Val was.

So Eagle answered for Val's edification, not Pammy's. Eagle pointed to her stupid Cinderella slippers.

"Let's just be practical, shall we?" she asked.

"Yes," Pammy said. "Which is why—"

"Don't argue," Eagle said. "I need you to act fast. We have medical issues."

They did—she really did need to deal with Val's face—but those medical issue were less of a problem than Pammy's shock, and the three of them, standing over a dead body.

"Move," Eagle said.

"Yes, right," Pammy said, and walked around the truck. She reached the other side, locked the door like instructed, and slammed it shut.

The sound reverberated in the small space like a gunshot. Eagle was shocked that no one had come over here from that restaurant on San Pablo.

"I got this one," Val said, holding the passenger door. She depressed the lock and eased the door closed.

Eagle stepped back and peered down the side of the building. They couldn't go back by San Pablo, not with all of that blood on Pammy's face. But there was a nightclub one block over, and no one would think twice about a woman with bruises near there. People would simply assume there had been an altercation inside.

There had to be a way around the back of the school. Eagle just had to trust it.

"Let's go," she said.

"We leave him?" Pammy asked, as she came around the back of the truck.

"Right next to the trash," Eagle said. "Exactly where he belongs."

VAL

We made it to 10th Street before I actually felt the injury. I knew it was there, of course, but something kept me going—adrenaline, excitement, shock. I wasn't feeling anything, and then, suddenly, my knees buckled.

Eagle caught me. She wrapped an arm around me, and logically, I should have balked. I'd been balking against touch ever since Vitel, but this time, having someone hold me up felt good.

I had fought back. I hadn't killed Lavassier, but I had slowed him down. I had bit him on that tender skin between the index finger and the thumb of his right hand, which was why he called me a bitch.

I wanted to tell Pammy that I had learned from her—*You go for the soft, squishy parts*—but she was in no condition to listen.

She walked with her head down. Thank heavens it had grown dark, because she had dots of blood all over her face.

Eagle was probably getting blood on her pretty new dress too, from my shirt. I had felt the warm splashes of it the first time Pammy hit Lavassier.

Not to mention the blood that had dripped from the side of my own skull when he slammed me against the truck. I had reached up

510

surreptitiously on the walk and found a cut, probably from one of the metal strips along the side of the truck.

Eagle's truck was right where I left it. I fished in my purse—Jesus, I still had my purse—and found the keys, extending them to Eagle. She took them and, bracing me against the truck, unlocked the driver's door.

Then she left me balanced there, and went around to the other side, helping Pammy in. Pammy hadn't been hit at all, but she seemed to be in a lot worse shape than I was.

I supposed, considering she had killed a man.

I used the side of the truck to guide me and walked around as Eagle was helping Pammy inside. I got in too, and Eagle closed the door. Then she went around to the driver's side.

"Where are we going?" I asked.

"The gym," Eagle said. "I'm taking us back to the gym."

EAGLE

Eagle parked the truck in the alley, grazing one of the trash cans as she pulled in. She didn't care. She unlocked the door, glad the light above it was out. They were in full darkness now, and she doubted anyone could see her.

Still, she was going to destroy all of their clothing. She would bag it and, later tonight, toss it, along with the purses, into the Bay. From where, she didn't know yet. That wasn't anything she needed to figure out immediately.

She doubted anyone was looking for them. Even if someone saw them, they wouldn't know who the three of them were.

On the short drive back, she had worried about loose ends. The motel room—which was under Lavassier's name—the fact she had been seen in the Golden Bear restaurant, the people sitting outside that restaurant on San Pablo.

But even if someone figured out who the three of them were, there was no way to tie them to Lavassier's death. Or there wouldn't be, once she got rid of the clothes.

The motel room would explain why he was in the neighborhood. If the cops figured out that a woman had rented the room, they probably would think she was the new assistant—if they even investigated that far.

And if anyone overheard Eagle's discussion with Lavassier in the restaurant, they would think her exactly as she had presented herself, a housewife who wanted to hire the man, not someone who had planned to kill him.

Eagle got Pammy inside and under a hot shower. Eagle was going to put Val in the shower too, after making sure she didn't have a concussion. She seemed to be pretty rational, but Eagle knew that meant nothing.

She went back to the truck and grabbed her main medical bag. In it, she had an ophthalmoscope so that she could look in Val's eyes. Val had sounded coherent, and she hadn't thrown up. She also wasn't complaining of dizziness, and she seemed to know where they were.

Eagle did a few tests and determined, as best she could, that Val didn't have a concussion. It looked like she had taken the bulk of the impact with the front of her face. Her right cheek and jaw were swelling. So far, Eagle couldn't feel any broken bones.

She got Val into the shower as well, then she sat for a moment on the bench, just breathing.

She felt bad. She had planned to be the one to stop Lavassier. She hadn't decided what exactly she was going to do to him. She had options— an LSD overdose, alcohol injected in his brain stem, or simply doing what Pammy and Val had thought they were going to do, leave him high and tied to the bed, awaiting the police's arrival.

She had planned to play that by ear.

But she hadn't expected Pammy to kill him. Pammy had never had anyone die at her hands. Pammy had been against this vigilante action in the first place.

Eagle looked over at the shower. Val was bracing herself against the wall. She had bruises all along her right side. No wonder her head wasn't as badly injured as Eagle thought it should have been. Val had taken some of the blows against her shoulder and arm.

Maybe she had learned a little from Pammy already.

Pammy shut off her shower and wrapped a towel around herself. She moved better than she had before.

"I killed him," she said, as she sat down beside Eagle. Pammy smelled of hot water and Ivory soap.

"I know," Eagle said.

"He was trying to kill Val," Pammy said.

"I know that too," Eagle said.

"I should regret it," Pammy said.

"Why?" Eagle asked.

Pammy shrugged. "I just should. But I don't."

Eagle looked at her. Eagle had thought Pammy was moving slowly from the shock of killing him.

"He killed Darla," Pammy said.

"Val told me," Eagle said.

"And he beat the crap out of Kelly MacGivers," Pammy said. "And tried to kill that gas station attendant."

Eagle nodded.

"I should regret it," Pammy said.

"Why?" Eagle asked again. "He was a son of a bitch."

"I didn't think I believed in vigilante justice," Pammy said.

"It wasn't vigilante justice," Eagle said. What Eagle had been planning—*that* was vigilante justice. "You saved a friend's life. That would hold up in court."

"If we stayed," Pammy said.

You can turn yourself in, Eagle almost said, but didn't. She wasn't going to give Pammy ideas.

"I don't like being judge, jury, and executioner," Pammy said.

"You weren't," Eagle said. "He was trying to kill Val."

"Thank God," Pammy said.

Eagle frowned at her.

"I don't mean that how it sounded," Pammy said. "I didn't want him to hurt Val. But by doing so, he made it easy."

Eagle nodded. She understood that.

"If we ever come across something like this again," Pammy said, "I'm going to the authorities. And if they don't help—"

"Just hope we don't come across something like this ever again," Eagle said. She didn't want Pammy to make a pronouncement she couldn't keep. Because she had clearly forgotten that Eagle had gone to the authorities *twice*. "I'd never heard of anything like this before, have you?"

"No, thank God," Pammy said.

"I doubt we will again."

Val shut off her shower. Eagle looked at her, trying not to stare as Val wrapped the towel around her too-thin body.

"I'm shocked you didn't break anything," Eagle said to her.

Val smiled. She seemed just fine with what happened. She seemed better than fine. She seemed to be at peace.

"It would have been worth it, even if I had," she said. Then she peered at Eagle. "You need a shower too. And fresh clothes. We need to get rid of this stuff."

"I already have a plan," Eagle said.

"I'll help," Val said.

Eagle wanted to say no, but she didn't. She didn't mind the company.

"We need to wipe down the inside of your truck," Pammy said. "There'll be blood in it."

"Got bleach?" Eagle asked. "That's the best."

"Bleach and old towels," Pammy said.

"Give it to me," Eagle said. "I'll do it before I shower."

She didn't mind cleaning up after an operation. And that had been what this was.

It hadn't been an operation that had gone by the book, but so few of them did. There was always something unexpected, always a twist or turn.

And sometimes the patient died on the table.

Not that Lavassier was a patient. He was the bomb, the mine, the bullet—the reason for the operation.

He was gone, and good riddance.

Eagle shuddered slightly. Pammy had no regrets.

Val didn't seem to either.

But Eagle did.

She was sorry that she had left her friends to fend for themselves. She hadn't protected them. Not that they had needed her.

They had defended themselves.

"Are you all right?" Pammy asked. She had obviously seen something on Eagle's face.

Eagle looked at her, then realized what was missing. The craving for oblivion. Yes, she felt bad that things had gone sideways. But it had actually worked out for the best.

And even though Lavassier had died, she hadn't murdered him while he was out cold. Or tortured him. Or disabled him in all those vicious ways she had considered.

She didn't need a drink. She didn't need a toke.

She was all right, here, in A Gym of Her Own, with her friends, defending their little piece of the world.

Because no one else ever would.

PAMMY

Monday morning, August 4, ten days later. Pammy had opened the gym around nine. She had had a long weekend. She had come to the gym on Saturday after seeing the headline in the *San Francisco Chronicle*. A man whom the paper called the Code Killer had confessed to killing two teenagers in Lake Herman and a girl in Vallejo on the Fourth of July.

Val had learned about that killing when she'd been tracking Lavassier and ruled it out as something he had done. But it became clear with that news story on Saturday that the area police had a big problem on their hands. Another killer, stalking the streets, looking for victims.

Pammy had a problem too. Whenever something like this hit the news, women flocked to her gym. The regulars came over the weekend to discuss the killer, and Pammy had listened silently.

No one had known what she had done.

Eagle had treated her with kid gloves these last few days, as if Pammy were going to break. Pammy even thought that she would at first.

But she hadn't. She'd slept well. She had no nightmares, even though she had killed a man with her bare hands. (Well, not bare—gloved—and with a concrete block.)

Sometimes she thought it was intent that cleared her mind. She hadn't meant to kill him. She had meant to stop him.

And as her father had said more than once, you do what you have to do.

Somehow she had always known she would be in one of those situations, and she had been prepared.

It helped that Val had been right in her prediction: The police thought Lavassier had been killed by one of the girls he tried to kidnap. Eagle's detective had called her and told her that Lavassier was dead and that she wouldn't see much about it in the papers. Apparently there were too many prominent families involved, and the BPD decided that letting Lavassier's history out would embarrass too many of them.

Typical, Eagle had said, and Pammy agreed. Whenever the prominent got involved, the local police protected.

Although Val pointed out that it was best this didn't hit the papers. If it had, it might have given some other bail bondsman the idea to run the same kind of scam.

Val hadn't arrived yet, although Pammy expected her. Val ended up bruised but all right. In the last week, she had redoubled her efforts to get stronger. Sometimes Pammy had to remind her to be patient.

Not that Pammy would have a lot of time to focus on individuals lately.

There were nearly a dozen women in the gym already this morning. Jill had shown up early as well, because she knew that they would be busy. She was signing women in, taking cash for the beginner class, which would be stuffed. She and Pammy had already talked about running two concurrent classes, although Pammy wasn't certain how that would work.

The students would hear both instructors and would probably end up confused.

So she was pacing the front of the gym, trying to figure out where best to hold a second class. She was near the door when it opened and a young woman hunched in.

Her protected posture caught Pammy's attention. The woman looked like she expected to be hit. She clutched a pile of books in one arm and glanced around as if the entire place terrified her.

Pammy knew better than to burst out with an enthusiastic hello. Instead she moved a few inches sideways so that she was in the girl's range of vision.

The girl looked at her, startled, and then smiled. "P-Pammy, right?"

It took Pammy a moment to place her, because she was out of context. The last time Pammy had seen her, she had been hiding in her dorm room.

"Kelly," Pammy said. "I'm glad you could come."

She kept her voice low and warm.

"Looks like you're busy," Kelly said. "I can come back."

"No, this is a perfect day," Pammy said. "We're starting a new class for newcomers. I would love it if you join it."

"I-I can pay." Kelly said, clearly remembering Pammy's offer. "In fact, I want to."

"Let's go to the counter and discuss this," Pammy said.

Kelly glanced over there and went pale. Too many people.

"Or my office," Pammy said.

Kelly shook her head. "I-I need to be—you know—stronger. Around people. They killed him, you know."

She blurted that last out.

Pammy's cheeks heated. "Him?"

"That guy," Kelly said. "The one you've been trying to find. A detective, he called me. Told me I was safe now. I had no idea how he even knew about me, but he did. He said one of the girls, or maybe a guy, they stopped the bastard when he tried to take them."

Pammy did not know how to respond to that. *Good* seemed lame. *It was me*, was something she didn't dare say, just like *I know*, revealed too much as well.

"Oh, thank heavens," Pammy said.

"I kept telling myself that was why I should come here. So you would know everyone was safe. But then I saw the papers, and I realized, we're not safe. There's always someone..." Kelly's voice trailed off. She swallowed hard. Then she squared her shoulders and started again. "There's always someone. And rather than hide in my room, I just have to know how to survive him. You can teach me that, right?"

Pammy smiled. "I can."

"Good," Kelly said, and smiled back. The smile was tentative and slow, but it was a real smile. "Thank you."

Pammy's breath caught. *You're welcome*, she thought. *Thank you for coming here and caring enough to tell me.*

Kelly nodded toward the counter. "I pay there?"

"Yes," Pammy said. "But the offer—"

"Is for someone whose parents aren't footing the bill for everything." Kelly's smile turned sharp. "They're going to pay for a lot of things they hadn't expected. So charge me extra if you want."

Pammy shook her head. "No need for that. But we have a fund you can donate to for others if you end up liking the classes. Wait until you've taken a few, though."

"Okay." Kelly threaded her way through the crowd of women who waited near the desk.

Kelly had stopped hunching somewhere in the middle of this conversation. She still hugged her books to her chest, but her shoulders remained back, her back straight, her chin out.

Not the frightened, damaged girl that Pammy had met, but a woman who had made a decision, a decision that would change her life for the better.

Pammy returned to her task. She needed to take advantage of the opportunity the sensational newspaper headlines gave her. She needed to make room for a whole new class, for women who needed to learn how to protect themselves.

Kelly was right: there would always be someone horrid—someone that Pammy, and Eagle, and Val couldn't find. But if others knew how to defend themselves, then those someones wouldn't have the upper hand.

Everything would balance.

Pammy nodded to herself. That was why she had no nightmares. She had known, deep down, that she was filling a void. Just like she had with the women who were in bad marriages. Just like she had when she taught girls how to fight.

Pammy believed in the gentle art of self-defense.

And she would offer it as long as she could, in the safest environment possible.

She would make sure that her women, at least, knew that they might not always win, but that they at least had a chance.

Which was more than most of them had before they came here.

She looked at the gym, filled with women she didn't know yet, and smiled.

Welcome to A Gym of Her Own, she thought. *Welcome. We hope you stay. And learn, and maybe, just maybe, teach.*

So that the word would spread, and grow.

Maybe she was seeing the beginning of what Strawberry would call a movement.

And maybe it would change the world.

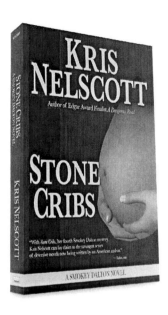

Learn more about Val's past in *Stone Cribs: A Smokey Dalton Novel,* on sale now from your favorite retailer. Turn the page for a sample chapter from that book.

After attending a charity fundraiser, private investigator Smokey Dalton and his powerful girlfriend discover a critically injured woman in his neighbor's apartment, and his neighbor missing. Smokey gets the woman to a nearby hospital which proves to be a mistake: the doctor won't treat the dying woman until she tells him what happened to her. Smokey works to save the woman and find his neighbor, but everything he does makes the situation worse.

Smokey has entered a secret part of America—the arcane rules of a hospital trying to follow the law as well as save lives. None of it makes sense, and all of it threatens everything Smokey believes in.

"Without the slightest hint of preaching, Nelscott brilliantly illuminates the ugliness of that era—which defines Smokey's world but does not destroy him. Because of Nelscott's strong hand, it also does not overwhelm the drama of this remarkable story."
—*Publisher's Weekly* (starred review) on *Stone Cribs*

1

W ind blew off Lake Michigan through the empty canyons of Chicago's Loop. The warmth of the afternoon was long gone, and the cold nights of early spring had returned.

As Laura Hathaway and I stepped out of the Sherman House Hotel, people surrounded us, talking and laughing. They were reviewing Ella Fitzgerald's concert, but not talking about the charity that had brought us all together.

The concert had benefited the Illinois Children's Home and Aid Society's new committee, the Committee for the Adoption of Black Babies. Events like this one overwhelmed me. Hearing about so many people in crisis—so many children in crisis—made me want to help all of them. Only to me, helping involved more than throwing money at a problem. Yet I couldn't see a real solution for orphaned and unwanted children, at least not a solution that I liked.

Apparently the benefit made the other four hundred and ninety-nine attendees uncomfortable as well. Even though the concert and dinner had raised more than fifteen thousand dollars, both in ticket sales and on-site donations, no one was mentioning the money or the children.

And neither were we. Laura and I were silent as we walked down the steps onto the pavement. I looked over my shoulder, an old habit, but I didn't feel as uneasy as I usually did in the Loop. All of the people around me, except Laura, were black. For the first time in this part of the city, I felt as if I belonged.

I slipped my arm around Laura, shielding her against the cold, and she stiffened, not leaning into me as she usually did when we were alone.

I wasn't sure if she was reacting that way because we were in a public place or because of the benefit. We tried not to touch when we were out in public—it simply invited too much trouble—but I didn't feel as if we were in public here.

Maybe Laura did. Or maybe she was still feeling stung from the reactions she had received inside the hotel. During the dinner, she had embarrassed me simply by being herself, and she had seen my reaction. However, I wasn't sure if she knew what she had done wrong.

She felt fragile against me, even though she wasn't. She wore her blond hair up, giving her an illusion of height. Her high heels and her elaborate hairdo made her seem almost as tall as I was, although flat-footed she was much shorter than my six feet.

The streetlights reflected off her pale skin. Her pretty features, accented by paler makeup, were set in a frown.

A dozen cabs, aware that there would be fares this late on Easter Sunday, lined up in front of the Sherman House's Clark Street entrance. Drunken patrons laughed as the valet whistled each cab forward.

The rest of us walked to our cars. Laura's was parked near the Chicago Loop Synagogue. From a distance, I could see the Hands of Peace sculpture hanging from the building's façade. They seemed appropriate somehow—helping hands—and I almost pointed that out to Laura. But one more glance at her expression reminded me to remain silent.

Her Mercedes 280SL was the only car on that block. It looked like the Hands of Peace were pointing at the vehicle.

This part of the street was empty. The other patrons had veered off, and Laura and I were alone.

The feeling of comfort left. The emptiness made me nervous, particularly since we were so well dressed. I was wearing a new suit, tailored to fit, and a topcoat of a type I'd only seen in movies. Laura wore a shimmering blue pantsuit that looked like a formal evening gown until she walked. Her shoes were open-toed. Her feet had to be cold now that we were outside.

In the distance, car doors slammed, a few taxis honked their horns, and people called good-byes and Happy Easters to each other. A man drunkenly sang the title line from "Between the Devil and the Deep Blue Sea," and a woman sang the next line, her voice not as drunk or as out of tune. Neither singer sounded like Ella Fitzgerald.

She had made the entire evening worthwhile. The dance floor in the old College Inn restaurant was lit with soft lights, the orchestra behind it. She used the space as if it were her own private stage until she got irritated that no one was dancing. Then she invited people forward.

And of course they came.

Laura's heels clicked on the concrete and my tight new dress shoes answered with solid taps. I wondered what Laura was thinking. Maybe Ella Fitzgerald's rich voice was reverberating in Laura's head the way it was reverberating in mine.

It wasn't the closing number that kept threading its way through my thoughts. Much as I liked "A-Tisket, A-Tasket," it wasn't my favorite Ella Fitzgerald tune. Instead, "Slumming on Park Avenue," with its sly lyrics about spying on the rich the way they slummed to spy on the poor, had captured my mood.

Ella Fitzgerald had segued into that song after an ill-advised set of rock 'n roll tunes. When she introduced "Slumming," she had done so with a wide smile, knowing she was in a crowd of like-minded people.

"It's Irving Berlin's way of letting all those rich white folks know how despicable their behavior can be," she said, her eyes twinkling, the orchestra playing a musical backdrop behind her.

At that moment, several people glanced at Laura. She was well known among people who followed the society pages, and apparently a lot of the upper-class blacks who shelled out fifteen dollars per person to come to this event read not only the *Defender*'s society pages, but the *Tribune*'s as well.

As Laura and I reached the Mercedes, I scanned the area, looking for people in the shadows. Not a lot of pickpockets turned up for a black benefit, but I knew better than to ignore the silent streets.

I saw no one. The synagogue's stained-glass walls and street-level glass reflected the lights, the car, and nothing else.

Laura slipped out of my grasp. She pulled her keys out of her purse, brushed an escaping strand of blond hair away from her face, and walked toward the driver's side.

She unlocked her door, and peered at me over the car's dark blue roof. Her makeup hollowed out her cheeks, giving her a patrician air.

"You're angry at me, aren't you?" she asked.

"No," I lied and jiggled the car handle. I wanted to go home.

She pulled her door open and got inside. She braced an arm on the gearshift between the seats and leaned over, reaching for the lock. In the passenger-side window glass, my own image was superimposed over hers, and I looked as out of place as I felt—a burly, six-foot-tall man stuffed into a suit. The new scar I had along the left side of my face made me seem tougher than I felt. If it weren't for the topcoat, people would think I was a bouncer at a trendy night club.

Laura's fingers pulled lightly on the lock, clicking it open. I grabbed the door handle and pulled as she sat up, sticking the keys in the ignition. I slid inside.

The car's interior was warmer than the street had been, even though the leather seats still creaked with the cold. The solid metal frame blocked the wind. We weren't even rocking from its force.

I settled back, my knees bent under the dash. It felt awkward to sit on the passenger side, even though the car was hers. I was used to driving.

But Laura had insisted, just like she had insisted on everything else about this night. She had bought the tickets, helped me find the suit, and even managed to check the official guest list to make sure that there would be no one in attendance that I would have to avoid.

She had known that Easter was going to be a difficult holiday for all of us, and she had planned this to cheer me up.

Last Easter, I had been driving back roads with Jimmy Bailey, trying to keep him away from the FBI and the Memphis police. Jimmy had witnessed the assassination of Martin Luther King, Jr., and the shooter Jimmy had seen was not James Earl Ray. Jimmy, who had been only ten at the time, had reported the shooting to the large contingent of police officers nearby and they had tried to kidnap him on the spot.

If I hadn't arrived at just that moment, I have no doubt that Jimmy would be dead now.

We were hiding here in Chicago. No one except Laura, and Franklin and Althea Grimshaw, knew Jimmy's name was James Bailey or mine was Smokey Dalton. No one knew that Jimmy and I weren't blood kin. Everyone here thought we were related to Franklin, and I had identification in my wallet, claiming my name was William S. Grimshaw—a man with an eleven-year-old son named Jimmy.

I had focused most of my energies these past few weeks on Jimmy. The articles in the papers about King's assassination, the constant reminders on the television set, had made Jimmy's nightmares return. I had hoped the actual anniversary of King's death—which had been, ironically, Good Friday—would make the nightmares go away.

But they hadn't.

So I had agreed to let him spend Easter weekend with the Grimshaws', hoping that the celebratory church services, the Black Easter parade, and Althea's delightful Easter dinner would help Jimmy focus on the present, rather than the darkness in his past.

It also gave me time with Laura, time we badly needed. In January of this year, we had resumed the relationship we began in Memphis, and it was proving as difficult as I had thought it would be. I was working with Laura now on a per-job basis, inspecting the buildings owned by the company she now ran. Laura had an amazing streak of somewhat naïve color-blindness, but no one else in Sturdy Investments did. The fact that she and I had an equal partnership disturbed almost everyone we came into contact with.

Then there was the personal relationship, which we were having trouble finding time for. I had Jimmy to care for, and Laura worked long hours. Sometimes we went a week without seeing each other, especially since I rarely went into Sturdy's offices.

Tomorrow morning I was supposed to pick up Jimmy, along with all of the Grimshaw children, and take them to school, so Laura and I were staying at my place to make the drive easier. I had wanted to spend the entire evening at home, but by the time I realized Laura was making plans, it had been too late.

Laura knew I longed for the music that had been part of the air in Memphis. My offices there had been on Beale Street, home of the blues, and every bar, every restaurant, had some form of music in the evenings. Even though Chicago was also a big blues town, it had its own style—a darker, moodier, more urban style that wasn't as accessible to me. The westside clubs were far away from my home and office, and I wasn't as free to go out at night as I had been in Memphis.

But I didn't want to go to a benefit. I had never liked the pretentiousness of the events, always wondering why people needed a special reward to give to charity.

I hadn't told Laura that, but she had sensed my mood on the way over. We pretended we were enjoying the evening, until we got up to dance. Then I felt the tension in Laura's body. She hadn't put her head on my shoulder like she had in the past. Instead, she had watched everyone around us, probably feeling the hostility they were directing at her.

She hadn't realized when she bought the tickets that she would be crashing an affair designed for blacks only. And I hadn't prepared her for the cattiness she would be suffering because she was a white woman who was clearly involved with a black man.

"It seems like you're mad at me," Laura said, obviously not willing to let the topic go. She checked the car's mirrors and turned on her lights before pulling into Clark.

I was annoyed at the entire evening; I didn't like small talk and I had been subjected to hours of it. I had also been on alert for the first hour, making certain that no one who might have known me from Memphis, someone who hadn't been on the initial guest list, was in the room.

"I would have thought after my donation that people would have understood how serious I am." She kept her gaze on the road ahead, her hands in a perfect driver's V on the wheel.

In the middle of the evening, the organizers called for donations. People verbally pledged an amount, and most wrote checks to cover it right away. Laura had done so, and the hostility had grown worse.

I had no idea if she had noticed, however. I wasn't going to tell her. But I didn't know how to respond to her statement without patronizing her or starting a real fight.

Laura and I came from completely different worlds. She had been raised the wealthy daughter of a small-time crook who became a self-made businessman. She had been pampered and protected her entire life, stepping out of that world only after her mother had died, when a strange clause in her mother's will had led her to me.

My parents had been lynched when I was ten, and after that, I was sent away from everything I knew. My adoptive parents were good people, and they raised me well, but they could never erase the memories I held of my first ten years or of that time I spent hiding in an upstairs closet while my real parents were being dragged out of the house to their deaths.

"I understand that some people there found my question offensive," Laura said. "But I didn't mean it that way. I mean, if we're going to be a truly integrated society—"

"It was offensive, Laura," I said.

She looked at me. The dim light of the dash revealed the shock on her face. She hadn't expected me to side against her.

But she hadn't understood the situation. Even after listening to the speeches, the points apparently hadn't struck home. I had no idea how she had missed the evening's subtext, since the first speaker had outlined it with one sentence:

If we are really serious about black pride, if we really believe that black is beautiful, if we really believe that we are somebody, we black adults will do something about the adoption of black babies in Chicago.

Apparently Laura hadn't heard the phrase "black adults," or if she had, she had misunderstood it. I had a good view of her as I watched the speakers, and her eyes teared up more than once at the thought of over a thousand children who were unclaimed because of the color of their skin.

She had stood, hand up, during the question-and-answer section of the presentation, and waited a long time to be called on. I tried to get her to sit, but she shook me off. When the speaker finally turned his attention to her, Laura asked why no one had thought of finding white families to adopt black children.

The silence in the large restaurant had been deafening. For a moment, I had thought the speaker wasn't going to answer her. Then he had said, "It simply isn't feasible," and had moved onto the next question, leaving Laura red-faced.

She had sat back down and, to her credit, hadn't brought up the issue again the entire night. Until now.

"What did I say that was so wrong?" she asked.

I didn't want to have this discussion. I had imagined leaving Sherman House, driving to my apartment, and taking her in my arms. The last thing I wanted was tension between us.

I sighed. Laura wasn't going to let me brush her off the way the speaker had.

I said, "Let's leave out the fact that a hundred years ago, white people controlled the destinies of blacks and their children, often separating them and selling the children like cattle. Let's also forget that the social services available to whites, like maternity homes and other such places, are not usually available to blacks. And let's not even discuss the way the legal system treats black families who somehow find themselves in court. Let's just talk about what you suggested."

"Okay." Her tone was cautious, like Jimmy's often was when he knew he was about to get a lecture for something he didn't completely understand.

She turned the car onto Lake Shore Drive. Lake Michigan looked black against the night sky. Only the headlights, rippling in the water, gave any indication that the lake was there.

"If we allow white families to take black children, then we must assume that black families will take white children," I said.

"They won't?" she asked.

"They won't be allowed to," I said. "But that's not even the point. The point is that our children will leave our culture and our nest, and once again, white people will be determining our future."

"But the black children aren't being adopted," Laura said. "No one's taking them. I listened, just like you did."

"And there were some things we all knew but which weren't spelled out for people outside of the community," I said.

"Like what?" She kept her gaze trained on the road, but her jaw was set. She was angry too.

Cars passed us. The street was busier than I would have expected at 10:30 on Easter Sunday.

"Black families do adopt black children, but have a tougher road of it," I said. "The model for a stable family is white. The woman is a home-maker and the man is the breadwinner, which is not the norm in black families. In black families, both parents work, and right there that makes the court assume that the household is unfit. If by chance the woman does stay home, then the white inspectors come and judge everything by their standards. They assume the neighborhood is bad because of the preponderance of blacks—"

"That's ridiculous," Laura said.

"I don't care if it's ridiculous, Laura," I said. "It happens. When I lived in Memphis, I used to do investigative work for attorneys who sometimes handled adoption petitions. More than once I had to prove that a black neighborhood, which looked dangerous to a white inspector, was actually safer than its economic counterpart in the white community."

Laura sighed. "So my donation made it seem like I was patronizing everyone there, then."

She finally understood. But I didn't want to upset her further, so all I said was, "I'm sure they knew you were sincerely trying to help."

"One thousand children without a place to go." Her voice was quiet. "That's a crime all by itself."

"I know."

We were heading into Hyde Park now, getting close to my street.

"I'm sorry," she said. "I wanted this to be a pleasant evening, Smokey."

I placed my hand on top of the one she had resting on the gearshift. Her skin was warm and soft.

"It was pleasant," I said, and it wasn't a complete lie. "It was fun to hear Ella again, and dancing with you—"

"Again?" Laura looked at me. She had chewed the lipstick off her lower lip, and more strands of hair had fallen around her face.

"I saw Ella a few times in Memphis."

Laura's carefully plucked eyebrows rose. I recognized the look. It was a combination of fear and panic.

"Does she know you?" Laura asked. "Could she have recognized you?"

I smiled. "Only as a familiar face in the crowd. We never spoke. I was just another nameless fan bebopping to the music."

"Bebopping." Laura smiled, too, and returned her gaze to the road. "I can't quite imagine you doing that."

Maybe not any more. I hadn't had the lightness and relaxation I had enjoyed on those nights in Memphis for more than a year.

Laura had never seen me comfortable or lighthearted. From the moment I met her, I had been on guard, and then events conspired to make me serious, protective, and justifiably paranoid.

She turned the car onto my street, saving me from having to comment on my past. She expertly eased the Mercedes into an empty parking space a few yards from my apartment's main sidewalk.

Half of the streetlights were broken, sending uneven pools of light throughout the neighborhood. Most of the buildings were former houses turned into apartments or pre-World War II six-flats which had been allowed to run down.

I lived in an older building on the second floor, in the apartment first rented by the Grimshaws. Laura had found them a home more suited to their needs, and now Jimmy and I lived in three-bedroom comfort, at least compared with last summer's crowded conditions.

Still, the apartment was small and meager, especially when I thought of Laura's penthouse suite on Lake Shore Drive. Even though Laura claimed the difference didn't bother her, it bothered me. Every time I brought her here, I kept seeing how mean my circumstances were—and it made me wonder if each of us wasn't slumming in our own separate ways.

As she parked, worry must have shown on my face. Laura shoved the gearshift into Park, shut off the ignition, and then smiled at me.

"It's all right, Smokey." There was amusement in her voice. "I'm insured."

I never doubted that she was, but insurance wasn't really the point to me. I was used to taking precautions, and leaving a valuable car on a street filled with poor people didn't count as one to me. Sure, my rusted Impala wasn't pretty, but it belonged here.

I opened the door and got out. She did the same, and I waited for her to come around to my side. As she approached, I held out my hand, and wondered if she would take it.

She did. Her fingers were surprisingly warm. We walked up the sidewalk, hand in hand.

The six-flat regained some of its elegance in the darkness. The unkempt lawn was harder to see and the chipped paint covering the brick looked almost clean.

Still, this building was clearly a multi-family dwelling, with different curtains in each window, and the air of public property outside.

The door to the building was propped open, something I wished the other tenants wouldn't do. But as the weather got nicer, people liked to have a breeze fill the hallways, which got stuffy in the afternoons. Once the door was open, no one bothered to close it.

Laura and I stepped onto the porch. Last summer, I had discovered a body here, and each time I walked up the porch steps I thought of it.

Tonight was no different. Little ghosts haunted me everywhere.

We stepped inside. The hallway was wide at the entrance, with a staircase to our right—a wooden staircase with an elegant banister that once had been polished and lovely. Now it was dingy with years of dirt.

The main floor had two apartments, the first near the metal mailboxes that had been built into the wall. Both apartment doors were closed, and each had extra deadbolts, just like mine did, even though the neighborhood was considered safe by Chicago standards.

The hall smelled faintly of baked ham and melted chocolate. The remains of a chocolate bunny was mashed against the doorknob of the nearest apartment. Foil Easter egg wrappers glittered on the floor, proving that someone had had a sweet holiday.

Laura smiled when she saw the mess. Her hair was losing its height, and the change made her seem more like my Laura, instead of the glittery society woman I had taken to the benefit.

She headed toward the staircase, careful to avoid the foil wrappers.

"Don't touch the railing," I said. "Who knows if sticky little hands were there first."

"The chocolate should be hardening by now," she said, and reached for the banister.

Above us, something thudded. Something heavy had fallen. I didn't like the sound. Laura looked at me, a slight frown making a line between her eyebrows.

I shrugged. This apartment building had its share of odd noises. I had owned my own house in Memphis, and even though I'd been here nearly a year, I still wasn't used to all the sounds that neighbors could make.

I turned, closed the front door, and latched it, like all of the tenants had agreed to do after dark. Then I joined Laura on the stairs.

She slipped her arm through mine. The tension from earlier had fled, and we were heading into that perfect moment I had initially imagined when we had left for the benefit. We took our time climbing up, as if we were heading toward a glorious suite in a fancy hotel instead of my dingy apartment.

Halfway up, she let go of my arm, and reached into the pocket of my topcoat for my keys.

Even though she and I had grown closer these last four months, I had not given her keys to my place, nor had I asked for keys to hers. Since I did most of my work out of my apartment, I wanted to be cautious about who came into my apartment and why. Keys to her place wouldn't have mattered, since I never would have used them. Even though the current building security was used to me, I was worried that some new overzealous employee would see a black man trying to open Miss Hathaway's door and act before thinking.

She managed to grab the keys, laughed, and with surprising agility for a woman in high heels, ran up the remaining steps. She thumbed the keys, looking for the square one that unlocked the top deadbolt.

The thud came again, closer, this time followed by a cry of pain. A door banged softly, as if it had been partially opened and had suddenly slammed closed.

Laura turned. She had obviously heard the sound, too. "Isn't that where your neighbor lives?"

The question wasn't as inane as it sounded. The only neighbor of mine that Laura had met was Marvella Walker, a stunning woman who had set her sights on me the moment I had moved into the building. Last winter, Marvella did her best to make Laura's visits hellacious, until I let Marvella know I wouldn't tolerate her behavior.

Laura was looking at the thick wooden door across the hall from mine. I took the last few steps two at a time, and reached the top. There I could hear a woman's voice, making short sharp cries.

"I think she's calling for help," Laura said.

I didn't wait. I hurried to the door. The sounds were louder here. In between the cries were moans.

"Marvella?" I asked, reaching for the knob. "Marvella, it's me, Bill. Is everything okay?"

"Help…me…please…" This cry was louder than the rest, but I still wouldn't have been able to hear it if I hadn't been nearby.

I turned the knob and to my surprise, it opened. Marvella was usually as meticulous about using her deadbolts as I was. But the door jammed, as if something were pushed against it.

Through the crack in the door, I could see a woman's bare foot on the hardwood floor, a bit of satin robe, and a blood stain that appeared to be growing.

"Marvella?" I tried not to let the panic I suddenly felt into my voice. "Can you move away from the door? I can't get in."

She grunted. The foot moved, braced itself, revealing some leg. Blood coated the inner thigh, and had run down to the ankle. As she moved, the blood smeared against the hardwood floor, and I realized the stain was really a puddle.

"What's going on, Smokey?" Laura had come up behind me.

I held up a hand to silence her, and pushed on the door. It finally opened far enough for me to slip inside.

When she saw me, the woman on the floor moaned in relief. But she wasn't Marvella. She was small, her features delicate and elfin. Her skin had gone gray, and the area around her eyes was almost bluish, indicating a great deal of blood loss.

"Thank God," she whispered when she saw me. "I need some help."

"Where's Marvella?" I asked, uncertain what had happened. Most of Marvella's tidy living room was intact. The wooden sculptures, all of faces in an African style, remained on the surfaces, and the plants still covered the window seat in front of the large bay window. But the add-on kitchen was a mess of glasses and dirty dishes, and Marvella's normally pristine brown couch was covered with blankets, towels, and even more blood.

The woman shook her head, then closed her eyes, and lay back down, as if all that movement had been too much for her. Next to her, a half-melted bag of ice added to water to the blood puddle.

Laura pushed her way in behind me.

"Oh, my God." She crouched beside the woman, and put a hand on her forehead. "She's burning up. Smokey, we have to get her help. Now."

The blood was coming from between the woman's legs. She wore Marvella's white satin robe, and it was partially open, revealing a slightly distended stomach.

"Get towels from the kitchen," I said. "See if you can stop the bleeding. I have to make sure Marvella's all right."

I had visions of her dead or dying in the bedroom. I hurried toward the narrow hallway, wishing I had my gun. My topcoat flowed behind me, catching on the small table Marvella used to accent the space between the bathroom and bedroom, and knocking it over. The sculptures on top of it scattered.

Laura moved behind me, making soothing noises to the poor woman as she gathered towels.

The bathroom light was on. Drops of blood covered the white tile around the toilet, and more blood stained the orange rug in front of the bathtub. The brown and orange shower curtain was open, revealing a mound of wet towels in the tub. No towels hung on the racks, and a bloody handprint stained the white porcelain of the sink.

But Marvella was not inside.

I moved quickly to the bedroom, and flicked on the light. I had never seen this room, but it continued the browns and oranges Marvella used to decorate the rest of the place. Instead of sculptures, though, big oil paintings of tribal figures covered the walls.

One painting was so large and narrow that the figure on it was life-sized. I caught it out of the corner of my eye, and had to do a double-take to make sure it wasn't a real person.

My heart was pounding. I made myself take a breath and slow down so that I could scan the room.

The batik bedspread had been pulled back and someone had removed one of the matching pillows. Women's clothing pooled near the closet, unusually sloppy in a very tidy room.

The bedroom smelled of Marvella's sandalwood perfume, and I realized that it was the only place in the entire apartment that didn't smell of fresh blood.

I checked the closet just in case, and saw nothing except rows of brightly colored clothing. Then I lifted the bedspread. Boxes of shoes, neatly labeled, were stored beneath the bed.

No one was in there either.

Marvella was missing and a woman was bleeding to death in her living room.

Something awful had happened here, and I had no real idea what that something was.

ABOUT THE AUTHOR

Kris Nelscott is an open pen name used by *New York Times* best-selling author Kristine Kathryn Rusch.

The first Smokey Dalton novel, *A Dangerous Road*, won the Herodotus Award for Best Historical Mystery and was short-listed for the Edgar Award for Best Novel; the second, *Smoke-Filled Rooms*, was a PNBA Book Award finalist; and the third, *Thin Walls*, was one of the *Chicago Tribune's* best mysteries of the year. *Kirkus* chose *Days of Rage* as one of the top ten mysteries of the year and it was also nominated for a Shamus Award for The Best Private Eye Hardcover Novel of the Year. The latest novel in the series, *Street Justice*, was also nominated for a Shamus Award.

Entertainment Weekly says her equals are Walter Mosley and Raymond Chandler. *Booklist* calls the Smokey Dalton books "a high-class crime series" and *Salon* says "Kris Nelscott can lay claim to the strongest series of detective novels now being written by an American author."

For more information about Kris Nelscott, or author Kristine Kathryn Rusch's other works, please go to KrisNelscott.com or KristineKathrynRusch.com and sign up for her newsletter.

Also by
Kris Nelscott

CPSIA information can be obtained
at www.ICGtesting.com
Printed in the USA
LVOW11s1642291217
561233LV00002B/325/P